LP FICT WARREN
Warren, Susan May, 1966-
author.
Wild Montana skies [text
(large print)]

WITHDRAWN

DEC 29 2016

DURANGO PUBLIC LIBRARY
DURANGO, COLORADO 81301

WILD
MONTANA
SKIES

**Center Point
Large Print**

Also by Susan May Warren and available from Center Point Large Print:

When I Fall in Love
Always on My Mind
The Wonder of You
You're the One That I Want

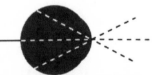

**This Large Print Book carries the
Seal of Approval of N.A.V.H.**

MONTANA
RESCUE
— 1 —

WILD MONTANA SKIES

Susan May WARREN

CENTER POINT LARGE PRINT
THORNDIKE, MAINE

This Center Point Large Print edition is published in the year 2016 by arrangement with Revell, a division of Baker Publishing Group.

Copyright © 2016 by Susan May Warren.

All rights reserved.

This book is a work of fiction. Names, characters, places, and incidents are the product of the author's imagination or are used fictitiously.

The text of this Large Print edition is unabridged. In other aspects, this book may vary from the original edition. Printed in the United States of America on permanent paper. Set in 16-point Times New Roman type.

ISBN: 978-1-68324-203-1

Library of Congress Cataloging-in-Publication Data

Names: Warren, Susan May, 1966– author.
Title: Wild Montana skies / Susan May Warren.
Description: Center Point Large Print edition. | Thorndike, Maine : Center Point Large Print, 2016.
Identifiers: LCCN 2016041256 | ISBN 9781683242031 (hardcover : alk. paper)
Subjects: LCSH: Women air pilots—Fiction. | Helicopter pilots—Fiction. | Rescue work—Montana—Fiction. | Large type books. | GSAFD: Love stories. | Christian fiction.
Classification: LCC PS3623.A865 W55 2016b | DDC 813/.6—dc23
LC record available at https://lccn.loc.gov/2016041256

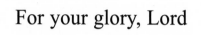
For your glory, Lord

– 1 –

Kacey didn't want to raise eyebrows and alert the entire town to her return. She simply hoped to tame the beast that had roared to life when she spotted the billboard for the Gray Pony Saloon and Grill, off Rt. 2, on the outskirts of Mercy Falls.

The home of the best hickory rib sauce in the West.

From the look of things, the hangout on the edge of town hadn't changed in a decade.

Dim streetlights puddled the muddy parking lot, now crammed full of F-150s and Silverado pickups. The twang of a Keith Urban cover swelled as the door opened. A cowboy spilled out, his arm lassoed around a shapely coed, probably a summer intern for the park service. She wore Gore-Tex pants, a lime-green Glacier National Park T-shirt, and a too-easy smile on her face. Kacey watched as the cowboy wheedled her toward his truck. The coed tugged his hat down, and he braced his hands on either side of her, leaning down to steal a kiss.

The sight had the power to stop Kacey cold, reroute her down the country road of regrets.

Maybe she should simply keep going, head north to Whitefish, back to the anonymity of a town that couldn't catalog her mistakes.

Still, the brain fog of two days of driving, not to

mention the drizzle of a nagging rain, could be the recipe for disaster on the winding roads that journeyed north through the foothills.

The last thing she needed was to drive head-first off the highway and die in a fiery crash here in her own backyard. Some welcome home that would be.

Kacey parked just as thunder growled, lightning spliced the darkness, and rain began to crackle against her windshield. The soupy night obliterated the view of the glorious, jagged mountains rising on the horizon.

Another pickup rolled up next to her, the running boards caked with mud. A fleet of what looked like army types piled out, garbed in mud-brown shirts and camo pants. Fatigue lined their grimy expressions, as if they were just returning from a two-day march in full field gear.

The nearest army base was over 150 miles away, so the appearance of soldiers had her curiosity piqued. She watched them go in, and a reprimand formed on her lips about donning utility wear off duty. But, like her army psychologist had suggested, some time away from her fellow soldiers might help her heal.

Keep her from derailing twelve years of distinguished service with an ODPMC discharge—or, to her mind, the old Section-8, Maxwell Klinger designation.

She wasn't crazy. Just . . . exhausted. Maybe.

She couldn't let the war follow her home. Let it destroy the best part of herself, the part she'd left behind in Montana.

The part of her that desperately needed a definition of life that included words like *safe* and *normal*.

Instead of, oh, say, *deployment* and *Afghanistan*. And acronyms like *PTSD*.

Which meant she had to start living like a civilian and keep her military secrets safely tucked away if she intended on putting herself back together and returning to base, healed and fit for duty, by the end of the summer.

Kacey scrubbed the sleep out of her eyes, then got out, hunting ribs and a frothy homemade root beer.

The Pony might not have updated their exterior, with the rough-hewn porch, the Old West–style sign, and neon beer ads in the windows, but inside, they'd overhauled for the next generation.

The honky-tonk tones of some country musician met her as she opened thick double doors, and she walked into the distinct intoxicating aroma of hickory barbecue.

She glanced to the front and almost expected to see cowboy crooner Benjamin King on stage at the back of the room, past the gleaming oak bar. Work-hewn muscles stretching out his black T-shirt, one worn cowboy boot hooked onto the rung of his stool, and wearing his battered brown

Stetson over that unruly dark blond hair, Ben would grind out a love song in his signature low tenor, wooing every girl in the room.

His devastating blue eyes fixed only on her.

Kacey blew out a breath, letting the memory shake out, settle her back into reality.

Stopping for dinner at the Gray Pony would be a very bad idea if Ben hadn't long ago sprung himself from the grasp of Mercy Falls, his guitar slung over his shoulder, nary a glance behind. No, she wouldn't find him, a big star now with the country duo Montgomery-King, back in this one-horse watering hole tucked in the shadow of Glacier National Park.

Now, Kacey scanned the room, getting her bearings. Roy had kept the taxidermied moose, rainbow trout, and black bear still posed over the bar, but the rest of the joint, from the themed barrel tables to the sleek leather barstools, suggested an upgrade. Along the wall, every few feet, flat screens displayed sporting events—bull riding, a UFC fight, a golf tournament, and a fishing show. And the adjacent hall that once hosted a row of worn pool tables now sported a shiny mechanical bull-riding pit.

Judging by the cheering of the fellas gathered at the rail, more than a few wearing Sweetwater Creek Lumber Co. shirts, the girl in the center of the ring offered up quite a show.

The saloon seemed to have upgraded their

clientele from the obligatory cowboys and park workers to a large conglomeration of army, local law enforcement, and even what looked like young, long-haired hippies hoping to spend their summer in yurts and hiking the craggy routes of the Rocky Mountains, cameras hanging from their necks.

Waitresses squeezed through tables packed with hungry patrons, their trays stacked high with wings, onion rings, and nachos. An "oo-rah!" rose from a table of soldiers as one of the UFC fighters went down.

She recognized no one, which, of course, could be providential. Because they might not recognize her, either.

Kacey squeezed past a group of hikers perusing a map and nabbed the only empty barstool. She climbed up, took a napkin, and mopped up the remains of a frothy beer puddling on the counter.

"Sorry about that." This from the woman behind the counter, her dark hair pulled back in a long braid, her brown eyes quick as she surveyed the activity behind Kacey. She took a rag and wiped the counter. "I think the person sitting here stiffed me." She glanced at the door.

"Where did she—"

"He. I dunno. I don't see him. He wasn't in uniform, but he could be with the guard." She tossed the rag under the counter, grabbed a coaster. "We have specials on tap—"

"Do you still have the house root beer?"

A hint of a smile. "Home brewed, my daddy's recipe."

Her *daddy* . . . seriously? Ah, sure, Kacey saw it now. Hair dyed black and about fifty pounds thinner. And of course, a decade in her eyes, on her face. She couldn't help but ask, "Gina McGill?"

The woman frowned. "Do I—"

"Kacey Fairing. I used to—"

"Date Ben King, yeah, wow, how are you?"

Kacey was going to say that she'd sat behind her in Mr. Viren's biology class, but she supposed Gina's version might be an easier association. "I'm good."

"I haven't seen you since, uh . . ." And there it was. The prickly dance around Kacey's mistakes. The ones that had driven her out of Mercy Falls and into the army's arms.

"Prom," Kacey filled in, diverting, trying to make it easier for both of them. "Nice of your dad to let us host it here. One of my favorite high school memories."

"What are you up to?" Gina said, pulling out a frozen mug from the freezer, filling it with frothy, dark, creamy root beer from the tap.

"I'm a chopper pilot. For the army."

"Really? Wow. I suppose they called you in, huh? Rescuing people off rooftops?"

Kacey frowned. "Uh, not sure what you're talking about."

Gina set the mug on the coaster. "Oh, I thought you were here with the rest of the National Guard. The Mercy River is flooding, and all these guys are working twenty-four-hour shifts sandbagging upriver all the way down to the bridge."

Ah, that accounted for dinner in their field dress.

Kacey took a sip of the root beer, let the foam sit on her upper lip a second before licking it off. "Nope. Here on leave for the summer, although, yeah, I'll be doing some flying for Chet King's PEAK." See, that came out easily enough, no hitch, no hint at the past. No irony.

And no suggestion that she might not be fit to fly. Keeping her chopper in the air had never been her problem, thank you.

Besides, she needed this gig, if only to keep her sanity during the daylight hours. Too much idle time only invited the memories.

Gina offered her a menu. "Well, don't be surprised if Sam Brooks comes knocking on your door. The Mercy Falls EMS department has the PEAK team on full alert, and he's recruiting volunteers for the sandbag brigade."

Kacey perused the menu offerings. "Why is Sam doing the recruiting? Is Blackburn still sheriff?"

"Yeah. He'll be in office until he retires, probably. Sam is the deputy sheriff. So, the smoked BBQ ribs are half off now that it's after 10:00 p.m., and I think I could score you a basket of the fried calamari on the house."

"The ribs sound perfect, thanks, Gina," she said, handing her the menu. "And I'm game for the calamari too."

Kacey grabbed the mug, sipping as she turned in her chair, glancing at the band on stage, the lead singer now leaning into the mic, plucking out another Keith Urban ballad.

"I'm gonna be here for ya, baby . . ."

Young, dark-haired, and not a hint of Ben's resonant twang. And yet just like that, Ben showed up, almost tangible in her mind, even after all these years. The smell of fresh air in his flannel shirt, his arms around her, lips against her neck.

Nope. She wrapped her hands around the cool glass.

She should probably also remember that Ben had made her believe in a different life. In the full-out happy ending. She should probably hate him for that.

On the dance floor, the cowboy and the coed from outside locked themselves in a slow sway. A few more couples joined them, and Kacey turned away, rubbing her finger and thumb into her eyes, slicking away the exhaustion.

"Working the flood?"

She looked up into the striking, blue eyes of the man who had slid onto the stool next to her. Brown, neatly trimmed hair and a smattering of russet whiskers, neatly clipped but just long enough to suggest a renegade attitude in a cultured life. He wore a camel-brown chambray shirt open at the neck, sleeves rolled up over strong fore-arms, a pair of faded jeans, scuffed cowboy boots, and the smell of money in his cologne. A rich, cowboy-wannabe tourist. And he had a low, rumbly voice that should have probably elicited some response, if she weren't so tired.

Really tired. "Nope."

From the end of the bar, a huddle of hikers roared as one of them landed a bull's-eye into the dart target. The man seemed to follow her gaze, frowned.

Huh.

"I suppose the rain's cutting short your vacation," she said.

This got a laugh. Or a harrumph, she couldn't tell. "Naw. I'm over the park."

"That's a shame. So much beautiful country."

Did she imagine the shadow that crossed his eyes? Maybe, because in a blink it vanished. Instead, "Gina talked you into the calamari, huh?"

Gina had deposited the deep-fried squid, sided with creamy aioli.

Kacey reached for a twisty piece. "Why? Something I should be worried about?" She took a curl, dipped it into the spicy mayo.

He shook his head, took a sip of his own root beer. "I tried to tell Roy that nobody north of Denver has ever heard of calamari, but he wanted to add it. Something for the tourists . . ." He lifted a nicely sculpted shoulder. "I think I'm the only one in five hundred miles ordering it."

So, not a tourist. But not exactly a local either.

"Rubbery." She wrinkled her nose. "Yeah, probably Roy should have stuck with cowboy food." She shoved the basket his direction. "Help yourself."

"Not for you?"

"I'm spoiled," she said, rinsing down the flavor. "I've spent the past year in Florida, seaside."

He seemed like a nice guy—maybe the right guy—to help erase old memories, find new ones.

Not that she was looking, really, but maybe, away from her rules on base, and with a longer stint home than normal, she might . . .

A shout on the dance floor made her turn, and she saw that the cowboy she'd seen before on the porch was tussling with one of the hippies, this one wearing a park-logoed shirt.

Oops. Apparently that cute coed in his arms had cuddled up against the wrong demographic.

"We're dancing here," Cowboy said.

"And she's not your girlfriend!" the hippie retorted.

Next to her, the man, Mr. Rumble Voice, rose. "That's not pretty."

She glanced at him. "They'll be fine."

He wasn't the only one on his feet, however. A couple of the hikers on the far end of the bar separated from the group and edged toward the dance floor.

And the table of USC fans stopped cheering, eyes on the spectacle.

She took another sip of her root beer.

The voices raised, a few expletives thrown.

When Cowboy pushed the hippie, Rumble headed toward the dance floor.

And, shoot—like a reflex, Kacey found herself on her feet, as if still on duty, the cool-headed soldier she'd been for twelve years.

Stay out of it. The voice simmered in her head.

"Hey, guys," Rumble said, moving closer, hands up. "Let's just take this outside—"

Cowboy threw a punch at the hippie, and the room exploded. The hippies emptied their table, and of course Cowboy had a few hands he'd dragged in off the ranch.

And just like that, Kacey was dodging fists, zeroing in on the coed who started the mess. The girl held her mouth where someone had accidentally elbowed her.

Kacey maneuvered through the fray, caught the girl, and pulled her back toward the stage. "Are you okay?" If she remembered correctly, there was an exit just stage left . . .

"I didn't mean to start this."

Kacey threw her arm over the girl's shoulder and ducked, heading toward the exit.

She didn't see it coming.

A body flew into her, liquid splashing over her as the weight threw her. Kacey slammed into the stage; pain exploded across her forehead.

The room spun, darkness blotchy against her eyes.

She sat there, just a moment, blinking.

Pull back, Kacey! Your position is compromised!

She shook her head to rid it of the voice but felt a scream rising when arms circled her, lifting—

"Oh no you don't!" Kacey shouted.

She thrashed against the embrace, elbowing her captor hard.

He made a sound of pain, but she followed with a hard uppercut to his jaw.

And landed on the floor.

The jolt of hitting the floor, the sense of movement around her, brought her back.

"What?" She blinked, clearing her vision.

Rumble peered down at her, holding his jaw. "You have quite a right hook, honey."

Oh. Boy. She made a face, but her forehead burned, and she pressed her hand against the heat of a rising bump. "Sorry. But—"

"My bad. But you need to get off the floor."

Voices now, loud, punching through the tension in the room.

He hesitated a second, then held out his hand.

She made a face, shook her head, and climbed to her feet. "I don't need help, thanks."

But she swayed, trying to find her balance on the wooden floor.

"Seriously, you look like you could go down."

"I'm fine." Only then did she realize the wetness down the front of her white T-shirt. And . . . oh no. The odor of beer from her soaked shirt rose to consume her. That would play well when she arrived home. She pulled the shirt away from her body and removed her hand from her head. Then, "Wait . . . that girl—"

"Jess has her."

Jess? She looked around and found the girl being led to a table by a pretty blonde, one of the hikers.

Rumble seemed to be debating grabbing her arm, but she gave him a look, and he simply led the way back to the counter. On the dance floor, the factions had separated, the musician was setting his mic back to rights. The hippies, angry, a few of them holding back their champion, congregated at their table. The cowboy stalked out of the bar, holding his hat, his posse shouting epithets as they trailed.

"The flood has everyone keyed up," Rumble said.

A man walked by, wearing a two-day scraggle of whiskers, dressed in a tight black shirt, Gore-Tex pants. Another one of the hikers. "Thanks, Ian," he said, clamping her not-needed rescuer on the shoulder.

Ian nodded after him. "Miles."

Apparently, this guy knew everyone in the saloon. "Ian? That's your name?"

He nodded while reaching for a napkin. He fished ice from his water and folded it into the napkin. "You've got a nasty bump there." He made to hold the makeshift ice pack to her head, then simply handed it to her.

"Thank you." Kind. She should have seen that earlier. "Sorry I hit you. It's a . . . well, a reflex."

"What, from your years cage fighting?" He raised an eyebrow, and she couldn't help a smile.

"No. Just . . . nothing."

He frowned a second, but it vanished.

She anchored the ice pack in place, too aware of the fact that she should be attracted to this man who seemed so clearly interested in her.

Or maybe she was simply so out of practice she didn't know how to flirt, or what flirting even looked like. Maybe he *was* simply being nice.

And she looked like a fool. She knew better than to dive into the middle of a barroom brawl—resurrect all her nightmares in broad daylight, or at least under the dim lights of a bar. Her specialty was picking up the pieces, not preventing the disaster in the first place.

Or at least it had been.

"I should go," she said, pulling the ice away, fingering the bruise, testing it. "I still have an hour of driving tonight."

Ian raised an eyebrow. "I don't think so. You're injured, and you've been drinking."

Huh? "Hardly." She picked up her glass. "This is *root* beer. Besides, I've been hurt worse than this and still managed to airlift eight marines out of a hot zone. Trust me, I can keep my Ford Escape between the lines from here to Whitefish."

"You still can't go."

"*Enough* with the gallantry. Listen, I'm exhausted, I've just driven for two days without sleep, and I have to report for my new job in the morning." She turned to Gina just emerging from the kitchen with her ribs. "Can I get those to go?"

Gina nodded, turned back to the kitchen.

"You don't understand—" Ian started.

"No, dude, *you* don't understand. I'm simply not interested, and frankly, you don't want to get messed up with me. Trust me on that one."

He frowned then, but then reached out and cupped his hand over her keys.

And that was just . . . it. So what if he had six inches on her, looked like he worked out regularly, and knew how to handle himself. She only *appeared* helpless.

She schooled her voice, kept it even but with enough edge for him to take her seriously. "Ian. I know you don't know me, and right now, I sort of wish we'd never met, but trust me . . . You let go of my keys or that little altercation on the dance floor will look like a warm-up."

And he actually, seriously, smiled?

"Huh. Okay." She slid off the stool.

"Slow down, I'm not trying to start another fight." He moved his hand. "You can't go home because . . . you can't. Highway 2 is washed out just north of Mercy Falls. Unless you want to drive three hours back to Great Falls, then two hundred miles to Missoula, then finally north on 93 for another one hundred or so miles and end up arriving home around dawn, you're hunkering down here tonight."

Here. In Mercy Falls. She sighed and found the fist she'd made loosening.

"I was just trying to save you hours of driving."

Gina came back out, plunked the bag of ribs on the bar. "Okay, here you go. By the way, Dad says hi. And that dinner is on the house for your service to your country. I didn't know you won a bronze star."

Kacey glanced at Ian, who raised an eyebrow. She turned back to Gina. "Tell him thanks." She didn't follow up on the medal comment. Because, really, she had her doubts about the validity of giving someone who'd just barely kept it together a medal.

"Listen," Ian said. "The hotels from here to Great Falls are full of National Guardsmen and volunteers trying to keep the river from flooding.

Why don't you come home with me? I have a ranch not far from here."

She stared at him. "You've got to be kidding me. What—do I have the word *desperate* tattooed on my forehead? Or *easy,* perhaps?" She grabbed the bag, her keys. "This may be a shocker, but no, I won't come home with you, thanks." She slid off the table, bumped her way through the crowd.

"Kacey!"

She ignored him, skirting past his friend Miles, who turned at his voice. She pushed outside, gulped in the fresh air. Wow, did that go south fast.

Apparently, it still wasn't over because Ian emerged through the doors right behind her. "Stop, Kacey."

She rounded on him. "And now this is starting to get a little stalkery. What's your deal?"

But the way he was looking at her, something like determination in his eyes . . . Now a little concern reached in, tugged at her. Her breath caught. "How do you know my name?"

"Take a breath. I'm not a stalker." He held up his hands as if in surrender, his jaw tight. "But I'm right, aren't I? You're Kacey Fairing?"

She found herself stepping back, wishing she had a sidearm. She dropped her takeout bag onto a bench.

He noticed and softened his voice. "This is my fault. I should have explained myself better. I heard you mention PEAK and then figured it out when Gina mentioned the medal, which is, of course, exactly what Chet said when he told me about you."

She took another step back. "Chet King told you . . . about me?"

Which would only stir up questions, she had no doubt. The last thing she needed was for her reputation to precede her.

"What did he say?"

"That you were exactly who we needed to take over flight ops for PEAK. Military hero . . ."

Oh. That. Still, that meant maybe she was safe from anyone grounding her based on false assumptions. Just because she was a little jumpy didn't mean she couldn't still handle a bird.

Ian lowered his hands but kept them out, away from his body, where she could see them. "You *are* the new pilot for PEAK Rescue, right? The one Chet hired to replace him and Ty?"

She nodded.

"Let's start over. I should have introduced myself earlier." He stuck out his hand, as if meeting her for the first time. "Ian Shaw. Local rancher and, well, founder of the PEAK Search and Rescue team."

Founder.

She swallowed, wrapping her brain around his words, even while reaching out to take his hand.

He rubbed the other hand over his jaw, now red, even a smidgen swollen.

"In other words, I'm your new boss. Welcome home."

Of course Ben knew that his father hadn't really caused the flood.

Sure, it did seem sometimes as if the Reverend Chet King possessed a direct tin-can-and-shoestring line to the Almighty that could call down divine forces. After all, Ben had seen it happen on more than one occasion—his dad hit his knobby knees and suddenly the sun began to shine, people got healed, and the town of Mercy Falls shouted hallelujah.

But certainly Chet's petitions hadn't caused the warm spell that thawed the snow cap off the Livingston Range, swelling tributaries and flooding the Mercy River. He hadn't created the three-day thunderstorm that saturated already drenched fields and creeks, turning them to torrents. Hadn't triggered the river to crest, to take out the Great Northern Bridge, wash out Highway 2, and threaten the existence of the small cowboy town of Mercy Falls.

Most importantly, he hadn't purposely trapped Ben in Mercy Falls while his music career fell to shambles around him. Not that his father actually cared, but at least he could acknowledge Ben's attempt to get himself back on his feet, stop being so stubborn, and most of all, refrain from calling down the wrath of God.

Thanks, but Ben got it already. He knew exactly what God thought about him.

Ben turned his F-150 onto the muddy frontage road edging the Shaw ranch.

Even if his dad could claim responsibility for the divine catastrophe, it wasn't going to work. Ben wasn't going to fall for the need to stick around and help his hometown dry off and rebuild. He had his own life—and frankly, his father's—to piece back together.

So what if he'd spent the night hunched over, hauling fifty-pound sandbags and trying to save the mobile home of Arlene Butcher. Not just Arlene's double-wide, of course, but the entire neighborhood of Whitetail Park that bordered the Mercy River. And, beyond that, the Mercy Falls Main Street, the high school, and even the Mercy Falls Community Church.

Which he supposed he should care about saving instead of wishing the place might be swept away.

He hit a rut in the muddy ranch driveway, and it sent a spear of pain through Ben's already aching back. And, wouldn't you know it, the tire spun in the muck, spitting out grime.

Ben shoved the F-150 into park and got out, stepping into ankle-deep soup. The sun hovered just above the horizon, bleeding through the gray veil of dawn, and the hint of more rain hung in the misty air, still too warm for June, which had caused this problem in the first place.

He pulled out a board that he kept in the bed of his truck just for this purpose and shoved it under the tire to give it traction. Then he stood, stretched, and simply breathed in the fragrance of the ranch.

Billionaire Ian Shaw's land sprawled through a bowl at the base of the western edge of Glacier National Park, in and over foothills striped with craggy streams and runnels of canyon, bordered by rolling meadows lush with foamy white bear grass, crisp alpine daisies, and pink fireweed. Behind it all, the northern Rockies rose in rugged, glorious backdrop, the Flathead Range to the east, the Swan Range to the southwest, their ragged peaks blue-gray and unyielding in the haze of the morning.

Ben could stand here forever, caught in the view, the sound of chattering bobolink, the rush of overflowing creek behind the house, the hint of all things summer in the air. Once upon a time, he had craved this life, relished the honesty of it. He could have built a happily-ever-after on the sense of accomplishment gained one day at a time, if he'd wanted it.

But therein lay the problem. He hadn't wanted this life. Just Kacey.

Ben got back into the truck, eased the truck out of the mud, then exited to retrieve his board.

He noticed the black outlines of Shaw's cattle, pinpricks on a hill on his northern forty, munching happily on the soggy table of wheat grass.

Ben ran his hand behind his neck, kneading a stiff muscle as he crawled the truck through the muddy track toward the highway.

The problem with sandbagging was that, at best, it kept the water from destroying homes, businesses, and yes, maybe even saved the lives of a few household pets. Which, of course, should be enough.

But it didn't actually fix anything.

Didn't repair the Great Northern Bridge, now eaten away and washed downriver, lodged at the apex of where the Mercy River met Hungry Horse Creek's south fork.

It didn't put the cabins at Moccasin Pass back on their foundations, nor keep the campers at Swiftcurrent Lodge from being stranded, having to be carted out by the army.

No, when a guy spent the night sandbagging, one backbreaking, fifty-pound bag at a time, he clued in to the raw-edged truth.

He had to do more than sandbag if he wanted to rebuild his life, his career. Which meant figuring out how to get his groove back, pen his own songs, then get into the studio and resurrect his solo game. Hollie Montgomery had another thing coming if she thought he'd just step aside for her to steal everything he'd sacrificed for.

He shot a glance at his watch hanging from the rearview mirror. Shoot.

His dad might be up already, trying to make breakfast, banging his chair into the table, upsetting the juice, refusing to let life sideline him. Ben longed to refit the house to accommodate Chet's injury, to help his old man *just be patient* as he healed from his dual broken hips. He kept pushing forward too fast, reinjuring himself, and now risked his long-term mobility.

But Chet never did well with *sit still*. Worse, Ben could admit he probably inherited the restlessness from his father and that he might be just as frustrated if he'd lost everything he'd loved.

Maybe he understood his father better than he'd thought.

Ben pulled up to the house, got out. Behind the log cabin A-frame, the creek tumbled over boulders, cresting to the edge of the wide bed. The porch swing facing it rocked in the morning breeze, and he half expected his mother to be sitting there, her Bible open or her knitting on her lap.

Overhead, the gray sky hovered low, thick with clouds. More rain in the forecast.

Maybe sandbagging was the best they could expect at the moment.

He came onto the porch, opened the entry room door.

Jubal met him, barking, upset, the hair on his neck ruffed up. "What is it, pal?"

Then, the acrid odor of burning metal rushed over him. A light haze clouded the entry, and he heard sizzling. "Dad!"

"In here!"

Ben charged inside, found the kitchen engulfed in smoke.

His father sat on the floor, dressed in his pajamas, his robe open, gripping a spatula like a weapon. "It's over. I got the fire out."

Next to him, on the melting linoleum, lay the overturned cast-iron pan, black oil puddling around the base.

Across the room and out of reach lay the overturned wheelchair, discarded, or maybe even shoved in disgust.

Ben picked it up, set it right. Leaned over the table to open the kitchen window. Glanced, one more time, at the stove, just to make sure.

"Stupid chair. I leaned too far forward and the thing flipped on me."

"Dad, that's one of the best chairs on the market. It doesn't just—"

"It flipped, son." He tossed the spatula in a perfect arc into the sink, began to scoot across the floor to the wheelchair.

There had been a time when Ben considered his father superhuman—lean, toned, one of the strongest men he knew. At sixty-five, Chet still had the strength of a bear, hands that could rip an apple in half or pull a birthing calf from its mother's withers. He possessed the stamina to outlast a breaking colt and a look that could stare down a bull. He'd been a hero too, evidenced from his stories of flying rescue choppers in 'Nam.

But seeing his father grunt as he wrestled himself onto his chair, his legs a nuisance more than a help, Ben just wanted to pick him up by his armpits, set him back into place.

Stop him from suffering one minute longer.

His father shouldn't have to spend the rest of his days shackled to a chair, and the injustice of that could cause Ben to shake a fist heavenward, even if he knew the consequences.

Frankly, Ben had run out of second chances so long ago, it didn't matter anyway.

"I'll get the pan," Ben said, reaching for the handle.

"Careful, it's—"

Hot. Ben jerked his hand back, shook it. Reached for a towel.

"I fell, and before I could get up, the bacon started burning," Chet said, now wheeling his chair to the table. "I tried to reach the handles on the stove, but I think I turned them the wrong way. I finally decided to move the pan off the heat, but it wouldn't budge, so I finally just yanked it down—"

"It could have fallen on you." Ben took the pan, wiped out the bacon grease, set it back on the stove.

"Naw. I knew where I wanted it to land."

"Then you might have gotten it closer to the carpet, because it burned the linoleum." Ben took a rag, wiped up the mess. "How about I fix us breakfast?"

But his father had already started cracking eggs into a bowl. He reached for a fork. "I'm not dead, kid. I'll whip us up an omelet. You grab a shower. You're filthy and I could smell you coming from Great Falls."

For the first time, Ben noticed the mud he'd dragged into the house. "Sorry."

"Your mother would've had your head," Chet said, and grinned at him. Ben wanted to match it, but how could his father so casually, so easily drop her name? Like she might be in the next room?

As usual, the old man could read him. "I miss her too, son. But she's just waiting for us. We'll see her again."

And there was the chaser, his father's casual, easy faith statement.

"Right," Ben said. He walked back out to the entryway, used a jack to yank off his grimy work boots. He returned to the kitchen. "I'll grab a shower if you promise not to burn the house down."

His father threw the towel at him. Ben caught it and threw it back, trying for a smile. *I'm trying, Mom.* But wow, Dad didn't make it easy.

Still, he'd made her promises . . . *"Come home once in a while, okay? He needs you."*

Right.

He turned toward the bathroom, then stopped, her words lingering. "You know, Vanderbilt Stallworth Rehab Center in Nashville is one of the best rehab centers in the country. And I've already lined up a therapist for you—"

"I'm not leaving Mercy Falls, Ben. I told you that."

Ben paused, not able to say the words—that maybe they should consider the fact he might never get out of that chair.

He hated that thought as much as his father did.

Besides, he knew how to pick his battles.

"Then what if I made some changes to the house —put in handicap-accessible appliances, modified the kitchen so you can get around. That's why I came home—to help you adjust to this life."

His father rolled the chair over to the stove. He reached for the cast-iron pan and Ben tried not to lunge for it, to help.

Chet turned on the flame. "Is that why you came home? Really?" He didn't look at Ben as he poured the egg mixture into the pan. The omelet began to sizzle.

Ben frowned. "Of course that's why. You needed help."

Chet just pursed his lips, nodded. "Huh. Because it looks a lot like running to me."

Ben refused to flinch. His father had never pulled his punches, and apparently without Mom around to temper him, he went right for the heart. "I'm not running. In fact, if you'll listen, I'm trying to get you to come to Nashville—"

"I'm not moving to your fancy digs in Nashville so you can shove me in rehab. I'm just fine here—"

"Dad! You nearly caught the house on fire."

Chet made a noncommittal noise that Ben didn't know how to track, then opened a drawer, grabbed a flat spatula, and tested the eggs. "You'd better be getting into the shower if you want breakfast."

"Listen, I'm just trying to help—"

"Then stop talking about me leaving and start unpacking—for real."

In other words, *stay.*

"You know I can't do that."

"You can do anything you want, son. It's never too late to start over."

Ben stared at him. "I don't want to start over. I've spent the last thirteen years building something—I'm not going to lie down and let someone take it away from me."

But yes, maybe it had taken him a month to figure out that he wanted to fight for it.

Betrayal did that—took the wind out of his sails, kept him gasping.

It took him three years to recover, find his feet last time. A month seemed record time, frankly.

But Chet's words bit at him. Especially as Ben moved to his tiny bedroom in the back of the house. He'd thrown his filthy clothes in a corner, the pile marinating with ranch odors. His clean laundry sat in a basket available to sift through on a daily basis.

Maybe it did resemble running—a bit. He had simply dumped his duffel bag out on the floor, made some not-so-tidy piles, and dove into some long-overdue house repairs.

Reverting back to his ranch-hand roots, the ones he sang about, the ones that had launched his now-in-jeopardy career.

Ben found a clean pair of jeans and an old Bluebird Café T-shirt, then headed to the shower down the hall.

Five minutes later, he braced himself against the tile, letting the still-warming water cascade over his aching muscles, lifting his face into the spray. Another thing his father couldn't do—shower. The old man somehow levered himself into the tub in his master bedroom, a feat the home health nurse probably assisted him with. Despite his father's disappointment over his music career, he noticed his father hadn't turned down the fancy, comfort wheelchair or Ben's offer for nursing help.

Thankfully. Ben wasn't good at that caretaking stuff.

But he could probably pick up a hammer and start modifying the house.

Ben scrubbed off the mud, let the heat massage the stress out of his back, then turned off the shower and climbed out, drying off. He wrapped a towel around himself, ran a hand across the mirror to clear the steam, and peered at his bloodshot eyes. He looked like he'd just come off the road after playing a month of back-to-back gigs, catching just a handful of winks between stops.

Grabbing his toothbrush, Ben stood at the window and cleaned his pearly whites, checking out the sky for rain. Two hundred yards away, on the far side by a creek and nestled in a grove of towering lodgepole pine, Ian Shaw's unassuming but gorgeous hand-tooled log home gleamed under the caress of morning.

With wide-planked wood floors and arching beamed ceilings, stuccoed walls, opulent leather furniture, five private bedrooms and baths for each, and a top-of-the line chef's kitchen.

So much house for a single guy, but of course, Ben was one to talk. His own place sat on thirty acres outside Nashville, with five bedrooms, a pool, and enough space for the family he'd always thought he'd have.

Maybe that's what he and Ian had in common— the hope for family. If they built it, it would happen. Or not. From the talk Ben could scour up, Ian preferred to be alone, or at least surround himself with just a handful of confidants—Chet, his personal assistant Sierra, and Deputy Sam Brooks, who swung by to check on the place when Ian jet-setted off to manage one of his many companies.

As if Chet and Ben weren't right across the yard to keep an eye on the place.

Even after more than a decade away, Ben still knew nearly every person in the town of Mercy Falls.

Or so he thought.

Ben moved the curtain aside to get a better look at the silver Ford Escape, a newer model caked with the appropriate layer of dried mud to have driven up in the night.

So Ian Shaw had a new friend. Interesting.

Ben spit into the sink, rinsed his mouth out. Decided against running a comb through his dark blond hair. Or trimming his whiskers. He had a feeling he'd be heading back out to the sandbagging team for a fresh layer of grime.

He pulled on his jeans and T-shirt, then headed out barefoot to the kitchen to find his father at the table eating an omelet.

Chet shoved a plate toward him. "I added mushrooms and picante sauce."

Chet had turned on the news of the day—the police scanner squawking reports from the local

EMS. Flood updates, a few calls from worried locals checking on the height of the river.

"Reminds me of the flood of '64. I was about sixteen, and Dad was working the Marshall ranch, closer to Great Falls. Mom looked out the window and saw this wall of water coming at us, way off in the distance. Dad threw me and Ham into the truck, and we went to the bottoms to move the yearlings. We got them to higher ground, then headed back to the house."

Ben retrieved a cup of fresh-brewed coffee.

"We got to the creek—it was about three feet wide when we'd crossed it an hour before. It had turned into frothy whitewater about thirty feet across, sweeping away cattle and horses, uprooting cottonwoods. And the worst part was my mom, trapped in the house on the other side of the creek, waving at us, holding Ike and Lucille on each hip.

"My father nearly lost it. He tied one end of the rope to a cottonwood, the other to his waist, and dove into the water. I thought he would drown, but he somehow made it to the far bank. He tied that rope onto one of the cottonwoods, and then Ham and I had to go hand-over-hand through the river.

"I took Lucy on my shoulders, and Dad grabbed Ike, and we ran in our bare feet up the bluff behind our house. The river simply ate our house, engulfing our front porch, breaking windows, tearing it off its foundation. It took everything, the cattle, the horses, and the lives of thirty-one people. We were lucky."

Ben had forgotten about his food. "What did you do?"

His father took a sip of coffee. Set it down to stare into the past. "We thanked God we were alive. And then we figured out how to keep going."

"Is that when you moved here?"

"Mmmhmm. Dad worked this land for Mr. Gilmore. And that's how I met your mom. Ruthie Gilmore. See, God can fix even the worst disasters, make something new and whole out of them."

If he expected agreement, Ben couldn't acquiesce. Instead he dug into his now-cool omelet. "The creek is nearly over its banks, but I don't think it'll rise much more." He shoveled in a forkful of eggs. "But the crest did take out the Great Northern Bridge last night—"

"Shh. That's an EMS call."

Huh? But Ben piped down, watching as the old man's head cocked toward the static of the radio. Ben hadn't a clue how to decipher the code.

"Get the phone," Chet said, gesturing to the ancient wall-mounted rotary next to the fridge.

"It hasn't even rung—"

And as if his father had magical powers, the old powder-blue phone jangled. Ben picked it up and, to make things easy, handed the receiver to his father. He ducked under the cord and settled back in his seat.

"Yes, Nancy. I think so," Chet said, then, "No, not yet. But I'm expecting the new pilot today."

He glanced at Ben, as if assessing him. "Yes, on four-wheelers, I suppose, but according to Sam, Swiftcurrent Creek is completely flooded, no access into the pass."

Ben put his plate on the table. "Is someone trapped in the Swiftcurrent Basin?"

Chet shot him a quelling glance, held up his hand. "Okay, if the National Guard changes its mind, give me a yell. I'll try to track down our new pilot and get back to you."

He handed the phone to Ben to hang up.

"I'm going to get you this nifty new gadget called a cell phone," Ben said, hanging up the handset. "What's going on?"

His father was digging into his robe pocket. "Youth group. Went camping up in the Swift-current area and haven't returned. They were due back yesterday, but with the rains, they should have pulled out sooner. They were supposed to take the Swiftcurrent Nature Trail up to the pass, but it's washed out all the way to Bullhead Lake. Parents are worried." He pulled out a piece of paper. "Dial this number, then hand me the phone."

Ben took the paper, picked up the receiver. "Is the National Guard going in?"

"Not until the campers are located. The army can't spare the manpower to look for them. They've got one chopper, and it's busy hoisting people from rooftops." He held out his hand for the phone. "But you know that area well."

"Yeah," he said woodenly, and his father didn't have to mention her name for Kacey to appear in memory—long auburn hair, mountain green eyes, the kind that could find him in a crowd and stop his breath. She swooped into Ben's head, lodged right there. No, worse, she sank down to his heart, where a fist tightened.

"Good," his father was saying, "because if you can locate the group, we can fly them out."

"In what, exactly, Dad? Your chopper is in pieces."

Chet grinned, winked, as if letting him in on a secret. "Insurance—and Ian—made sure we got a beautiful new dual-engine Bell 429."

Ben finished dialing and handed the receiver to his father. "Wow. So, want me to get Ty on the line?"

"Ty's still shaken from the crash. Hasn't even been in the simulator since it happened. No, it's going to be a busy summer, and we need some-one at the helm who is seasoned, who knows what she's doing. I hired us a new pilot."

She?

The word must have come out of Ben's mouth.

"Yes, *she*." His father held the phone to his ear. "Do you have a problem with that?"

"Of course not, but . . . I don't know. I thought with the accident, you were done with PEAK

41

Rescue. I mean, who will take over the team?"

"Maybe you could."

Oh, Dad. "I have a job."

His father shrugged, and it opened up the scab.

"Why would I come to your concert, Ben? You sing about beer, women, trucks, and fast livin'. That's not my life, and it shouldn't be yours."

Well, that life paid the bills—his and his father's.

More, people lined up for days to get tickets to his concerts. Or at least they had, once upon a time.

Right then, whomever his father had called picked up. "Hi, yeah, this is Chet King. I'm just checking that you're headed in this morning? You can stop by the house . . . super. See you soon."

He handed the phone back to Ben. "Now we have to call Miles. I suspect the team is already busy working the flood, but maybe Jess can ride along in case there are any casualties."

"Okay, fill me in here. Who is this new pilot?"

Ben might have imagined it, but he thought he saw his father turn a shade gray. "Before she gets here, I need to talk to you, son."

"Dad, are you okay?"

Through the window over the sink, he saw a figure move out from Ian's house, climb into the Escape. From this vantage point, it looked like a woman.

Really, Ian?

But he didn't have time to think that through, sort it out from what he knew about Ian, because his father had turned to him.

"Son, I know you say you're not hiding, but the fact is you've never been the same since you and Kacey split up—"

Ben's gut tightened. "Dad, stop."

The Escape pulled a U-ey, started their direction.

"And I know there's a lot of hurt there, but—"

"Hurt, Dad? That's how you're framing it?"

"I know you have unfinished business."

"I can promise you we don't."

"And I think the reason you've never been truly happy in Nashville is—"

"I'm happy in Nashville! I have a great career, fans, a house that's five times this size—"

"Because you never stopped loving her."

And now Ben had nothing. His father stared at him.

Chet's voice dropped. "You're still running from your mistakes, refusing to forgive yourself."

"No, *Kacey* couldn't forgive me."

Although, what good would it do to forgive himself, really? It was over, either way.

The Escape rolled to a stop in front of their house.

"That's the thing. What if you gave yourself a second chance?"

43

His dad's words dug in, even as the car door closed.

"There's no second chances, Dad. You can't go back and fix the past."

Chet's grin was rueful. "Well, I guess we'll see about that."

Boots scuffed on the porch, and now his dad's expression changed. Hardened. "Listen, sometimes you just gotta have faith. See that it can work out for good. There are second chances. Even grace, son, if you'll open your eyes to see it. To let it in—"

"Hello? Mr. King, are you here?"

Ben simply froze. The voice, sweet, bright, carrying so much of the past and too many fragmented hopes, rushed over the threshold, flooded through the house, and caught him by the throat.

No. His father did *not* call—

"In here!" his father hollered.

Ben stared at his father even as the footsteps stole his breath, stopped his heart. And yes, he had the crazy urge to get up, push away from his father, and simply, well, run.

Put this town and his father's meddling behind him.

He didn't want to rehash the past. Didn't even want a second chance.

"Dad . . ." His voice shook.

"This is why you came home, Benny," his

father said quietly. "Not for me. And not for you. For *her*."

Then he looked up, past Ben, and smiled. "Kacey Fairing. Finally. And, I might add, just in time."

He glanced at Ben, grinned as if he hadn't just put a fist through his son's chest.

"You're a sight for sore eyes. Right, Ben?"

— 2 —

It simply wasn't fair that seeing Ben King could shear open the scars, rip through thirteen years of healing right to the bone.

Kacey refused to let him unravel her, wouldn't let him see her flinch.

The jerk stood with his hands on the hips of his faded low-hanging jeans, dressed in a black T-shirt still clinging to his wet chest, his dark hair damp and tousled from a recent shower. Worse, he smelled clean and fresh, despite the scruff of a night's whiskers, a dark layer on his chin.

She hated to admit it, but Ben King in person was every inch as stunning as his album art, the in-the-flesh embodiment of his dazzling CMA accolades.

But country megastar and local legend Ben King had no business standing in the middle of his father's A-frame kitchen staring at her as if she owed him an explanation.

She wasn't the one who'd run off in the middle of the night. Who'd left her to pick up the pieces while he became an international star, with swooning fans, computer wallpaper, and albums dedicated to "the ones who gave my music life."

Once upon a time, she thought that had been her.

For a second, his expression tightened into incredulity.

Yeah, well, she had her own feelings of disbelief, thanks. Disbelief and not a little latent fury. But she could get to that later.

She narrowed her eyes at him, a reflex she instantly regretted, before she turned to Chet and squatted to pet the chocolate lab that insisted on making friends.

A sight for sore eyes. Sweet. As for Chet, the sight of him nearly undid her. Trapped in a wheelchair, his once-robust body withered under the destruction of his accident, his leathery, lined face evidence of the fatigue of doing daily battle with his uncooperative body.

But although his body had aged a century since the last time she'd seen him, his brown eyes still held the same warmth, lit by an internal fire, a joy in his expression that made her feel instantly home.

"I'm glad to see you too, Chet," she said quietly,

meaning it. She got up and hugged him around the neck, and for a second sank into the grip of a man who had known her and loved her anyway.

She stood up, Chet's hands still clasped to her forearms. "I'm so sorry about Ruth."

He nodded, and for a second grief flashed in his eyes. "She fought hard, all the way to the end."

Of course she did. Ruth had taught them all what it meant to stand tough.

"Thanks for coming over so quickly," Chet said, and she had the feeling he didn't realize she'd spent the night in Ian Shaw's guest room.

However, Ben clearly knew, because he instantly threw her under the bus. "She was next door, Dad." And his tone didn't suggest anything other than something lewd.

He was one to talk. Her mouth tightened. "I came into town last night and found out the bridge to Whitefish got knocked out. I met Ian, and after he introduced himself as my new boss, I took him up on his offer."

A decision she'd doubted the wisdom of until she slept like the dead in his plush, queen-sized guest bed. Two days of exhaustion plus her requisite Ambien made for instant, blessed unconsciousness.

Still, she'd locked the door, just in case her subconscious decided to take a midnight stroll. Thankfully, she woke still clutching his thousand-count Egyptian cotton pillows.

"He could have been a murderer," Ben muttered.

She glanced at him, shook her head. "I know how to take care of myself, thanks."

Ben quirked an eyebrow. "Is that why you're nursing a goose egg?"

Her hand went to her head. She moved her hair to cover the gray-green lump. "It's just a bump, in the line of duty."

"Kacey's done three tours in Afghanistan," Chet said to Ben, and the frown that creased his brow suggested he hadn't known.

He didn't know?

Well, how could he? How soon after Audrey was born had he hightailed it to Nashville to pursue his dreams? A week and a half?

Ten seconds?

"Wow," Ben said, and that one little word, the accompanying tone of respect, saved his sorry hide.

"She flies Black Hawks," Chet elaborated. "Which is why I asked her to sign on to the PEAK team for the summer."

"I'm home on leave for a few months," she added. She didn't follow up with a question about where Ben had been, because, well, the pitiful fact was she already knew.

She had this little issue with downloading his songs, listening to them until they turned her to ash, then, like a crazy person, deleting them.

Rinse, repeat for the past thirteen years.

He, on the other hand, had left her so far behind his father had to inform him of her military service.

For the first time, she wanted to thank her parents for moving them an hour north, to Whitefish.

Speaking of, probably she should cut this reunion short, considering she had five hours of backtracking to do.

"I'm ready to get started anytime, Chet, but first—"

"Good, because we have a situation," Chet said. "A bunch of campers—kids with a church youth group—are caught in the park. We think they're up on the Highline, near the pass. It's possible, with the rain, it's too treacherous to descend."

Highline. She refrained from glancing at Ben, but certainly he experienced the same flash-back. The dusty trail etched into the side of a granite mountain that dropped three hundred feet to Bullhead Lake. The moraine blue sky, the taste of ruby-red thimbleberries on their tongues, culled from their hike up, and the clean smell of wind over lingering snow.

She could almost hear his voice, feel the warmth of his hand on her shoulder as he directed her to turn around to catch the magnificence of Swiftwater Glacier caught in a bowl of a faraway mountain.

For a long second, the sense of being very alone

amidst all that magnificence, with only Ben to hold on to, swept through her.

Such a long, long time ago.

"At some points, that trail is only three feet wide where it cuts into the mountain. And it drops hundreds of feet," Ben was saying, clearly, yes, remembering.

He looked at her then, as if to catch her gaze, but she looked away.

Chet saved her. "Ben, go get the truck—I want to head over to PEAK headquarters."

Ben reached for the grips to his father's chair and moved toward the entryway, but Chet swatted Ben's hands away, fighting for control of the chair.

Ben surrendered, then shook his head, grabbing his boots and heading outside.

She walked out, holding the door open as Chet pushed himself through. Ben sat on the stoop, pulling on grimy socks, his muddy boots. Without looking back, he strode off to the earth-caked truck parked nearby.

Chet looked up at her. "He's had a rough go of it."

Ben had a rough go of it? Excuse her if she didn't cry him a river. A retort formed on her lips, something about abandoning his fiancée on the night she gave birth, leaving his daughter to be raised without a father, but Chet followed up with, "Give him a chance to get used to the idea of you being home," and the words just left her flattened.

Give him a chance.

Hardly. Um, *never*.

And then, a dark feeling crested over her, and she reached out, touched his chair. "Chet . . . wait. Are you telling me that I'm going to have to work with Ben? Is he"—oh, no, *no,* and her voice went a little weak—"part of the PEAK team?"

Chet glanced up at her, even as Ben pulled up the truck. "Of course."

Of. Course. The words lodged like a fist in her chest as Ben came around the truck, strode up the steps. He leaned down, put his arm around his father's waist.

"On the count of three," he said and then eased his father to a standing position.

"I can do it," Chet barked, but Ben ignored him, practically carrying him down the stairs to the truck.

Kacey looked away.

Ben settled him in the cab, then came back for the wheelchair and folded it up. He kept his voice low. "He won't let me build a ramp. Says he's going to be running by the end of the summer." He made a face, like "what do you do?" Then carried the chair to the truck.

She shook her head as she walked over to her Escape, climbed in. *You do what's right. You deal in reality and not take off to chase a dream, leave everyone behind.*

Her hands tightened around her steering wheel as she followed him through the muddy drive, out past the ranch land, and onto the dirt road that traversed the property. Rain drizzled against her windshield, and she turned on the wipers.

She hoped Chet was patched into the nearby airport for weather updates.

She bumped over a drainage ditch, then cut through a grove of willows and finally emerged to a driveway that led up to the former owner's house and barn.

The words PEAK Rescue, painted red, emblazoned the front of the white barn. Beside it, the modest two-story house had been updated and painted a crisp white, with a new green tin roof. A porch wrapped around the outside.

She parked next to Ben, who was unloading his father's chair. She held it as Ben retrieved Chet, again half-carried him up the steps, and settled him into it.

Chet looked away, his jaw tight, adjusting himself in the chair when Ben returned to the truck.

She couldn't help but notice that Ben had lifted his father without even a grunt of strain.

Apparently being a country music star required a regular workout. She noticed Ben had filled out, his shoulders wider, his body thicker, his forearms stronger.

And with that arrived another rush of memory that only confirmed that no way would she spend the rest of the summer in close proximity with Ben King.

Besides, she'd also noticed he hadn't once asked about Audrey.

Out of sight, way out of mind, apparently.

She followed them into the house/headquarters and found the old Gilmore place had been turned into a firehouse of sorts. A long center island doubled as a worktable in the updated kitchen, complete with stainless counters, a sub-zero fridge, and a chef's stove.

Apparently Ian didn't settle for anything but the top of the line.

On the other side of the room, on a grouping of desks, two computers hummed, one of them hooked up with the weather service, now flashing updates on one of the flat screens affixed to the wall. The other flat screen played an update of the news from the area. A massive, intricately detailed topographical map, probably ten feet wide and half as tall, covered the opposite wall.

"I've got the latest weather report," said a woman emerging from a room in the back. "The weather seems to be clearing up over the park, for now. Ceiling is at 2400, wind out of the east, 10 mph, 35 percent chance of rain. Hey, I'm Jess." She came over to Kacey and extended her hand.

Dressed in a pair of green Gore-Tex pants and a white shirt with PEAK Rescue monogrammed on the pocket, she had a confidence to her gait and wore her long blonde hair down, a smile in her blue eyes.

Kacey recognized her from the night before, at the Pony.

"I'm the team EMT," Jess said. "Chet has told us a lot about you."

She saw Ben shift, his jaw tighten. He shook his head as if in disbelief.

Kacey ignored him. "Great to be here. I hear we have a bunch of trapped kids up by Swiftcurrent Pass?"

"Maybe. Or they could be down by Bullhead Lake. That's what their hiking plan suggested, and the river may have flooded behind them, cutting off their route back." Jess walked over to the oversized map and traced her finger across the map, starting at the West Glacier entrance, past Lake McDonald, over Logan Pass to the Continental Divide, then over the Garden Wall, and down to Redrock Falls. "According to the wife of the pastor—"

"Pastor?" Kacey said.

"Oh, it's a church group." Jess glanced at Chet. "They hired a couple park guides, so they probably made it to higher ground, but with the rain and cloud cover, we haven't been able to contact them."

"Mercy Falls Community Church," Chet said. "I know the youth leader—a solid guy named Jared North." He turned to Ben. "He played football against you and Sam, remember? For Hungry Horse?"

Ben's mouth tightened, and he gave a nod. "Running back. A bit of a showboat, if I remember correctly."

Jess's mouth tweaked up as she turned back to her map. Kacey liked her.

"Well, he's up there, with a couple guides and about twelve hungry lost kids, so let's hope that he's left the showboating behind and has them hunkered down somewhere. With the glaciers melting and the runoff from the mountains, who knows but they could find themselves in a flash flood trapped on the side of a cliff."

And that put a fine point on their mission. "Right. With the ceiling being so low, we can't fly Visual Flight Rules over Logan Pass. But you said this was a Bell 429, right, Chet?"

Chet nodded. "Brand-new, 150-knot top speed, with single pilot Instrument Flight Rules and WAAS precision approach capabilities. Holds three people during a medevac, but seven if we remove the basket. And it has a dual engine, so we've also got a winch."

Kacey glanced at Chet, and he grinned up at her, a spark in his eyes, not unlike when he used to talk about Ben making a catch on the goal line or even sometimes when Ben played guitar for youth group.

So much pride, and Ben had never really seen it.

It didn't matter anymore, however. She couldn't fix Ben, didn't even want to.

Kacey walked over to the map, checking altitudes, mapping a route to Swiftcurrent Basin. "Okay, the weather report predicts the ceiling will hang around 2400 during our window, which still means we'll need an MIFR flight plan. Jess, you get the chopper loaded with supplies, I'll get us mapped, filed, and cleared."

Silence.

She turned. "What?"

"Kacey, I think Ben should go with you," Chet said.

Every fiber of her body thrummed, steel hard.

"Ben could stay and man the radio." She thought it a good concession, considering she'd have to listen to his voice in her ear.

"No. I'll man the radio. You'll need Jess in case anyone is hurt. And Ben knows the Swiftcurrent area."

"So do I." She shot a look at Ben. "I don't need him."

"Clearly," Ben said, his tone dark. "You never have."

She rounded on him, the words scurrying to the surface. "And whose fault is that?"

Ben's mouth tightened.

"What's going on here?" Jess asked.

Ben glanced at Kacey, but she turned away. "Nothing. Sorry."

But she could feel Ben's eyes burning her neck. Then, finally, "She's right, it's nothing."

She closed her eyes, the word a punch to her heart. *Nothing.*

His daughter, now thirteen, nothing. The girl he'd loved through high school, asked to marry, nothing.

Yep, that felt about right.

She took a breath. Twelve years in the military schooling her emotions and she was right back to holding her heart in her hands while Ben walked away.

Not anymore. This was just a job, nothing more, and she didn't have to let him unravel her. She turned, found the voice that had saved her and her soldiers, kept her sane. "Let's get this done. We have kids to rescue."

He wanted to strangle his father. *"This is why you came home, Benny."*

Uh, no, no it wasn't.

Ben had not come home for Kacey, and even if he'd ever harbored the dream, the faintest hope that they might find their way back to each other, it had died from the hypothermia radiating his direction.

She'd spent the last forty minutes neatly ignoring him, and frankly his head still spun just a little from the fury in her tone.

"And whose fault is that?"

Uh, well, hers, actually.

He still sometimes replayed his happiest moment, when he'd gotten down on one knee, handed her a ring purchased with every cent of the tip money he'd earned from playing at the Gray Pony for four years, and pledged to marry her, provide for her and their baby, and most importantly, love her for eternity.

And, to his recollection, she'd said yes.

So, according to his math, she owed *him* answers. But he harbored a queasy tightening in his gut that she didn't quite see it that way.

So, yeah, what she said—the faster they got in the air and located the campers, the sooner he could get back and figure out how to talk his father into going to Nashville with him before the man came up with more bright ideas.

"She looks like she knows what she's doing," Jess said as she carried a pack full of emergency blankets. They had hiked out to the barn, where the sleek white Bell 429 chopper sat on a retractable pad that moved it from the hangar to the helipad. Outside, a blue and red paint job on the back added color, the words PEAK Rescue outlined in white.

Kacey had already walked around the chopper, inspecting it inside and out.

He'd watched her out of the corner of his eye, a little undone by the transformation in the girl he'd once known, who could barely find a pencil in her locker. Now, she'd designed an IFR flight plan through the park, as best she could given their SAR parameters, moved the chopper onto the pad, and reconfigured the seats inside to make way for a litter, should they need it.

Meanwhile, Ben weighed and loaded the chopper with first aid supplies, blankets, rain slickers, water, and food. He added a haul line, a spider rescue strap rig, and just in case, a rescue litter as well as helmets, gloves, and a heli-tack harness should he or Jess need to rappel.

He hadn't always been a country star. Once upon a time, he'd even harbored his own SAR aspirations. Loading up the chopper stirred the old preclimb adrenaline.

Jess came up, carrying another pack of blankets. "I know this sounds a little crazy, given our mission, but . . . I have all your albums. You're one of my favorite singers."

He glanced at Jess and she made a face. "Is that weird?"

"Naw. Thanks." He hadn't experienced many fan moments since his return—mostly, he'd hung around the ranch and lately spent his hours covered in mud and grime, grateful the paparazzi hadn't found him yet.

"I didn't realize you were from around here. I mean, yeah, I guess I knew that from your interviews, but I didn't know you were actually, well, that your dad was Chet King." She caught her lower lip, her eyes wide. "I'm babbling, aren't I?"

He lifted a shoulder.

"Your dad said you worked the Esme Shaw search. Ian's missing niece?"

"Yeah." Then, glad to talk about anything but his careening music career, "Those were dark days. Shaw nearly lost his mind when the EMS teams stopped looking for her. And then the SAR volunteers went home and it was nothing but Shaw and his money. That's when he started PEAK Rescue. Apparently, we were the first to have a chopper that could haul people out of the Bob, or off a cliff in the park, or even track them down in some raging Cabinet Mountain river. I only worked the one summer before heading back to Nashville, but it was busy."

"That was about the time the first Montgomery-King album launched. I know—I flew down for the concert in Denver."

He found a real smile then. "That was a great tour." Back when he was Hollie's mentor, when she thought he could fly. Before she'd turned on him.

Apparently, he possessed the stellar ability to make the women in his life betray him.

"I loved how you brought local bands on stage. So cool," Jess was saying.

Actually, that was Hollie's idea, but one he easily agreed to. He clearly remembered what it felt like to sleep in his car or in a ratty motel, traveling from one gig to the next, hoping to be discovered.

Holding on to hope, one neon-lit bar gig at a time.

"Hey, baby, when I see you smile . . ." Jess was humming out the first stanza of one of Montgomery-King's many chart-topping singles.

Aw, what the heck . . . *"I know you're mine, for a little while . . ."*

"To have and to hold, and life is right . . ."

He gave a chuckle, but the song died and he gave a rueful smile. "At least it's catchy."

"I still have it on my playlist. I can't believe you're actually here for the summer."

Is that what his dad had told her? He blew out a breath. Right, well. "We'll see. I need to get Dad into rehab."

"He looks better," she said, adding MREs to another duffel bag.

He did? "He's getting around more. Misses flying."

"I'll bet. He and Ian are pretty close. Ian probably needs a friend—poor guy. I can't imagine losing someone you love like that."

"There were some who thought she might have run off with her boyfriend. But we gave it our best effort. Spent the entire summer searching nooks and crannies of the forest." Ben loaded in the blankets. "I couldn't help but wonder if she had run away."

If he'd known Kacey would be part of the

homecoming package, he might have run away too.

"So, you've done a lot of hiking in the park? Your dad said you knew the Swiftcurrent area," Jess asked as she pulled her blonde hair back into a quick braid.

Thanks, Dad, for bringing that up. He nodded.

But his conscience nudged him.

"Actually, Kacey and I hiked the Swiftcurrent Pass when we were kids."

Jess raised her eyes to him.

"We were on a camping trip—not unlike these kids. And Kacey and I sort of got separated from the group." That was the most delicate way to say it, he guessed.

Mostly, he'd wanted to see the view from the Swiftcurrent Fire Lookout tower. A view that included Kacey in his arms.

"We'd hiked up ahead of the group—they were on their way to Granite Park Chalet—and I figured we'd see the lookout, then meet them back at the chalet. We stayed too long, and I got mixed up, and we nearly found ourselves stuck on the mountain with night falling and the temperatures dropping. We made it back to the group, but everyone was pretty shook up. Dad and a couple of the other leaders got worried and started searching for us."

"So, did you get that kiss you'd hoped for from Kacey?" Jess said quietly.

"What?"

"I'm not stupid. I know guys." She winked.

He lifted his shoulder in a shrug, managed a quick smile. "Maybe."

She picked up the container of MREs. "So, did you and Kacey date?"

He nodded, not sure how to correct her. Date? No. Believe that he'd found his soul mate? So much so that when she got pregnant, he'd asked her to marry him, believed in his naive seventeen-year-old hope that they could live happily ever after on love.

Apparently one of them had come to their senses.

He, on the other hand, made a living singing the lie that love was enough.

"We went out a few times," he finally said.

Kacey came out of the house wearing a borrowed jumpsuit and holding a clipboard and her flight helmet. Maybe it was the freshness of old memories, but the sight of her, tall, shapely in her uniform, that auburn hair tied back to reveal her high cheekbones, her no-nonsense expression —all of it stirred up memories of a different version of her sitting on a stool at the long bar of the Gray Pony, swaying to one of his songs, looking at him like he could save the world.

Made him believe it.

"We need to get going before the ceiling deteriorates," Kacey said. "We don't know what we'll find in Swiftcurrent Pass."

Aye, aye, Captain. But he bit back the words. She was right—they had kids to find.

The uniforms hung from wooden lockers in the back room, helmets shoved on the shelves overhead.

He dug through the old uniforms and located the one he'd worn three years ago, during the summer of the great search. However, his helmet had clearly disappeared. He dug out one with the initials P.B.

Jess, too, donned her uniform and grabbed her helmet.

Kacey was in the cockpit, going through her preflight check.

Yes, once upon a time, he thought he couldn't breathe without Kacey looking his direction. But they'd both moved on, clearly, and maybe his dad was right. He just had to keep going. He didn't have the right to ask God to fix anything anyway, so maybe this was the best he could hope for.

He climbed into the back of the chopper, tested the radio in his helmet. Kacey's voice came through crisp and sharp.

"Keep an eye out for those kids," she said.

"You just keep us away from any mountains," he responded.

"This will be fun," Jess said, and Ben couldn't tell if she was being sarcastic.

Ben eyed Kacey as she turned on switches, connected with the airport out of Kalispell. A precaution more than permission, but probably she was used to following regs. She checked in with Chet, then told Jess and Ben to buckle in.

Check.

He'd flown with his father so many times he knew the feeling as the chopper lifted vertically from the ground, of losing his stomach like he might on a roller-coaster ride. Kacey held the cyclic stick between her knees, her left hand on the collective lever, which appeared very much like an emergency brake on a car but acted like a motorcycle handle to increase lift and accelerate their ascent.

She maneuvered the tail rotor blade with her foot pedals.

They levitated, then gathered altitude as the bird found speed.

She angled them away from the base, over the barn, the house, then pointed them northeast toward the park.

He never grew tired of flying over Glacier National Park. She skimmed them over the vast meadows blanketed with scarlet red Indian paintbrushes, pink fireweed, sunburst yellow glacier lilies, and gold and purple daisies as she hovered below the clouds, the mountains looming ahead. Then she switched to IFR and flew them up through the clouds to where the peaks jutted above the cotton. Jagged-edged mountains, spires rimmed with snow reaching to the heavens, the blue vault of sky arching over-head, almost peaceful.

And that's when their conversation from earlier revived, found purchase.

"What's going on here?"

A good question, asked by Jess. And he'd been scrambling for an answer when Kacey came up with it.

Nothing.

That's what she thought? That they'd been *nothing?*

But maybe Kacey was right. He'd spent too long dissecting his mistakes, trying to figure out why she'd gone from saying yes to marrying him to deciding to give their child up for adoption and refusing his calls.

And she thought *he'd* betrayed *her.* Wow.

He held on as they veered down, dipping again through the clouds, emerging into a bowl, the trees cascading down in a slope of green fir to a dark blue lake pooling at the bottom. He could make out the Highline Trail etched into the Garden Wall as she descended.

"We'll land near the pass. We'll have to go through the clouds again. Hang on." Kacey's voice, calm, no stress as she maneuvered the bird toward Swiftcurrent Pass, to the saddle where she could put down.

They landed in a patch of white daisies, the wind buffeting the chopper, and she instructed them to wait until she had the bird shut down before they got out.

The wind whistled in his ears as he opened the door and hopped out, searching for the group.

"Granite Park Chalet is just down the trail. My guess is that they've holed up there," Kacey said, walking over to retrieve one of the duffel bags of MREs. "Ready for a hike?"

He grabbed his backpack and the bag of blankets while Jess fitted on her EMT pack.

Too many memories for him to answer.

He took off down the trail instead, on his way to the chalet.

More of a rustic way station than a traveler's paradise, the Granite Park Chalet perched on top of a mountain on the west side of the Continental Divide, at the apex of two trailheads. Ben had more than once found his way to the remote outpost to listen to the songs in his head.

Like three years ago, when he thought he just might end up in Mercy Falls for good.

And, of course, right before he left for Nashville that first time, trying to undo the knots Kacey had lodged in his brain.

He hadn't realized he'd left Jess and Kacey behind until he spotted the stone buildings gleaming in the midmorning sunshine. Built of ledge rock by the railroad over a hundred years ago, with a main eating area equipped with a stove and rough tables and second-story bunk rooms that emerged onto a hand-hewn deck. The view from the lodge felt a little like swallowing the world whole. More than once Ben had repressed the wild urge to swan dive into the expansive valley and hope the wind might catch him and carry him aloft, over lakes and black pine, the wind a song in his ears.

"Do you see them?" Kacey had caught up, barely breathing hard.

"Nope," he said, "but there is a wisp of smoke from the chimney."

He headed down the path. Far away, on the edge of the horizon to the west, black cumulus gathered, edged with the finest flash of gold, and he thought he heard thunder rumble.

"We'd better hurry," Kacey said.

Although the sign directed visitors to the back, he entered from the front, onto the front porch and into the main eating area.

The door opened on ten teenagers sitting around the stove, some of them with their sleeping bags wrapped around them, eating Doritos and playing Monopoly.

Apparently *not* in need of rescue.

Except, from the group rose a woman, mid-twenties, her dark blonde hair in braids and held back with a floral handkerchief. She wore green army fatigues, a vintage Pac-Man T-shirt, and Keens. "Oh good, you're here!"

Huh?

Kacey had come in behind him and now pushed past him, toward the woman. "Willow? What are you doing here?"

The woman aptly named Willow climbed over bodies, directing someone not to cheat, and came over to them. "I'm so glad you're here—and wow, really? Ben King too?"

He frowned, felt a smile lift. A fan, here on top of the mountain?

"I guess that's a good thing, right? Because now you're both here and you can look for her together."

Look for . . . ?

"What are you talking about?" Kacey said, her pack dropping onto a table.

Willow stared at her, and something about her expression made Kacey still. Her hand touched Willow's arm. "Who are we looking for, Willow?"

"Oh, of course, you don't know. Sorry—I figured that's why you came."

Kacey's mouth tightened into a tight bud of impatience.

"Audrey. She's lost. Jared is out looking. I think he took the Loop Trail down, but I don't know. He left hours ago to look for her—for them."

Kacey had stiffened. "Them?"

Willow made a face at Kacey. "I'm sorry. She took off yesterday with one of the guys in the group, and they haven't been back."

"Audrey is with one of the *guys?*" Kacey took a

deep breath. Held up her hands as if trying to wrap them around Willow's words. "Who is she with?"

"Just another camper—his name is Nate. He's her age, promise."

"Nice. Two teenagers out on the mountain by themselves. That's fantastic." Kacey turned, pressed both hands on the table.

Enacted some deep breathing.

Ben hadn't a clue what might be going on here. "Who's Audrey?"

And that's when everything around him stopped, went silent. Willow stared at him, blinking, and then, slowly, Kacey rounded, her eyes wide, her mouth opening.

He heard only the thunder, maybe out of the approaching storm, but more likely deep inside, his heart knocking to get out. To run.

Because even as the words formed on Kacey's lips, even as she put voice to the truth, he realized his father had been right.

This is why he'd come home.

"Audrey is only your *daughter.*

— 3 —

As much as she wanted to throttle Willow—and Audrey, for that matter—Kacey didn't have a thought beyond trying to decipher if Ben might actually be asphyxiating.

He had his mouth open, his eyes widening, his breath hitching—maybe not about to perish, but as his mouth closed, he looked very much like he'd had the wind knocked out of him.

"My . . . *daughter?*" He cast a look at Willow, then back to Kacey.

She narrowed her eyes at him. "Are you serious right now? That you didn't know, for the past thirteen years, that you had a daughter? Wait, don't tell me. Did you miss the fact that I was pregnant? Don't tell me you have selective amnesia right now, because I remember every detail, from the pickles to the ice cream runs." She had other details she remembered too, but she wouldn't bring them up in front of a group of within-earshot teenagers.

"Yeah, I remember, thanks," he said, his voice sharp. "And yes, I know you had a baby." He cleared his throat, cut his voice low. "Know *we* had a baby, but—"

"What did you think happened, Ben? That she *vanished?*"

71

And that was when he caught her around the elbow and, before she could recover from her shock, dragged her outside.

He pulled the door shut behind him.

"What?"

"Are you kidding me? If we were in cell phone range, those kids would be tweeting right now."

"Tweeting—that's what you're worried about?" And now she would have to dismember him. "You have a daughter."

"Stop talking." He held up his hand. "Just give me a second here."

And then he bent and grabbed his knees, as if his head might be spinning.

Seriously? "Ben, what is going on? You didn't know about Audrey? At all?"

"I can't believe you didn't tell me." He walked away from her, running his hands through his hair.

Seriously?

Her mouth opened, even as he whirled around.

She had no response for his stripped, incredulous expression.

"I called," he said on a wisp of voice. "I called and called and—"

"You didn't show up for her birth! You were sitting in jail, drunk! I know, because my father told me."

He sucked in a breath. "That's not the whole story." And he wore such a broken expression she had to turn away.

She refused to feel any sympathy for him. Instead, she blew out a breath, hands on her hips. A low-pressure system gathered in the west, evidenced by the low-hanging thunderclouds. She didn't like it.

"It doesn't matter. It's over, and now we have to find Audrey," he said, as if reading her mind.

"Agreed." She stepped back inside the cabin, her entire body trembling.

Thankfully, it seemed that despite an outburst that felt like shouting to Kacey, the youth group had been oblivious to the revelation. Small mercies.

Willow, however, had turned ashen. "I'm sorry. I didn't know that Ben didn't know."

She could hardly blame the sister of Audrey's godmother. After all, for all Sierra knew, Ben had walked out on them the night Audrey was born.

So much for the abandonment story. Although, until this very moment, it had been true.

"It's okay," she said to Willow. "But I don't understand—what is Audrey doing with the Mercy Falls youth group? She attends church in Whitefish with my parents."

Willow's mouth made a silent O. "Well, that probably has something to do with Nate."

"Nate."

"Oh, they are so cute. Nate's had a thing for her since—"

"Willow! Who is Nate?"

"Sorry. They play in a band together at their middle school, and since she doesn't have a youth group at her church in Whitefish, she started playing for us and attending some of our extracurricular events. Like this hike."

"Perfect. Where did they go?"

The door had opened, and Ben stepped in behind her. She felt his presence, solid, a wall of anger and not a little frustration, and it raised the little hairs on her neck.

But she'd spent twelve years in the military, in hot spots around the globe, and a little ire from Ben wasn't going to faze her.

Her biggest concern, right after locating Audrey and Nate, was keeping Ben quiet.

The last thing her confused thirteen-year-old daughter needed was her absent, superstar father rising from nowhere to complicate her life. And what would Kacey do if Ben sang her daughter a song, made her fall for him, then walked out of her life the millisecond she actually needed him?

Nope. Audrey already had a semi-absent mom. She couldn't be saddled with a disappearing father.

"I don't know. It was supposed to be a three-day trip. We hiked the trail up here two days ago, and when we went to leave yesterday, we realized the trail had been washed out. With the rain on the mountain, Jared suggested we lay low in the chalet for another day. He was thinking we'd hike out today via the Loop Trail. They must have sneaked out yesterday afternoon—we didn't notice them missing until last night, and we went looking, but it got dark so fast, and we didn't know what to do—"

"You don't leave two kids out in the elements overnight!" Ben snapped. "It *snowed* in the park last night."

"I know. We walked down the Highline Trail as far as we could and didn't see them. We weren't equipped to search in the dark and had no way to contact anyone. That's why Jared hiked out today—to get help." And now Willow looked like she might be unraveling, her eyes shiny. "Listen, we didn't know what to do. Nate's dad is a forest ranger, so hopefully he has some sense about him."

"It's Audrey who has the sense," Kacey said. "She's been backpacking with me numerous times—she probably found them a place to hunker down." She noticed that Jess had joined their conversation. "Can you pack me a survival first aid kit—water, food, blanket, simple splints? If they haven't returned, it might be because one of them is injured."

"Want me to go with you?" Jess asked. "The kids are good here—mostly just dehydrated."

"No. Stay here, on coms. If we find them and need to pack them out, we'll need you to go back to the chopper, meet us with gear."

Jess nodded and turned to repack her bag.

Kacey glanced at Ben. "I don't suppose I can talk you into—"

"I know where they are."

She stared at him, words dropping away. His mouth tightened, and he raised an eyebrow.

Oh.

He raised a shoulder. "Why not, right? If his dad is a park ranger, he's heard of the place. And if you've told your daughter—*our* daughter—anything about—"

"No. I haven't."

And that clearly hurt him, because he flinched. Then, "Right. Well, it's worth a shot."

Willow was staring at them, and now, as Jess returned with the pack, asked, "Where?"

"The fire lookout tower," Kacey said. She grabbed the pack, pulled on the straps. "Stay on the radio, Jess."

Ben had already pushed through the door.

She had to run to catch up to his long strides carrying him away from the chalet. He strode with purpose, a darkness in his expression.

Now was probably not the time to . . . "Ben, can we talk?"

"About what? Or rather, where do we start? Maybe with the fact that you told me you were going to put the baby up for adoption?"

Ho-kay. She slowed her breathing. If he wanted to run all the way to the tower—wait. "Adoption? Why would I—"

"You know why. Because of your mother."

And that hurt, a blow right to her solar plexus. She fought the urge to press her hand there, ward off the ache. "I only suggested it once. And I didn't mean it."

"It sounded like you meant it. And when your dad showed up and told me—"

"What do you mean, when my dad showed up?"

The sky had turned a greenish black, the wind carrying an edge as it slid through her jacket. When Ben stopped, rounding on her, she could have sworn he carried the change of weather in his expression. "I called him, hoping he'd get me out of jail. And by the way, I wasn't drunk. I'd been fighting."

Something in his expression contained a dare. Always did, in a way. She could never ignore it.

"Who were you fighting, Ben?"

He shook his head slowly. Took a breath. Met her eyes.

His blue-eyed gaze always had the power to sweep her breath away, to make her heart stop, to still the world around her and center it on just him.

The wind shrilled, whipping between them.

"It doesn't matter anymore," he finally said. "But your dad came down to the jail and told me that you never wanted to see me again. That you were going to put the baby up for adoption and that I should leave."

He turned back up the trail, striding hard. "He said I had nothing to give you and that I should make something out of my life and let you do the same. And, if I didn't leave town, he'd make sure I ended up in prison."

She ran up next to him. "My dad would never do that."

He lifted a shoulder in a shrug. "Ask him." He topped the ridge, stopped, and pointed to a building a mile ahead. "There's the lookout."

Not an impressive building, save for its view overlooking the Swiftcurrent Basin all the way to Grinnell Glacier to the southeast and Iceberg Lake to the north. But with windows on each side, the fire lookout could spot smoke for hundreds of miles into East Glacier.

The perfect place for a teenage boy to take a girl if he wanted to impress her.

Kacey's mouth tightened.

Ask him.

"I don't care what my dad said to you. You shouldn't have left."

"I'm thinking that very thing right now," he said quietly as he moved up the trail. "But I was seventeen, scared, hurt, and frankly you weren't taking my calls."

"I'd just had the most traumatic experience of my life—giving birth—without the father of my child. I was angry. But then you left . . . you just . . . left."

He said nothing as he climbed over another ridge, set down the trail.

"I hated you," she said, a sort of confession that took the edge off her anger.

"I guessed that."

"I told her you'd abandoned us."

She'd caught up to him and now saw his jaw had tightened.

"I suppose there's truth in that." His voice was tight, calm.

It only sparked her ire. "What is your deal?"

He rounded again on her so fast she slammed right into him. He caught her by the arms, and she realized how much he'd grown, taller by at least a couple inches, and he had a fierceness to his features she hadn't seen before. His beard had filled out, and his eyes nearly glowed with something unnamed. She stepped back, a little unnerved.

His voice was whisper-low, steel-edged. "I'm so angry at you right now, I can't breathe, okay? I can't believe that you didn't write to me, didn't take my calls, and didn't even think that I would want to know that I had a daughter. I can't believe that after all these years you never once let me into her life. Frankly, I'm trying to keep myself from throwing you off this mountain."

She stared at him, trying not to be undone, rattled.

Then he turned and headed again up the trail.

Shoot.

"Ben!"

But he didn't stop.

"Ben, listen, here's the thing. I know you're angry—okay, I get that. You're right, I should have contacted you. But you left—"

"We'll just go round and round on that, Kacey. It's not going to help."

"Fine. But I had to go on. To do something. So I got a job."

"You joined the army." He caught his breath then, glanced over his shoulder. "Which effectively means you abandoned her. Our daughter. What kind of mom does that?"

She recoiled, his words a slap. "The kind who is serving her country."

"Your country shouldn't come before your family."

"Tell that to the over 1.3 million active-duty soldiers out there protecting your freedom!"

His voice turned lethal. "Tell that to your daughter, who is lost out there, cold, maybe hypothermic—"

She didn't think, her arm moving nearly on its own as she reached out to slap him.

As if on reflex, he caught her wrist, jerked back.

But the movement shocked them both as he recoiled. He clenched his jaw, his chest rising and falling.

She swallowed, jerked her arm from his grip, shaking. "Sorry, but—"

"No. I shouldn't have said that. I'm sure she's fine."

She looked away, her eyes blurring.

Then, quietly, "You could have called me. I would have come home, taken care of her—"

"And sacrificed your brilliant, amazing, star-studded country music career?" Oh, she didn't mean for all the derision to fill her voice. Really. "Don't tell me you would have given up your dreams to come home and babysit." She turned back to him, didn't mask the accusing expression.

His eyes narrowed, but maybe she'd finally landed a blow in truth. He turned away, striding again down the path.

She stalked after him. "I know what you said, but let's just get really honest here. Admit it—the idea of a child and a wife depending on you probably scared the stuffing out of you. You didn't want the responsibility, the burden of providing for a family. You wanted your freedom and were all too happy to let my dad give it to you."

And that was when he whirled around again, his expression black.

His fists balled at his sides, released, tightened again. "I loved you. I wanted you. And yeah, I might have been scared, but I meant it when I asked you to marry me."

Oh.

His gaze held hers. And, shoot, if her eyes didn't start to burn. Stupid wind, whipping over the tundra, cutting through the rocks.

"Ben." Her voice trembled, so she schooled it, tried again. "I have to ask you not to tell her."

He blinked then, the fury on his face dissipating to what she guessed was disbelief.

"Oh, you've got to be kidding me." He turned away. "Not on your life."

"Ben!" She put a hand to his arm, tugged, and with something that sounded like a stifled curse, he relented.

"What?"

"She's going through puberty. And she's . . . well, clearly she's not thinking straight because why else would she run away with this boy?"

He raised an eyebrow. Then bit the inside of his mouth, considering her. "Huh."

"You know what I mean. It'll just confuse her. And I haven't even seen her yet—"

"Doesn't she know you're coming home?"

She made a face, and he rolled his eyes, looked away. "Nice. Wow, Kacey. So, the first time she's seen you in, how long . . . ?"

"Six months—"

"And you're tracking her down while she's on a romantic escape with her boyfriend."

"He's not her boyfriend, and by the way, you might consider being a little protective here. She *is* your daughter, after all."

His eyes widened. "Make up your mind. Is she or isn't she?"

She licked her lips, then caught her bottom one between her teeth. "I—"

"Geez, Kacey. What do you want from me? Do I get to be her dad or not?"

"I don't know, okay? I never thought this day would come."

"You thought I wouldn't ever find out? Sheesh. I live in Mercy Falls too. Which is weird. Why did my dad not—wait, *does* he know?" A hand went up around the back of his neck. "Oh my gosh—"

"I don't know, Ben. My parents moved to Whitefish right after Audrey was born. I always thought your folks knew and didn't care but . . . maybe not."

The look he gave her could have turned her to ash. "My mother died without knowing she had a granddaughter."

Kacey winced. "I'm sorry."

"Mmmhmm."

"Please, Ben. I know you're angry, but this isn't about you. It's about Audrey. If you tell her, she'll just get attached, and then when you leave, go back to your life in Nashville, it'll destroy her."

She didn't know how to interpret his grim look, the tightening around his eyes.

And that's when she heard it, a voice, light

and crisp, hanging on the wind. "Mom? *Mom!*"

She searched for it, and there—thirty feet below, on an outcropping of rock—Audrey stood waving, jumping up and down, then yelling as she scrambled up toward the trail.

Kacey headed down to her, over tundra and rock, trampling wildflowers and climbing over boulders as Audrey worked her way up to her.

An ugly scrape reddened her chin, her chestnut hair lay in tangles, and she'd been crying, evidenced by the swelling around her beautiful blue eyes. "I knew you'd come—I knew it. I know it was crazy, but I prayed and asked God to send you and he did." She flung herself into Kacey's arms.

Kacey didn't know what she'd done to curry God's favor, but she agreed her beautiful daughter deserved all the breaks she could get. She pulled the girl to herself, tucking her head over her daughter's, trying not to cry, failing.

Audrey looked up at her, ran a hand under her runny nose. "We were walking back from the lookout in the dark, and it started to rain and snow, and then Nate fell—"

"Fell?" Ben, of course. "How far?"

"He's down below the ledge. I think he broke something. He's in so much pain, I was afraid to leave him. And then . . ." Her gaze had turned to Ben, and she frowned, blinking.

"Do I—wait. Do I know you?"

Kacey froze, looked at Ben, her eyes wide.

Ben seemed unable to respond because his mouth opened, closed.

Kacey silently begged him. *Please.*

"Wait, I *do* know you."

Audrey stepped out of Kacey's embrace, her hand over her mouth.

Oh no, *no*. "Honey, I can explain—"

"Oh, Mom. I can't believe it!" Audrey's hand trembled as she grabbed Kacey's arm. "This is, this is . . . Benjamin King!"

Ben had experienced awkward fan moments in his life, but nothing compared to having his own daughter list her favorite songs off his albums, rattle on about the concert she'd attended last summer at Countryfest in Kalispell, and ask to take a picture with him once they got Nate off the mountain.

Nate, too, seemed to recover a smidgen when Ben scrambled down behind Audrey to his resting place. He'd fallen some forty feet from the ridge-line—not a straight drop but steep enough for him to tumble hard, until he finally landed on an outcropping about ten feet wide.

Beyond his perch, the mountain dropped fast another two hundred feet or so to another hilly descent of razor-sharp ledge rock, spires of black pine, and tangles of blueberry brier.

Ben hated to think what might have happened

had Nate's ankle not caught on the rocks. It was broken, but it had saved his life.

Apparently, Audrey had chased him down the hill, tried to make him comfortable. "Then the sun set and it started to snow, and I couldn't leave him," she said. "This morning, he didn't want me to leave, but I finally decided that I had to if I wanted to save us both."

Audrey had led them to their bunker, where she'd managed to pile rocks around them for a windbreak. She'd also scraped up tundra and spread it out for a bed and warmth and ripped up scrub branches for a meager ceiling.

By huddling together in the shelter, they'd survived the chilly night.

Now, Nate sat with his back to the hillside, his ankle grotesquely swollen, his face ashen. But he managed a smile, a flash of interest when Audrey announced that country music star Benjamin King had shown up to rescue him.

Not exactly, but the facts still fit.

Ben noticed that Kacey watched it all with a wary, gimlet expression. He still couldn't believe she'd nearly slapped him. Her impulsive violence had probably shaken her as much as him, given her expression.

It had also, for a second, jerked him back to reality. To his stinging words. *What kind of mom does that?"*

He might have deserved a slap.

But she gave back in kind. *"You wanted your freedom and were all too happy to let my dad give it to you."*

He refused to let those words rattle around his brain, unseat his anger.

For thirteen years, she hadn't reached out to him. He'd missed seeing his child take her first steps, lose her first tooth, read her first book, and call him Daddy.

"I have to ask you not to tell her."

No. It wasn't fair—and she knew it.

Kacey hunkered down next to Nate, probing his ankle after cutting open his pants leg. "I'm not an EMT, but I think you did more than sprain this. It clearly looks broken." She tugged off his sock, and Nate let out a moan, but even Ben could see the gray, mottled skin. Bruised, and perhaps a lack of blood supply.

Ben reached out to touch the ankle, hearkening back to his first-responder training that SAR summer three years ago, and found the appendage icy cold.

"We're going to need a stretcher," he said, and got up. They'd already tried to contact Jess, but the mountains had turned their coms to static. "I'll take Audrey back to the chalet, get the litter from the chopper, and be back as soon as I can." He glanced at the gathering clouds and saw the gunmetal sheen of rain over the far western mountains.

Kacey seemed to read his mind. "Hopefully it'll head south, but if we don't move fast, we could get trapped here."

Ben handed her his water bottle, glanced at Audrey. "Ready for a hike?"

For the first time, her fan glow faded and she glanced at her mother. "I want to stay with you."

He knew the debate on Kacey's face had nothing to do with her daughter's pleading tone. No, as she flashed Ben a tight-mouthed glance, he knew she heard his words: *"What do you want from me? Do I get to be her dad or not?"*

He met her gaze, and then, despite the roar inside, gave her a quick shake of his head.

Okay. Fine. I won't tell her. For now.

She turned back to Audrey, took her hand. "It's okay, honey. I promise to take good care of Nate. You go back to the cabin with Ben and let us focus on rescuing Nate."

Audrey nodded despite the tears edging her eyes. Smart girl.

Ben had the crazy urge to pull her close, to hold her and tell her everything would be okay.

That Daddy would take care of her.

He shook that thought away before it bubbled out.

Instead, he held out his hand. "C'mon. Let's get going before we lose the sun."

She took his grip, and he closed his hand around hers, so small and delicate in his. He pulled her up the hill, then put her in front of him as they hiked back to the chalet.

He made contact with Jess halfway there, and she was waiting for them, pacing outside as he came down the trail, the sun at his back, a sweat under his jacket. Willow came out to enclose Audrey in a hug, then draw her inside the chalet, listening to the story.

Ben updated Jess on Nate.

"Nate isn't the only one who needs medical attention. I have one of the girls here who is insulin dependent. She just used her last shot. She'd packed extras, just in case, but that what-if is here, and she won't last until tomorrow. We need to get her out tonight."

But with the ceiling falling and the sun fading . . .

Jess had already assembled her first aid pack and hiked/ran to the chopper with Willow to retrieve the litter. Together, they climbed back to the pass, and he and Jess hiked to Kacey and injured Nate.

Kacey had already splinted his ankle, applied body warmers to his core, and cleared the area for the litter. He and Kacey lifted Nate into the basket, then covered him in blankets. Jess took his blood pressure, gave him a quick assessment.

"Okay, we're ready."

Ben didn't like the pallor on the kid's face. He grabbed the back of the litter. "I'll try and keep him as level as possible—you just keep climbing."

Kacey and Jess took the head and they worked their way up the hill, silent, breathing hard as Nate groaned and cried out as they jostled him.

By the time they reached the chalet, the wind had turned Ben's fingers numb as flurries pecked at his cheeks and neck.

A fire blazed in the stove of the chalet dining area, the room cozy and safe from the elements. Still, the aura of fatigue and not a little fear bullied the mood as they set Nate on the floor.

Audrey and the rest of the youth group gathered around him as Ben drew Kacey and Jess aside.

"I'm not sure it's safe to fly out of here."

"The ceiling is dropping, but I don't see what choice we have," Kacey said. "I can fly us out, but not if we wait much longer. His ankle is bad. It has a scant blood supply, but he could lose his foot."

"Then I think you and Jess should fly out with Nate and the diabetic girl. I'll stay the night with the kids and we'll hike down the Loop Trail in the morning."

Kacey frowned at him. "I'm not leaving without Audrey."

"She's fine, Kacey," Jess said. "A little banged up, but I checked her out. She's not hypothermic, and she's safe here with the kids. There's really no room for her in the chopper."

Kacey's mouth formed a bud of disagreement.

"I promise, she'll be fine, Kacey." Ben didn't

exactly know how else to say it without giving her away. *No, Kacey, I won't tell our daughter, who seems to think I hung the moon, that I'm her father.*

"We're running out of daylight," Jess said quietly.

Kacey shook her head. "I don't like it."

"I promise," Ben said again quietly.

The words seemed to register, and Kacey finally nodded. She stepped away from him. "Audrey, c'mere, honey."

Whatever she said to her daughter as she pulled her away from the group had Audrey shaking her head, throwing her arms around her mother. Hanging on.

And the sight of it did crazy, unbidden things inside him. He couldn't place the emotions that churned up. Jealousy? Compassion? Frustration?

Then, Kacey looked his direction and back to Audrey, and Audrey's eyes widened.

His breath caught. Kacey didn't . . .

Kacey stood up and walked over to him, her arm around Audrey. "I told her that you might be willing to sing her a couple of your hits," she said, offering a small smile. "I didn't realize she was such a big fan."

A concession, he knew it. But he couldn't place the odd rush of relief. Didn't he want her to know?

"Be glad to," he said to Audrey.

Audrey grinned at him, and right then, his world stopped. Sure, he recognized Kacey in the shape of her face, oval with strong cheekbones, and those freckles on her nose. Her chestnut hair seemed the right blend of Kacey's auburn and his dark brown. And she had Kacey's body, just a hint of curves at this age. In fact, if he stepped back, he could easily make out the girl he'd once known when he'd run off to show her the view from Swiftcurrent Lookout.

But for all that, the girl before him had *his* eyes. Blue and shiny, so much hope in them.

He recognized a dreamer's expression.

He dredged up his own smile. "We'll have a regular sing-along if that helps keep us warm."

He turned to Kacey. "Let's get you loaded up."

They hiked with Nate and Jess's diabetic patient to the chopper, and he secured Nate in, then stepped back to watch as Kacey lifted them off the hillside. The storm had moved south, but night crept up around them to meet the pewter sky. The chopper dropped away from the mountain pass, then soared across the basin before gaining altitude and disappearing into the clouds.

Ben stood alone on the mountain, the wind in his jacket, listening to the whump-whump of blades calling him a fool.

How did he expect to spend the next twenty-four hours with his daughter without telling her the truth?

Willow had fed the stove, turning the room toasty warm. He heard her in the kitchen area, humming, and when he took off his jacket and unzipped the neck on his jumpsuit, he followed the smell and found her stirring up a pot of beef ravioli procured from some opened MREs. "I found some dried oregano and garlic powder—that'll liven it up," Willow said as he bent over the pot and inhaled.

His stomach jumped to life, growled.

Willow grinned at him. Then, quietly, "Sorry about that, back there. I didn't know that, well, you didn't know."

"I understand," he said and fought to keep the derision from his voice. "Kacey thinks she has her reasons, but . . ." He lifted a shoulder. "She wants me to keep it to myself for now. Doesn't want Audrey to know until—I don't know. Maybe until she turns thirty-five?"

Willow gave him a look. "Or maybe until she can tell her? It isn't like you've been around."

"I've been back to Mercy Falls three times since Audrey was born. And I was here the entire summer Ian Shaw's niece went missing. I promise, I've been around."

"And that might be the problem. Because it's not like you're just some cowboy down on the ranch. You're Benjamin King, chart topper, CMA host, and the lead singer of Montgomery-King. You have to admit that it couldn't have been easy for Kacey to see you and Hollie Montgomery together."

"We're not together."

"It sure looked like you two might be. And the tabloids—"

"Lied. Hollie and I flirted, sure, but she didn't really want me. She wanted what I could give her—and frankly, the feeling was mutual."

Okay, the smallest of lies—because early on, he'd thought they might be more. His manager, Goldie, had found him the perfect match for his husky, country tones with Hollie's blonde, country sweet soprano. She was flirt to his ballads, flash to his cowboy persona. And he supposed she'd injected life into his nose-diving career.

Willow considered him as she stirred the ravioli. "Rumor has it that you two broke up."

"This time, the press got it right. She's going solo."

"And you?"

Reeling. Regrouping.

"Helping my dad get back on his feet."

Willow nodded. "Sierra keeps me updated. Said you moved in with him."

"Just until I can get him to pack up and head back to Nashville with me."

"Good luck with that. PEAK Rescue is his whole life."

And that, thank you, he knew all too well.

He headed into the dining area and sat on one of the picnic table benches, listening to the chatter. Audrey sat cross-legged on the floor, her hands moving as she told the story of Nate's fall and their treacherous night on the mountain.

She possessed a sort of energy, a charisma in her storytelling that had him hearkening back to his early days when he'd step up to an open mic and summon the courage to sing a song.

If not for Kacey, he might not have even opened his mouth. But she'd believed in his dreams, even if they seemed crazy and out of reach.

He'd held on to that belief despite the wounds, working the honky tonks and dives until he got his break. And even then, he'd spent most of those first five years on the road, touring, one venue after another to earn sales, fans.

Snapping pictures with mothers and daughters, not unlike Kacey and Audrey, signing autographs, and generally building a persona that paid the bills.

Making him a better man than the one he'd left behind.

Audrey finally finished talking, then looked over at Ben, grinning. "And then, all of a sudden, I realized that not only had Mom found me but she'd brought along Benjamin King!" She got up then, and walked over to him and sat down opposite him at the table. "And it's been bugging me all day. How do you know my mom?"

Ten pairs of eyes on him, but he only saw Audrey's—blue, piercing, shining—and he wondered if she was clinging to some idea that he and her mother might be . . . well, exactly what they were. Old sweethearts.

"My family lived in Mercy Falls, so I knew your mother growing up. We were . . . school friends." True enough. "I came home to help my dad and got called in on the SAR team today. I didn't know she flew helicopters."

"Oh yeah," Audrey said. "She got a medal a couple years ago for saving some guys in Afghanistan."

Ben tried to wrap his head around that, and again regretted his words about Kacey serving as a soldier. Of course she was a hero.

"So you and my mom were friends, huh?" Audrey said. "Did you, like, hang out?"

Why not? He'd discovered from his press interviews that if he could give them something, they'd stop digging so deep. "Yeah. We even went hiking—this very pass. I took her up to the lookout."

Oops. Audrey's eyes widened, her mouth opened. "Really?"

And right then, he knew exactly what she'd been doing with Nate.

He stilled, rocked by the sudden flash of anger—something proprietary and dark.

But he couldn't rightly reprimand her—not here, not now. But wow, it didn't take him long to turn into a hovering father.

"Yeah. But we were just . . . well, we got lost too. So I guess—"

"You got lost?"

"Didn't you say you wanted to hear a song?"

To his great relief, the other members of the youth group rose to his suggestion. One of them got up, found a guitar next to the bookcase, a troubadour's offering, and handed it to him.

He set it over his knee, avoiding Audrey's blue-eyed gaze on him. He could almost hear her questions forming.

"I recorded this song about ten years ago, on my first album. You were all probably too young to know it, but it's a song about a kid just like you, who dreams of something big."

"I know this one!" Audrey said. "It's 'Mountain Song,' right?"

A swell of warmth rose through him, choked him, and he barely pushed out his voice. "Yep."

He wished for a banjo, a violin, or even his drummer as he played the intro riff. To his surprise, Audrey began to beat the table, in time, the other hand hitting her leg in the offbeat.

The girl—*his* girl—had his rhythm.

He hummed a few bars, then opened up the song.

Early riser, gonna catch the sun
Gotta start 'er early, gonna get her done
Rounding up the herd, putting on the brand
Then I'll kick off my spurs and head out with
the band

By now, the kids were clapping, a few of them humming along. "C'mon, now, those who know it."

I've got a Mountain Song
I'm cowboy strong
Working all day
It's where I belong
But after the work's done
I'm gonna sing my song
Waiting on a break, hoping on a star
Believin' that the dreamin's gonna get me far
I've got a Mountain Song

He glanced over at Audrey, and she was grinning, bobbing her head, singing along.

This was how it should be. Father and daughter, singing together in tune.

"Okay, Audrey, the next verse is all you."

Her eyes widened, and she shook her head.

"C'mon," he said, waiting for her, humming.

"I can't."

"You can. Okay, let's do it together."

After the big game, the bonfire's on
I got my pretty gal, doin' nothing wrong
Wishing on stars, hoping in the night
Someday everything's gonna work out right

Audrey mouthed the words, and he was almost there, Kacey tucked in his embrace as stars spilled into the night. His lips against her neck, the smell of autumn in her hair, the feeling that, yes, everything would be perfect.

The memory jolted him. Somehow he kept his smile. Caught up to the song.

As he finished the last verse, he looked to the darkness pressing against the window, seeing the girl he loved sitting on a high-top at the Gray Pony, her beautiful green eyes staring into his. *"I believe in you, Ben. Someday, you're going to make it."*

I find my tomorrow in the words of a song
All my dreamin' is suddenly gone
I traded the mountain for Music Row
And everyone's expecting me to put on a show

His voice grew soft, and the song turned into a ballad as he looked at his audience, now quiet, listening. He slowed, let the tenor that had won him two Grammies wind through them.

Somewhere back there, the mountain waits
Sorry, darlin', but I'll be home late
I've got a song to sing, the dream demands
C'mon, boys, let's warm up the band

He let the chords nearly die out before he wound up with the final chorus.

The kids cheered as he ended with a hard, fast

lick. The final notes hung in the air as he put the guitar away.

"Another one!" Audrey said, clapping.

And wow, he'd do just about anything to see that look on her face.

"It's dinnertime," Willow said from where she leaned on the doorframe. "I need helpers."

A handful of teens rose to help her. Audrey got up, picked up the guitar, propped her leg on a bench, and set the guitar on her knee.

"I've always wanted to learn how to play the guitar." She thumbed the strings, one at a time. "I keep trying to get Grandpa to let me take lessons, but . . ." She lifted her shoulder.

Grandpa. Aka, Judge Robert Fairing, the man who had lied to him, kept him from meeting his amazing daughter.

Ben barely kept himself from offering to come over, have a little face-to-face chat with Judge Fairing.

"Really?" Ben said instead. He came over, sat down on the bench next to her, and positioned her hand on the neck, her fingers on the fretboard. "That's the G chord."

She strummed, made a face.

"You'll get it. Keep your strum loose, a down and up pattern for right now."

She leaned over, catching her lower lip in her teeth.

Oh my—yes, she looked just like Kacey when

she did that, and his heart nearly stopped beating.

Then, she looked up at him, her expression earnest. "Do you think . . . I mean, would you . . . could you teach me?"

And then his heart did stop. Because the yearning for it, the sudden *yes* that swelled inside him could crush him.

This so wasn't fair.

"Yeah, sure." He heard the words before he thought to stop them.

Shoot. She responded before he could pull the words back, temper them with something like, "I think we need to ask your mom."

"Oh, that's awesome!" She rushed into the kitchen. "I can't believe it! Benjamin King is going to teach me how to play the guitar!"

Kacey was going to kill him.

As if reading his mind, Willow looked up from where she was serving ravioli, raised an eyebrow.

He got up, walked away. He didn't have to answer to her. Didn't have to answer to anyone. Audrey was his daughter, thank you.

He needed air.

Grabbing his coat, Ben headed toward the door, then stepped outside into the cool breath of night. It had stopped raining, but the air caught his breath, held it in a puff, and his nose burned with the frigid wind. Overhead, however, the clouds had parted, and stars winked from the dark, velvet vault.

He hummed the song, wondering if it was possible his dreams had gotten him *too* far.

Or maybe, in fact, they'd somehow inexplicably led him home.

He was standing there, the wind tucking around him, chilling him, pressing him to return inside, when he saw a light wink at the top of the trail leading down to the chalet.

More lost hikers? He waited, and another light, then a third appeared. Head lamps.

They came closer, and he made them out—one dressed in a lightweight green jacket, the other two in the heavier coats of PEAK Rescue.

"Ben King—no way. Is that you?"

This from the first guy, in the green jacket, who turned off his head lamp. Without the glare, Ben recognized his face, that too-confident smile. "Jared?" Ben held out his hand for the youth group leader. "Where did you come from?"

"I made it down to the foot of the Loop Trail and met up with some campers. They had a working radio, and we called in our position to the EMS. They sent up these two troublemakers."

He gestured to the PEAK team members behind him, and only then did Ben recognize the wry smile of Pete Brooks and the chiseled, dark expression of team leader Miles Dafoe, both former classmates at Mercy High.

"Dude!" Pete thumped him on the back. "Sam didn't mention you were back in town."

He refrained from saying the same to Pete, who'd spent the last few summers working as a smokejumper out of nearby Ember, Montana.

"Just here for the fun," Ben said.

Miles grinned, held out his hand. "Glad to have you back." He motioned to the cabin. "Kids in there?"

"Yeah."

Jared had already gone inside. Ben could hear the cheers of the youth group as he entered. Their hero, with more stories to keep them busy.

Probably a good thing. Ben wouldn't survive another round of digging up memories and what-ifs. However, "Did you get an update on Kacey, by any chance?"

"Yeah, Chet updated us. She landed at Kalispell Regional Medical center about an hour ago."

He hadn't realized he'd been worried until a band released in his chest. "I was going to hike down with the kids in the morning."

"We were already on our way—weren't sure what we'd find. If the weather's good, Kacey will chopper some of the campers out in the morning," Miles said. "But we need to get back, and pronto."

He frowned, especially at the way Pete's smile vanished into a dark, grim line. "Why?"

"A body washed up in the flood. Probably caught in the Mercy River somewhere, and the flooding jostled it loose. It's pretty decayed, but . . . well, Sam is afraid that it might be the body of Dante James, the boy who disappeared three years ago . . . with Esme Shaw."

Ian Shaw's fresh start would begin tonight.

After three years of fruitless searching for a girl who clearly didn't want to be found, meeting Kacey Fairing had woken him up to the hope of a new beginning.

Kacey Fairing, despite her initial cold shoulder, was exactly who Chet had portrayed. Level-headed, able to untangle chaos to do her job. When Ian had seen her beeline through the fight at the Pony to rescue the distraught girl in the corner, he knew it in his gut.

Time to let go of his grip on the past. To move on, begin anew, put the last three years behind him.

Which included releasing the reins of PEAK Rescue.

Which then made room for his brainchild of epic proportions—the one that solved his current problem of how to *not* say good-bye to his assistant, Sierra Rose.

Especially when she showed up this morning, bedraggled, sleep deprived from spending the night in the community center shelter—and despite it all, still looked as beautiful as she did every single day. He couldn't believe her home had been flooded by the crest of the Mercy River.

Which meant maybe she needed a fresh start too.

He allowed himself a smile at her surprise this morning when he'd announced his plan to take her to New York with him for the Charity dinner and auction. He wasn't sure why the idea hadn't occurred to him earlier—Sierra, with her long black hair, her pretty hazel-green eyes, could easily fill in as the necessary plus one without making it awkward.

Without her suspecting ulterior motives. Or knowing that she could take his breath away. Something he'd had to get used to reining in over the past five years.

He glanced at Sierra standing in the back of the gala room under the sparkling chandeliers, looking, well, radiant, her paddle with his number at the ready. His secret weapon, armed with enough cash to disentangle him from any designs some random, albeit beautiful, woman might have on his company for the evening.

Just because he'd agreed to be sold off in the annual children's charity bachelor date auction didn't mean he couldn't end up with the woman he really wanted to spend time with.

Ian sat on his chair sandwiched between Aaron Ellington, the CEO of some IT company, and former NFL pro Michael Stram, part of the lineup of eligible bachelors being auctioned off. Actually, not Ian, but a date-with-Ian, including a rooftop dinner—a five-course meal prepared by one of New York's finest chefs—and an open carriage ride through Central Park.

On the stage bedazzled with bouquets of peonies, irises, and lilies, the announcer took the podium and introduced the fun for the gala event.

Ian handed his empty appetizer plate—he'd loved the savory cheese puffs—to a waiter and let his gaze drift back to Sierra. He'd booked her into a suite down the hall from his, arranged for a personal hairdresser, and called in her measure-ments during the five-hour flight. He could admit fearing he'd stepped over the line again as he donned his tuxedo, but when she'd appeared in a dazzling white strapless Givenchy gown with a beaded bodice and a chiffon skirt, her hair pulled back and flowing down her back, yeah, he wanted to give himself a high five.

Yes, best assistant ever.

No. Best *friend* ever. Even he wasn't so stupid as to not notice just how much he relied on her, for more than filing and arranging his appoint-ments.

She knew him. Had seen him at his worst—and stuck by him as he'd bloodhounded every lead that might help him uncover the cold, dead trail left by a girl who clearly didn't want to be found.

Unless, of course, Esme *hadn't* run off with boyfriend Dante James and had instead been lost forever somewhere in the wilds of Glacier National Park.

Ian couldn't shake the idea that he knew Esme —knew she had plans to attend college, pursue a medical degree.

She might have loved Dante, but Ian thought she was too smart to sacrifice her future for him.

Sierra, however, was convinced that Dante and Esme had run off together, and because of that, she never let Ian go down that dark road of despair and grief.

Yes, so much more than an assistant.

Sierra was looking at him from across the room, gesturing with her head. She'd caught him daydreaming again, thinking back to those early days after Esme's disappearance when he barely slept, ate whatever food appeared in his fridge, and generally ran himself ragged on the desperate hope that he hadn't lost the niece entrusted to his care.

He glanced at the announcer on stage and smiled, apparently the right reflex because the emcee of the event smiled back, stepping back to clap.

Oh. They must have announced his yearly donation to the charity. He wished they wouldn't do that—it always dragged up questions, digging by reporters, and inevitably the story of his wife, his child, and a rehashing of the tragedies of Katrina.

But he lifted his hand, acknowledging the crowd's applause.

Met Sierra's eye, and she nodded. Good boy.

Strange how her smile could stir in him an unexpected warmth. Then again, of course he'd have affection for the one person who never gave up on him, never thought him crazy.

He didn't deserve her, he knew it.

And now, true to form, she was going to save him from his own stupidity by agreeing to "buy" his dinner date. Her expression contained humor, her eyes shone. She held a glass of champagne, and now sipped it.

He should have taken Sierra along on his many events earlier, more often. But he'd been afraid to ask without making her feel, well, that he might be stomping over that line of boss-employee.

Which he'd promised himself he'd never do again.

But he couldn't imagine moving to Dallas without her. Which was step three in his recovery plan—a relocation of his headquarters to Dallas. Step one was handing over PEAK Rescue to the EMS control of Mercy Falls. Namely, deputy sheriff and EMS liaison Sam Brooks.

He'd jumped right over step two—asking Sierra to join him—because, well . . .

Because he was batting at two strikes when it came to women wanting to be in his life. First his deceased wife, and then, maybe even Esme.

If Sierra was right about her running away.

Next to him, Mr. Football popped up, his name on the block. Ian moved chairs, one over, and watched as his cohort stood on stage, not a little uncomfortable, listening to the bidding rise for his seafood dinner at Le Bernardin, then box seats to a Yankees game.

The woman who bought him, a shapely red-head, came right up to the stage to help her "date" off, tucking her hand into the crook of his arm, already possessive.

The emcee turned to Ian next and nodded at him to join her on stage. "We're so excited for our next bachelor's date. Ian Shaw is the founder of Shaw Oil and the head of Shaw Holdings. With holdings in petroleum, communication, and technology, Shaw Holdings is one of our biggest donors, and Ian Shaw serves on our board. We're grateful Ian has agreed to join us on the platform tonight."

Ian had the sense of standing naked before a room of gawkers. He wanted to bolt, and only Sierra's firm gaze on him from the back of the room kept him planted.

The bids began. He waited for Sierra to add her bid, but she stood silent. He noticed a woman in her midforties, a little plump in her blue sequined dress, ardently driving the price up, fighting with a younger woman, probably the daughter of someone important. A third woman—oh shoot, he recognized her as the wife of Harry Waverly, a board member—began waving her paddle.

C'mon, Sierra, bid.

He looked at her, imploring, and she just smirked.

She wouldn't.

"Okay, we're at thirty thousand, from Mrs. Waverly."

Thirty *thousand?*

Wait—weren't the Waverlys in the middle of a divorce? His hands began to sweat.

Sierra!

"Okay, if there are no more bids—going once, twice—"

Sierra flicked her paddle. "Thirty-one!"

Finally. Sheesh.

"Thirty-two." Waverly, shooting a glare at Sierra.

Sierra shrugged. "Forty."

Forty? Forty thousand for—

"Forty-five."

Had she lost her mind? He wanted to turn Waverly's wife to ash, but he forced himself to smile.

Sierra was looking at him, an eyebrow raised. Apparently she could read his mind.

Except, wait, he'd told her not to go above forty, never dreaming the bidding could get over ten.

He gave her an imperceptible—maybe too imperceptible—nod.

"Going to—"

"Fifty thousand!" Sierra yelled.

He wanted to leap from the stage in joy as Sierra came forward, leveling an "I dare you" gaze at Mrs. Waverly. "I'm telling you, ma'am, I'll keep outbidding you, because he's mine."

She had a little fire in her eyes, and he couldn't help the strange quickening of his pulse.

Not that she meant anything by it, but—

"Sold! To . . . who are you, ma'am?"

She glanced at Ian, grinned. "I'm his date for the night."

Right. He climbed off the stage as she came over and, just like the redhead, put her hand through his crooked arm.

He leaned down to her. "Way to make me sweat."

She laughed, looked up at him, her eyes gleaming. "Oh, I could do worse than that if I wanted. But for now, I'm hungry."

As if reading her mind, a waiter zipped by, and Ian snagged one last savory puff from the tray, this one different but just as tasty as the cheese version.

Sierra dropped her auction paddle off at the door, and he stopped by the cashier in the back, pulled out his card, wrote the amount on the back. "I'll have my accountant send the money in on Monday."

Then, before he got into any trouble, he led

Sierra outside, to the lobby. "Dinner is at the Hotel Americana."

"Oh, is it?" She looked at him, winked. "Right."

Something about her seemed different. Delightful, almost giddy.

On the street, his driver got out and held open the door to the limousine. Ian took her hand, helped her in. She scooted to the far end of the couch. "There's a moon roof!" She leaned up, moving the glass back. "Hello, New York!"

He got in, laughing.

She settled back, kicking off her shoes. "Oh, that was so much fun! I've never been to such a fancy event. Did you see the ice sculpture? In the shape of a unicorn?" She wrinkled her nos at him. "This is some shindig! And those appetizers —salmon puffs, and I don't know what the other one was, but wow. I wanted to fill my dinky little purse with them."

He laughed. She had pulled her legs up under her dress and now reached back as if to pull the pins out of her hair.

"What are you doing?" He caught her hand. "Don't take your hair down."

She raised an eyebrow. "Uh, why not?"

"Because the evening's not done. We have dinner and . . . what?"

She was frowning then, moving very slowly as she pulled her hand away. "I don't understand.

I thought this was just for show. I didn't think you *really* made reservations."

Oh. His chest tightened. "I have something to ask you."

He suddenly felt not so brilliant.

In fact, his words clogged, and for some reason he couldn't push them out.

He leaned back in the seat, his hand on his suddenly tightening chest.

She sat up then, considering him. "You're sweating. Are you okay, Ian?"

Come to think of it, he wasn't. In fact, his chest continued to burn, his throat to tighten. He swallowed, found it harder to breathe.

"I'm going to touch your forehead. Oh, you're burning up. Ian . . ." She reached for his bow tie, had it off in a second. "Are you having trouble breathing?"

He nodded now, and for the first time considered it wasn't because of the words still lodged inside.

She turned in the seat, opened the door to the driver compartment. "We need a hospital, *now!*"

"I'm, fun . . ." Huh, his lips felt fat, hot.

"You're not fun. Your lips are swelling, and I think you're going into anaphylactic shock."

"Huh?" That came out clearly. "I wah—"

"Stop talking. Just breathe." She turned in her seat. "Hurry!"

She undid the buttons on his shirt, opened his collar. "I think I know what was in those cheese puffs—and it wasn't just cheese." She leaned down and pressed her head to his chest, listening.

He had the crazy urge to wrap his arms around her. The words, all of them formulated into three, and he pushed them out in a rasp. "Don . . . lef . . . meh." Shoot. *Don't leave me.*

She sat back up, his words lost to her. "Mushrooms. I sent them your allergy list. I can't believe this!" She shook her head. "Don't you die on me, Ian. That is *not* on our itinerary!"

He managed a feeble chortle, then began to cough.

"Where's your epi pen?" She put her hands on his jacket, then searched his inner pockets.

"I don't—"

"It's probably back at the hotel—I shouldn't have let all this fancy stuff distract me! Shh, stop talking. Breathe."

It wasn't fine. Not at all. Because it couldn't end like this.

Not with him being such an idiot. "Don—" *Leave me. Don't—*

Then his airway cut off. He gulped, trying for a breath, but nothing gave.

"Ian?" Her voice rose. "Ian!"

They'd pulled up to the hospital.

And then she was on her feet, screaming through the moon roof.

114

He grabbed her ankle, holding on to her, a lifeline, his only sure thing, fighting as the world closed in—shadows, then striations of light, and finally, black.

— 4 —

Kacey leaned her head back against the cool wall of the PEAK Rescue barn, staring up at the folds of night. The sky had cleared, and the air was crisp and filled with the soggy redolence of cattle droppings and the scent of pine combed from the nearby mountains.

She pressed her finger and thumb against the bridge of her nose, the fatigue layering her voice as she spoke into her cell phone. "I promise, she's fine, Mom. She's with her youth group."

"She was with that boy Nate, wasn't she?"

Of course her mother had somehow already found out about Audrey and Nate—how, Kacey couldn't know, but then again, she never understood how her mother found out anything. She secretly believed her mother had a network of spies scattered throughout Mercy Falls—and had probably enacted her sleepers during this particular crisis.

"She was, but—"

"And this is why we asked you to come home, Kacey. It's time you talk some sense into her."

Kacey could imagine her mother dressed in a pair of yoga pants, maybe a workout jacket—her preferred outfit around the house, even this late at night. Her blonde hair cut into a blunt bob, she would be pacing her newly remodeled kitchen in their five-thousand-square-foot whitewashed log home situated on forty acres of pristine Montana forest.

Or she might be standing in the middle of her vaulted great room, with the two-story river rock fireplace, the expansive view of the Haskill River basin.

No doubt Kacey's father, the Judge, would be sitting in a nearby wingback, whispering instructions on what to say, how to say it, and generally critiquing the entire phone call.

Not that her mother needed any help delivering her opinion. "I know, Mom. But I'm not sure what kind of sense you mean. She seemed fine—glad to see me. Kept her head on her shoulders all night long as—"

"She was out all night with him?"

"On a ledge. On a mountain. She made them a shelter, pretty much kept him from going into shock. I'm not trying to be dramatic here when I say she may have saved their lives."

"Yes, but *why* was she out there with him in the first place? You know how this happens, what this leads to." On the other end, her mother sighed, and Kacey closed her eyes, squeezing tight to keep her voice from spooling out for the second time today.

"Mom. Let's just not jump to conclusions. I'm flying back up the mountain to pick up Audrey in the morning. Then, hopefully there will be a makeshift highway bridge across the Mercy River and we'll drive home by midafternoon. Let's save our recriminations until tomorrow."

"Kacey, you need to take this seriously. You weren't much older than she was when you took up with Ben. And we both know how that derailed your entire life. I don't think you want that for Audrey. I know we don't."

Her mother knew how to reach through the phone lines, grab her by the heart, and inflict pain.

"Yep," she said, not willing to fight. "Listen, I'll call you tomorrow on our way home. I just wanted to let you know that we were both okay."

"And thank the Lord for that."

"See you tomorrow, Mom." Kacey clicked off, tapping her phone on her leg as she let her mother's words sift through her.

"I don't think you want that for Audrey."

She couldn't help but cast her gaze to the park, where, right now, Ben could be betraying her. This day had gone south way too fast.

Please, Ben.

Six hours of rescue. Flying had helped the panic, the frustration, and frankly, the disbelief to settle to a low simmer of worry.

She no longer required just a strategy to survive the summer in close working contact with Ben King. Now she had to figure out how—or if—she should let him wheedle his way into her daughter's life. Although, deep in her gut . . .

A small, mustard-seed-sized part of her knew he deserved to know his daughter. That he might even be good for her.

After all, every girl needed a daddy, right?

She pushed up from the wall of the barn and headed toward the PEAK ranch house, where lights from the windows pushed out past the porch, illuminated the soggy ground. Next to the house, a couple pickups caked with grime evidenced some of the team had gathered inside.

She stopped by her Escape, pulled out her backpack, then headed inside to the warmth and smells of the headquarters.

Jess sat at the long counter, eating a plate of spaghetti, dragging garlic bread through the sauce. She'd changed out of her jumpsuit into a pair of jeans and a black pullover, had her hair back in a loose ponytail, and had one leg under her as she leaned into the counter.

"Hey, Kace," Jess said, apparently okay with instant familiarity.

Kacey toed off her boots at the door.

A man Kacey didn't recognize turned from where he was serving himself noodles at the stainless stove. Dressed in a green T-shirt, a baseball cap perched backward on his head, brown hair flowing from the back, he looked like a surfer who'd taken a wrong turn. He was barefoot, and his jeans were clean, albeit faded. His dark brown eyes took her in a second, assessing before he smiled.

"Hey," he said, setting down his plate on the counter and heading over with his hand outstretched. "I'm Gage Watson. I'm the other EMT around here. Sounds like you and Jess had all the fun today."

Kacey met his grip.

He picked up his plate and finished ladling up his sauce. "Jess said you were pretty boss flying IFR out of the park." He looked up, glanced across the room. "Did you hear that, Ty? Competition."

Her gaze followed his gesture to another man sitting on the sofa against the wall. He wore a jean jacket, and his stocking feet were propped up on the worn coffee table as he watched the local news. Black hair, cut short, a gray T-shirt. He looked over at Gage, and one eyebrow dipped down. Then, his gaze caught on Kacey, and he took a breath, blew it out, and leaned up, taking his feet off the table. "Hi," he said. "You must be Kacey."

She nodded.

"I'm Ty. The backup pilot, apparently."

Oh.

But he got up then, came over to her with a sort of cowboy swagger, and held out his hand. "Ty Remington. Glad to meet you." He glanced then at Gage, narrowed his eyes. Gage grinned at him, shrugging.

"Pretty good spaghetti," Gage said to Kacey. He slid onto the barstool next to Jess. "Chet's special—he always makes it when we come in from a call. Ruth's recipe."

"With the fresh basil?" She walked over to the pot, took a whiff. Yes, that might heal a few aches. She found a plate in the cupboard and dished herself up dinner, trying not to feel guilty.

The crew up on the mountain had probably eaten rehydrated goulash.

"Apparently, Jared, the youth pastor, came down the trail and got in contact with Chet. He couldn't get us on the radio, so he sent Pete and Miles—you'll meet them—up the trail," Jess said. "They're probably camping out with Ben and Willow tonight. He said you could fly out Audrey and a few of the younger girls in the morning. Ty can go with you—"

"I need to head back to the ranch," Ty said. "Unless Kacey desperately needs me." The way he said it, she had the feeling she might never desperately need him.

"Depends on the weather, but I can handle it."

Ty got up, headed out of the room. She heard footsteps on the stairs.

"Ty's just knocked out of place because Chet hired *you* to take his spot," Gage said.

"*She* didn't crash a 1.3-million-dollar helicopter," Jess said. Then she looked over at Kacey. "Right?"

"Not recently," she said, deadpan.

"Chet says you earned a bronze star."

Kacey offered a smile and reached for the Parmesan cheese. "Where is Chet?"

"He's in the office, in back. Probably assembling weather reports or talking to Sam. Apparently there was a body that washed up today south of town. Ty helped with the recovery."

"Thanks. I need to check in with Chet," she said, picking up her plate. She slipped down from the high-top and headed over to the office.

The back office—once a bedroom, she supposed—housed a twin bed, a table on cement blocks, a computer on said table, and a host of communication equipment. A giant map of the park papered one wall, whiteboards with personnel updates on the other.

Chet sat in his chair at the table, reading through weather reports.

"Knock, knock," she said, and he turned, offered her a smile.

"I thought I heard you out there."

He motioned for her to sit on the bed. She came in, cradled her plate on her lap.

"So, how was your first trip out?"

Where to start? She lifted a shoulder.

"Good. I was hoping in the morning you might go back up, bring some of those kids home. Their parents are pretty nervous."

She was one of those parents. But she spoke to herself as much as to Chet. "They're fine. Ben's with them."

"I sent up Pete and Miles too—you remember Miles, right?"

"And Pete. He played football with Ben."

"Oh yeah." Chet grinned. "That kid could run when he had the ball." For a moment, he wore a faraway look, as if caught back in the stands, watching Ben toss a perfect arc to his receiver.

He would have been a wonderful grandparent. The thought caught her up, made her jerk.

"Are you okay?"

She nodded, looked away, blinking back a sudden rush of heat in her eyes.

"Can I ask you something? How did you find me? I mean, when you called, I assumed you'd contacted my parents."

Chet had his own plate of spaghetti, now finished, but he picked up a cup of coffee, took a sip. "I read that article about you in the *Mercy Falls Register*—about getting the bronze star. I didn't know your parents were in Whitefish until then. I gave them a call, but your dad wasn't that keen on giving out your location. Probably for security reasons."

Kacey nodded, as if that were exactly it.

"But I did get out of him that you were stationed stateside. It was just a matter of contacting the right people, old friends in the military. Florida, huh?"

"For the past eighteen months." She had lost her appetite and now put the plate on the table. "So, you haven't talked to my parents for, what—thirteen years?"

Chet frowned, as if thinking. "Yeah. I thought maybe Ruth had kept in touch, but really, after you moved away, I figured, well . . . There was a lot of healing that needed to be done, I know. I wanted to give you space. Time to put your life back together." He gave her a warm smile. "And you certainly did. If I haven't told you already, I'm so proud of you, Kacey."

And now her stomach twisted, threatening to give up her meal.

"Thanks," she managed, the sudden urge to tell him everything lumping in her throat, nearly choking off her air supply.

"And now that Ben's back . . . I know that was a surprise. I should have told you, but there was so much between you two, and I don't know about you, but Ben has never really been the same since you two broke up."

"Really?"

"I know I shouldn't meddle, but I think it's because you two never really said good-bye.

Never, well, resolved things. If anything, you two were friends—good friends. And I thought that maybe you could sort it out if you spent some time together. Sorry if I overstepped . . ."

He sat there wearing the benign smile of a pastor, and she suddenly wanted to stand up and let him have it.

Overstepped? Try a giant, Paul Bunyan–sized overstep.

But she'd been trained to keep her voice even, her emotions fisted. "Do you know how long Ben plans on sticking around?"

Chet set his coffee down. "He's got it in his head that he wants to move me back to Nashville as soon as possible. And I suppose with his partner bugging out on him, he probably needs to figure out what's next."

"His partner—you mean Hollie Montgomery? She left him?"

"And took one of his original songs with her. Or so he says. He won't talk about it much, but I know he's tore up inside. Feels betrayed, I suppose . . ."

Oh my. She looked at the night pressing against the glass.

"So, I don't know how long he'll be here until he gives up and realizes I'm not moving to Tennessee anytime soon."

She glanced at him. "But you need . . . um, I mean—"

"I need help? Yep, I suppose. But not in the way Ben thinks. He wants to check me into some fancy rehab facility when all I need is time and prayer. God is going to put me back together, honey. It's just a matter of time."

She wanted to smile, nod, agree. But from her vantage point, once you derailed your life, once it shattered, there was no putting the pieces together again. You had to live with the broken pieces the best you could.

Except she wasn't Chet, was she? Maybe God simply sorted out the worthy from the unworthy, and gave whom he chose a second chance.

She knew where she landed—had always landed.

"You get some rest. There's a couple bunk rooms upstairs—men's and women's dorms. Hunker down and we'll get those youngsters off the mountaintop in the morning."

The main room was empty when she returned. She emptied her plate, then loaded it in the dishwasher, turned off the kitchen light, and debated.

Upstairs to the bunk room, to stare at the ceiling —or worse.

Or, down here, maybe catching up on her classic movies.

But she had to fly tomorrow.

She grabbed her backpack and headed upstairs.

Two bedrooms, one to the left for men, the right, women.

She eased open the door and found Jess sitting on the lower bed of one of the four bunks, pulling on wool socks. "I know it's summer, but my feet get cold. I keep a drawer of socks here, just in case I have to pull an overnighter."

Kacey sat on the other bunk, noticed it was covered with a homemade quilt. Probably Ruth's touch. "How often do you stay here?"

"Oh, it depends. If there's a snowstorm, or maybe rain, or if there's fire in the park—situations where Chet thinks we might get called out. And definitely after a callout. I'm so tired, I just bunk here. Besides, my new place doesn't have running water, so I'm partial to the showers here." She winked, then pulled herself under the quilt.

"No running water?"

"I bought a fixer-upper—an old Victorian in town. Needs a few repairs. Like plumbing, electricity. A roof and a floor."

Kacey laughed. "Seriously?"

Jess pulled the covers up to her chin. "What can I say? I like projects."

Kacey unzipped her jumpsuit, thankful she'd worn a pair of leggings and a thermal shirt underneath. She climbed into bed. Glanced at Jess, but she had her eyes closed.

She pulled out the Ambien, popped one out, and downed it dry.

Please, let her sleep hard and dreamless.

She sighed, probably too loudly, because Jess rolled over and propped her head on her hand.

"Okay, I know it's none of my business, but Ben says that you two used to date? And, I'm so sorry, but am I mistaken in making the connection that Audrey is your daughter?"

"My daughter, yes—"

"Not Ben's? Because—"

"Yes, I know she has his eyes."

"Oh. Actually, I was going to say that Willow mentioned that she and Nate played in a band together, and it made me think that maybe she had inherited Ben's love of music."

Oh, shoot. Yes, of course she had. The girl had been singing since she could talk. Kacey pulled the covers up over her head. "This is a nightmare."

"What?"

Kacey sighed, put the covers down, and looked at Jess; the Ambien had kicked in enough to relax her. "Can I tell you a secret?"

Jess nodded, made a little cross over her heart, a poke in her eye.

"Yes, Ben and I dated. In fact, we were engaged, although that part was a secret. I got pregnant at seventeen, and he and I were—well, at the time I thought we were in love." She'd skip over dissecting the emotions, the words, the foolishness of believing in true love and soul mates and the rest of that emotional quagmire.

"Ben got a job working down at the Sweetwater

Lumber Company, and we were going to live"—
she finger quoted the rest—"happily ever after.
Except, he didn't show up the night Audrey was
born. I thought he'd gotten drunk, and I was
furious. I didn't take his calls. And then, when
Audrey was about a week old, he just left town.
Just like that, moved away. I only found out
where a few years later when his first album
came out."

"Oh boy."

"Yeah. I had just gotten my rating, was being
sent to Iraq for my first tour, and there he was,
on the radio, singing a song he wrote for me."

Jess's eyes widened. "What song?"

" 'Mountain Song'?"

"Oh, I love that one!"

Her too. "I thought he was the one. And then,
suddenly, he abandoned me and my daughter,
and I didn't know what to do. So I joined the
military and went on with my life. Until today."

"I don't understand. Why today?"

"Apparently, Ben thought I gave up our baby
for adoption."

Silence, and yes, it only confirmed that it was
as bad as it sounded.

"You mean, he found out that you kept the
baby . . . today?"

Kacey winced, nodded. "And he's really mad."

Jess said nothing.

"I know that maybe I should have contacted

him—but he walked out. Moved away. That sent a pretty clear message."

Jess only nodded.

"And now he wants to tell her that he's her dad—and I get that, I really do. But according to Chet, he's not sticking around here. I know Audrey would like to have a dad, even if she's never said it. And it killed me, knowing he'd turned his back on her. But the fact is, if he could walk away from us once, despite what he believed, then he could leave us again. I don't think she could take that. She's thirteen. And according to my parents, she's had some trouble at school . . ."

No. "The real truth is that I had something happen to me at Audrey's age that I just couldn't deal with. And it led me to right now. To a daughter who doesn't know her father, and a mother who is—well, more comfortable in a cockpit than making cookies."

It was a revelation she hadn't expected to make, but in the shadows of the bunk room, after spending the last six hours saving lives together, Jess just might have the makings of a real friend.

It occurred to Kacey, then, that probably she should have called Sierra, let her know she was back in town. So much for being a real friend.

"I'm no good at cookies, either," Jess said.

Kacey glanced at her, and Jess was grinning. Then, her smile dimmed. "Listen, I know a bit about life blindsiding you and people walking away. And I know that if I had a chance to redo some of the big events of my life, I would go back, give certain people a chance to make different choices. I don't know Ben, but if he is serious about knowing his daughter, then maybe the question isn't if, but how."

Kacey tucked the covers up under her chin. The room was starting to blissfully swim.

"Be the one who invites him in, on your terms. Tell him that you'll tell your daughter the truth when you think she's ready, when you can trust him. She's already pretty dazzled by him—"

"I know. She's apparently a fan."

"Who isn't? Benjamin King won Entertainer of the Year a few years ago, and he's been on a few most-eligible lists on the internet."

"I know. But what if he swoops in, dazzles her, and then . . ." And then she could hardly breathe. "What if he sues me for custody? Tries to take her away?" She put her hand to her head. "I don't have his money, his resources—"

"You're her mom. Just take a breath. Like I said—you control this. Invite him in."

Kacey swallowed, refused to let the panic spread.

"Besides, you can't keep this secret forever. And you don't want to. Trust me on that—secrets only tear relationships apart."

She had nothing for that except a nod.

"This doesn't have to go south. There could be a happy ending out there, somewhere. Maybe even for you two."

But to that, Kacey shook her head. "We had our chance at happy endings. Trust me on this one—there's nothing left between us but a sad country song."

For five years Sierra had been telling herself one thing.

Ian Shaw was not her entire life.

Even if sometimes it felt that way. Why else would she rise before dawn, her body knotted after sleeping in the community center on a cot, and hike out to her rattletrap Aveo and force the little four-cylinder hatchback over sidewalks, down alleyways, and generally fight to untangle herself from the sandbagged and fortified perimeter of Mercy Falls?

Maybe because while Ian Shaw was not her entire life, she was his. Keeper of his schedule, manager of his domain, and organizer of everything that kept Ian's life running.

Okay, that might be an overstatement, but she did help him stay sane, and cement his persona as one of the wealthiest, eligible—and let's not forget devastatingly hot—bachelors in the country. And one with a heart of gold, evidenced by his yearly giving statement. The man thrived on supporting lost causes.

And, of course, it was the least she could do, frankly, after the consequences of keeping Esme's secret.

So yeah, when Ian had asked her to help disentangle him from his bachelor-gala nightmare, what did a good assistant say?

Especially an assistant who felt like a homeless vagabond in her muddy jeans and ratty T-shirt—the only clothes she managed to grab in the wee hours of the night when Deputy Sam Brooks and his cadre of volunteers decided to oust her from her cute 1910 Sears kit Victorian a block from the river.

So, sure, dress her up, fly her to NYC, feed her gourmet food, and drive her around in a limo. The sacrifices she made for her job.

Except Sierra hadn't counted on her heart getting ripped from her body as she watched Ian expire before her eyes.

Breathe! Don't die! Her own words echoed back to her inside the hollow cavity of her chest.

Everything that came after that she easily justified.

The scream from the open ceiling of the limo.

Panicked mouth-to-mouth resuscitation.

The lie that gave her access to his bedside.

Fiancée.

Well, she *was* dressed the part, and it worked for Sandra Bullock in *While You Were Sleeping*.

Besides, she knew enough to be his fiancée;

she'd filled out his intake papers, from his insurance information to his past injuries, surgeries, and yes, his allergies. All one of them, including the Most Important, Life-Threatening One that she'd for sure faxed to the hotel over a month ago.

Not that they could amend the food list for every patron, but for one who donated over six digits a year?

Now Sierra stood at the end of Ian's hospital bed, watching as the nurse took his vitals, part of her wee-hours-of-the-morning routine. She ran her hands together, listening to his oxygen pump. He looked so . . . so *frail* laying there in his bed.

It scared her. Reminded her of those early days after Esme went missing. How he'd disappear for long rides across the ranch and she'd take the four-wheeler out, just to make sure she could spot him on the horizon. Or call Chet for a quick heli-trip across the ranch.

Ian had so thoroughly blamed himself, and she hadn't known him as well back then.

He lay bathed in the half-moon light, pale and wrung out, his face still puffy despite the meds they'd pumped into him. She couldn't help but wind her arms around her waist to keep from shaking.

Ian Shaw had nearly died.

What if he'd been alone?

Or with someone who didn't know him, didn't understand—

And that's when the thought caught her up, ran fingers around her throat.

Ian Shaw *was* her entire life.

She knew better than this. Knew better than to go there, to step in that emotional place where she saw him as more than a boss.

More, even, than a friend.

Her stomach knotted, and she walked over to the window, clenching her jaw.

No, no, *no,* she could not be in love with Ian Shaw. She'd tried so hard to keep her distance.

She pressed her hands on the cool glass. His fifteenth-floor room looked out over Central Park and the glittering skyline on the west side of Manhattan, so far from the grandeur of Montana.

She wanted to go home. Back to normal where she could tuck away her feelings and find her footing as his perfect, dedicated assistant.

Keep his world together, without worrying what might spill out and threaten everything.

They'd put him in a private room, and only the sound of the oxygen tank feeding life down his throat and the beep of his pulse monitor convinced her he was alive.

He'd nearly died. He would have if not for a quick-thinking ER doc who responded to her screams, armed with an epinephrine pen.

Somehow she'd ripped the pretty dress he'd

given her. Stupid investment—she'd tried to tell him that. But he'd been acting weird all day, from the sudden decision to take her with him, to the dress, to the hair appointment, to even the idea that they'd actually have dinner on top of the Americana Hotel.

It didn't make sense, and now it didn't matter.

The nurse left, and she walked over to him, put a hand on his leg.

Held on.

Because she'd started to shake. She blew out a trembling breath, closed her eyes. She couldn't lose him. Couldn't. "Oh, *Ian.*"

She didn't know where that voice, that tone, came from, and it shook her. She got up then, stalked to the corner of the room, trembling. Pulled out her phone. Dialed. *C'mon, Willow.*

The phone flipped to voicemail. Willow's way too perky voice.

Sierra glanced over to Ian, then sank down, her back to the wall.

"Willow, I really wish you'd pick up. I did something stupid. Really stupid. And I don't know what to do."

She paused, waited for the beep to cut off her message, but nothing came.

She sighed then, her voice broken. "Ian nearly died tonight. He ate mushrooms, and before you turn that into one of Mom's stupid jokes, I'm serious. He's in the hospital and . . . I nearly lost him. And not just my job—but *him*. Which . . . oh, you're going to kill me but . . . I think I'm in love with him."

Sierra bent her head, breathing hard, her eyes burning. "I know I said I wouldn't but . . . he turned all gray and I just panicked. And—I can't lose him, Willow. Shoot! I'm in so much trouble." She ran her hand under her nose, found it running, tears now coursing down her cheeks.

Behind her, the machine started to beep, and Ian lurched in his bed, choking.

"Ian!" She dropped the phone, ran to him. His eyes flashed open, and he writhed in the bed, fighting his breathing tube.

"Don't move—your throat was swollen, and they feared it closing up again. Just calm down." She slammed her hand on the nurse call button, then pressed down on his shoulders, found her assistant's voice, the one that kept their lives in order. "Stop thrashing. You're fine—you're just *fine*."

She forced a smile.

The door banged open, and the night nurse strode in, followed by another.

"He's awake and fighting his breathing tube," Sierra said as she stepped back.

The second nurse turned to her. "Okay, you— step out. We need to take out his tube."

"I'm staying." She backed up to the wall.

Maybe the nurse believed her, or maybe she

simply didn't have time to argue. "Okay, Mr. Shaw, we're going to call the doctor, see if he can take this tube out."

She left while the other nurse took his pulse.

Sierra walked over and slid her hand into his. He gripped it, weaving his fingers into hers.

Oh boy.

Then he focused his blue eyes on hers, as if he needed her, and she simply couldn't move.

How could she leave this man who so clearly needed her?

She offered another reassuring smile, and the doctor entered the room.

Flicked on the light.

And there went the relative obscurity of her meltdown.

But she held Ian's hand as the doctor explained what had happened, how they'd had to resuscitate him, intubate him, and flood his body with epinephrine and albuterol. He'd been on IV cortisone and antihistamines for the past three hours. "We just want to make sure you don't have another, delayed attack. But we can take out your breathing tube and just keep you on oxygen."

She hung on to Ian's hand as he coughed and the doctor pulled out the tube, leaving him gasping, white, and nearly retching.

He finally fell back into the pillows. Looked over at Sierra.

"Don't try to talk," she said softly.

The nurse removed the blood pressure cuff, charted the results, and suggested that she go back to the hotel.

Sierra responded with a look that earned a chuckle from Ian.

"What? What if you don't like your Jell-O? Someone has to be here."

"My hero," he said, his voice sandpaper.

"I said stop talking."

He gestured for water, and she moved the cup and straw to him.

"Not too fast."

But, of course, he didn't listen.

She pulled it away. "Enough. You keep that down, I'll give you more."

"The meds will make him sleepy," the nurse said, in a final attempt to get her to leave. But really, where would she go?

"Thanks. I want to be here when he wakes up."

The nurse gave a tight nod as she left.

Ian leaned back, and Sierra stifled the urge to press his sweaty hair back from his head. Oh, shoot. She had to get these feelings under control or—

"You were crying," he said, his voice a little slurry.

She froze, then affected a frown. "Naw, I wasn't—"

"You were crying, I can see it on your face."

Oh, that. She shrugged.

"And I heard you."

She barely suppressed a wince. "I called my sister. Just to let her know—"

"You said . . . I thought you said something about being in trouble. Is everything okay?"

She froze, then scrambled. "No, I said I think the gala is in so much trouble. I can't believe they gave you mushrooms."

He made a funny face, and even in this light, it might've been about the most attractive thing she'd ever seen. Ian, with his beard growing in, dark red to match the highlights in his hair, looking at her as if he wanted to rise from his near deathbed to solve her problems.

He couldn't save her from her sad, pitiful self.

"Thank you for what you did tonight. I know you saved my life."

He had such a warmth in his eyes, she had to look away. Run, actually, except she couldn't let go of his hand. "Of course. That's what assistants are for."

Oh, how lame. But what else could she say?

"I'd say that's over and above. But that's what I wanted to talk to you about tonight." He slid his hand out of hers, sighed. Closed his eyes as if in pain.

And her brain rushed to a thousand conclusions, settling on one.

Oh no. She simply had to do the math, starting with the expression on his face as he'd faded, all the way back to the insistence that she bid on him, to the fact that he actually expected them to have dinner on the Americana Hotel rooftop.

She knew better than to suspect anything romantic. He'd made her promises, after all. So that only meant . . .

He was letting her go. This was her final huzzah, the send-off, the thank-you for a great job.

She nearly put her hand to her chest to cover the wound.

But in truth, she'd seen it coming, what with him handing over PEAK Rescue to the Mercy Falls EMS. It was only a matter of time before he turned his frequent trips away from the ranch into a permanent change of address.

Which meant that cutting it off now, before her heart got even more desperately entangled, was best for everyone. "Ian, stop. Before you go any further, you should know you don't have to do this. I'm already—um, well, I know that I like working for you, but I think it's time for me to—"

Her cell phone buzzed from where it lay on the floor, moving as if it were alive.

She sucked in a breath. "Hold that thought."

"Sierra—"

She held up a finger to shush him as she chased down the phone. Willow?

No. She frowned as she answered. "Sam?"

"I'm so sorry to call you this late at night, Sierra,

but I've been trying to get ahold of Ian. I know you keep his schedule, and I know it's late, but I really need to find him."

She glanced at Ian lying in the bed, his eyes closed, as if drifting back into sleep. And why not—the guy was drunk on meds. She supposed that Sam might be a little surprised, should she simply hand the phone over.

"Uh, why? Is there a message I can pass on to him?"

"Actually, yeah. If you can track him down, it's pretty important." She could imagine Sam, his dark blond hair in spikes from dragging his hand through it, going on a handful of hours of sleep, thanks to the flood. She could hear the fatigue in his voice.

"I can probably find him," she offered. She walked over to the bed. Yes, most definitely conked out. Their conversation—and her resignation— would have to wait until morning.

"Good. Tell him to call me as soon as he can— or better yet, get back to Mercy Falls. We dragged Dante James's body from the river tonight. He and Esme clearly didn't run away together."

Everything around Sierra went silent—her heartbeat, her breath, even Sam's voice in her ear.

Esme hadn't run away with Dante.

The words banged around in her head, even as she said, stupidly, "What?"

"The flood must have loosened his body from wherever it was caught in the river and floated it down. A rancher found it just south of town lodged in a drainage canal. It's pretty decomposed, but he's still wearing his class ring. It's Dante."

Dante was dead. Her knees turned weak, and she reached out for the nearby chair before she fell.

Oh no.

"We need to talk to Ian and see if he wants to reopen the search for Esme."

And she knew, without asking, just what that answer would be.

She turned and stared at Ian, old, secret words rising up to surround her.

"I love Dante, and I'm going to be with him, even if we have to run away. Don't tell him, Sierra, promise me you won't tell Uncle Ian."

"He'll be back in Mercy Falls by tonight," she said quietly, and hung up.

— 5 —

Somewhere in the night, Ben had landed on one clear, resolute thought.

He wasn't going to let Kacey steal his daughter from him. Not again.

"Ben, slow down. You're going to break these kids' necks!"

Miles's voice reached out from up the trail, echoing over the valley and slowing Ben's gait. Probably Miles was right—the switchbacks heading down from the Loop Trail, although not as treacherous as the Highline Trail drops, could still derail a camper if they tripped.

The tumble downhill could lead to another broken ankle, or worse.

And he had a responsibility to get the remainder of the kids—the ones who hadn't flown out this morning with Kacey—back to Mercy Falls. He could admit that after being out in the elements overnight, Audrey seemed worn out, probably wouldn't have made it back down the mountain.

Leaving him, Jared, and the other two PEAK Rescue personnel to hike down the Loop Trail. Overhead, lazy, wispy cirrus floated high, depleted by the three-day thunderstorm, the sky a light, airy blue, the sun healing the soggy land.

God setting the world right after the storm.

For the first time in his life, Ben thought maybe the Almighty might finally be doing the same for him.

If, in fact, that were possible.

He took a breath and stopped to let the group catch up and survey the view. Not a spectacular vista compared to the Highline Trail, but one could hardly discount the breathtaking rise of Heaven's Peak to the south and Mt. Oberlin to the east, shaggy-edged with green pine, snowcapped and jagged against the blue horizon. A fragrant mountain breeze caressed the wildflowers that covered the mountainside, and soon they'd descend into the fireweed and the scraggly pines and aspen of a young, recently burned forest.

Ben's thighs burned with all the downhill pounding, and, going first, he kept an eye out for grizzlies rooting in the huckleberry bushes.

A large part of him just wanted to leave the group behind—they were safe in the capable hands of Jared, Pete, and Miles—and do an all-out sprint down the mountain, all 3.8 miles to Going-to-the-Sun Road, where he'd flag down some tourist and somehow catch up with Kacey and the PEAK chopper.

Stop her before she packed up Audrey and drove her away, out of his life.

He'd spent the night replaying their fight, her words finding the crannies where he parked his shame.

"The idea of a child and a wife depending on you probably scared the stuffing out of you."

He lay in his springy bunk, chilly under a blanket as the moonlight dragged across the floor, dredging up his memories. He'd tunneled back through time and took a good look at the seventeen-year-old sitting in the jail cell, his knuckles raw, his jaw aching, one eye egg-sized, listening to the honorable Robert D. Fairing, judge of Flathead County and apparently ruler over his future, tell him that the girl he loved didn't love him.

Didn't want him or his child.

More, that by attempting to build a future with her, Ben would only destroy it.

He had been scared, he could admit that.

Miles caught up to him. "You in a race, buddy?"

He glanced at Miles but didn't answer.

Miles hadn't said a word to him about Kacey and Audrey, but maybe he didn't know about her. Still, Miles lived in the area, had grown up with both of them.

Ben was trying not to feel betrayed by everyone he knew.

"Have you kept in touch with Kacey Fairing?" Ben asked.

"I guess I might have heard she joined the army. I haven't been around either, really. I've been over with the Jude County Wildland Fire Department for a few years. But with Kelli expecting our second—"

"Kelli's expecting?" Ben remembered her from high school—cute, petite, a couple years younger than him, which put her at least four years younger than Miles. "She finally decided to marry you?"

Miles offered a grunt. "Yeah, but . . . Actually, we were separated for a while. She was tired of me fighting fires and spending the winters chasing the rodeo game. Gave me an ultimatum."

Ah. Miles never did well with an "or else."

"So what brought you back?"

"Kelli. And my kid—Huck. He's a regular little bull rider like his dad. Should have seen him riding the lambs in the county fair. Kelli said she'd give me another chance if I was really going to stick around. I'm trying to be worthy of that, I guess."

Worthy.

Maybe that's what Kacey needed—something other than his word that Ben would show up, stick around in their lives.

He took out his canteen, downed some water, then glanced back at the teens now catching up.

And that, really, was the problem, wasn't it? He couldn't rightly just lie down and surrender everything he'd built. But if he wanted to be in his daughter's life, that would require him changing his life—or hers. Which meant sending her life into upheaval.

He wiped his forehead, waiting while the kids all took drinks.

One of the kids had his phone out and was holding it up for reception. Ben hadn't even checked—and now pulled his cell out of his pocket.

Three missed calls, all from Goldie Davis, his manager.

He shoved the phone back in his pocket, not quite ready to hear bad news.

The next two miles down took another hour, and by midmorning he was loading the kids into a van driven out by the EMS department of Mercy Falls.

He hunkered down in a seat in the back with his cell, thumbing through his Twitter feed.

While he'd been saving kids and discovering secrets, his former partner had decided to release her new single on iTunes.

It had blown up to number one, and she'd announced her new single album with Golden Heart records.

Which left people asking, *#whereisBenjamin King?*

He leaned back in the seat, closed his eyes.

"Play me a song, Benj."

He could almost feel Kacey's long auburn hair twining through his fingers, taste her lips as they brushed his, hear her laughter as she backed away. They were sitting in the back of his pickup, a horse blanket spread out on the bed. Her beautiful green eyes shone, her smile pure and sweet. "I can tell you've been working on a new one."

What he wanted to do was trace the freckles dotting her nose, down her cheekbone, then catch her face in his hands and kiss her. To lose himself in her touch and the fact that with her, he wasn't the poor kid of the town pastor but already a star.

Already someone with his name in lights,

proving to the one-horse town of Mercy Falls that he didn't need any more handouts.

Instead he pulled out his guitar and picked out a chorus.

When you need a friend
A shoulder you can cry on
Someone who understands what you're going
  through
Just look over here, see me standing closer
Nobody will love you the way I do

A jolt as the van slowed over a rutted section of the highway, and Ben jerked awake. He had the sickening feeling he'd actually been humming, judging by the way one of the campers eyed him. He sat up, adjusted his gimme cap, ran a hand over his beard.

They were coming into the southeast end of Mercy Falls, past the Gray Pony Saloon. The gullies and ditches were filled with muddy water, the road eaten away in parts. The VFW hosted a few regulars in its parking lot. Cars were abandoned by the side of the road, a few power lines down, and every single greenhouse at the Mercy Falls nursery had caved in, the yard submerged under three feet of standing water.

They turned south before they hit town, toward the PEAK headquarters, skirting the destruction on Main Street, the flooded church, the destroyed Safeway grocery store, the trailer park now simply debris.

And, of course, the Great Northern Bridge in splinters, halfway into the river.

Sandbags held back more destruction, but it would take months, if not longer, to rebuild the town.

They headed south, and just outside the city limits a couple miles of split-wood fencing paralleled the road. They finally turned into the PEAK entrance, driving under the crossbeam.

The blue and white PEAK chopper sat on the pad, and worried parents waited in groups, nursing coffee.

His father held court on the porch.

And no sign of Kacey's silver Escape.

The van pulled up and the kids piled out, running toward their worried parents.

Ben unfolded himself, climbed out, and then headed toward his father for some answers.

He was intercepted by one of his rescuees wanting a selfie and managed to tamp down his frustration for a photo op that might earn him some favor in Twitterland.

It started a rush, and he spent the next ten minutes smiling, meeting parents, and giving autographs.

No sign of Kacey or Audrey.

He finally disentangled himself and headed for the house.

Chet sat on the porch, watching the parents

drive away. He looked up at Ben. "Kacey left an hour ago."

Of course she did. He leaned against the post. Considered his father. The man wore grizzle on his face, bags under his eyes. "Were you up all night?"

"I caught a few winks on the office bed, but . . . I woke up early, saw Kacey outside loading the seats back into the chopper, and never got back to sleep."

Probably anxious to get on with her escape from his life.

"How was your night?" Chet asked. "By the way, Nate is going to be okay. He had surgery on his foot, but they were able to set it, and he hadn't lost circulation, thank God."

Ben nodded, because for the first time, he agreed.

"How did you and Kacey get along?"

Ben looked away, not sure where to start. Or how to wrestle his voice under control. He finally swallowed and turned back to his dad. "How did you know Kacey was a soldier?"

"I saw an article the *Register* did about her. I called her dad—tracked her down. Why? She asked me the same thing."

Huh.

"Did she mention why she moved to Whitefish?"

Chet shook his head. "I thought maybe she wanted a fresh start. You know—so much between you two—"

"She had a baby, Dad."

Chet nodded, something slow. "I know, son. I do remember that part."

"Did you know she *kept* the baby?"

He couldn't help but test his father's expression. But by the frown . . . "What are you saying?"

Yep, the old man didn't know. Which only eased the band of betrayal just a fraction. At least his dad hadn't kept the truth from him.

"Did Kacey by any chance leave with one of the teens?"

"Yeah, I think so . . . oh. Are you saying . . . ?"

Ben's jaw tightened. "Yeah. That girl with the pretty brown hair has my eyes. She's your granddaughter, Dad. Audrey." His throat tightened. "And she doesn't know that I'm her dad."

"What do you mean, she doesn't know you're her dad?"

His dad, catching up. Ben looked at him, and he imagined that Chet's expression matched his own twenty-four hours ago.

"Kacey thought I walked away from her, so she told our daughter that I . . . um"—he could hardly say it—"*abandoned* them."

Chet frowned.

"I didn't abandon them, Dad. I didn't know."

"But you *did* leave. And not too long after the baby was born."

"Because she wouldn't see me! She wouldn't take my calls—and I thought that she was giving up the baby for adoption. That's what her dad said. He told me I'd just destroy her life."

Chet still hadn't met his eyes.

"What?"

"I remember when you told me about the adoption, son. And I remember thinking that I thought I knew Kacey better than that." He looked at Ben. "And so did you."

He'd hoped his father, of all people, might be his ally, just this once.

"She lied to me."

"She didn't lie—she thought you had abandoned her."

"You should be on my side."

"I am, but Ben, you've always been, well, impulsive—"

"I'm not impulsive, Dad."

Chet said nothing as he looked out over the land, maybe letting the fact he was a grandfather sink in.

"Fine," Ben finally said, the silence tugging it out of him. "But I was hurt."

"And you had a dream calling you. And you've never been good at taking things slowly. Or waiting." His dad raised an eyebrow, and the old judgment, the shame pricked Ben's heart.

"I know we made mistakes, Dad. *I* made mistakes. But I was willing to stay here and work, build a life for us."

More silence.

"She took that from me. And now, she wants to keep Audrey from knowing me—"

"Now that makes sense," Chet said. "She asked me how long you were sticking around."

Ben stilled, nonplussed. "What did you tell her?"

"That you were probably headed back to Nashville as soon as possible."

Perfect. He leaned against the railing, scrubbed his hands over his face.

"Isn't that what you want?" Chet said. "To rally, fight for your career? You've been prowling around the ranch for nearly two weeks, your cell phone plastered to your ear, fighting with your manager."

As if on cue, his cell phone buzzed in his pocket. Probably another text from Goldie.

"I guess I want it all. I want to get to know my daughter. I want my career. I want . . ." *Kacey*. Or at least he used to. "What I really want is for life to stop betraying me. For once, can't things just work out? It would be a lot easier if God was actually on my side."

He didn't care that his words might feel like a slap to his father. Maybe he even wanted it.

Chet stared at him, frowned. "Son, God *is* on your side."

"Yeah, right. If he was, then my career wouldn't be stolen by my former partner, my daughter would know my name, you wouldn't be in a wheelchair, and Mom would be alive."

Chet recoiled at that, and Ben hated himself a little. But he leaned up from the porch.

"Just forget it, Dad. If I want back in my daughter's life, I'll have to make it happen." He pulled out his phone.

"Son, don't make this worse."

"It can't get worse."

He glared at his dad, who stared back, unflinching.

"You might consider that if you want to be in your daughter's life without ripping it to shreds, you should slow down. Stop fighting your way through life and start trusting God."

"Yeah, right." But he pocketed his cell. "Kacey doesn't want Audrey knowing about me. Not until she's ready."

"That seems fair," Chet said, and Ben tightened his jaw.

"Listen, there's grub inside. Get yourself put together, take a shower, and then take my truck and go see Kacey. And Judge Fairing."

Hopefully he wouldn't end up in jail this time.

Ian could admit to having a bit of a struggle sorting out the events of the past twenty-four hours. From the charity gala, to his limo, to a private hospital room, to flying home in his private jet. He still felt wrung out and not a little bruised from his mushroom-allergy ordeal.

But despite the crazy twenty-four hours, he clearly understood that something was not right in Sierraville.

His assistant, dressed in her jeans, a yellow T-shirt, her hair now back to its normal straight-and-behind-the-ears style, sat opposite him, fiddling with her empty coffee cup and staring out the window.

Not talking to him.

Not laughing, teasing, ordering, or berating him for being so stupid as to not check his food before he popped that last mushroom-cheese puff into his mouth.

Which only meant . . . "Am I trouble? Because last I checked, I was the one in the hospital, the one in need of sympathy and kindness here."

They flew above the clouds, at fifteen thousand feet. He could feel the plane start its initial descent as the Rocky Mountains came into view.

He tried a smile as a chaser, and she responded with a quick flash of light.

"No. Sorry. Thinking. Can I get you anything?" She was already rising from her seat, and he put up his hand.

"No, I'm fine. Freshly hayed and watered. But you look . . . what's going on? You're acting very . . . was it about what happened?"

He didn't want to bring it up, but maybe one of them should. "About our conversation? Because I know I was a little medicated, but I had the distinct impression you were, well—you're not quitting on me, are you?"

"It was a long night, boss." She offered a quick smile. "I was tired and maybe a little freaked out. It's all good. We just need to get you back into your own bed is all."

"I'm fine, Sierra. And hardly going back to bed when we land. But we should talk."

In fact, if she was going to say what he thought . . .

"I don't want you to leave. I . . . don't know what you were going to say, but . . ."

She looked up at him with those enormous hazel-blue eyes, and his voice just caught, right there.

For a second, he was back in the limo, watching her unravel. And he could still feel her mouth on his as she tried to keep him alive.

Beautiful, amazing Sierra, always beside him, holding him together. The feelings now took him with a rush.

He was still in love with her.

Had been long before that night when he'd let grief take him to the edge, found solace in a bottle of bourbon.

And yeah, he'd toed the line since then, but none of those feelings had really died. He'd just tucked them away, hoping he could keep them hidden.

But not if she was going to leave him.

Ian studied her as she sat in the seat across

from him, drumming her fingers on her lap, her eyes luminous, her mouth tight, as if holding in— what? Frustration? Fear?

"Sierra, I know that it's been a rough three years, but things are different now. I realize I'm not going to find Esme. And I can't keep living my life trapped there. I'm ready to move on."

She had sat up. "Mr. Shaw—"

"What? Since when do you call me . . . what's going on?"

"Nothing. It's just that, I know you need to move on. And I understand—"

"No, you don't, Sierra. See, it's more than just moving on emotionally. I want to sell the ranch and actually *move*."

"You can't move!"

He stopped.

And then, with a rush, it came back to him.

"I think I'm in love with him."

Did he hear that or dream it?

Did she think he was going to move without her?

"Sierra, that's the thing. I *am* going to move, but I want to . . ." He softened his voice. "I'd like to take you with me, if you'll have—"

"What—no! *No*."

Oh. He closed his mouth, cleared his throat. "I see."

"No, Ian, you don't see." She considered him an eternal moment, and he felt like a sixteen-year-old asking the girl he had a crush on to prom. Then, "I have to tell you something."

Ah, what an insensitive clod he was.

"No, that's okay, Sierra. I understand. You have your sister, and your mother—"

"That's not it."

Oh.

She had someone else. And now he was an idiot.

He held up his hand to stop her right there.

He wasn't a desperate man, but yeah, he'd blame the antihistamines. He wanted to slide out of his leather seat, slink down the hallway, and lock himself in his back cabin office.

"I get it. We made a deal, long ago, and I—"

"Ian, I'm not leaving you."

Huh?

"But I have been keeping something from you." She reached into her bag and pulled out his phone. "I answered all your messages. And responded to your voicemails." She sighed. "There's something you need to know."

"What, did someone get a shot of me dying on the sidewalk?"

He meant it as a joke, but it fell flat, given her expression.

"Check your voicemail."

He frowned, then opened the app. "I have one from Sam."

"Yeah, you do. Which is why we're heading home so soon. It's pretty important, but I wanted you to be, well, fully cognizant when you heard it."

And now she had him worried. He pressed the voicemail, listened to Sam's strained, tired voice asking him to call him back.

Which he would, if he weren't in a jet at fifteen thousand feet.

"What does he want?" Ian said, deleting the message.

"He should probably tell you," she said quietly.

"I want *you* to tell me."

And that's when her face started to crumple, when her hands shook. She pressed her hand over her mouth as tears filled her eyes.

"Sierra, what in the world?"

"I'm sorry . . . I'm so . . . sorry." Her voice trembled, and then she turned away from him, covering her face with her hands.

Sierra. He couldn't help it—he moved off his chair and pulled her against himself.

And although he'd been feeling hollow and wrung out, something about holding her, her body melting against his, roused some latent protective instinct. He smoothed her soft hair. "I don't know what it is, but I'll fix it. I promise, I'll fix it."

She leaned back from him, shaking her head, her hand in his jacket lapels. "You can't fix this, Ian. Because . . ." Her face crumpled again. "This is my fault."

He stilled. "I don't understand."

She wiped her cheeks with her hands, smearing whatever makeup had remained from the night before. "I . . . oh, Ian. They've found Dante James's body."

"What?" He sat back, feeling punched.

"It was in the flood—I don't know all the details, but that's why Sam called. He thinks—"

"That Esme didn't run away. Instead, she died."

She nodded, then pressed her hands to her mouth. "I'm so sorry, I'm so, so sorry—"

"Sierra, shh. Okay, yeah." His breath caught. "Okay, I thought I had prepared myself for this . . ."

"I'm sorry, Ian." Her voice shook. "If we'd kept looking . . . we stopped because I told you to."

He frowned, nodded. "Yeah . . ."

"I told you I thought she'd run away. But I didn't tell you everything. She was in love with Dante. They were going to elope."

He frowned.

"She told me she was going to run away with him."

He blinked at her, trying to catch up. "Wait—what? When?"

"A couple days before she ran away. She didn't want to tell you that she didn't want to go to Yale."

He backed away. "You knew she was going to elope and you didn't tell me?"

She looked stricken, nodded. "I know. I didn't

think she'd really do it—I tried to talk her out of it. And then . . . then she went missing, and I didn't know what happened."

He stared at her. "You *knew* she was going to leave. And you didn't tell me. If you'd told me, I could have stopped them."

"I know. And yes, I should have told you, right away. But when she first went missing, I didn't know what had happened. And then, when we didn't find her, I thought maybe she did run away to elope."

"And still you didn't tell me!"

She opened her mouth, not sure what to say.

"We've searched the entire world for them, Sierra—you *helped* me."

"I didn't know where she went—and I really wanted to help . . ."

"You just wanted to make yourself feel better."

Tears coursed down her cheeks. He looked away.

"Ian, I'm so sorry. I've been sorry for three years—and wanting to find her too. I know I should have told you—"

"You were an adult, she was a kid. And you worked for me. Yes, you should have told me. And now, she's probably dead. What if she was out there all that time, hoping we'd find her, and I gave up because of you?"

She opened her mouth, closed it, not wanting to point out that if Esme had been in the park, she might have died of exposure long before Ian quit the search. "I know. You're right, I should have told you. And that's why I told Sam that we'd come home and reopen the case. We'll figure it out, Ian, I promise."

He couldn't look at her. *I gave up because of you.*

His words emerged almost as a reflex, the hurt biting at his tone.

"No, actually, we won't." He sat back in his chair, picked up his phone.

She stilled, caught her lower lip in her teeth.

He ignored the tightness in his chest, kept his tone even, despite the vitriol that rose inside him. "As soon as we land, you're fired."

If Kacey had to spend one more minute listening to her daughter wax on about Benjamin King, she just might drive right off the road screaming.

"Then he sat down and played 'Mountain Song.' And he let me sing along—even harmonized with me during the chorus. It was so cool, Mom. Mr. King is totally boss."

Audrey sat sideways on her seat, grubby, tired, but alight with excitement, her Benjamin-blue eyes shining. She was talking with her hands—that, too, like Ben.

Shoot. Until now, Kacey hadn't exactly seen the resemblance.

Or hadn't wanted to.

"And then later, he showed me how to play

the guitar. He taught me how to strum, and the G chord, and then he said he'd even teach me how to play!"

Kacey's hands whitened on the steering wheel, her jaw tight.

"He's so nice, Mom. A whole bunch of us played charades, and then he taught us the game of spoons. I really like him."

Oh boy. "Yes, well, I'm sure he thought you were nice too. But let's remember, he's a big star—"

"He said he might be staying the entire summer!"

She let out her breath. "Okay. Well, we'll see about the guitar thing. He's a busy guy."

"He said you were friends. In high school or maybe middle school. I can't remember, but were you, Mom? Friends with Mr. King?"

Yep, she would slowly dismantle him next time she saw him. "We knew each other." She measured her words. "His father was the pastor of our youth group and we would sometimes hang out. In a *group*."

The western side of the Mercy River seemed less damaged, although downed branches and other litter lined the ditches. Her stomach growled and she guessed she probably should have grabbed lunch.

Or maybe it was simply the roil of dread, knowing that she'd have to corner her father and pry the truth out of him.

"Your dad came down to the jail and told me that you never wanted to see me again. That you were going to put the baby up for adoption and that I should leave."

And then her father had neatly moved them away, shortly after Ben left, with the hope, maybe, that he could stop her from seeing him again.

How could you, Dad?

She hadn't exactly thought that all the way through, her hands full of midnight feedings, dirty diapers, and figuring out how her life had turned from happily ever after to, well, blinding.

She'd never been cut out to be a mother—she'd told Ben as much. But he hadn't believed her, made her question her own gut and stirred an unfamiliar desire to try.

Thankfully her parents had stepped in, helped her get back on her feet. No, they hadn't loved the military idea, but at least it paid the bills. And she'd found a job she could actually excel at.

"That must have been so cool—hanging out with Benjamin King. Was he hot? I'll bet he was hot."

She glanced at her daughter, frowned. "I guess."

"Did you like him?"

"Um . . . I don't know," she said, fighting a rising panic. "We were . . . just friends."

Oh, what was she doing? But Audrey wasn't ready for the truth—maybe neither of them were yet.

"Listen, what were you doing out with Nate, anyway?"

"Oh."

And just like that, her daughter shut down.

Kacey glanced over at her. She'd turned toward the front, looked out the opposite window. "Audrey?"

"It's nothing, Mom. Nate goes to my school. We're just friends."

Huh. Like Ben had been just a friend?

"Well, honey, the thing is, apparently you've been skipping classes, and you can't do that in a private school. You'll get expelled."

She hadn't exactly been around for the so-called change in her daughter that her mother had described, but suddenly, that girl emerged, a full-out clone of Kacey at that age. "*That's* why you came home. I thought you were here because of my birthday!"

Oh. And that only drove the dagger a little deeper. Stellar mother she was. Kacey had completely forgotten her own daughter's birthday just a week away.

"You're only here because Grandma and Grandpa freaked out about Nate and school and said I was in trouble, didn't they? Wow. That's great, Mom. How about listening to *my* side of the story?"

Oh, how she wished that twelve years rescuing hurting, broken, scared soldiers might have

165

kicked in to her response. Instead, she looked at Audrey and saw a girl who'd skipped class, probably for this Nate kid, and didn't want an adult telling her how to live her life.

Because she was in love.

Just friends indeed.

"Audrey, I'm here because none of us want you to make a mistake. It wasn't easy getting you into Glacier Christian Academy—"

"I get straight As. So I missed a couple classes. I wasn't out getting stoned, I was in the music room practicing with my band."

Her what? "You have a band?"

"Yeah. We call ourselves Stalemate."

"Who's in this band?"

"Me. And Nate. And sometimes Ally Marshall and a couple other people. I'm the lead singer."

Of course she was. Kacey shook her head, looked away.

"What? Sierra knows about it. Willow is one of the youth organizers, and she thinks it's great."

"This is why you're attending the youth group events in Mercy Falls, right? Because of this boy?"

"No. Mom, c'mon. It's the band. And yeah, Nate plays in it, but they don't have a youth group at the church Grandpa and Grandma go to. And I like the Mercy Falls church. Besides, half of the kids from the Academy go there—and it's fun."

"I just think you need to be careful about this, um, relationship with you and Nate. You're too

young to be hiking out to lookouts with him."
She looked at her daughter, raised an eyebrow,
gave her a gimlet eye.

"Mom!"

"Well, am I right? Do you have a crush on him?"

Audrey folded her arms and looked away
from Kacey, and Kacey's heart fell.

This was how it started. Thirteen years old.
A boy playing a guitar for a girl. Wooing her
with his voice, his charm, the idea that nothing
was right in his life until she came along.

Unbidden, a song rose softly inside.

When you need a friend
A shoulder you can cry on
Someone who understands what you're going
    through

She shook it away, but the tune held on, and
with it the memories.

Ben, sitting on the end of the pickup, his guitar
over his knee. His smile as the last of the tones
finished, something sweet, even husky, in it.
The late-afternoon sun gilding his hair and
sliding over his shoulders. He wore his faded
jeans, his flannel shirt rolled up to the forearms,
his cowboy boots, and looked every inch, even
then, the megastar he'd become.

But then he'd put down the guitar, crawled over
to where she sat, ran his thumb down her nose,
her cheek, and around the back of her neck and

cupped her face as he drew her lips toward his.

Sometimes, she could still taste him, feel his touch, sense herself sliding her arms around him, surrendering, wanting to belong to Ben King. Her Ben.

"Mom, are you crying?"

Kacey sucked in a breath, ran her thumb along her cheekbone. "I'm just tired."

Well, she *was* tired. She'd dropped off last night into a hard sleep, only to awaken in a slick sweat, a scream on her lips.

She'd gulped it back before she could terrify Jess, got up in the wee hours, and headed out to the chopper.

Strangely, one of the few places she still felt safe.

"And . . ." she reached out to touch her daughter's hand, "I'm so glad to see you."

Audrey drew her hand away. "You just don't understand, Mom. Nate and I—we're, like, I don't know. More than friends. We're *soul* mates."

"Oh, honey, you don't even know what that means."

"I do know! Just because my dad left you doesn't mean that Nate will. Yeah, okay, I love him. And I'm going to marry him."

"You're thirteen years old! You shouldn't even be thinking about boys."

And great. Now she sounded like *her* mother.

"Why not? Just because you don't want to fall

in love and get married doesn't mean I don't! I don't want to be you. Yeah, sure, you got a medal, but I don't want that. I want a house in Whitefish and a dog and kids and *Nate*. That's what I want. And you're not going to make me break up with him, no matter what you say."

"Honey—"

"And you know what? I almost wish I knew my dad. Because I'm probably more like him than I am you, and I'd bet he'd agree with me. He'd be on my side."

That was just *enough*. "You don't know what you're talking about."

A dozen words gathered behind her pressed lips, fighting for release. "Yeah, you might be a little like your dad. But I guarantee that he'd say the same thing—you're too young to date, to fall in love, and to think you're going to marry Nate whoeverheis."

Audrey folded her arms, stared out the window at the passing pastureland. "I wish you'd just go back to Florida and leave me alone."

Kacey stayed perfectly still, refusing to flinch. Instead, her voice flat, she said, "Yeah, well, we don't always get what we want."

They drove in simmering silence all the way to her parents' forested land, just northeast of Whitefish. She wound her way up their mountain, through the wooded pine forest, until she finally emerged on their circle drive.

The front of the whitewashed log house seemed unassuming; all the grandeur was located in the back, with the view of Big Mountain ski area, the smoky outline of the Livingston range in the distance, and Haskill River running at the foot of the property. Snowy grazed in the pasture, and Kacey's heart warmed to see the sweet palomino.

Audrey got out, slammed the door behind her.

Nice.

The front door opened then, and her daughter ran into the arms of her current, albeit fleeting, ally, her grandmother.

Laura Fairing looked up over the head of her granddaughter and frowned at Kacey.

Kacey shook her head, retrieving her duffel and Audrey's backpack from her back hatch. Her daughter had pushed her way inside, probably running up to her room by the time Kacey lugged them both inside. She dropped the bundles in the entryway and met her mother's embrace.

Her mother had easily dropped ten pounds since Kacey saw her last, and she felt feeble, despite the way she held on to Kacey. "I'm so glad you're home." She pressed a kiss to Kacey's cheek, and for a moment, Kacey wondered if she knew.

Had her father betrayed her by himself, or was her mother a cohort?

She leaned back. "Is Dad home?"

"Not yet. He had a full docket today. But I have a nice roast in the Crock-Pot, and he'll be home for dinner." She stepped back, surveyed her. "Why don't you get changed?"

"Um, okay. But you should know—I saw Ben King in town today."

Her mother's eyes widened. "Oh, Kacey." She glanced up the stairs, then back to Kacey. Pitched her voice low. "Does Audrey know?"

"No, Mom, but the bigger question is—why didn't Ben know?"

Her mother frowned. Shook her head. "Know what? That you were back in town?"

"No, Mom." She barely kept the horror from her tone. "That he has a daughter."

Any remnant suspicion that her mother had been in cahoots with her father died at the confusion on her face. "*What* are you talking about?"

"The fact that he didn't know about Audrey. He told me that Dad told him that I was going to put her up for adoption. He told me that Dad said I didn't want to see him."

"Oh no. Kacey. Your father would never do something like that. He knew how much Ben meant to you."

And now Kacey didn't know what to think.

"Why wouldn't he know about Audrey then, Mom?"

Laura took her hands. Gave her a sad, pitying look. "I don't know. But it's best that he left.

Ben wasn't cut out to be a father, and he knew it."

She left off the rest: *And you're not cut out to be a mother.*

Her mother gave a sad nod, then dropped her hands. "We both know that Audrey is better off without him. And so are you." She cupped Kacey's cheek. "You've done so well for yourself. We're so proud of you."

"Thanks, Mom."

"Listen, Audrey has softball practice this afternoon—their last game is Saturday, so I'm glad you'll be home for it. But I can take her to practice if you want to get cleaned up. I made a bed in the guest room for you."

Kacey picked up the bags, climbed the stairs, and found her daughter's bedroom door closed. She knocked, but when she didn't get an answer, she dropped the backpack in front of the door.

She found the guest room, aka, the room she'd occupied that summer after her parents moved. A picture of her and Audrey at Walt Disney World hung on the wall; another from two summers ago, at SeaWorld, sat on the hickory bureau.

She dropped the duffel on the floor, eyed the queen-sized bed with some envy, then opened the bag and dug out a T-shirt, a pair of jeans.

Then she turned on the shower in the guest bath.

The steam filled the room as she stared at herself in the mirror, her auburn hair unruly and wild after two days in the bush. She looked wrung out, circles under her eyes, her face sallow. She could drop and sleep right here on the bathroom mat. Which probably accounted for the way her mother's words needled her.

Ben wasn't cut out to be a father, and he knew it.

Probably that was true. But she could still see him on one knee, holding out a ring, asking her to marry him.

See his face as he'd brought home a bassinet he'd found at a secondhand shop.

"We both know that Audrey is better off without him. And so are you."

Kacey got into the shower and let the heat massage her sore, tired muscles. Then she leaned against the tile and simply hoped the water might wash away the last twenty-four hours.

Return her to the world where her heart didn't feel freshly battered, kneaded, and stripped.

But maybe her mother was right. *Of course* her mother was right. Kacey well remembered how her own life had derailed when she was just about Audrey's age. The last thing they needed was to drive Audrey into the arms of a boy who could, well, land her exactly where Kacey found herself now.

She finally shut off the shower, got out, dried off, and got dressed. She was standing at the sink, trying to untangle her mess of hair, when she heard a vehicle drive up.

She looked out to the driveway and froze.

No.

He did. *Not.*

She didn't bother with shoes, just ran downstairs and straight outside, closing the door behind her just as Ben climbed out of the cab of his father's truck.

"Go away," she hissed and came off the porch, right onto the driveway. "You shouldn't be here."

"You left and we weren't finished."

He looked like he'd showered too, although he hadn't bothered to shave; the sun picked up the copper and gold in his whiskers. He wore a black T-shirt, jeans, and his fancy cowboy boots.

"We *are* finished. Listen, Ben—"

"*You* listen, Kacey. I kept my promise. I didn't tell her—"

"Keep your voice down!"

"You're the one shouting."

Oh. She clenched her jaw, looked back at the house, and saw her mother at the window.

Thankfully, Audrey's room looked out the back, toward the mountains. But she'd be leaving for practice any minute. "Get in," Kacey snapped.

"No."

She was already around the front of the truck. "Please, Ben."

He tightened his jaw but climbed in.

She slid in on the passenger side. "Let's just drive."

He turned the truck over, put it into drive. "Talk and drive."

"That's what I meant." Except she didn't want to talk. Not yet.

She just wanted to sit here, in the cab, with him driving, and try to figure out the tumult of emotions.

They drove down the winding drive, back toward the highway.

He turned left, as if he had a plan.

"You told her you would teach her the guitar?" She didn't know why she started there, but it felt like a betrayal, and frankly she needed all the ammunition she could get.

Or felt like it.

"That just came out." He glanced at her, his blue eyes dark, clearly in a fighting mood. "But she wants to learn. She's got pipes, and musical talent —*my* musical talent, Kace. I should teach her."

She held up a hand. "Just let me think."

He shook his head, then turned at the stop sign, crossing the railroad tracks.

Oh. He was bringing her here.

He stopped outside the chain link fence to the Glacier valley municipal airport, with the sleek private jets parked at their hangars.

"You're not playing fair." Of course he'd take her to the place where she'd first gotten the bug to fly. Remind her of the hours they'd spent here, watching the planes take off, land.

"This isn't about fair," Ben said. "It's about the

fact that I know you. And I should have realized you wouldn't give your baby up for adoption. *Especially* not you. My dad didn't know, Kacey. But he did suggest that he suspected something wasn't right, and that I should have suspected that also. And he was right. I wasn't thinking. I was hurt and angry and, well, scared."

She leaned back, put her feet on the dashboard, watching as a plane began to taxi out to the runway. "My mom didn't know either. Not to call you a liar, but my mom said my dad would never—"

"I was in jail because I beat up Cash Murdock. And I called your dad to help get me out."

Oh.

She glanced at him. The name sparked old hurts and a strange sense of satisfaction at his revelation. "You did? Really?"

He nodded.

"I hope you broke his nose."

That got a flicker of a smile. "I shouldn't have called you a bad mother, Kacey. But you can't shut me out of her life. Please. I get wanting to go slow. I agree the timing isn't great, but when exactly will it be? When she's eighteen and I've missed every major event of her teenage years?"

Kacey drew in a breath. "You'll probably miss it anyway, Ben. You can't have your career in Nashville and go to your daughter's softball games in Montana."

"She plays softball?" The smile grew.

"She is half mine too," Kacey said, but felt her own smile blooming, something sweet passing between them.

Finally.

Then his expression turned solemn. "I haven't figured it all out yet, but I'm not going to step into her life only to walk away, and don't look at me like that."

"I'm not—it's just, you have a busy life."

"And so do you. You've made it work."

She looked away.

"Kacey?"

"I don't know, Ben. I don't know what I'm doing, really. I've always been, I dunno, Fun Mom. I get some leave, so I come home and we go skiing, or to Disney World, or off to Hawaii, and then I disappear again and leave the hard stuff for my parents. What kind of mother does that?"

"One trying to serve her country."

She wanted to give him points for that, and when she looked over, he gave her an expression that urged a conceding laugh. "Stop it."

"Well, you were right about that too. I know it's not easy. I shouldn't have been so—"

"Self-righteous?"

"Angry."

Right.

"Okay. I agree we should tell her, but I'm not quite ready to drop the bomb on her yet. She already worships you."

177

"Hey, that's a good thing."

"Not so much, because, see, she's also in love with Nate, the kid we rescued, and seems to think he's her soul mate. If she finds out that you're her father and that we knew each other in middle school, she'll suddenly start thinking that Nate is her happy ending. We just need to slow her hormones down a little here."

And suddenly he was all nods, on board, clearly remembering himself at that age too. "I hear you."

She ignored the slightest twinge at his agreement, that he so easily realized the danger looming before her—their—daughter. Their need to slow her down before she made a mistake she couldn't fix.

"So how about we take it one day at a time? I'll think about the guitar thing, but . . ." She took a breath. "Would you like to attend her last softball game? My mom said it's later this week. And then we'll go from there. Will that work for you?"

He sighed. "It will have to."

She looked at him, and he sat there, his hands on the steering wheel, his blue eyes in hers, his mouth a grim line.

A jet had spooled up its engines, started take-off. Kacey watched the bird lift into the sky, white against the blue arch overhead.

"Maybe," she said quietly, "if we do this right, we can both figure out how to be good parents to our daughter."

— 6 —

"Lieutenant Fairing, tango at your two o'clock." The voice issued the warning in a sibilant whisper, to her left, wheedling through the ink of O-Dark-Hundred. The low-hanging clouds blotted out the stars and any hope of a glint of moonlight on a Taliban weapon.

But they were out there. She hadn't moved in hours, her bones burning as she pasted herself to the bunker they'd made just outside a yaw of rock, where five army rangers, she, and her gunner fought to stay alive. She became the rocks, searching her sector for movement.

"Affirmative, Corporal," she said under her breath. Ten feet away, her gunner, Cpl. Morgenstern, wore the thermals and was scanning the craggy outline of this pocket of the Spin Ghar Mountains for heat signatures.

"Duffy, O'Reilly. Sit rep." She kept her voice barely above a whisper.

"I count two hostiles," SPC Duffy responded across the darkness, some six feet away.

"One in my sights," said O'Reilly, to her right. He, too, wore thermals. She affixed the NVGs to her helmet, noted her hands shaking.

Five hours to dawn, and hopefully by then the clouds would lift enough for a fire mission.

They just had to survive until—

An explosion lit the far side of their bunker. A scream from Duffy.

Gunfire peeled back the night. She heard a huff behind her, turned.

Her NVGs showed Duffy tangling with an unknown tango, his face obscured by his shemagh.

Duffy had his knife out, fighting, yelling.

On her other side, O'Reilly unloaded his SAW at the thermal-lit tangos.

She reacted without thinking; her gunshot blinded her, the kick slamming her back into the rock, even as the enemy jerked, slumped on top of Duffy.

Duffy raked him off and lurched back to his position, picking up his weapon.

Pain in her shoulder punched through her adrenaline. She'd cut herself, or—

"Kacey!"

She didn't know whose voice—maybe Captain Johnson, rousing from his wounds in the darkness of the cave—but something hard clamped down on her arm. She reached up, found purchase, a fire in her throat—

"Kacey."

She jerked, scrabbling for her bayonet knife. She wasn't going to die here on this mountain—

"Kacey! Wake up."

She stilled, and the dream faded as she blinked it away and came to in the lamplight of her living room.

One hand on the back of the sofa, the other fisted into her father's bathrobe. He regarded her with some distance, a wary expression, but held her arm in a tight grip.

"You were whimpering," he said quietly.

She let him go. Looked around just to confirm.

No. She wasn't fighting for her life in the wee hours of the night deep in the Spin Ghar Mountains, the feral scent of blood and death mixing with dust and the sulfurous odor left by gunfire.

Although the taste of fear definitely layered her throat, hot and acidic, and her heart thundered.

She stood in the living room, the night pressing through the soaring windows, moonlight tracing the wooden floor. Her father had flicked on a side lamp and stood, looking old and not a little worried. He wore his pajamas and a blue bathrobe, his gray, thinning hair rumpus on his head. She recognized the signs of insomnia on his face.

"What are you doing up?" She untangled herself from his grip.

Shoot. She'd hoped that her string of two nights without sleepwalking might be a sign of progress.

"I should ask you the same thing," he said, leaning down to scrutinize her face. "Where were you?"

She sighed, shook her head. "I'm home now, and that's what matters."

He nodded. "I'll make us some chamomile tea."

She doubted the efficacy of a few leaves to combat her night terrors, but she followed him into the kitchen.

He filled the copper kettle. Turned on the gas stove as she slid onto a high-top stool.

"Dad. I didn't want to say anything tonight, at dinner, but . . . Ben King is in town. He was with me when we went into the park to get the kids. He met Audrey."

Her father drew in a long breath, the corners of his mouth tightening.

"He said"—and she lowered her voice, because she didn't want it to find its way upstairs, into Audrey's bedroom—"that he didn't know."

Her father looked at her, frowned. "Didn't know what?"

"C'mon, Dad. You told him that I was going to give Audrey up for adoption. He didn't know that I kept her."

And then, because it still felt too loud, she got off the stool, walked around the counter, leaned against it, arms akimbo. "He said you went down to the jail after he'd gotten into that fight with Cash and told him I didn't want to see him. That he should leave town."

Her father turned back to the flame, watching it

flicker as a gasping sound emanated from the copper pot.

She expected a denial—something that would tell her that Ben had lied, that her father would never—

"Yes. I did."

She recoiled, nonplussed.

He tucked his hands into his bathrobe pockets, turned to her. "You know why he and Cash had that fight?"

How could she forget the crass word Cash and his cronies had spray-painted on the cute yellow VW bug her parents had bought for her on her sixteenth birthday?

"To avenge my honor?"

"That's one way to put it. And maybe that was his purpose, but I think it was deeper. I think Ben knew that he could never give back what he'd stolen from you, and his fight with Cash was just a reminder of that."

He walked over to the cupboard, took out the box of tea.

"He called the house hoping I'd get him out of his mess. You were just starting labor. I remember thinking his timing was pretty uncanny."

She didn't dispute that she'd been afraid he'd track Cash down. Never considered that he'd end up in jail the night she gave birth.

And, in her youth, she simply couldn't forgive him for that.

She should have talked to him, taken his calls. She blamed herself for that part, at least.

He took out two mugs, set them next to the tea. "So I went down to the jail. He was pretty roughed up, angry, and frankly smelled like a brewery."

"Ben was never a drinker, Dad."

"Maybe not, but he wasn't himself that night. We can agree on that."

Maybe.

He pulled out two tea bags, added one to each mug.

"I saw him sitting there, and I thought . . ." His shoulders sagged. "This is not the life my daughter wants. I know you thought you did, but how many air shows did we attend? How many times did we sit outside, stare at the stars while you told me how you wanted to fly?"

She looked away, unable to dispute that.

"And Ben—I remember listening to him sing. That talent show that he won when he was a sophomore?" Her father shook his head. "That boy had what it took. Clearly."

"Dad, please don't tell me you did this to help—"

"I wasn't just thinking of you, Kacey. I was thinking of *both* of you." The pot started to whine, and he turned off the heat before it woke the house. He poured water into the cups. "And frankly, I was hoping, back then, that maybe you *would* put the baby up for adoption."

"Dad!"

He held up a hand. "Not now. Of course I'm so thankful for Audrey. But I remember how thrilled we were when we adopted you. I was overjoyed to be your father, and I thought . . . I just didn't know how you were going to take care of a baby on your own. I agree that maybe I just didn't want to see your life derailed."

He lifted his mouth in a sad smile. "But it wasn't—not really. You're an amazing pilot now, and Audrey is a wonderful young woman, despite a few recent missteps."

She didn't know what to say to that. Except, "But Dad . . . Ben said that you threatened to put him in prison."

He drew in a breath. "I'll cop to that. I was pretty rattled, and yeah, I might have overstepped. But in my defense, the next day I released him on his own recognizance and later dismissed the charges."

"He missed Audrey's birth."

"That wasn't my fault."

No, to be fair, it wasn't. Ben would have had to sit in jail until his court appearance anyway.

"Ben deserved to know about Audrey."

"I know."

His response brought her up, swept away her anger. "Then why?"

"I never said you shouldn't tell him, honey. I just didn't want him in and out of your life. I know how you felt about him, but I also knew he was destined for a different life than you wanted. So, yes, when he called here after Audrey was born—you were so angry and tired and overwhelmed, I just knew that he would confuse you. You needed time." He stirred his tea, then hers. "I never thought he'd leave town without looking back."

Oh.

He handed her the mug. "And then you left for the military, and I didn't see any need to involve him in Audrey's life. Not when his seemed a little . . . he hasn't exactly lived the life of his Christian upbringing."

"Dad—"

"I'm just saying that he's made some choices that I wasn't thrilled to bring into Audrey's life. I'm still not. He's got fans and paparazzi and a very public life, and you and Audrey . . . well, you don't need that. Especially if you want to keep flying missions in Afghanistan."

He sipped his tea.

She considered hers. "What if I don't want to? What if, I don't know . . ." She'd let her thoughts float to the surface, bubble out, and now wanted to take them back. "It's just that coming home this time has been harder."

He took another sip. Drummed his fingers on the mug. "Or perhaps leaving it behind is the problem?"

She looked at him, at the tight, sad smile on his face. "Yeah."

He surprised her then, by putting his mug down, reaching out for her.

She put hers down and walked into his embrace, feeling the comfort, the safety of his protection as she closed her eyes. "I don't know if I'll ever get better," she said. "And if I don't, I can't go back. They can't have a pilot who walks in her sleep."

"Then maybe you don't go back," he said quietly.

She sighed. "I don't know what else to do. I look into my future, and . . . it looks blank."

He ran his hand down her hair. "Just take one day at a time." Then he kissed the top of her head. "You don't have to decide today."

She leaned back, drawing away. "And in the meantime, what do I do about Ben?"

His shoulders rose and fell. "I think you need to consider the evidence you see. Can he be a dad—a real dad—to Audrey? Or are you setting her, and you, up for heartache?"

"But she needs a father."

His mouth tightened. "One who will only disappoint her?"

"A case could be made for the fact that Ben only left because you told him to."

"You really believe that?"

She heard her words on the mountain, about him being scared. Remembered Ben's apology in the truck—that he should have trusted the person he knew and loved.

"He made his choice."

"And you have to make yours. But remember, whatever you do, it can't be undone."

That she knew all too well.

He picked up his mug. "Don't let the what-ifs from the past cause you to make a mistake today."

Then he touched her cheek, a gentle good night before he headed upstairs.

She stood at the counter, sipping her tea. She thought about Ben in the truck earlier today, assuring her that he wouldn't leave, that he deserved to be a father.

She finally put the cup in the sink, turned out the light, and headed upstairs.

She stopped, however, at Audrey's door. Eased it open.

Moonlight cascaded through the window, along the carpet, illuminating the row of stuffed animals at the foot of Audrey's bed—the orca she'd picked up at SeaWorld, a Mickey Mouse, of course, and the worn teddy bear Kacey had brought home after her first deployment, the fur on its belly rubbed nearly clean.

Her daughter lay on her side, facing away, silvery light sliding over her humped form. Kacey sat on the bed, longing to touch her daughter's hair, maybe curl up beside her, something she might have done even six months ago.

Today, however, her daughter bore the hints of womanhood; she was a girl caught between childhood and who she would be, complete with her own decisions, rebellious or otherwise.

Kacey wasn't ready for this version of her daughter. She didn't know this person. Not really.

Kacey got up, a sheen of unexpected tears rimming her eyes.

She couldn't explain why she reached out for the threadbare teddy bear and snatched it from its demotion at the end of the bed.

Nor could she pinpoint why she stole it back to her room, locked the door behind her, and climbed into bed.

But she resigned herself to the idea that she simply felt better with her face buried into the fur, holding it tight as she stared into the long night ahead.

Ben stood outside the PEAK Rescue HQ, the sun on his neck, covered in sawdust and sweat as he listened to his father's new personal physical therapist give him a rundown.

"The problem is, Ben, that although your father had inpatient rehab after the accident, and although you checked him into the nursing facility, he wanted to be at home. He checked out way too early—which meant long hours in his bed, the home health nurse feeding him, taking care of him. And then him, in frustration, getting up, falling, and dislocating his hips, again. It wouldn't be so bad except he had a double fracture—both hips. It's just going to take longer."

"How much longer?"

He didn't mean it the way it sounded, and glanced away, toward the guys—Ty, Pete, and Gage working on the ramp to the deck.

"It's hard to say." Pretty, maybe thirty years old or so, Charlotte Teague came highly recommended from Ty, who'd worked with her while getting his knee back in shape.

"The problem is, people generally don't do well with at-home rehab. He has plenty of desire, but he's short on patience. Physical therapy is a day-by-day, small increments type of activity. Your father wants to get up and run, now."

"I know," Ben said. "He's furious that I'm building this ramp—thinks he'll be able to vault it in a week or so."

"He needs to take his time, get on a schedule, and stay at it. The brutal statistics are that within two years of a hip fracture, about half of the patients are either dead or living in a long-term care facility. He also has a higher risk of heart failure, as well as blood clots. Your dad needs to get up, yes, and start using his walker—"

"Which he hates."

"But also needs to give himself time to rest, and that means using the chair too."

Ben shook his head. He should have been here

instead of leaving his dad's aftercare to a nurse. Sure, he'd come home after the accident, stayed with him during surgery, checked him into the nicest care center in the valley. And he'd even flown home for a weekend and settled his father back into his house, but that had been two months ago . . .

Right about the time Hollie had been whining about his lack of inspiration in the studio.

And then the old man had fallen, ended up back in the hospital, and Ben packed his bags.

"It's one day at a time, Ben, and someone needs to be here to remind him of that. I'll be back tomorrow."

She stepped off the porch, and Ben took off his gimme hat, rubbed his arm over his sweaty face, and debated heading inside to talk to Chet.

He noticed, however, that the guys had broken away from work. Ty sat on the deck, drinking a Coke, his Stetson pushed back on his head, shouting encouragement to Gage, who'd picked up a rope to lasso the fake steer on a hay bale, a remnant from Ben's youth someone had dragged out from the barn.

Ty's instructions wicked up a memory of himself standing in the yard, his father standing behind him, instructions in his ear as he swung the loop around his head. *Keep it angled toward the horns. If you swing too high, you'll miss the right horn; if you don't follow through, you'll miss the left. Keep it tight and fast.*

He shook the memory away and grabbed a drink from the cooler, sat on an Adirondack chair, and watched Gage's progress. The guy was all hips.

"You look like you're slow dancin' out there," said Pete, clearly reading Ben's mind. He'd stripped off his shirt earlier; a slight sunburn layered his shoulders. Gage threw the lasso at him and caught Pete around the arm; Pete grabbed it and pulled.

Gage skittered across the yard but didn't fall. "Good try, Brooks."

Pete shook off the lasso. Came over to sit by Ben.

A truck pulled in the gravel drive. Sam Brooks got out, retrieved his tool belt from the bed. "Need help?"

Ben nodded, and Sam came up to the porch.

"I thought you'd be saving the town of Mercy Falls," Pete said, something Ben couldn't place in his voice.

Sam regarded him a second, then grabbed a drink from the cooler. Turned to Ben. "The city had to condemn a couple houses near the river—foundations crumbled. Unfortunately, one of those was Pete's rental."

"Mom is thrilled to have me back at home," Pete said, and again, Ben couldn't read his tone.

"Yeah, well, the Sweetwater Lumber Company

might be in business with all the repairs. Which is good because about half of the businesses just south of Main Street are closed indefinitely, including quite a few B&Bs and the Grand Hotel. We could use a boost in our economy."

"Running for sheriff already?" Pete said.

Sam turned to Pete. "Funny."

Pete lifted a shoulder.

Sam sighed, then sat down on the edge of the deck, regarded Ben a long moment. "I still can't figure out how you went from throwing footballs to hosting the CMAs."

Ben smiled.

"Is Carrie Underwood as hot in person?" Pete asked, now smiling.

"Everybody looks hot with a couple layers of makeup, but yeah, she's pretty enough."

Pete raised an eyebrow, and even Ty looked at him.

"So, tell us about Hollie. I certainly wouldn't forget her if I saw her in a crowd," Pete said.

Ben gave a chuckle. "Goldie says she adds the sassafras to the act."

"Have you and her, uh . . ." Ty gave him a look that finished his sentence.

Ben shook his head. "No."

"Seriously, dude. That's not what the magazines in the grocery store say." Gage had given up his attempts to lasso the hay bale. "Apparently you're hiding out after your big breakup."

"No breakup. We might have flirted a little . . ." Okay, a lot. And for a little while, he considered she might be the one to take his mind off Kacey.

It took just one after party to realize that he'd need more than a near tryst with his singing partner to get his mind off the woman who'd been the real thing.

Besides, he had mistakes he didn't wish to repeat.

"Listen, sure, I'm not a monk. I've dated. But no one . . . well, my career takes up a lot of time. Mostly I've never found . . . *loved* anyone like I loved Kacey."

And he couldn't believe he'd just admitted that. It earned a sort of silence among the guys.

"Weren't you hooked up with that actress, Mackenzie Grace?" Gage said.

"We were just friends. Guys, you can't believe everything you read."

"It was on the internet," Gage said.

Ben gave him a look.

Gage held his hands up. "So, you're saying you haven't even been tempted?"

Ben finished his Coke, tossed the can into a paper bag they were using for garbage. "I didn't say that. I just . . . I have enough baggage."

Pete gave him a look, nodded. He and his big brother Sam might be the only ones who knew what he was referring to. And even then . . .

He looked at Sam. "Did you know Kacey has a daughter? Audrey?"

Sam frowned. "Really?"

"Yeah."

"Hmm." Sam considered him now, and Ben couldn't help it. He met Sam's eyes and nodded.

"Really," Sam said. "Huh."

"I know. But the thing is, Audrey doesn't know her father. At all. He hasn't been around in her life."

Sam said nothing, and Ben knew he'd inadvertently opened old wounds. Because, probably no one got over losing a parent, especially one who died way too young.

Still. He glanced at the steer head on the hay bale. "What if she had a chance to know her father? Do you think Kacey should let her? I mean, it's been . . . a lot of years."

"No doubt," Gage said.

Ty was picking at his can of Coke. "Depends on who he is. If he's a jerk or in prison or something, probably not. But if he's a decent guy, I guess it depends on what's best for the kid. How old is she?"

"Thirteen. She'll be fourteen in a week or so."

He couldn't look at Sam.

"That's a tough age," Gage said. "Hormones and all."

Sam leveled a look at him. "I think the father would have to ask himself if it's in his daughter's best interest. Or is it going to add problems to her life?"

"Why would it add problems?"

"Say, if the father were, I don't know, someone who people watched, who could have his personal life dragged through the don't-believe-what-you-read tabloids."

Ben's mouth tightened, and out of the corner of his eye, he saw Ty cock his head.

Ben threw a glance at Sam, ready to end the conversation, but Sam had his gaze on him. "I guess, if it were me, I'd make sure I didn't do anything that might hurt someone I loved."

Yes, well, Sam would say that. But he struck a chord of truth.

Kacey was right about the blowout this could cause—and not just because of Audrey's age and hormones but because it would change everything.

It was one thing to be the cool, country star dad.

Completely another to subject Audrey to a life under scrutiny. No thirteen-year-old survived that unscathed.

"If we do this right, we can both figure out how to be good parents to our daughter."

He had to figure out how to do it right.

— 7 —

"Please tell me I haven't just made the worst decision of my entire life." Kacey never really returned home until she had tracked down Sierra and met her for soup at the Summit—their favorite sandwich and soup café.

Sandbags still closed off Main Street all the way to the bridge. After a week, the water had begun to recede, muddy and gray as it rippled in low-lying parking lots on the sunny Saturday morning. The sandbags lining the sidewalks protected the downtown shops—gift stores, a used bookstore, a barbershop, the historic Grand Hotel, and of course the Summit Café.

Kacey had parked her Escape in the Safeway grocery store lot and hiked down the cracked sidewalk to the café.

Now she sat across from Sierra in a red vinyl booth as her high-school bestie sipped her regular—a banana chocolate shake—and almost ignored her Reuben sandwich. She wore a loose sweatshirt, and her black hair was tucked into a jaunty beret. "I don't know, Kacey. Don't ask me. Apparently, I am the queen of abysmal decisions."

Hmm. "Does that have anything to do with the chocolate overload?"

"Barkeep, get me another!" Sierra called out. Rick, at the long soda counter, looked up.

"She's lost her mind," Kacey said and waved him off. "But really?"

Sierra hit bottom with her straw, sucked up the remains.

"Wow. That bad?" Kacey picked at her turkey club, her own appetite in the dregs. She was living on Diet Coke and energy bars. Locking her door at night to keep herself in.

Staring way too long at the shadows on her ceiling before surrendering to the Ambien.

Sierra wiped her mouth. "Yes. It's that bad."

Unless she was mistaken, her friend's eyes glistened. "What happened between the two of you?"

She watched as Sierra blinked, hard, fast, and forced a smile. "He fired me."

"Fired you? Fired? You don't get fired. You're the best personal assistant on the planet."

"Not anymore. I am un-em-ployed. I'm pretty sure I'm not going to get a reference, either."

She looked away, blinked again, then reached for the ketchup. "Which is fine, because I am done being at someone's beck and call. Probably I need to take some time off and air out the house. You should see my backyard—I think frogs have taken up residence in my new swamp. And the flood took out my deck in back. It's hanging off the house in pieces, falling into the river that used to be my backyard. And, my driveway is a swamp. I need Wellingtons just to get to the door. I just hope that Sam doesn't show up, put a big con-demned sign on the front door."

She affected a sort of laugh that had Kacey reaching out, touching her hand. "Sierra—"

"Nope." She pulled her hand away. "I'm good. Believe me, I've lived in worse conditions and survived unemployment. I don't need Ian Shaw. I'm over losing my job. The sad part is that the man could actually use my help right now."

"Why?"

"Oh, because . . . well, you weren't here, but when his niece went missing three years ago, a lot of folks"—she pointed at herself—"thought she'd run off with her boyfriend, Dante James. But . . ." She made a face. "Dante's body washed up in the flood, and suddenly Ian is thinking that maybe she was killed. Or murdered."

"Murdered?"

"I don't know. Apparently Dante was arrested once for assault."

"So was Ben. That doesn't make him a murderer."

"Ian is upset, and he doesn't know what to think now, but apparently I'm not invited to help." She lifted a shoulder. "Leaving me free to worry about you, my friend, and how you're in a heap of trouble."

Kacey took a bite of the sandwich, then pushed

her plate away. "So, as long as we're planted firmly in denial, could you please confirm to me that I haven't lost my mind about letting Ben attend Audrey's softball game?"

"Can't do that. You've totally lost your mind." Sierra smiled and picked up the Reuben.

"I knew it! What aren't you telling me? Is Audrey really in trouble? You're supposed to be my eyes here—"

"Calm yourself, Lieutenant. Audrey is fantastic."

"What about this Nate guy?"

"Nate is great too. His dad is the associate pastor, for crying out loud. Nate plays in the worship band, and frankly, he and Audrey probably spend their time reciting verses—they spent ten years in Awana together, after all, and attended Bible Study this year."

"I doubt they're reciting Bible verses."

Sierra laughed. "Well, I don't think it's serious. Not like you and Ben after you saved that guy from the bear mauling."

Yes, everything had changed after that night in the park. "I think things were probably changing before that, but yes, spending a night saving a life—I think that was when I really started to fall for Ben."

"You had a crush on him since he took you hiking on Swiftcurrent Pass. To 'show' you the fire shelter." She added finger quotes for effect.

Kacey managed a smile. "Maybe. But it became something more after that."

"Which is why you are in heaps of trouble, my friend. Because I know you. Ben King is the only guy you've ever loved. You haven't even looked at another man since he left."

"I'm a mom. And a soldier. I don't have room for love."

"No. You don't have room for anyone else but Ben. And now he's inching his way back into your life and . . ." She lifted a shoulder.

"And what?"

"And you know what my mother says. Never give a man control over your heart or he'll run away with it and you'll never get it back." She dragged a French fry through ketchup. Sighed as she looked at it a long moment. "I've gained ten pounds in five days, I'm sure of it."

"Really, Sierra, if you want to talk about it—"

"I'm just an idiot, that's what. But it's you I'm worried about. Ben's leaving tore you apart. I would dare say he *did* take your heart with him and never gave it back. The military put you back together, mostly. And that was a good thing. But it's different now. You're different."

"What do you mean?"

"Seriously." Sierra stopped midswipe with her next fry. "I don't know what the military does for people like you who have to save the day—to the detriment of your own safety and sanity—but it doesn't take a doctor to recognize the dark circles under your eyes, the way you're main-lining that Diet Coke. You're still not sleeping, are you?"

Kacey looked away.

"Please. Do I need to bring up the bronze star and why you got it? You deserve more than a four-month break. Maybe it's time for you to think about retiring, so to speak. And yes, while Audrey's doing just fine, *really,* you might consider sticking around."

Kacey finished her Coke. Frowned at her empty glass. "I love Audrey, you know that. But flying helicopters is my life. I'm not good at anything else."

"You could be, if you wanted to. Besides, the guys at PEAK are great. Did you meet them all?"

"I met Jess and Gage, the EMTs."

"Gage is awesome. He's a world-class snow-boarder—even taught lessons for a while."

"I liked him. And I met Ty too."

Sierra made a face. "Ty. Yeah. His dad runs one of the biggest spreads in Montana. Ty grew up cowboy rich—trucks, horses, big toys, and lots of rodeo. And he was the one who was with Chet in the crash. We haven't gotten the full story from either of them, but speculation is that Ty caused the crash. He did keep Chet alive, however, so he gets credit for that. But he hasn't been up—even in the sim—since the accident."

"He looked a little bent out of shape that I was there."

Sierra nodded. "Pride. When do you start?"

"Chet said he'd give me a few days to get settled, but I'm itching to get going, start some training. It's been a long week at home."

Sierra frowned.

Kacey shook her head. "Audrey is withdrawn, and I can't quite get my footing with her. Ben asked me, out there on the mountain, what kind of mother abandons her daughter? He apologized later, but maybe he's right. I'm not cut out to be a mom. I have the wrong genes."

"Are you serious? You're not your mother. No, I don't mean your perfect mother, Laura. I'm talking about your *other* mother. You're not remotely like her, and don't let your fears tell you otherwise."

Sierra knew her too well. "Her grandmother is more of a mom to her. And I feel like she's changed so much since I saw her last."

"It was just five months ago, for Christmas."

"I know, but . . . she's growing up so fast. Did you know she's in a band?"

Sierra nodded. "They play for the youth group sometimes."

Kacey picked at her napkin. "Maybe I should just head back to Florida before I make things worse."

"What? No. Audrey needs you—she loves you, and frankly, she needs a mom who understands the challenges of being thirteen."

Kacey leaned back, sighed. "Maybe I can keep her from making my mistakes."

"Like Ben?"

Kacey nodded.

"I don't know, Kace. Ben might have been a mistake when you were seventeen, but you're not seventeen anymore. I'm not seeing the draw-backs."

"How about the fact that he's a *star*. He has a life in Nashville—one that he isn't going to leave for a daughter he barely knows. And—"

"And you don't think you can compete with all the female attention?"

Kacey's mouth opened. Uh. Then she frowned, shook her head. "I don't care about Ben and the female attention. I'm over him."

Sierra choked on her food, then grabbed a napkin and covered her mouth.

"What?"

"Oh, Kacey." She continued to cough. "Like . . . I said . . . heaps of trouble."

"Do I need to give you the Heimlich?"

Sierra's eyes were watering. She shook her head and took a drink of water. Cleared her throat. Finally, "But if you want, I'll be glad to give you a whack upside your head. You invited him to your daughter's softball game."

"And?"

"Don't tell me this isn't some crazy dream of yours to sit in the stands with Ben while your daughter plays softball."

"What . . . no. I never—"

"Kacey, sometimes you don't know yourself."

Kacey blinked. "I don't need Ben King in my life to be happy. Most importantly, I don't *want* him in my life to complicate it. I will not fall in love with him again."

Sierra held up her hands in surrender.

"Besides, ten bucks says he doesn't show."

"I'll take that action. I think you're giving him too little credit here."

"Yeah, well, in my worst nightmares, he shows up, does something spectacular, then breaks my little girl's heart."

Sierra made a humming noise, something that sounded like assent.

"All done here?" Rick came over, smiled down at Sierra. "Hey, Kacey. I heard you were back. Welcome home."

"Thanks, Rick," Kacey said. She glanced at her watch. "Game's in an hour. I gotta run." She looked at Sierra. "Wanna join us?"

"And watch you *not* fall in love with the man who still carries your heart in his pocket? Yes, I'm in." Sierra slid out of the booth. "Besides, if your old man is going to be there, along with Ben, we could sell tickets."

Kacey froze. "Oh no."

"Oh yes, my friend. Oh yes."

"We've got to get ahead of this thing, Benjamin."

Ben paced the edge of the baseball park, the sun winking overhead, the smell of fresh-cut lawn and grilling hot dogs stirring up memories. He fought to keep his voice low. "No, Goldie, I won't go on the *Today* show. Why would I do that? It only makes Hollie's betrayal seem okay."

"You need to start being okay with it."

He could imagine Goldie pacing her fifth-floor office on Music Row. In her fifties, a platinum blonde, she'd discovered him plunking out songs at the Bluebird and turned him into a star.

"What part of Hollie recording her own album in secret and releasing my song is okay? She had a contract, too, with me."

"We both know that Hollie's been itching to launch her own career, and the contract she had with you allowed for individual efforts."

"She still shouldn't launch it by betraying me."

"She claims you two wrote the song together— or started to. That you abandoned it halfway through. Which we've talked about. You lose enthusiasm for something, and suddenly you walk away. Frankly, Benjamin, Hollie Montgomery was the best thing that happened to your act in a long time. You couldn't afford to lose her."

He stopped, pinched his finger and thumb into

his eyes to rub away the sleep. His body ached, worn out from building the ramp, then adding three days of cleanup around town, a favor to Sam he couldn't say no to. But the honest work felt like a vacation away from the internet and the buzz of his dying career on social media.

Not dying—just at a full-out halt. "I don't need Hollie."

"You need to get back to Nashville and into the studio. It's make or break time, Benjamin. We need to wow the label with something fresh and new from you if you want to hang on to your future."

"I don't have anything fresh and new!" Aw shoot, and there it was, out there for Goldie to scrutinize. He cut his voice down before she jumped on his words, his tone. "I'm just a little blocked is all."

"Give it up, Benjamin. You haven't written anything original since the *Mountain Storyteller* album. But we promised the label something amazing from you and you're going to deliver if I have to come up there and drag you down to Nashville myself. You know how this business is—out of sight, out of mind, and you've been out of sight for too long, my friend. If you don't want to disappear completely, we need to give the press something. Tell them you're back in the studio."

"I have things to take care of—"

"Then take care of them, and then get back

and get busy." She schooled her voice. "Listen. Dig deep, find something sing-along-able, like 'Mountain Song'—"

"That was a one-of-a-kind song."

"No, Benjamin, it wasn't. You have more of that in you. You just need to find it."

He heard voices and glanced over to the field, spotted the team arriving. Girls dressed in blue T-shirts, softball pants, cleats. He located Audrey, her chestnut hair pulled back in a ponytail, a silky mane through the hole in her baseball cap.

He nearly lifted his hand in a wave, but suddenly the sight of her, the immensity of walking into her life, of her knowing—

He couldn't screw this up. Not only for Audrey, but suddenly it felt like this might be his chance to hold on to something that mattered.

"I gotta run, Goldie. You're right—time to move on."

"Benjamin—"

He clicked off, pocketed his cell phone, and walked over to the backstop where Audrey and her teammates took practice hits from their coach, a middle-aged man sporting a Sunday afternoon couch-surfing paunch and a worn cap over a bald head. Ben guessed that his daughter probably played for the team.

Ben hadn't tried to go incognito today, just wore the first things he grabbed out of his bag— a gray T-shirt, faded jeans, cowboy boots, his old Mercy Falls Mavericks baseball cap, aviators.

He didn't expect her to notice him, although he could admit he hoped it as he hung a couple fingers on the chain link, watching as she came to bat, touched the bat to the plate, assumed her stance.

For a second, she became Kacey, the sun catching the gold strands in her hair, the determination in her jaw so cute he couldn't help but smile. Then, Audrey raised the bat and Ben was back in the present, watching her swing.

Whiff.

He must have made a sound because she turned, frowned. Then stepped back from the plate.

"Benjamin King? You're here at my game?" She came over then, grinning, tipping up her hat. "What are you doing here?"

"Your mom invited me." He didn't think before the words came out, and when her jaw dropped, he thought he might have come better prepared "I mean, she mentioned you had a game today, and I'm still in town, so I thought I'd stop by . . ." And that sounded lame, but thankfully she bought it.

"Wow, really? Okay." She glanced at the dugout, where a couple teammates had come out, curious. "Just to let you know, we're pretty bad. And I'm not that good of a hitter."

"Aw, I just love a good softball game," he said, wanting to ease the embarrassment in her expres-

sion. "Although, if I can give you a pointer—
you're too far choked up on the bat. Hold it
further down—you'll have more power."

She moved her grip as he spoke, and now he
came around the fence. "Can I show you?"

She nodded and handed him the bat. He drew a
square in the dirt, then got into position. He
showed her his grip. "Grip the bat where your
calluses are. Your left hand or bottom hand
controls the bat. The top one gives it stability
and direction. Keep your wrists flexible." He
wiggled the bat.

He stepped up to the plate and signaled to the
dad on the mound. "Pitch me something."

The man gave him a look but looped the ball to
him.

He connected with a satisfying crack that split
the morning air. The ball arched up, and the right
fielder held her mitt high, one hand over her
face to block the sun.

The ball soared over her head, hit the far wall.

"That was awesome! Did you play baseball or
something?"

Audrey's voice raised behind him, and he
allowed himself a grin. "Something." Years of
watching Kacey perfect her swing, practicing
with her over and over.

He turned and handed Audrey the bat. "You try."

She assumed the position, worked through a
couple swings. He adjusted her grip on the bat,

then stepped behind her and guided her swing.

Then she stepped up to the plate.

Her first swing parted the air, missed.

"Eye on the ball, Audrey. You're looking good."

She glanced over her shoulder, grinned at him, and his heart felt like it might burst.

The next pitch came in low, but she adjusted and connected, a pop fly into center field.

She dropped the bat, squealing. "I did it!"

He grinned, held up his hand for a high five.

"I can't believe Benjamin King taught me how to hit!" She picked up the bat, ran back to the dugout.

He didn't know why his heart sank just a little.

No. Her *dad* had taught her how to hit.

Still, he kept his smile as he turned to the bleachers.

He startled, though, when he saw Kacey standing just beyond the chain-link fence. She wore a blue and white shirt with baseball sleeves, a blue cap, and a pair of faded jeans, her auburn hair down, curly and blowing in the wind.

The sight of her could still stop him cold, turn his entire body to a live wire. Except for her expression—her mouth was a tight bud of disapproval, her arms folded akimbo.

"Really?" she said as he walked over.

"What?"

"This is how you ease into her life? By making yourself her softball hero?"

"Did you see that hit? Hey, Sierra."

He should have guessed that Kacey's best friend might show up to offer reinforcements. And it occurred to him then that Sierra, who'd helped him search for Ian's niece three years ago, clearly had known about Audrey.

And lied to his face. Or at least left out pertinent information. His realization must have shown in his expression because she gave him a quick smile, something sheepish in it. And went right to her defense, as if she could read his mind.

"You never brought it up, and it wasn't any of my business."

He shook his head. "How many people in Mercy Falls know what a fool I am?" he asked as he followed Kacey onto the bleachers.

"Just Sierra. And Willow, probably. But let's remember that I thought you knew." Kacey climbed up on the bleachers. "And thought you just didn't want to be in her life."

"Well, now I want in," he said, sitting down beside Kacey.

He didn't miss the look exchanged between Kacey and Sierra.

"What?"

"You don't have to sit with us," Sierra said from beside Kacey.

He was about to chase her words with a "why not?" but he followed her gaze.

Oh. Across the lawn, carrying folding chairs,

came the honorable Robert Fairing and his lovely wife, Laura, dressed in their softball fan gear.

Right.

He looked at Kacey. "Did you ask him about what happened?"

"Of course I did. And he claims he did it for our good—yours too."

"And you believe him."

"He said he never dreamed you'd just leave town."

Maybe he would go sit somewhere else.

"Kacey, seriously. He destroyed—forget it. I'm talking to him. He owes me—us—an apology. Accountability. He is a *judge,* after all."

He made to rise, but Kacey's hand fell to his arm. "Just sit here, please, Ben."

Something about her tone stopped him.

"If you go over there, you and my dad are going to have a big fight. Which will only attract attention—Audrey's attention. And then suddenly we'll have a very public personal family moment that she—we—don't need."

He watched as Audrey ran over, wrapped her arms around Judge Fairing's waist. He adjusted her cap, and Laura bent down to give her a kiss on the cheek before Audrey ran back to the field.

They walked past them and set up camp down the field, near third base.

And then the Judge cast a look toward Kacey.

It took only a second for his gaze to fall on Ben,

and he was ready for it, met it with a steel eye. Yes, Kacey had nailed it—there would be a very ugly public fight, and then the truth would come out.

Ben took a breath and looked away. "Fine."

He might have imagined it, but it seemed as if Kacey let out a breath she'd been holding in.

The stands had filled, and he noticed Jess saunter in with Gage Watson. She lifted a hand to them and climbed up on the bleachers to sit in front of them. "Gage's kid sister is coaching for the other team," she said, pointing to the brunette stationed at first base.

"Batter up!"

Ben had forgotten the simple joy of sitting on the bleachers, watching his girl play softball. Yeah, the guys might have laughed at him, but he didn't mind sitting in the sun, cheering on Kacey, dreaming of hanging out with her after the game. The sun soaking into his skin, the smell of brats sizzling on a nearby grill, the cheer of the crowd, the sweet taste of anticipation as Kacey took the field.

"Audrey plays shortstop," he said quietly.

"Mmmhmm," Kacey said. "She's got my arm."

Indeed. Two at bats later, Audrey scooped up a line drive and threw the runner out at first, ending the inning with no runs.

"Wow." He pressed his hand to his chest, against a strange swell of pride.

"I know. She went to softball camp last summer."

He sat through the next three innings without speaking, listening to Kacey and Sierra cheer, catch up on schoolmates, and comment on Willow's latest beau.

Audrey's team scored a run off a bases-loaded hit, and he found his feet, cheering wildly.

Kacey high-fived the other parents around her.

How easily Kacey slipped back into this life. As if she belonged.

He wanted that—to slip back into a life where he belonged. But the fact was, even after years in the music industry, he didn't know where—or if—he belonged.

Sure, Benjamin King and his larger-than-life persona still had a foothold in Nashville, but the Ben King who just wanted a basket of fries and a brat off the grill, to take his girl down to the Gray Pony and sing her a song from the stage, to go stargazing from the back of his pickup after-ward—*that* Ben he'd somehow lost along the way and didn't know how to find him again.

Unless . . .

"What if I stuck around?" He said it softly—so softly that he thought Kacey didn't hear him.

But she'd stilled next to him. Then, quietly, "What do you mean?"

"I mean, what if I hung up my music career for now and moved back for good. Stayed here to be a real dad to—"

"Shh!"

He recoiled and glanced at her. Her widened eyes, the way she glanced around to the scattered crowd, made his jaw tighten.

"We can't keep this a secret forever."

"No, but this is a small town," she said under her breath.

"And that's what I'm talking about. I want her to find out—I'm *dying* to tell her, Kacey. And I know that you're freaked out about me leaving. But what if I didn't leave? What if—"

"Seriously?" She turned to him, and her expression made him recoil.

"What?"

"Now I'm the bad guy? You're going to give up your entire career so I'll let you drop a bomb in my daughter's life."

"Our daughter."

"Whatever."

And that was just not right. He grabbed her hand, leaned over to Sierra. "We'll be right back."

Then he turned to Kacey. "We need to talk."

She rolled her eyes but got up and followed him off the bleachers. "I'd better not miss anything."

But he still had her hand and pulled her behind the opposing bleachers, then all the way to the end, near right field, out of earshot of the fans.

He finally let go. Took a breath. "Kacey, it's not whatever to me. I've had five days to think about this. I want to be on that field helping coach

216

her, showing up for the games, and then spending the evening teaching her how to play the guitar."

Kacey folded her arms. "You want to be Fun Dad. Of course you do—because that's what you do best. Show up and put on a show. You're all about the performance, whether it's rescuing kids off mountains or singing a country song."

Her words stung, and he gaped at her, just long enough to get his footing. "No, I'm ready to be not-Fun Dad too. Did you hear the part about me sticking around?"

Kacey raised an eyebrow. "I'm sure you think so. But I know better than anyone how hard it is to be a part-time parent. I haven't been good at it—and I'm trying to change that. But it hasn't been easy for her, for any of us. And yeah, you might be able to go back to Nashville and still be a big star, but at some point, she'll need you and you'll eventually have to choose. And that's when you'll turn on me, remind me how I've destroyed your life, your dreams."

He stilled. "What do you mean, destroyed my dreams?"

"Oh, don't tell me that thought didn't go through your head when you found out I was pregnant."

He glanced across the field, his gaze settling on the Judge and the Mrs. "Is that what your dad said?"

"No . . . yes, but it doesn't matter. Being a parent isn't just a part-time job. And I know this from firsthand experience. You can't just whiz in and out of her life. She deserves better, from both of us. But you've worked hard for your career, and I don't want you to give it up—"

Top of the ninth inning, one run behind, and he heard the crack of a bat as the other team landed a hit. He watched the ball line-drive to right field. The runner from second slammed into Audrey, flattening her into the dirt.

"Hey!"

Kacey's hand tightened on his arm.

"She's fine." Kacey wore a small smile. "Calm down."

Audrey had popped back up to her feet, dusting herself off.

But he turned to Kacey, suddenly hot. "Let me decide what I want to give up, okay?"

She stepped back, hands up. "Fine. But I swear, if you break her heart, Ben—"

"I won't." He met her eyes then. "I promise."

She blinked then, clearly rattled by his words. "Okay. But you still have to wait to tell her until I think she's ready."

"How about on her birthday next week?"

Kacey stilled. "You remembered."

"Of course. Every year, on the 16th, I remember." He couldn't place the strange curl of hurt at her tone. "Just because I walked away doesn't mean I didn't care."

"Right."

But her expression softened when she turned back to him. "Okay. Her birthday. But only if you mean it, Ben. I'm not going to upset her entire world without some promises."

He held up two fingers, Boy Scout style, and for the first time since he'd seen her again, she gave him a smile that he recognized, one that accompanied a shine in her eyes, the kind of smile that could find its way inside, make him believe that everything would be okay.

Another hit behind them, and he turned just in time to see Audrey field the pop fly and then run in to the dugout.

He glanced at Kacey, and they took off for the bleachers. He sat beside Sierra, Kacey on the other side.

Sierra looked white, her expression drawn. She wasn't watching the game.

He followed Sierra's gaze over to the form of Ian Shaw, who stood near the backstop fence, talking with Sam Brooks, who was dressed in his uniform.

"Are you okay?" he asked.

The first at bat took first base on a walk.

"Audrey's up to bat!" Kacey's hand squeezed his arm.

His pocket began to buzz, and he dug it out, one eye on Audrey.

She whiffed on the first pitch—strike one.

"Eye on the ball! Keep your shoulders loose!" He glanced at the display. Oh no.

Hollie Montgomery.

The second pitch came in—a ball.

He hesitated a moment, then answered the phone. "What?"

"Seriously, Ben?"

He wasn't sure who said it, Kacey or Hollie, but he climbed over Kacey and jumped off the bleachers. "I'm in the middle of something—"

"Oh, Benji—I think I made a terrible mistake!"

He stilled. "Hollie, are you okay?"

"I—"

"Strike!"

He turned back to the game, saw Audrey's shoulders slump.

"I need you, Ben. I know I screwed up, but I'm in over my head. I need—"

He put his hand over his ear. "I can't hear you, Hollie."

The next pitch came in wide. He walked to the back of the bleachers, caught her words.

". . . quit on me, and now I don't have anyone. And I'm so sorry that I hurt you and won't you please forgive me. We can work it out."

A crack, like a shot. He turned in time to see the softball clear the head of the right fielder.

The crowd erupted, on their feet as Audrey dropped her bat and took off for first base.

"Benji?"

"Run, Audrey!" He ran to the fence, leaned over

it. He windmilled his arm as she headed for second. The first runner rounded third.

The right fielder picked up the ball next to the fence, threw it in a wild arc toward second. It landed halfway down the field, and the second baseman ran out to pick it up.

One run in, and Audrey headed to third.

"Run!"

Kacey appeared beside him, screaming as the second baseman threw the ball to the pitcher, as cutoff.

She turned, looked at the catcher.

"Slide, Audrey!" He wasn't sure who said it, him or Kacey, but suddenly Audrey hit the dirt.

The ball hit the mitt of the catcher just as Audrey took out the girl at the knees.

They fell together in a heap.

"Safe!"

Kacey turned, and as natural as breathing, leaped into Ben's arms.

He likewise caught her up, whirled her around, and when he set her back down, he felt it all click back into place. The smile in her eyes, the way she looked at him like he could save the world, save *her* world.

Then she ran out to the field to join the celebration.

Only then did he realize he still held his phone. But when he put it to his ear, Hollie had hung up.

●●●

Ian didn't want to begrudge a team of thirteen-year-olds their first victory of the season, but it seemed a sort of sacrilege for the sun to keep shining, the world to putter on when his niece lay decaying, lost in Glacier National Park.

And after three days of hauling out the maps, tracing the hiking path the youth group had taken three years ago, sorting out where Dante's body might have floated in from, Ian itched to get eyes on the park and start surveying the river.

Hopefully the coroner would have some clues as to where to start.

"We're still waiting for the report, Ian," Sam said, watching the celebration on the softball field behind him. The fact that Sam, in uniform, had decided to take his lunch break at the game—when he should be out interrogating Dante's friends and family—irked him.

Ian turned to take in the celebration, or whatever had Sam's interest piqued, and his gaze fell on Sierra.

High-fiving Kacey Fairing, then hugging one of the team members.

She wore a tank top under a baggy wide-necked sweatshirt, her hair tucked back in a beret, a pair of painter pants rolled up at the cuffs, her old black high-top Cons. And he could hear her laughter from here, trickling inside him, buzzing under his skin.

"It's been almost a week—"

"And we have our hands full tracking down every last resident, making sure people are safe and accounted for." Sam turned to him, peering at him through his aviators. "I know Sheriff Blackburn packed up Dante's body and sent it to the Flathead County medical examiner. He said he'd call you when he got the report."

"And in the meantime, my niece is who knows where."

"I'm sorry, Ian. I know this is upsetting. But maybe you can finally have some closure."

"You think this is better than believing she's out there, living happily ever after?"

A muscle pulled in Sam's jaw. "No."

Ian shot another look at Sierra and froze when he saw her gaze on him. Her smile fell, her face suddenly drawn.

And he had the crazy urge to go over to her and . . . and pour out his frustration. The nights that stretched out too long, the what-ifs chasing him into sleep.

It's my fault.

He let those words burn inside him as he turned back to Sam. "Listen, I don't want to wait. I want the team to take up the chopper, start searching the river—"

"I'm sorry, Ian, but with the flood, the funds are used up. We don't have money for a body search. Especially one that's three years old."

223

"PEAK Rescue belongs—"

"To the city as of a month ago, Ian. You signed it over."

"I still fund over 50 percent of its operations."

"I know. But it doesn't mean you're in charge anymore." He held up a hand to Ian's obvious retort. "Take a breath. Listen, just because we don't have funds doesn't mean you can't privately hire some of the team. I need Pete, Gage, and Miles, but you can have Kacey. And maybe Jess, or—"

"Ben. I need Ben. He knows the park, and he was there that summer." He nodded at Ben standing in the infield.

"Fine. Ben's not even a part of the team. But listen, SAR is first priority. If I need Kacey and the chopper, I reserve the right to pull her in."

Ian's chest rose and fell, loaded with a tangle of emotion.

But Sam had turned away from him. "Hey, Sierra."

She walked past Ian without looking at him. "Sam."

"Could I talk to you . . ." Sam followed after her.

Ian longed to spy on their conversation, but he forced himself to stay put, simply watch as Sam strode up beside her, as she looked at him, laughed. As he walked her out to her rattletrap car, held the door open for her.

Wait—Sierra wasn't *seeing* Sam, was she?

Ian turned his back on the spectacle and headed for Ben, weaving through the parents and the girls still hugging each other.

Ben stood with Kacey, talking to one of the players.

"Ben, hey, can I talk to you a minute?" Ian turned to Kacey. "And you?"

Kacey turned to the girl. "Get your stuff, honey, and meet me at the car. We'll hit Scoops for an end-of-season treat."

"Can Mr. King go with us? Please, Mom?"

Ian watched as something passed between Ben and Kacey.

"Uh, well, your grandparents will probably tag along . . ."

"I've got some calls to make," Ben said. "Maybe another time."

But the girl's expression clearly had Kacey regrouping. "It's okay, Ben. My parents won't mind."

Ben's eyebrow went up, but he glanced at the girl, nodded. "Okay."

"Oh, thank you, Mr. King!" She ran off to retrieve her equipment.

Mr. King. Ian had forgotten that Ben had a name for himself in music circles; he was used to seeing him in a completely different world here in Montana.

Ben shoved his hands into his pockets. "Ian, how can we help you?"

Ian suddenly felt like the storm cloud on their parade. "I need your help with a missing person search."

Kacey suddenly turned all ears. "Who's missing?"

"My niece, Esme."

Ben's eyebrows went up. "Ian—"

He held up his hand. "I know it's been a while, but Dante James's body washed up in the flood."

"I heard that," Ben said, toeing the dirt with his boot. "I'm sorry."

"Then you know what that means," Ian said. "Listen, I know that it's a long shot, but I need you guys to dig in, retrace steps, and see if you can locate her."

Even to his own ears, he sounded tired and not a little desperate. Frankly, it added an edge to his voice. "I'm tired of dead ends. I need answers."

Kacey frowned. "We'll do our best."

"I know. I'll see you both tomorrow morning, first thing."

Ben frowned. "Tomorrow?"

"First thing." Ian turned and headed out to his truck.

Across the parking lot, Sam had finally shut Sierra's door. He stepped back and she waved out the window as she pulled away.

Ian watched her drive away, then turned his vehicle toward the ranch.

The late-afternoon sun simmered over the horizon as he drove, spilling gold over the standing water in ditches and submerged fields.

He pulled onto the frontage road and spotted Chet sitting on his front porch in his wheelchair. He lifted a hand and waved, and Ian slowed, then put a foot on the brakes. He leaned over, rolled the window down. "You okay, Chet?"

"Just enjoying the sunshine after a week of storms. But the home health aide Ben hired was just here and she brought a batch of cookies." He gestured to a plate on a table next to his chair. "Want one?"

In truth, just the mention of food had Ian's stomach churning. With the flood in town, his housekeeper hadn't made it out to the house, and he'd pretty much eaten his supplies down to the crumbs.

He parked, got out, walked up the steps, and took a cookie from the proffered plate. Stared out at the land. "They found the body of Dante James," he said quietly.

"Sam told me when he stopped by to ask me where we searched. I gave him the rundown, but I still have the notes and grid if you're interested."

"That would be great. I'll send Sierra—I'll be by tomorrow to pick them up." He finished his cookie. "Thanks."

"Ian, wait. I know it's none of my business,

but according to the rumors around town, you fired Sierra."

"You're right, it's none of your business." He didn't mean for the words to emerge so sharp. "She lied to me about something. Or rather kept something from me, and . . . well, I can't have someone I can't trust on my staff."

Chet gave a slow nod. "So then I shouldn't hire Sierra to run our communications center?"

"What—no . . . I mean, yes. She's . . . great." He didn't know why Chet's words burned a hole through him. "She'll be awesome."

"Really. But not trustworthy?"

"She's . . . well, she's the best assistant I ever had."

"So you fired her."

Ian took a breath, his mouth settling into a tight line.

But Chet didn't seem to be done. "Ian. I'm not just your neighbor, I'm your friend. And you look like you haven't slept in a week. Stop punishing her—and yourself—for making a mistake. I don't know what she did, but certainly it's not worth starving to death." He gestured to the plate, where Ian had grabbed another cookie. "Or destroying your working relationship."

He considered Chet. "I just need someone who will obey me."

"Oh, I'm sorry. Maybe I should give you old

Jubal here. He's super obedient." He looked over at the yellow lab lying on the deck. The dog didn't move, simply looked up with curious brown eyes.

"Point taken. But I need someone I can depend on."

Silence.

"I'm never stopping for cookies again."

Chet smiled. "Listen. The one thing I can still do is pray. So God and I chat all day. I haven't forgotten you, and neither has he, Ian. You're not alone if you don't want to be. And that includes Sierra."

Ian's smile had faded. "Don't pray for me, Chet. I don't need any more attention cast my way. God's already wreaked enough havoc in my life." He put the cookie back. "Hire Sierra. She's a great employee—just not for me."

Then he got in his car and drove back to his ranch, Chet's words a burr under his skin.

"You're not alone if you don't want to be."

He shut the door behind him. The silence of the house sank into him like the afternoon rays now turning the reclaimed floors a dark umber.

No. He was utterly, painfully, wretchedly, safely —and probably deservedly—alone. And that's how he was going to stay.

— 8 —

A new day and a fresh perspective could change everything.

In fact, if Ben got the words right, he and Kacey might find their way back to becoming friends.

Ben sat in the copilot seat of the PEAK chopper, strapped in; the rotors hummed through his helmet as Kacey dipped down into the gorge carved out by the Mercy River, following it upstream. A moraine blue and edged with cutledge rock on one side and shaggy evergreen on the other, the wide, overflowing river glistened under the wink of sunshine high and bright.

After an hour of flying up the middle fork of the river, they'd unearthed nothing but an occasional fisherman. Now, Kacey flew a route upstream to Lake McDonald, headed for Avalanche Creek deep into the mountains.

"I don't know how Dante's body would make it all the way from Avalanche Creek through Lake McDonald, then into the Mercy River." Kacey spoke through the headset.

Indeed, the route seemed improbable, and Ben had pointed that out to Ian, who had met them this morning with such dark circles under his eyes he resembled an extra from *The Walking*

Dead. "We promised him we'd be thorough," he said. Ben looked out the side, scanning the shoreline.

Nothing but tree debris, frothy residue, and jagged granite boulders spilling down into the river.

"What's that song you're humming?"

He glanced at her, but she didn't look over.

"I like it."

He hadn't noticed he'd been humming but realized now that he'd also been tapping his finger on his jeans. "Nothing. Just something I woke up with."

"It's nice. Catchy." She picked up the tune, and something stirred inside him, filled his chest with warmth.

She angled the chopper toward a falls and hovered there as he surveyed the pool of water until he shook his head. She continued upstream.

"What happened, exactly?" she asked into her mic, through the headset.

"With Esme?"

"And Dante."

"Well, no one really knows. Esme and Dante were on a hiking trip to Avalanche Falls. My dad was leading it, along with Sierra and a couple other leaders from Mercy Church. Esme and Dante sneaked off during the night—or that's the word. The next morning they were both gone, and no one could find them. Vanished without a trace. Speculation was they ran off together, but Ian couldn't accept that. He spent all summer searching the park for them and the past three years hunting every hint of a lead."

"Sad. It's hard to hold out so much hope for something."

He tried not to let her words find roost, and instead nodded.

"What did he mean when he said for you to retrace your steps?"

"I was in the original search three years ago."

"You came back to Mercy Falls? Why?"

Oh. He didn't expect the sudden rush of heat.

The answer gathered right there, sticky on his tongue. He'd come back, success in his grip, and in the back of his head, regardless how unlikely, and the fact he knew she'd moved away, he harbored the dream that he might find her again.

But she couldn't know that. Not when she'd so clearly moved on, forgotten him.

Ben cleared his throat. "My mom got sick. She was diagnosed with cancer, so I came home to talk about options. She sent me back to Nashville at the end of the summer."

"So you weren't here for—"

"No. She didn't want me around—and really, she didn't tell me how bad it was until the end." He tried to keep the edge from his voice. "My dad finally called the day before she passed. I was on tour and jumped on the first plane I could get. Made it home before . . ." And now he couldn't breathe.

Kacey reached over, gave his arm a quick squeeze. "My mom wrote to me when she passed. I was in Iraq, otherwise I would have come back for the funeral."

He glanced over, gave her a tight smile. She met it, same expression.

Her hand returned to the collective, and he felt the absence like a sudden chill.

"I know she was proud of you. I remember her sitting in the front row of the sophomore talent show, cheering her heart out."

A happy memory. "I should probably blame her for my belief that I could sing."

"You could—can sing. You stole the show."

"Thanks." He also remembered Kacey in the audience. Almost mentioned it, gulped it back.

No need to stir the coals. She had a life, a future, something that didn't include him.

But together they did have Audrey.

"Have you given any more thought to guitar lessons?" he asked.

She nodded as they followed the fork to McDonald Creek. "Maybe after her birthday."

She left the rest unsaid. Yes, he could teach her, if everything went well and Audrey didn't react to the news about her father with an outraged sense of teenage betrayal.

He watched as the river narrowed, scanning the shoreline, acid lining his throat.

"You should know that I wish I'd been there that night. I was—"

"Leave it, Ben. It's done. We can't go back."

So much for the right words.

They rode in silence as they came out to Lake McDonald. She climbed to soar over it.

For a moment, he simply breathed in the beauty, Howe Ridge to the north, Snyder Ridge to the south, the historic brown and white outline of McDonald Lake Lodge on the southeast shore, the glistening falls at the northeast end. The lake spread out below, striations of blue and aqua, almost translucent to the rocky bottom. A slight wind rippled the water, and a few boaters waved. Probably inlanders or the residents of the handful of cabins grandfathered in.

Kacey arched over the lake, then slowed as she worked her way back up the river. She hovered over the ledges of McDonald Falls, the mist rising. "I don't know how we're going to find her. The river narrows from here."

Indeed, the gorge narrowed, the water frothy and choked with debris after the flood.

Still, she dogged on, searching her side of the tangle of forest.

"I checked—Audrey does have all three of your albums. She's been singing them constantly since the softball game."

He allowed a smile. "Thanks for letting me tag along for ice cream." As it turned out, her parents had opted out of the celebration, a decision that tempered his lingering fury at Judge Fairing. A little.

"Audrey's amazing, Kacey. You've done a great job."

Silence. Then, "She loves that song you sing with Hollie—what's it called?"

"Which one?"

"Something about starting a fire?"

His gut tightened. "Oh no, not that one."

"What?" She started to sing it. " 'Golden tan, a laugh for the band, I see you in the crowd, waving your Coke can—' "

"Stop. No. You can't let her sing that."

"Why not?"

"Because it's not an appropriate song for a thirteen-year-old girl."

"Why not? How does it go?"

"I don't remember," he lied.

"But it's on your album."

"Yeah, I know. But I didn't write the song."

"It's catchy."

He turned in his seat then. " 'I like your smile, stay for a while. Huddle up around the fire.' " He added the tune. " 'It's all right, stay for the night. Let's chase away the cold and do it right. C'mon, baby, let's start a fire.' "

She went quiet.

"Yeah. You really want our thirteen-year-old daughter singing those lyrics?"

"Why did you sing a song you don't want people to sing?"

"The entire album is full of songs we didn't write."

"But you—you're an amazing songwriter, Ben. You could always write songs that made people feel and cry and . . . I have your first album, and . . . you should write your own songs. The kind you want people to sing."

He couldn't breathe. She had his first album.

Before he could follow up, she added, "Hollie was a good addition, though. She's a cutie."

He snorted. "Hollie is cotton candy with blonde hair and an amazing voice." Cotton candy that had just destroyed his career.

"Wow. That's harsh."

"Okay, she's not exactly cotton candy. But she's . . . well, let's just say that she's not necessarily known for the dark ballads."

"That's all your department?"

He wanted to nod.

"She hasn't written a song her entire career. Her skill is belting out the high notes and putting on a show. And not that it matters, but Hollie and I split up. She's going solo."

More quiet as they angled up the river, and he focused on the shoreline, eyes on the edges in his fruitless search.

"She hurt you."

He stilled. Sighed. "No. She stole something from me. Betrayed me."

She angled up another falls, and that's when he saw it—something tangled in the edge of the river. White flesh, decaying legs. "Kacey, look."

She turned the chopper around, angled back toward the spot. Hovered over it for a better look. "I don't know, Ben. It could be a deer corpse."

"Can we put down, take a look?"

She added altitude. "Get out the map. The nearest place is probably Avalanche Creek Park. But mark these coordinates down." She gave him her reading.

They rose higher, and he leaned back in the seat, his heart thundering.

"That was her on the phone on Saturday, wasn't it?"

Oh, they were still talking about Hollie. He nodded.

"She wanted you back."

He frowned. Then shook his head. "It doesn't matter. I can't sing with someone who's going to stab me in the back when I'm not looking."

Silence, and he couldn't tell if he'd hurt her.

Until, "No, I suppose not."

Great, Ben, so much for making friends.

Kacey absolutely refused to be jealous.

And really, how silly was it to be jealous of someone Ben had called cotton candy.

Except Kacey had seen Hollie Montgomery. That "cotton candy" came with curly, lush blonde hair, pretty blue eyes, and curves that looked good in Daisy Dukes, a cutoff black T-shirt, and red boots.

She didn't believe it for a moment when she told herself he hadn't liked her.

They'd probably had a fling and Ben had skedaddled north, nursing a broken heart.

Well, he wasn't bouncing back into *her* arms, thank you.

But Kacey could admit that it irked her, just a little, that while she'd been flying rescue missions and watching her back for snipers, he'd been singing love songs with a beautiful woman in front of thousands.

Overhead, the sun had reached its apex; the smell of the river mixed with the piney scent of the forest. They'd follow the trail along Going-to-the-Sun Road, cut in toward the river as they got closer.

She'd put them down about six miles from the sighting, near the campground area of Avalanche Creek, radioed in their position, and now grabbed her own backpack of supplies.

He hadn't said much since his revelation about Hollie and the fact that he hadn't written his last album of songs—something she hadn't expected, given his love of sitting in his truck, penning lyrics. Now he set off, leading the way back down the trail along Avalanche Creek without a word.

Something—not Hollie, exactly, but maybe someone else—had him on edge.

But it wasn't her problem to fix him anymore—not that she ever had anything to give him except her ear—but the old tug remained, to reach out, to listen.

To care.

She did care, but she couldn't let old memories wheedle open her heart, let him get a toehold.

Not that she could escape it with him walking ahead of her on the path, looking like a hero in his faded jeans, hiking boots, and a blue SAR T-shirt stretched out by his sculpted shoulders. The sight of him stirred up forbidden feelings, like an old song suddenly revived, her body humming to the long-familiar beat.

"We're going to have to hurry if we hope to check out that—something—and get back before dark." Ben glanced over his shoulder at her.

Blue eyes, and they could simply swipe away her breath, like they had so many times when she'd spotted him watching her across the dance floor at the Gray Pony, or when he'd glance into the stands at a football game. Always searching for her. Finding her.

Seeing her.

It had taken her years to find *herself* after he left. She couldn't be lost again.

"I forgot to pack bear spray," she said, catching up. "This is bear country."

He patted his pack. "Armed," he said, and his glance contained memories. "I got this."

"Good," she managed, painfully aware that a part of her she'd forgotten—or perhaps had simply eradicated from her life—stirred at his easy protection.

He always had a way of making her feel safe, and she hated that, despite her years of survival training, she leaned into it like a reflex.

He walked along the path, clearly a man who had grown up in the shadow of the park, his gait sure as he stepped over ruts in the trail. But that was Ben—as comfortable in the woods as he was on the football field or under the bright stage lights.

He was born to show up, be a hero.

Oh boy, she was in such big trouble.

As if reading her thoughts, he glanced over at her, his eyes warm. "You remember that night we rescued that hiker, how dark it was? I still can't believe Lulu found us. Or that we made it back to her cabin."

"You did have that head lamp, but I kept waiting for the bear to follow up, jump us in the middle of the forest. All that blood."

"I know. They say bears can smell a human from five miles away. And they can run forty miles an hour. I'm pretty sure God had an army of angels looking out for us that night."

She let his words fall, not sure what to say.

He too went silent, his boots thumping the ground. A squirrel ran across the trail.

"You were amazing that night. I still can't believe you carried that guy over a mile—"

"We couldn't stay there, and besides, you helped."

"I was just trying to keep up. You acted so fast —probably saved his life."

He lifted a shoulder. "The one time my impulsiveness came in handy."

She gave him a tight smile, let his comment pass.

"Did you know that Ken still comes out every year, hikes this trail, just to prove he lived? There's some kind of bear attack survivors' club, and they make a point of revisiting the place where they were attacked every year."

"I don't see the point of revisiting the past," she said.

He glanced at her, fast, then nodded, looked away.

"I didn't mean—I don't mind . . . Anyway, you were amazing that night. So cool under pressure."

"Hollie says it's my superpower. I never get stage fright."

And they were back to Hollie. Nice.

"I wish I had your steel nerves," she said.

"What are you talking about? You fly rescue choppers. In Afghanistan. You won a bronze medal. That says steel nerves to me."

No, that just said she'd lived.

"I still can't believe you became this amazing pilot, Kace. I'm really proud of you. You're a hero."

Crazy, hot tears pricked her eyes. She blinked them away. Clearly she needed more sleep. But again, last night she'd spent too long staring at her parents' ceiling before finally surrendering to a sleeping pill.

"I'm just a chauffeur. The real heroes are the guys on the ground who defend the villagers and build wells with targets on their backs."

"You didn't earn a medal for being a chauffeur—"

"Yes, actually, I did." She winced at the edge in her voice.

He frowned, and she couldn't bear the look of concern in his eyes.

She ignored it and headed down the path in front of him. Two hours they'd been hiking, and if they didn't find the body soon, they'd have to camp out here for the night.

"Kacey?"

"I don't want to talk about it."

"I Googled the article. I know what happened."

"I wish you hadn't."

The breeze lifted the smell of earth and decay, mixing it with the scent of the river. "Up ahead is an overlook," she said, remembering the trail.

The sooner they got off this mountain, the better. He caught up to her. "Kacey, what's going on?

You should be proud of what you accomplished."

"And you should be writing your own songs." She rounded on him. He took a step back. "You want to tell me why you quit writing?"

His mouth tightened. "No."

She stood there, a little nonplussed. Then, "Right. Okay. Let's just get this done."

She led the way toward the overlook, the mist of the falls rising and iridescent in the mid-afternoon sun. On the opposite side of the river, a similar overlook, higher and just downstream, jutted out over the falls.

She scanned the frothing river. "We're still a mile or so away."

"We can cross the river down at the Avalanche Creek Bridge, work our way back up. The body might be easier to spot from the opposite side."

Indeed, with the overhanging cliffs dropping twenty feet in some areas, rocks, scrub bushes, and shaggy pines obscured the view of the shoreline below.

"Once we find it, we can probably find a place to cross, or at least get a better look, take pictures, and bring back a recovery team."

She returned to the path, not looking behind her, feeling his eyes on her. They walked in silence for so long that she glanced back once to see if he was still following her.

He wore a solemn, tight look. "I wonder if Lulu still lives around here."

"She was already ancient fifteen years ago. I doubt it."

"Did you know that her great-great-grandfather owned the property, back in 1890? Used to trap this area. She's fifth generation in that house."

They came to the bridge and crossed it. The trail headed southwest, to McDonald Lake, but they turned east, back up the trail, scanning the far bank. In places, the river narrowed, dropping through the gaps in rocks that resembled bowling balls stacked on each other, covered in yellow and green lichen. In other places, the river flattened out, flowed flat and clear over a wide, stony bed.

"I don't see anything," Kacey said, finally standing at the edge of a cliff with the river ten feet below. Spray licked her face.

Ben stepped up beside her. She'd forgotten how tall he was, a good six inches towering over her. The wind picked up his scent—the finest hint of sweat, the cotton of his shirt, the remnants of his morning shower. The late afternoon had added to the layer of golden whiskers on his chin.

And just like that, her memory circled her back in his arms, and the taste of his lips on hers, whiskers against her chin, his kiss asking for her surrender. She felt his chest under her hands, the way he wrapped her up in his embrace, made her feel safe.

Her throat thickened with the rush of memory, the heat tingling her skin.

Yes, very dangerous to revisit the past.

"What's that?" He pointed downstream to an eddy, the late afternoon shadows turning the water a deep indigo. Caught against a stripped-downed log—a body. Most definitely a body.

She hadn't realized she'd grabbed his hand until he squeezed back.

"Is it her?"

"We need to get back across the river, see if we can work our way down."

"Maybe we should call in the team. We don't want to destroy any evidence."

Ben nodded. "Take a picture, and I'll see if I can get reception somewhere." He pulled out his phone and held it up, searching for bars.

She took a few shots with her cell, a familiar quickening inside her. This might be a body recovery, but at least someone—Ian—would have answers. Closure.

No one would be left on a mountaintop today.

Ben came back to her. "No signal."

"I think we need to get down there."

"We're running out of daylight, Kacey. I don't think we're going to make it back to the chopper before dark."

"We'll climb down, get a good look, hike back to the campsite—"

A scream tore through the rush of the river, the wind scurrying through the trees.

Kacey froze, looked at Ben.

He'd already turned, pocketed his phone.

Another scream and he grabbed her hand, pulled her back to the path. "It's coming from upstream."

She should have expected it; Ben ran right toward the scream.

— 9 —

Fifteen years ago, screaming had erupted through the woods, and Ben and Kacey had tracked it down just in time to see a grizzly take his final swipe at a hiker. With a punctured leg, a broken collarbone, and a gash that opened up his skin along his back to the bone, the man was close to perishing on the side of the trail.

Thankfully, Lulu Grace had also heard the screaming. With the twilight deepening the layers of danger in the forest, she'd found them and convinced them to bring the man back to her cabin in the woods, let her doctor him, then wait out the night in case the bear decided to turn them all into prey.

That night, Ben had seen for the first time the side of Kacey that made her not only a soldier but a rescuer.

No one stood between Kacey and someone in need of saving.

No wonder she'd earned a medal.

Now, Ben watched as she knelt next to the

injured hiker they'd finally tracked down a half mile up the trail. His wife—Ben placed her in her early seventies—paced the trail behind her injured husband, shaking.

Ben stood up, walked over to her, and without thinking, simply drew her into a quick embrace. "He's going to be okay. It looks like a broken ankle."

"He has a heart condition," she said softly.

"What's your name, ma'am?"

"Mary Beth. And this is Howard."

Howard wore a Glacier Park baseball cap, a yellow sweatshirt, and a pair of rain pants, and his face grimaced in pain. Kacey had already draped her blanket over Howard and was now taking his pulse.

"Mary Beth, why don't you sit down?" Ben went over to his pack and pulled out his blanket. He tucked it over the woman's shoulders, just in case the trauma of seeing her husband fall into the river and nearly get swept away sent her into shock.

"How did this happen?" Ben said quietly, holding her hands. Her skin felt paper thin, soft. She too wore hiking attire—Gore-Tex pants, boots, a windbreaker, a pair of binoculars around her neck.

"We saw a ruby-crowned kinglet, and Howard wanted to get a picture, so he climbed down onto one of those boulders and slipped."

Ben didn't want to tell her how many people slipped, fell into the froth, and drowned, especially now with the rivers swollen.

"I think he wedged his foot on a boulder. How bad is it?"

He had taken a look at the leg, seen the angle of the foot, the swelling around the ankle as Kacey worked off his boot.

Bad.

"I don't think he can walk on it," Ben said. "Stay here—let me take a look."

He left her on the boulder, glanced at the darkening sky, and for a second wished Lulu might miraculously show up.

But they weren't fifteen and alone. Surely Kacey knew how to save lives, and Ben could pull out his rusty first-responder skills. Besides, this injury didn't look nearly as bad as Nate's had been.

Ben knelt beside Kacey as she searched for a pulse in Howard's ankle, her voice calm. "So, you're a birder," she said. "Did you know that Glacier has the largest concentration of Harlequin ducks in the Lower 48?"

"Yeah," Howard said, his breath tight with pain. "We were hoping to get a glimpse of a nesting Black Swift."

"They roost behind waterfalls," Ben said. Kacey had taken off Howard's sock, and now Ben pressed on the appendage, watching the refill. "It seems to be getting blood," he said quietly. He turned to the man. "Can you feel that, Howard?"

He nodded.

"Wiggle your toes for me," Kacey said.

He winced but managed movement.

She leaned back on her haunches. "I don't think it's broken, but there is no way he can walk."

Ben dug around his pack, found the ice pack, and snapped it into use. He wrapped it around the man's ankle, keeping it gentle as he heard Howard groan. "Sorry, pal." He secured it with the Ace bandage.

"Maybe one of us needs to hike out, get help." She looked up at the sky, then checked her watch. "I can do it."

"You should stay here with him. You have more medical training."

"I can fly the chopper out."

"In the dark?"

She gave him a look.

"Listen, I get that you flew all over the mountains of Afghanistan, but this is Glacier, with its own weather patterns. Besides, I don't like you walking alone this time of year—we haven't seen a grizzly yet, but twilight is not the time to hike solo. Besides, we're hours from civilization—even if you hike out to the road, the Logan Pass Visitors Center closed an hour ago. There's not going to be any traffic until morning."

She sighed, nodded as if his words made sense.

She glanced over at Mary Beth. "She's really upset. And his pulse is high. We need to get them to some shelter. It's still early enough in the season for the temps to drop into the low thirties."

He dug into his pack, pulled out his windbreaker, rolled it up. "I'm going to splint it."

He bent down, moved the jacket under the man's foot, easing the foot into a ninety-degree position. Kasey handed him lengths of medical tape, and he secured the jacket to the foot and leg.

The sun had dipped below the ridgeline, and fine gooseflesh raised on his arms.

Kacey glanced at his bare arms. "It's going to be cold out tonight."

"We're going to Lulu's cabin."

She caught his gaze, as if assessing his words. Then, "Yes. Can you carry Howard?"

He put the man at about 180 pounds. "Do you remember the way?"

"I dunno."

"We'll find it." He winked then, and the look she gave him came with so much hope that he felt as if they'd tunneled back to a time when she actually believed in him.

He and Kacey helped Howard to his feet, then he bent and Howard climbed on his back.

Ben wrapped his arms around the man's legs. "Can you hang on?"

"Sorry about this, son," Howard said, something sheepish in his tone.

"It's all good. It's what we do."

When Kacey glanced at him with a smile, he felt he could have carried Howard to Canada and back.

The shadows lengthened, drawing out from the forest as night settled around them. With it came the chill of the mountains, gathered in the forest, borne on the spray of the river, the breath of the wind scurrying down the mountains into the gorge. He longed for his head lamp, but Kacey pulled out a mini Maglite and held it out for him as they walked.

To his recollection, Lulu's cabin was a half mile beyond the Avalanche Creek Bridge, just off the path near the northwestern edge of Lake McDonald. But the forest was overgrown, and as he passed the roar of the falls, somewhere out in the blackness, his back aching from Howard's weight against him, he stopped.

"What's the matter?" Kacey said behind him.

He didn't want to admit it, but . . . "Just give me a second here to get my bearings." He let Howard slide onto a boulder. Stretched.

"Nothing looks familiar," Kacey said quietly.

"It's been fifteen years."

Overhead, clouds covered the stars. Kacey flicked her light around the forest.

He took off his hat, scrubbed a hand through his hair. "I thought this was a good idea."

Kacey had gone strangely silent, wrapping her

arms around herself. Now, she looked at him, something wan in her expression. "Um, maybe we should head back?"

From the side of the trail, Howard cleared his throat. "If you two are finished panicking, Mary Beth and I are praying over here. We're not lost—we just can't see the path. But God can."

Ben glanced at Kacey, who stared at Howard with an enigmatic expression. But she stepped forward, took Mary Beth's hand.

Huh. He didn't want to argue, but he hadn't sensed God's presence in his life since the day he'd flattened Cash, ended up in jail, and walked out of Kacey's life.

Frankly, he didn't exactly deserve for God to show up.

Except, a strange longing burned inside him, and while he couldn't place it, he felt a nudge.

Fine. Ben refused Howard's proffered hand but took a step closer as he began to pray.

"The Lord is my shepherd . . ."

Oh, he knew this one. His father had made him recite it every night before bed.

"I shall not want."

Ben didn't speak the words, but they gathered in his head, his throat, as if wanting to push out.

"He maketh me to lie down in green pastures: he leadeth me beside the still waters."

He wanted to laugh at that, given their circumstances.

"He restoreth my soul."

Nope. He wasn't playing this game.

Ben walked away to the edge of the light, stood in the darkness, away from them. But everything inside him suddenly ached.

"He leadeth me in the paths of righteousness for his name's sake."

For some reason, Kacey's voice revived in his head. *"You should write your own songs. The kind you want people to sing."*

Yeah, well, he'd forgotten how, lost the ability to hear the songs in his head, feel the lyrics.

"Yea, though I walk through the valley of the shadow of death . . ."

He looked at Kacey, the way she now clung to Mary Beth's hand.

Something had happened to her in Afghanistan, something the article hadn't mentioned—he felt it in his gut, and seeing her lean into the words, as if thirsty . . .

"I don't want to talk about it."

"I will fear no evil: for thou art with me; thy rod and thy staff they comfort me."

Something flickered on the edge of the forest. A light. He turned, searching, but it had winked out.

"Thou preparest a table before me in the presence of mine enemies."

He walked down the path, searching for the light in the darkness . . . *there.* A dent of light deep in the pocket of woods, flickering.

"Thou anointest my head with oil; my cup runneth over."

He strode back to Kacey, took the light from her hand, and shined it against the folds of the trail. The trees parted, the dark brush shrank away.

"Surely goodness and mercy shall follow me all the days of my life."

He spotted the path cutting away from the main trail and followed it.

"And I will dwell in the house of the Lord forever."

Ben made out the clearing some fifty feet away, the small log cabin with the overhanging porch, and through the leaded window, the glow of lamplight.

Lulu Grace's historic home.

He tromped back out to the trail. Kacey had let go of Mary Beth and stood in the darkness, waiting.

"I found it."

Howard looked up at him. "I knew you would."

He frowned but didn't argue as he maneuvered Howard onto his back. "I think someone's there. I saw a light on."

Kacey held the flashlight as they headed toward the cabin. Constructed from stripped, pitched, and now almost black pine logs, the ancient, snug cabin sat in a clearing of towering black pine, the overhanging porch cluttered with hand-hewn chairs and pots. A pair of dry, gray moose antlers were affixed to the center of the porch, near the roof. Ben remembered the cabin being bigger, somehow, although from the outside it appeared no more than two rooms, a main cabin and a smaller addition off to the side.

He put Howard down on the porch, then knocked on the door.

No answer, and he took the handle, eased the door open.

The light in the window—the source a lantern in the center of a rough-hewn table—cast a glow over the small room. The aroma of brewed coffee was thick in the air, and Ben saw a propane cookstove topped with a coffeepot, and beside that, a counter with a sink, a drying rack, and a cupboard.

At the far end of the room, coals flickered in the hand-piled stone fireplace. Another door led to a back room—storage or another bedroom, he couldn't remember.

He walked in further. "Lulu?"

A book lay upside down on the deeply grooved leather sofa that faced the fireplace.

He walked over to the addition, eased that door open.

A single bed with a hand-stitched quilt and a mirrored bureau. He caught a glimpse of his unshaven self, then closed the door.

Walked back outside. "No one is here." He put

Howard's arm over his shoulder, helped him hobble inside, and settled him on the sofa.

Kacey closed the door behind Mary Beth, who sat next to her husband. Kacey set her pack on the table and pulled out a water bottle.

She handed it to Ben, who unscrewed the lid and was handing it to Howard when the door opened.

He saw Kacey freeze and followed her gaze.

An elderly woman, with her white hair pulled back in a handkerchief, stood in the open doorway. She wore a nubby brown sweater, a pair of canvas pants.

And in her grip, pointed in the general direction of Kacey and Ben, she held a double-barreled shotgun, circa 1950. "Who's here?"

Kacey didn't move. But her breath rose and fell.

Ben raised his hands. "Lulu? Is that you? It's me, Ben King."

The woman scrutinized him, as if clicking through her memories. Then she cast her gaze to Kacey, and a smile went over her face. She lowered the shotgun. "You're back. And you brought your sweetie."

Ben put his hands down, not sure what to say.

Yes, actually.

"And this is Howard and Mary Beth," Kacey said, filling in the gap. "Howard fell. We were hoping . . ."

Lulu had set her gun aside and now came around

the sofa and knelt before Howard, probing his ankle, testing the blood flow. "Can you move it?"

Howard shook his head but wiggled his toes.

Lulu stood up. "You can't bring him out tonight. But tomorrow I can get the truck going." She turned then, looking at Ben. Startled him when she reached up and took his face in her hands, scrutinizing him.

"Yep. Just like your old man." Then she patted him and walked over to Kacey. Touched her arms. "And you've grown up."

Kacey offered a smile.

"Okay, sit down. I'll bet you're hungry."

Kacey glanced at Ben, and he lifted a shoulder. He glanced at the sofa, where Howard had leaned back against his wife and closed his eyes. Mary Beth held his hand, gave Ben a shake of her head.

Yeah, well, he understood losing your appetite when you saw someone you loved get hurt.

Lulu opened a bread box on the counter and retrieved a half loaf of wheat bread. Then she opened an ancient icebox and retrieved a jar of raspberry jam. "I'll heat up some stew."

She produced a cast-iron pot right from the fridge and put it on the stove, then lit the fire in the box with a match. It blazed to life.

She turned then and grabbed the bread and a knife. "So, tell me. Did you two get married and have a pack of kids?"

Ben looked at Kacey, who seemed to go a little white.

He had the crazy urge to reach out for her hand. "Um—"

"Oh, please." Lulu dove into the bread, slicing. "You two were absolutely smitten with each other."

Kacey glanced at Ben, then back to Lulu.

"No. We—" Ben started.

"We have a daughter," Kacey said suddenly.

Ben stared at her.

"Oh, that's glorious." Lulu piled the bread onto a plate. "But you didn't get married?"

Ben looked down, away. And there it was, his sins out in the open.

"It's not too late."

This from Mary Beth on the sofa. She had turned and now put her arm over the back of the sofa while Howard rested. "Howard and I are high school sweethearts. But we both married other people and only found each other again last year." She looked down at him, something soft in her expression. "We're on our honeymoon."

Really?

"Congratulations." This from Kacey.

"We figured we never stopped loving each other, so we'd grab whatever time we have left and live like we have forever." She ran a finger under her eye. "I don't think you ever get over your first real love. You give your heart to it, all in, without knowing the perils. That's the person who knows your dreams, the person you want to be. If you're lucky, they can look through the clutter of your life and still see that young and hopeful person inside."

Kacey got up from the table. "Actually, Lulu, I'm not hungry. I think I'm going to try to get cell reception and call in our position."

Lulu picked up a piece of bread, dipped a knife into the jam, and layered the bread with it. Then she held it out to Kacey. "Go to the far edge of the property, stand on the boulder, and face the west. My grandson says it works for him."

Kacey paused, then took the bread and headed outside.

Ben watched her go, not sure why he felt a fist in his gut. But for a second, he heard his father's voice, the words he'd spoken over a week ago.

"This is why you came home, Benny. Not for me. And not for you. For her."

Somehow they'd ended up right back where they started.

Kacey just needed some fresh air, something to ease the knot around her heart that suddenly held it captive, strangling.

"I don't think you ever get over your first real love."

Yes, yes you did. If you left town, dove into a

different life, put the past behind you with the admission that it was just a mistake of youth.

If you never mentioned his name, refused to let the memories gather in the dark, secret places, and didn't take them out when you were afraid and alone.

Or facing death.

Kacey stalked out to the boulder Lulu had mentioned, her heart thundering, and stared at her cell phone for reception.

Of course, she'd done *none* of those things. Yes, she'd left town, but she'd hardly put her past behind her. Every time she looked at her beautiful daughter, memory swept her back to Ben down on one knee, giving her his heart.

Or her, weeping when she held their daughter, alone in the hospital room, making vows to herself to never forgive him.

Vows she seemed to be breaking with record speed. What was wrong with her that the minute Benjamin King walked back into her life she turned into a seventeen-year-old girl, hoping he would look her direction?

No, in truth, she wanted more than that. She wanted to see her reflection in his eyes, wanted his arms around her, his breath on her neck, his hands in her hair. Wanted to believe him when he said everything would be all right.

Oh, she needed to get off this mountain, and soon.

Kacey climbed up on the rock, held her phone up, and yep, one bar flickered. But when she tried to place a call, it refused to connect.

She should have brought the satellite phone from the chopper, but she hadn't been thinking they'd have to spend the night.

In fact, it was the last thing she'd expected. She thumbed in a text, pressed send, and held up the phone for the signal to connect.

Sent.

She turned back toward the cabin, saw the friendly glow of light, and couldn't go back. Not yet. So she sat on the boulder.

"You give your heart to it, all in, without knowing the perils." She pulled her knees up, rested her forehead on them, closed her eyes. Fatigue threatened to turn her body to slush, but she shook it away.

Still, the darkness washed over her, her mind relaxing, images flooding back.

Ben, coming out of the locker room, his hair still wet, curly behind his ears, his gaze landing on her.

He swung an arm around her shoulders, pulled her close, pressed a kiss to her forehead. "We can go to the Pony later. I want to show you something."

She wrapped her arms around his waist, walked with him to the truck, slid over beside him as he pulled out of the school lot, the lights of the field bright, the scoreboard still lit up.

He smelled of flannel and blue jeans and the clean scent of a shower, and she just hoped the Judge wasn't waiting up.

"Watch out, honey. That boy doesn't know what he wants, and he'll drag you away from your dreams."

But he didn't know Ben like she did. And she knew perfectly well what he wanted.

Her.

Besides, all *her* dreams included Ben.

He drove her over the bridge, then toward West Glacier, the sky sprinkling stardust along their path. The mountains loomed up around them as he cut off onto a dirt road, came out to an old river bridge.

"I found it this summer when I went river rafting with the youth group," he said. "We jumped off it."

"Don't get any ideas," she said, laughing.

The bridge spanned the middle fork of the Mercy River. He got out, retrieved his guitar.

She walked out onto the bridge, staring at the silvery moonlight tracing the black river.

He threw down a blanket, and she spread it out. Then she sprawled out on her back, watching the stars.

He sat beside her, facing her. "I have more of that song for you."

She rolled over onto her side, propped herself up on her elbow.

I need you, I need you, I need you
Don't say good-bye
I need you, I need you, I need you
Can't live without you
I need you, I need you, I need you

He began, and his voice had a way of tunneling under her skin, consuming her.

Just look over here, see me standing closer
Nobody will love you the way I do

He started to hum, then, playing the song out.

"Where's the rest?"

"That's all I've got." He lifted a shoulder. "It's just the bridge and part of the chorus, but what do you think?"

She sat up, wove a hand around his neck. "I think I love you."

Then she kissed him.

Ben made her feel wanted, whole. And with Ben, her future turned to the stardust above, sweet and right and breathtaking.

He put the guitar down, wove his hands into her hair. He tasted freshly showered, of toothpaste, and his touch was gentle, but she could feel him start to tremble.

He broke away, found her eyes. "I love you too."

His eyes glistened.

"What's wrong?"

"Nothing."

But she heard the tremor in his voice.

Around them the wind stirred up the loam of fall, the scent of pine. The river sounded like applause, rushing below them, and a mist rose, settled on her skin, raising gooseflesh.

He leaned her back on the blanket, stretched out beside her, wrapping his arms around her.

"Ben, are you okay?" She leaned up to look at him, one hand on his chest.

He nodded, a sweet smile tracing his lips. "You're so beautiful, it takes my breath away. I just can't believe I'm this lucky. That you're my girl."

Oh.

He kissed her again, pulling her down to him, then rolled over, cradling her in his arms.

She felt the strength of him, and felt safe in his arms. He kissed her like he needed her. Couldn't get enough of her. And she lost herself a little in his touch.

Him, too, because when he leaned up, he was breathing hard. He searched her eyes and said nothing for a long time.

Then, "We should probably go."

His fingers traced her face, caressing her cheek.

"Not yet," she whispered and twined her hand around his neck to pull him close.

Nobody will love you the way I do.

"Kacey, you okay?"

She looked up, knew that her eyes had widened at the sight of Ben standing just outside the glow of light. She couldn't see his face, just his outline, but she didn't need to.

She knew the texture of his blue eyes, the shape of his shoulders, the feel of his hand in hers. *"I don't think you ever get over your first real love."*

She put a hand to her cheek, found it hot, probably flushed, a little wet.

"Yeah. I . . . uh, sent a text." Her voice crackled as if she'd been crying. She blinked hard, fast.

Yes, she needed sleep. Except not here, not tonight where she could wander off, find herself in the river.

"Howard is asleep in Lulu's room with Mary Beth. Lulu took the cot in the storage room. She left you the sofa." He stopped closer. "She makes a mean venison stew. She saved you a bowl."

Kacey nodded, slid off the boulder. "I'll just keep watch."

He frowned at her. "Listen, if you're worried about Howard, I can keep an eye on him. You need some sleep."

She walked past him toward the house. Pocketed her phone.

"Kacey?"

She rounded on him. "I don't need sleep. I'm fine."

"Of course you do."

She turned around, but he caught her arm. "What's going on?"

She looked at his hand on her arm, back to him. "Nothing."

But he wouldn't let go, and the heat of his grip wheedled through her, turned her weak. "Okay, fine. I sometimes have a hard time sleeping." She worked her arm free, folded her arms across her waist. "It's just a little residue left from my tours."

"A little residue . . . Wait, are you talking about your crash, the attack in Afghanistan?"

"I don't want to talk about it." She pinched her mouth tight.

"Enough with that. Kacey, it's me. And I don't care how long it's been—I still care. I'm still your friend."

"That goes two ways, Ben. Why don't you tell me why you're not writing your own songs? Why you're recording songs you don't want our daughter to sing. And why you decided to go duo—I thought you were a solo act."

He recoiled, and in the dim light, his face turned dark. "I was never a solo act, Kacey. And that's the problem. I thought you, better than anyone, knew that." He strode past her then.

But halfway through the yard, he stopped. Turned. He wore such a stripped look on his face, it shucked the breath from her.

"I don't write songs anymore because everything good I ever wrote came from . . . from you, from *us*."

She stood there, nonplussed, frozen. And in that moment, he took a step back toward her.

"Now, how about you telling me why you can't sleep?"

Oh. She licked her lips, rooted around for an answer that wouldn't tear her open, expose her.

"I sleepwalk."

He frowned. "You sleepwalk?"

"Yeah. It started happening after the . . . after my chopper was shot down. Not right away, but later. I couldn't sleep right afterward—too many nightmares. And then I got dependent on sleeping pills. But if I didn't take them, I'd get up and wander. Find myself standing in my skivvies in the middle of the room, or worse, wandering down the hall. I always woke up with this sense that I was supposed to be going someplace. But I never knew where."

He'd taken another step closer to her. She rubbed her arms, suddenly chilled.

"What happened on that mountain, Kacey? What doesn't the article say?"

She took a breath, shook her head, walked past him to the cabin.

She felt him behind her, though, and when she reached the porch, she sighed. "Okay. But you can't tell anyone, Ben. Not a soul."

She turned, looked up at him.

The glow of the light swept away the years, and suddenly she was looking at the boy she'd run to when she'd discovered the truth about her biological mother. The teenager who'd held her in his arms, made her believe, at least for a season, in happily ever after.

The man she'd trusted.

He nodded, and she sat down on the porch, her hands between her knees.

He sat beside her, his leg touching hers.

"I never dreamed of being in the military—wouldn't have joined, but back then I was desperate. Everything we'd planned was . . . well, I hadn't thought beyond marrying you, building a life with you."

He drew in a breath, his jaw tight. And thankfully offered no words of self-defense.

"I knew nothing about being a parent, and I thought if I could just get a job, provide for Audrey, I could fix it. My parents were thrilled to take care of her, and they're good grandparents, Ben. They love her." She glanced over at him, and he allowed her a tight nod.

"I enlisted and immediately enrolled in the flight school trajectory."

"I should have never taken you flying with my dad," he said, nudging her leg.

She nudged him back, a sweet memory rising.

"I scored nearly perfect on my Flight Aptitude Selection Test. I got accepted, went through basic, then warrant officer candidate school. By the time I started flight school at Fort Rucker, I was feeling like maybe I had a chance at really being someone. Audrey was thriving with my parents, and then . . . I went up in my first Black Hawk. It was nothing like the simulators. Once I swallowed my stomach back down, it was . . . powerful. I could leave behind this girl who was running from her past and be this person who saved lives. Within a year, they deployed me to Iraq and I was flying SAR and medevacs, pulling soldiers out of danger."

She looked out into the darkness. "I talked to Audrey every week on my computer, and yeah, I missed her, but she was fine. And I was . . . better."

Better. Not whole, but enough.

"The military is a great place to forget yourself, even rebuild. You focus on one thing— your job—and I figured out how to put my heart in this safe little box." Or mostly safe—except when she started hearing Benjamin King songs on the radio.

"I'll never forget the first time I heard 'Mountain Song.' I was in country, and a bunch of guys were playing basketball with an iPod playing. And there you were, in Iraq, singing about stars and dreams and . . ." She cast him a sheepish smile. "I nearly threw the iPod into Kuwait."

He swallowed, his smile wry.

"Anyway, in a way it helped. I realized that you'd moved on, and I should too. I went home, extended my service, and headed to Afghanistan, did a fifteen-month tour, then another, and finally, the last one." She took a breath.

"The one where you crashed."

"We were in the Shajau district of the Zabul Province. It's an area thick with forest and mountains. A chopper of rangers had gone down, and we thought it was due to mechanical failure. But . . . when my team—three of us—got there, we came under fire, and I had to do a hard landing. We found the troops pinned down, four dead—the pilot and three others—the rest fighting a group of Taliban."

She stared up at the sky. "We fought them off for thirty-six hours. Two more men died, including my crew, and by the time the reinforcements came in, myself and two others had killed a dozen Taliban."

He said nothing.

"It was the longest night of my life," she said quietly. "They had the high ground and kept coming at us from everywhere. We kept calling in for air support and didn't get through until early morning. But they couldn't get to us—and we were trapped on all sides." She shook her head to shake free the memories. "I shot one in close combat."

"Oh, Kace."

"The worst part is that when we went down, my navigator was wounded. I got to the bunker and kept wanting to go back for him, but . . ." She could sometimes still hear the moaning, a low drill in the back of her mind. "He died in the rubble of the crash, alone."

"It wasn't your fault."

"Yeah, actually, it was. I was his pilot. I should have rescued him." She wiped her hand across her cheek. "I was just so scared. I kept thinking of Audrey, and how I wasn't going to die on a mountain in Afghanistan."

"How did you get out?"

"The PJs dropped in behind the insurgents and we coordinated an attack." She could see the rosy gold of the morning as the sun crested, hear the staccato of gunfire, smell the sulfur, dirt, blood. Taste her own fear piling up in her throat, bile and heat, acrid.

Ben reached out for her hand.

"At first, I was just grateful. So *painfully* grateful that I'd lived."

He wove his fingers between hers.

"And just like they said, eventually the daymares started to fade. I stopped jumping at the sound of a shot. But . . ."

"They come back at night."

She looked at her hand in his. "I feel like the tiny box I kept my heart in exploded into a thousand pieces, and suddenly I don't have anywhere safe to hide. I cry at stupid things—a box of animal crackers Audrey sent me in a care package. And a replay of the Seahawks losing the Super Bowl."

"We all cried at that."

She glanced up, and he wore such a sweet smile that she thought she might just cry again.

"I still haven't figured out how to rebuild the box. Maybe that's why I keep finding myself up in the middle of the night, wandering around."

He tugged her toward him, and although she knew better, she let herself lean in, let him wrap his arms around her.

Let herself close her eyes, breathe in the smell of him.

"I wish I'd been there—not in Afghanistan, but with you. I hate that you were so afraid."

"You *were* there, Ben." She looked up. "I know it's going to sound crazy, but in the middle of the dark, on top of that mountain, I heard you singing, in my head." She began to hum, sing the words. " 'After the big game, the bonfire's on. I got my pretty gal, not doin' nothing wrong. Wishing on stars, hoping in the night. Someday everything's gonna work out right.' "

He was staring at her, so much emotion in his eyes, that she stopped singing, looked away. "Sorry, I just—"

"I wrote that song the night we made Audrey," he said quietly.

She looked back at him, her throat full. "I thought so. Maybe that's why I sang it. Because I was thinking of her too."

His hand touched her cheek now, his thumb running over her skin, gentle. "I was such a fool to leave you." His gaze stopped at her mouth.

And he wasn't the only fool, because she leaned close and brushed her lips against his. Softly, like a whisper.

It elicited something of a groan inside him, as if he'd been holding his breath.

"Oh, Kace," he whispered. He wound his hand behind her neck.

Then he was kissing her, sweetly, a delicious familiarity, yet something new, more powerful in his touch.

The man he'd become, now returning to her.

She heard voices in the back of her head but ignored them, just for a second, letting herself go. She touched his chest and folded into him. Lingering.

He finally moved back, his breathing just a little ragged.

Silence fell between them.

A smile slid up his face.

And then it sank in . . . What was she *doing?* She moved away. "Oh. Wow."

"Kacey?"

She held up her hand. "I think, maybe . . . I'm just so tired, Ben. I don't know what I'm doing."

"Shh." He kissed her forehead, caught her eyes in his. "It's okay. You're safe here. Listen, just lie down." He scooted over to make room, and she hesitated.

"You're safe here," he said again.

And yeah, that did it. She curled up on the porch, her head against his leg, his arm on her shoulder. "I'm not going anywhere," he said quietly. "Just close your eyes."

And then he started to hum.

When you need a friend, a shoulder you can cry on, someone who understands what you're going through . . .

She sighed, let herself sink into the song, the blessed comfort of the warmth of his presence, the smell of the woods, the aura of the past.

Okay, just for tonight.

— 10 —

The aroma of fresh eggs and bacon could rouse Kacey from her grave. She opened her eyes and adjusted to the morning light streaming in through the leaded windowpane across the smooth oak floor. She lay on the sofa, her feet tucked up under a blanket. She had to concede that she'd slept like a corpse.

How had she gotten from the porch to the sofa without her recollection? She pushed herself up, heard the chatter of voices behind her, felt the heat of the pillow grooves in her face.

She pressed a hand to her mouth. She'd slept so hard, she'd drooled. Pretty.

"Over easy or scrambled, Howard?"

Lulu stood at the stove, with bacon sizzling in a black cast-iron pan; a plate of flapjacks in a golden pile were in the middle of the table. Howard sat on one chair, his foot up on his wife's leg. She sat in the other.

No sign of Ben.

Kacey ran a tongue over her shaggy teeth, made a face. She needed coffee, a shower, and tooth-paste, not necessarily in that order.

Instead she got up, folded the blanket.

"Oh, you're up," Lulu said, and as if she could read Kacey's mind, she came over with a hot cup of coffee, black. "I hope we didn't disturb you."

"Disturb—no. I was dead to the world." Apparently.

"You don't remember walking in here, standing in the middle of the room?"

Oh *no.*

"Well, you were pretty groggy. Ben guided you to the sofa, and you fell onto it like you hadn't slept in years. You've been out for a couple hours."

"Where's Ben?"

"He left over an hour ago, trying to track down some help. Pull up a chair—have some breakfast, then we'll see if we can coax the old Ford to life and get Howard to a hospital." Lulu set a plate down at the end of the table, and Kacey sat down, her stomach suddenly roaring.

Lulu's pancakes filled the hollow crannies inside, and Kacey ate three, topped with raspberry jam, without stopping.

She was working on two eggs over easy and a crispy strip of bacon when Ben opened the door.

He stood there, looking a little shaggy with a burnished swath of whiskers and his baseball cap backward, and suddenly their kiss rushed back at her.

Oh, Kace.

His voice, but she wanted to say the same thing. What had she done?

She looked away from him before she could betray her horror. She could not . . . could *not* fall for Ben again.

Not with her heart roaming around outside her body, unprotected, too easily crushed.

"I got hold of Sam. He's going to bring a body recovery team and alert Jess and Miles to meet us on Going-to-the-Sun Road."

"I can drive you out," Lulu said as she fixed Ben a plate.

He sat down opposite Mary Beth.

"I don't know, Lulu. I took a look at your truck. It doesn't look like it's been driven in a decade."

She served him a plate of eggs, sunny-side up.

"My grandchildren shop for me, but she's a runner. I drove a lost hiker up over Logan Pass all the way to Saint Mary a few years ago."

"A lost hiker?" Ben said, taking a sip of coffee.

"Yeah, a girl about seventeen or so. She'd been separated from her group, had gotten lost on the trails. I found her near the lower falls. She was pretty rattled, so I brought her back here. I wanted to bring her to the Apgar Visitor Center, but she insisted I bring her to Saint Mary. I dropped her off at the lodge there."

Ben had stopped eating. "Lulu, do you remember what she looked like?"

She picked up a towel, wiped her hands. "I don't know. Blonde hair. She had the most beautiful light blue eyes." She paused. "Wait, I have something of hers."

She turned to the windowsill, grabbed a bowl, fished through it, and plucked out a ring. She handed it to Ben.

"She left this behind. I found it on the bureau after I got back. I didn't know what to do with it."

Ben stared at it, then handed it to Kacey. "Recognize that?"

She held the ring in her palm. Gold band, with two hearts holding up the crown, each embedded with a diamond, and in the center, an emerald. Circling the crown were the embedded words "Mercy Falls High." "It's a class ring."

"You had one of those."

She nodded. "These are expensive. Why would she leave it behind?" She handed it back to Ben. "You don't think . . ."

Ben turned to Lulu. "Where did you say you dropped her off?"

"Saint Mary Lodge, on Highway 89, north of East Glacier."

"Can I hang on to this?" Ben asked.

Lulu nodded, and Ben pocketed the ring. "Thanks." He got up. "I think we need to start hiking out." He turned and took Lulu's hands. "Do you need anything?"

"I'm fine, Ben." She smiled up at him.

He leaned down and pressed a kiss to her cheek. The gesture caught Kacey's attention; the kindness in his eyes was something she knew but had forgotten.

In fact, it seemed she'd forgotten a few important key characteristics about Ben. Like his willingness to sacrifice himself for others. She didn't know where he'd slept last night, but she could guess it wasn't comfortable.

Given the fact that she'd fallen asleep on his lap, it could be he hadn't actually slept at all.

While she'd apparently had one of the best sleeps in nearly two years—no memory of sleepwalking, even if she had apparently wandered.

And the way he could listen, always knowing the right words, no judgment.

It was, in fact, the first thing that made her love him.

Love him.

No. *No* . . .

She watched as Howard struggled to his feet, balancing on his new bride's shoulder. Ben came around and hoisted him up on his back.

Okay, so she might still have feelings—yes, definitely feelings, all trapped inside a confusing tangle of memories and not a few might-have-beens.

And it didn't help that she could still taste his kiss, could still feel the old hunger stirring inside her. She couldn't deny the sense of peace that had settled over her as she sank into sleep.

But that was last night. Tomorrow, they had separate lives.

Except for Audrey.

She bound them together. Regardless of what mistakes they'd made thirteen years ago. Or last night.

Audrey was their Today.

And it was definitely time to tell her daughter about her amazing, superstar father.

She got up from the table. "Thank you, Lulu."

Ben was already outside waiting for her, the sky blue overhead, the bouquet of summer in the breeze. He looked young, strong, and his smile could light up her entire body.

Today.

Sierra could admit that she'd secretly harbored a belief that Ian would end up on her doorstep, forgiveness and a to-do list in his grip.

A week later she convinced herself she had successfully moved on.

Clearly not needing him.

"You just started, Sierra! One day on the job and you're already making cookies and spending every waking minute at the PEAK headquarters." Blossom Rose, aka, her mother, sat up to the yellow Formica counter in Sierra's house located just off Main Street.

"I like being there," Sierra said.

"But you're doing it again—giving your heart to something that can't love you back." Blossom reached over to the batch of fresh cookies cooling on wire racks. The kitchen smelled of chocolate chips and the kind of home that Sierra had always longed for.

For her part, she'd created it, with Willow, in this tiny two-story kit house. The furnishings might be from garage sales, but with the crazy quilt she'd made in high school home economics thrown over the sofa and an eclectic mix of refinished garage sale finds, the place felt homemade and cozy.

Audrey and Willow sat at the refinished pine table in the middle of the kitchen, playing a game of Dutch blitz.

"Chet and his team need me. Otherwise, Sam wouldn't have asked for help."

"Mom, you should see the place," Willow said, not looking up from her game. She'd never felt the need to call Blossom by any of her crazy monikers. But Willow was like that—sang her own tune, just like their mother.

Sierra was grateful that Willow never received Sierra's crazy, nearly unintelligible voicemail. Probably she'd simply rambled on, oblivious of the ending message beep, and all Willow got was a muffled voice, a request for her to pick up.

So, thankfully, no one knew how close she'd come to being another cautionary tale of giving your heart away.

"Sierra cleaned the entire kitchen, reorganized the office, filed all the reports by name, with a cross-reference system by date in the computer, created a schedule and a group texting system depending on the callout. Now she's working on stocking the freezer."

Sierra cast a glance at Willow, who looked up fast and winked at her. Her kid sister might be six years younger, but sometimes Willow seemed to be the older, protective one.

Then again, Willow grew up knowing her father, a soldier who still lived in Mercy Falls. Sierra's best guess at her biological father was that he was one of a handful of men who lived with her mother at a spiritual colony in Missoula.

Not that ultra-feminist Blossom made any attempt at clarifying. *"You don't need a father—just another man in your life to own you, call you his."*

"I have no doubt Sierra poured herself into serving the team—that's what she does," Blossom said. "I still can't believe you stayed with Ian for five years—I kept telling you that one day he'd move on, leave you with nothing."

Sierra pulled the last batch of cookies from the oven, set the pan on a hot pad. "We weren't dating, Blossom. He was my boss."

Blossom rolled her eyes. "You gave him everything—your time, your energy, your youth, your heart. And he took it, then gave you your walking papers."

And now, Sierra felt sure they weren't talking about Ian. "Aside from the fact that Ian was my boss only"—she simply ignored the squeeze of her words—"I didn't give him *everything*."

She flicked a glance at Audrey, hoping her mother didn't spiral into a feminist diatribe about men and "all they wanted from women."

"All I'm saying is you need to watch what you give your heart to. Only you can make yourself happy, despite what that crazy pastor friend of yours says."

"Chet isn't crazy. The Bible says to do nothing out of selfishness, but to be humble. You don't lose yourself when you serve others. It's what Christ did."

"And look what happened to him."

Sierra opened her mouth, but her mother continued. "Bible, *shmible*. It's just another rule book. Trust me—you give away your heart and you'll never get it back. And Ian is the worst—he never saw how amazing and beautiful my Sierra is." She slid off her stool, walked over, kissed her on her cheek. "Besides, it wouldn't do us any good to have a repeat of the Rhett Thomas disaster."

"Blossom—"

She held up a finger. "You know I'm right. In fact, you might think about taking a new name this time. Really wipe the slate clean."

Her mother switched her name—not legally but in casual usage—whenever she felt a change of breeze in the seasons of her life. For nearly six years, during Sierra's youth, she'd called herself Meadow. Then came the birth of Willow and a sweet stretch of time when Sierra had enjoyed what she believed might be a real family, with Willow's dad, Jackson, moving into her mother's cabin. With Willow's arrival, her mother renamed herself Lilly, and during the next seven years she resembled the other mothers who made cookies, showed up occasionally at school for a parent-teacher conference, and actually cared if their kids had clean clothes, food on the table, and a father in their lives.

Until a Vacation Bible School at the Mercy Falls Community Church roped in Sierra and Willow, finally luring Jackson to the altar. Suddenly, her pseudo-father got ahold of grace and decided to do something unforgivable—propose to Lilly.

Judging by her mother's reaction, he might as well have clamped a nose ring on her, and Sierra's dream of home shattered. Jackson moved out, taking Willow with him every other weekend and during holidays.

Lilly moved through a handful of quick hookups, emerging into Blossom after she moved them all to a forty-acre artists' commune north of Mercy Falls. Sierra learned to drive that year, and would pile Willow and two other kids into the community Ford truck and trek them an hour to school every morning.

Sierra simply refused to lose her grip on her taste of normal. She sneaked out to attend church, joined the youth group, and clung to the only real friend she had, Kacey Fairing. Because Kacey, for all her outward normalcy, knew exactly what it felt like to be the daughter of a woman with a questionable reputation.

Blossom swiped another cookie. "I'm late for my ride. Cooper is picking me up at the Last Chance."

Sierra shot a look at Willow, then back to Blossom. "Cooper?"

"He's a fellow artist. We're heading out to the salvage yard."

For all her mother's eccentricities, she made a

semi-decent living selling her metal sculptures—made from cast-aside tin cans, hubcaps, tools, rebar, and other items she picked up at the junk-yard. Her line of barnyard animals—goats, chickens, sheep, and even a cow—caught on with a few celebrities over the years and now graced the front steps of a dozen or more Hollywood homes.

She watched her mother go. In her early fifties, Blossom was the beautiful one, with long tawny brown hair and a body that she kept fit with long hikes into the park.

Audrey slammed her hand down on the pile of cards. "Blitz!"

"Oh!" Willow shook her head, tossing down her cards. "You're just way too fast for me."

"My mom taught me. She's really good."

"So is Sierra," Willow said. She gathered up the cards. "We have to run too. Youth group band practice."

"Actually," Audrey said, "I'm going to ride out to the PEAK ranch with Sierra. Mom's coming in with that injured hiker, and I'm hoping to see Benjamin King again and ask him about the guitar lessons."

Willow glanced at Sierra, the other Keeper of the Secret.

Now, Willow glanced back at Audrey. "Are you sure? Nate said you two were singing a duet this week at worship."

"We practiced today at school." Audrey got up,

pulled her backpack over one shoulder. "Besides, Nate . . ." She sighed. "Nothing."

Sierra looked up from where she was boxing cookies into a plastic container. "What's nothing?"

She lifted a shoulder. "Ever since he broke his ankle, he's been acting weird. Won't talk to me at school and ignores me at band practice. It's like . . ."

"He's just embarrassed, honey. You saved him—that hurt his thirteen-year-old ego," Willow said, gathering up her mesh bag and slipping into her Birkenstocks. "Men can be like that. They want to rescue us, not the other way around." She scooped up her keys, glanced at Sierra. "By the way, for once I agree with Mom—you gave your heart to Ian, even if he was *just* your boss."

Willow left, but her words lingered and pricked at Sierra as she packed up half the cookies, followed Audrey out to the car.

Audrey said nothing as they pulled out of the drive.

"Are you okay?"

"Who's Rhett Thomas?"

Oh. Sierra slowed as they crept through the muddy streets, out onto Main, and toward the Shaw ranch.

She needed to stop thinking of PEAK as Ian's. Just because it was located near Ian's ranch didn't mean she had to think of Ian wandering around the house in his stocking feet, his dark hair rumpled, wearing his workout pants and an old T-shirt.

"Rhett was the coach for the Mercy Falls Mavericks hockey team. You were probably too young to remember. He went on to play for the St. Paul Blue Ox. We dated while he was trying to get a shot at the majors." She had probably frozen a significant portion of her backside following him to games during those early years. "I was pretty young—just out of high school. Your mom had left for the military, and Rhett, well, he was very cute."

She looked over and winked at Audrey, a short and sweet way to end the conversation.

She'd just rather not elaborate on the protracted pain of watching him fall out of love with her and into the arms of a prettier, less clingy member of the Blue Ox ice crew.

Maybe she should have changed her name after that fiasco. Instead, she'd moved on to working for Ian.

And yes, maybe Blossom was right, had given the man her heart.

Not anymore. She had managed to land on her feet, her heart safely back in her chest, memories of Ian shut away into the past.

Sierra looked over at Audrey. "How are things with you and your mom?" she asked. Maybe Audrey needed a sounding board, someone who knew the situation.

Audrey stared out the window at the fields

dotted with cattle, the arch of the sky stretching blue overhead. She lifted a shoulder. "She's been really weird. Usually she's cool, but this time she's trying to tell me what to do. She actually went to school and met with my teachers. Like she's a normal mom or something."

She looked at Sierra. "I'm glad she's home, but she's freaking out about Nate. And I don't know why she won't let me hang out with Benjamin King. He's really cool."

"I know. But your mom just wants to make sure that you don't get hurt."

"Why would I get hurt?" Audrey turned in the seat, and Sierra scrambled for a reply.

"Because he's a big star?"

"And he might not have time for me? I know that. It's just . . . she thinks I'm a little kid and doesn't see that I'm all grown up and can take care of myself."

Sierra schooled her voice. "I'm sure you can, Audrey. But let your mom catch up, okay? She's just trying to be a good mom."

"A good mom would stop hovering and let me live my own life."

"I had one of those hands-off moms, Audrey. Trust me, it's not as great as you'd think."

"But you and Blossom are okay now, right?"

Sierra turned off the highway toward the PEAK driveway. The helicopter pad sat empty, the yard drying under the morning sun.

"Only because I no longer have to depend on Blossom to take care of me." She pulled in next to the house and caught Audrey's arm before she got out. "Just . . . keep in mind that whatever happens, every decision she made was for you. To help you have a great life."

Audrey frowned, then shrugged. "I know." She got out, shut the door, headed up the porch.

Oh boy.

Sierra got out, headed into HQ.

So what if she'd spent some unpaid hours yesterday giving the kitchen an extra scrub, adding some homey touches—daisies on the table, a bulletin board with a funny meme. And she'd even stuck around for the team meeting last night, getting an update on Ben and Kacey's overnight at Lulu's.

Next Sunday, she planned on making a "welcome to the team" cake for Kacey at the weekly SAR meeting-slash-barbecue.

She set the container of cookies on the counter and spotted Audrey talking to Chet. He had rolled himself out of his office and was now shaking her hand.

Sierra put her hand on Chet's shoulder, squeezed. "Have you heard from them yet today?"

Chet dropped Audrey's hand and reached for the cookies. "They're on their way in. The team met them on Going-to-the-Sun Road today, drove the hiker and his wife to Kalispell Regional

Medical. They also found a body. Sam sent a recovery team out to meet them. Ben and Kacey hiked back up to the chopper."

As if on cue, the hum of the Bell 429 diced the air. Audrey dropped her pack and ran to the window.

Sierra followed Chet over, then opened the door for him, and he wheeled himself outside. But she'd noticed his walker, folded and laying by the sofa. Hopefully he hadn't been shuffling around without supervision.

She'd have to keep an eye on him.

The blue and white bird floated down from the sky, settled on the pad near the barn. In a few moments, the rotors died and Kacey emerged from the cockpit. Ben came around the front.

"Mom!" Audrey waved, and Kacey grinned as she pulled off her helmet, waving back.

Audrey came off the porch, ran over to her mom, caught her in a hug around the waist. A person would have had to be blind not to see the look of longing on Ben's face. But then Audrey came over and high-fived him, and that garnered a grin.

Something passed between Ben and Kacey then, a look, something familiar, sweet even—

Oh no. And sure enough, Kacey came up the stairs and glanced at Sierra, guilt written in her expression as she brushed by her.

"Hey, Dad," Ben said as he greeted his father.

He clasped his hand, and they headed inside. "Have you heard from our hiker?"

"He has a mild fracture. His wife called and said to pass along her thanks."

Sierra listened to the conversation but longed to get a moment with Kacey, to back her into a room, dissect the look that had passed between her and Ben. Instead, Kacey had grabbed Audrey for a quick mother-daughter debrief.

Ben bit into a cookie. "These are fantastic," he said to Sierra.

He walked over to the map on the wall, then traced his finger across the park to the eastern side. Tapped it at Saint Mary Lodge, then traced it down to Highway 89 all the way to the entranc at East Glacier. "Did you know there's an Amtrak out of East Glacier?" he said to no one.

Sierra walked over to him. "Yes. The Empire Builder runs through there, from Chicago all the way to Seattle."

He finished off his cookie, then dug into his pocket. "We stayed with Lulu Grace last night."

"How is she?" Chet had rolled over to Ben.

"As spry as ever. Made us flapjacks with fresh eggs and bacon today. But most importantly, she told us a story about giving a lost hiker a ride to Saint Mary Lodge about three years ago. And that lost hiker left behind something." He dug into his pocket.

A cold hand closed around her throat as Sierra

stared at the gold class ring with an emerald center stone and diamond chips in the heart setting.

"That's Esme Shaw's."

Ben looked at her. "Are you sure? There's no name."

"I remember her wearing it." She picked up the ring. "I'm almost positive. Ian gave this to her for Christmas, her senior year." She looked at Ben. "Lulu gave her a ride to Saint Mary?"

Ben nodded. "The description sounded like it belonged to Esme." He looked back at the map. "I keep trying to piece it together. Why would she ask to be dropped off on the other side of the park?"

"Was she afraid?"

"Or guilty?" This from Kacey, who'd come over. "We have to ask—how did Dante's body get in the river?"

Silence.

"I need to tell Ian," Sierra said quietly.

She was halfway to the door when her words kicked in, turned her around. "Actually, no. I don't need to tell him." She held out the ring. "You should tell him, Ben. He asked you to hunt for Esme."

Ben shook his head. "I'm going to get cleaned up and go into town, see what Sam has found out. You go to Ian's, update him, and tell him we'll call him first chance we get."

He swiped another cookie, then glanced at Kacey.

There appeared that smile again.

And it might be Sierra's imagination, but did Kacey actually . . . blush?

"See you this weekend, Audrey?" Ben said. "For your birthday party?"

Audrey's smile could light the northern sky. "Yes."

Kacey steered her daughter toward the locker room in the barn, where she could change clothes.

Which left Sierra with the ring in her grip.

Perfect. *Fine.*

She'd simply stand on his front porch, deliver the message.

She got into her car and drove over to his beautiful house, her heart thundering.

His truck sat in the drive.

It was just a message.

But she had to wipe her hand on her jeans before she could manage ringing the bell.

She stood there, listening to the thunder of her heartbeat.

No answer.

She rang again. Waited.

And the longer she stood there, the more the image of him lying there passed out—or worse—took form in her head.

What if he . . . well, what if he hadn't been over to see her at PEAK headquarters because he actually, *truly* needed her more than ever?

She dug out her keys, found his house key, and unlocked the door.

The silence inside could deafen her.

"Ian?" Her voice echoed through the cavern of the house.

She toed off her boots, then padded into the living room. Stopped.

Papering the floor, the sofa, the long trestle table, the end tables, even the hearth, lay every paper, every report, every map, every sketch, every faint lead they'd ever followed on Esme.

As if he'd stepped right back into the middle of the search to let it consume him.

Oh, Ian.

And then she heard steps behind her.

She turned, and the sight of him stopped her cold.

He wore a beard—not an overnight stubble but an actual beard, russet with sparks of gold and copper. His hair was wet, spiked up as he toweled it dry, and he'd emerged into the room wearing only his sweatpants.

She'd only seen him without a shirt a handful of times, but she never quite got over his washboard stomach, the sculpted wide shoulders, biceps in his strong arms, the dusting of dark hair across his chest. He was always so proper—but in this instance, he looked wrung out and not a little feral.

He slowly lowered the towel and stood staring

at her, his blue eyes riveted to her, wearing an expression she couldn't place.

Anger? Shock?

Please, let it be relief.

"What are you doing here?"

Ian didn't mean for the words to snap out quite like that—sharp, lethal, as if he wasn't in fact simply blindsided.

If he could, he'd simply tuck his words back inside, stand there and hope she didn't see him.

He knew how he looked—and only the fact that he'd smelled like something that had languished in floodwaters for a week had coaxed him into a shower.

But he'd taken a long, painful look in the mirror, studying his bloodshot eyes, feeling as if he'd aged a decade in a week and realized . . .

He'd made a mess out of his life.

He'd dodged that truth for a few days, but as the days blurred together, the haze of information swilling his brain, tangling it, blotting out the sun, he came to the understanding that without Sierra, his world had turned to night.

And into that darkness, she'd appeared.

Standing in the middle of his family room, wearing a pair of leggings, a long striped yellow shirt, and those eyes that could practically see right through him, uncover every moment of stupidity.

Wow, he missed her. Needed her. So much so that one look at her turned his entire body to ache. But he'd fired her, and he couldn't, as much as he longed to, drop to his knees and beg her to stay.

Ian Shaw simply didn't do begging. He commanded, sometimes with money, but begging meant taking out his heart, offering it up.

And he simply didn't have the strength for that, not anymore.

But that didn't stop him from feeling the hollow burn deep inside as she frowned, her face darkening at his words.

"I'm here because . . ." She took a step toward him, cleared her throat. "I have news about Esme. And for your information, I didn't want to come, but Ben asked me to."

News? He wanted to ask, but his throat wouldn't work, caught on the rest of her words.

I didn't want to come.

He couldn't betray that her words had found purchase. Instead, he hung the towel over a chair and headed to the kitchen.

She followed him. "Ben and Kacey searched the river. They found a body."

"Oh." Although he'd hoped they'd find a clue to Esme's disappearance, the words still felt like a punch to the gut.

He ran his hand along the cool granite of the kitchen counter, balancing himself because all at once he was in very real danger of his legs buckling.

He managed to reach the fridge, open it, and blink against the bright light.

A container of orange juice, a piece of cheddar, a jar of pickles. He grabbed the OJ and drank it out of the carton.

Ran his hand across his mouth, a measure of composure returning. Then, "Do they think the body is Esme's?"

"They don't know. They also found this."

Something plinked on the counter. He turned, and the light caught it, the emerald in the center casting northern lights against the stainless steel of the fridge. He stared down at it, and his heart gave a lurch.

He picked up the ring, held it between his fingers, all breath gone.

"It's hers, isn't it?"

He must have nodded, because he felt her hand on his back. "Sit down."

"No." He put the ring back on the counter, took another swig of juice. Stared out past her to the mountains.

So God was really going to do this. Destroy his life yet again, despite his best efforts at earning forgiveness. "So then the body is hers."

She frowned. "Oh no, Ian. I'm sorry. No, this wasn't—I'm so sorry. I handled that badly."

She acted as if she wanted to reach out to him but pulled her hand back.

He could have used her, just for a second, to hold on to.

"Ben and Kacey ran into an injured hiker and had to spend the night with Lulu Grace. Remember her—she lives near McDonald Lake? She has that homesteaded cabin?"

"Yes, but—"

"She claims to have driven someone who left this ring behind and who matches Esme's description to Saint Mary Lodge."

He stilled, trying to sort the words out, categorize them. "When?"

"Three years ago. I don't know any more than that."

"What about the body?"

"Sam sent out a team to recover it. I don't know anything."

"So she could be alive?"

"I don't know. But Ben made the point that if she got a ride, she could have been dropped off at the Amtrak."

"What?" He rounded on her, then shook his head.

Woozy. Yeah, he probably needed to eat something. But he blinked away the spots and walked past her, into the family room, finally locating the map of the park on the sofa. He stood above it, tracing his finger loosely down highway 86. "That's a pretty wild stretch."

"Maybe. But we never even thought to check

the Amtrak. We focused all our searching on this side of the park."

He closed his eyes then, a wave of emotion rushing over him. "I don't understand. Why would she drive to the other side of the park?"

The voice didn't even sound like his own. Rattled, tired, broken.

"Ian."

"I just . . . wish I could understand." He turned and padded through the chaos of his room, his bare feet kicking up papers as he stood in front of the picture window.

From here, his land extended all the way to the far horizon, with the cut of the gray-blue mountains rising to the northwest.

His world, and yet Esme, like his wife, Allison, had run from him.

He heard shuffling behind him. Then, "Me too."

He turned then, surprised.

She lifted a shoulder. "I never understood why finding Esme was such an obsession with you. I mean, I got it, of course. You loved her. She was your niece—and you were taking care of her. She got lost on your watch and you were determined to find her. But those are just the obvious reasons." She touched his arm. "What's the real reason?"

He drew in a breath, looked at her hand on his arm. Then he closed his eyes. "Because she was my responsibility. Even my second chance.

And I didn't want to believe I was the most wretched man on the planet."

When he opened his eyes, she was still standing there, looking up at him.

"What are you talking about?"

He pulled away from her. "It doesn't matter."

"It matters to me, Ian. I know I was just your employee, but I actually do care about you."

Just your employee. Her words burned in his chest, and he longed to correct her.

But she'd betrayed him too.

Still, he needed someone. And apparently, Sierra was that person. "I drive away the people I love. And then God takes them away."

"What?"

He sighed. "I wanted to find Esme, because then I could convince myself that maybe God wasn't still punishing me—for what happened to Allison and Daniel."

She frowned at him, shook her head to disagree, as if the loss of his wife and child in Katrina *wasn't* God's punishment—but he kept talking.

He ran his fingers into the shag on his chin. "I hated that Esme was seeing Dante. I wanted her to go to college and I knew that anyone she met here would hold her back. You remember our fight. How I told her that after the camping trip, I wanted her to go out east. I hoped that she'd eventually forget about Dante.

Esme was smart, beautiful, and I didn't want her to make my sister's mistakes."

He looked away from her. "My sister married the first boy she fell for, and he left her pregnant and alone two years later. She nearly lost custody of Esme twice before I convinced her to send her to me."

"You're not to blame for her wanting to run away with Dante."

"I gave her an ultimatum." He shook his head. "I practically pushed her into his arms. And now she could be dead too."

He looked at her. "And I did the same thing to you."

She shook her head. "You don't control my life, Ian. And you had every right to fire me."

His throat closed, and he looked away. "Maybe, but I shouldn't have. I jumped to conclusions and led with my anger . . ."

"Is that why your hands are marked up again? The hanging bag in your weight room getting a workout?"

Oh, she'd noticed. He looked at his knuckles, the angry red skin.

"And without tape and gloves, I see."

He stuck his hands in his pockets. "The problem is, I'm just not good at personal relationships, Sierra. I sort of forgot that, with you." He looked at her. "You're too easy to be with. Too nice. And you took way too good care of me. I got that mixed up a little." He shook his head. "You were right to keep this all professional, because frankly, if you get too close, you just don't know what could happen. I'm probably cursed."

"Ian!"

He held up a hand. "Face it. I'm to blame. God has a right to punish me."

She just stood there then, looking stricken. "God is not punishing you."

"Then what would you call it?" He turned, walked back to the sofa, tossed the map on the floor, sat down. "Bad luck?"

"Well, right now I'd call you an idiot. And obsessed with punishing yourself. And frankly, a little bit narcissistic to think that God would let innocent people die because of you. By the way, if you think you're going to control a teenager in love, you really have a complex."

He couldn't tell if she was kidding, or . . .

She lifted her mouth in a smile.

"I suppose, however, you're just being you."

Was that a good thing? He didn't feel like it.

She came over to a chair, lowered herself into it. "Listen. I understand feeling responsible for Esme. But you've wrapped yourself up in finding her for so long, it's become a prison. Maybe instead of punishing you, this is God setting you free, showing you that you had no control of Esme's disappearance. Maybe he's trying to help you let go."

"What are you talking about?"

She reached over and picked up the map off the floor. "If she's alive, we have to ask, why did she go to Saint Mary? Why didn't she just come back? Especially if Dante was dead?"

He shook his head.

"Ian, maybe she didn't want to come home because she had something to do with Dante's death."

He sat there, unmoving. "What are you saying?"

"I don't know. I'm just trying to piece this together. But it might have absolutely nothing to do with you and everything to do with something that happened out there on the mountain. Something Esme is running from. And that something is *not* you."

He looked up, ran his hands down his face. Scrubbed. "I have to know if whoever Lulu drove to Saint Mary Lodge was her. That she's at least alive."

"Then maybe you'll shave?"

She smiled at him again, and the sense of her being here so filled him up, nearly choked him. Maybe . . .

"Listen, I know you're working for PEAK now, but maybe—"

"Yes, Ian. I'll get on the phone to Saint Mary. See if we can track down a connection." She stood up then. "But first, I'm making you some coffee and calling in for some sandwich delivery. And you are going to clean up this mess."

He glanced up at her, and she winked at him.

But he longed for her words to latch on, become truth.

Clean up this mess.

Yes.

Finally.

Somehow.

— 11 —

Ben hadn't been so nervous since his first arena show. He sat in his truck, Audrey's gift propped on the seat beside him, sweat trickling down his back in a single, hot line.

Today he became a father.

When exactly should they tell her? Before he gave her the gift—special ordered from Nashville? Or maybe after the party, when it could be just them, a family.

Family. The word swept through him.

He hadn't realized the enormity of his longing until this moment.

Ben had never been to the Fairings' new house before last week, but he couldn't help being impressed with the estate. A few other hybrids and SUVs parked in the circle driveway, and he'd spotted a parent dropping off a carload of kids as he sat muscling up courage.

He felt like he had the night he'd proposed. Even if he knew Kacey would say yes, so much of their future hinged on her answer. His heart had been in his throat as he'd driven her out to the old river bridge, to where he'd arranged candles, a blanket, a moment under the stars.

He'd hoped, by redeeming the mistake made there months ago, he might also erase the guilt that roamed behind his proposal.

Now, he had an even bigger redemption looming.

But he could hardly sit here all night, just hoping it would happen. He got out, pulled on his old brown Stetson, and reached for the gift.

The sun hung low, slipping just behind the mountains, twilight turning the sky purple and bruised. Laughter, music, and chatter lifting from the backyard suggested the party's location, and he steeled himself as he walked around the house.

"It's just a get-together, some ice cream sundaes, a movie outside, a few games."

Kacey's description of the event matched nothing of what spread out on the back lawn. Sofas, whether rented or hauled out from the house, lined up before a giant wooden wall draped with a long white sheet. Bowls of popcorn sat on wooden spools, arranged like cocktail tables in the lush grass. From the speakers scattered around the yard, he heard the pearly tones of a talented up-and-comer in the Nashville scene whose music, in his humble opinion, might be a little too old for a fourteen-year-old girl.

Kids stood in clumps of conversation, the girls laughing on one side, the boys on the other. He recognized Nate propped up on crutches, his leg in a cast.

A few parents congregated on the deck, and the smell of hot dogs and burgers sizzling on the grill seasoned the air.

He spotted the honorable Robert Fairing standing on the deck wearing a green apron and wielding a spatula.

Ben paused as the past put a hand to his chest.

"Leave, Ben, and make something of your life. And let Kacey do the same."

He stood there, trying to find his footing, reaching out for Kacey's words, the confirmation that, yes, he had permission to walk back into her life.

Maybe he'd read too much into her invitation, but even though he'd texted her twice, just to confirm, she hadn't suggested she'd changed her mind.

It did nothing to stop the crazy daydream forming in his mind, the one where he started over, stayed in Mercy Falls, rebuilt his life— one that included Kacey as his wife and Audrey living in a home he built for them.

The life he should have had.

Then he spotted her. Kacey walked out on the

deck carrying another bowl of popcorn. Her auburn hair hung long and loose, glinting copper and gold in the fading sunlight, and she was wearing a pair of cutoff jeans, cowboy boots, and a T-shirt topped with a flannel shirt tied at the waist.

She looked about eighteen, and his heart skipped, the memories so tangible he could nearly feel her lips on his, smell her skin, hear her whispering in his ear.

"I think I love you."

Oh shoot, yes, he wanted this way, way too much.

And then, as if she knew his heart had climbed outside his body, running full-speed ahead toward her, she turned and spotted him.

Smiled, her eyes shining.

He was a goner, and as she put down the popcorn and came over to him, he scrambled for words.

Her gaze went to the gift. "Really?"

He shrugged. "It seemed like the right thing."

She stood in front of him, and he wished he hadn't worn the suit jacket over his T-shirt and jeans, wished he might be in his comfy jeans, a cotton T-shirt and, while he was at it, sitting with her in the back of his pickup, singing her a song.

He might even try the one that kept churning through his head, almost nonstop for the last week. Something from the past that he'd revived, added a verse or two.

"You want to give it to her now?" Kacey asked.

"Really?" Oh, way too much hope in his voice.

But she didn't comment, just nodded. "A few of the kids brought gifts, but she opened them already. I think she'll love it."

She reached out to tug him forward, but he hesitated.

"What?"

He shot a look at the Judge, who still hadn't noticed him.

She followed his gaze. Dropped her hand. "He has his regrets too, Ben."

Sure he did. But Ben let her lead him toward a cluster of kids. He spotted Audrey standing in he middle wearing cutoff overalls and a pink T-shirt, barefoot in the grass, her hair pulled back into two braids.

He stood at the edge of the crowd, but it only took a second for her to look up, her eyes to go wide. "Wow. Hi."

"Happy birthday," he said quietly, the most profound, perfect words he'd ever spoken. Then he held out her gift.

Her mouth opened, and she looked from her mother, back to Ben. "Really? For me?"

"No time like the present, right?"

"You got me a guitar?"

He nodded, grinning, his heart exploding as she came over and took the instrument in its case into her embrace.

"I don't know what to say," she whispered, her eyes glossy.

Neither did Ben.

"Thank you," Kacey said, and Audrey glanced at her.

"This is the best present anyone has ever gotten me. In my whole *life*."

He raised an eyebrow. Grinned, still unable to speak. She brought it over to a sofa, set it down, and opened it. Almost reverently, she ran her hands over the fingerboard, the rosewood pick guard, the amber body.

"It's a vintage Gibson Hummingbird," he said. "The design is called a square shoulder dreadnought, the way they made guitars back in the 1960s. The top is made from spruce, the body from mahogany. And the pick guard is hand engraved, with the original bird and floral design. It's got a beautiful sound. May I?"

She stepped back, and he pulled it out of the case, propped his leg on the sofa arm. He'd already tuned it this morning and now played a quick lick. "The midrange is perfectly balanced, and listen to the treble."

He picked out another country lick, his fingers flying over the fretboard, and watched as her eyes lit up.

"Do that again," she said.

He laughed and repeated it, faster, extending it. "How about a birthday song?" he asked over the music. "I wrote you a little something."

"You wrote a song for me?"

"Just something silly." But he played the intro riff and launched into the song.

Thirteen years, already gone
Sweet little girl, sweet country song
So much more, she's just begun
Let's start with tonight, let's have some fun

Happy birthday, Audrey, it's true
The world had no song 'til there was you

He'd managed to get through the entire thing without his voice seizing up, but he segued fast into another impressive riff, then ended with a flourish.

She was clapping, her beautiful eyes shining. "I love it!" She turned, found her mother standing just outside the ring. "He sang me a song."

Kacey wore a strange smile, her eyes glistening. "I know, baby."

Then Audrey turned back to him, and he didn't know what to do when she flung her arms around his neck. "Thank you!"

He startled, and by the time he figured out to hug her back, she'd danced away, laughing, caught in the arms of a couple giggling girls. He put the guitar back in the case.

He was turning back toward the house when he

spotted Robert staring at him from the deck. Ben nodded at him, not wanting to give him reason to stride down, order him off his property.

Funny how one look could steal ten years of success and make him feel like a teenager sporting a black eye, swollen lip, and way too much shame to stand up for himself.

He searched for Kacey and found her coming up behind him. "That was . . . really cool of you, Ben." She whisked her hand across her cheek.

"It was nothing."

"You wrote a song."

"It was just a silly little somethin' . . . but . . ." He lifted a shoulder.

She made a noncommittal noise. "Why don't I put the guitar in the house, where it won't get damaged?"

He handed it over to her, then stood, watching Audrey laugh with her friends, feeling Robert's gaze on his neck. He noticed that Nate was standing away from Audrey, talking with a couple other girls. He kept sneaking looks at her, but when she glanced up, he would look away.

Yep, the kid liked her. Probably too much for his own good, although Ben knew exactly how it felt to be thirteen and in love with the most beautiful, amazing girl in town, feeling so out of his league it only stirred in him a desire to be better. Be more.

Be worthy.

"Did you get a burger?" Kacey had returned.

"I can't eat," he said and cast another look at Audrey.

Kacey grew silent beside him, then put her hand on his shoulder. "We'll tell her. Let's just wait until after the party, maybe?"

He nodded, unable to speak with the immensity of the emotions washing through him.

"Wanna take a walk?" she said, as if sensing the fact he just might do something crazy, like break out into tears.

He nodded, and she slipped her arm through his, guiding him away from the party.

"What movie are they seeing tonight?" he asked.

"Oh, probably *Star Wars*. Audrey is a crazy nut over the original series."

He took her hand as they wandered toward the paddock. A creamy palomino grazed in the field, its ears flicking back as Kacey whistled.

"That's Snowy," she said. "My parents gave her to Audrey a couple years ago. I think it was my dad's attempt to make good on a promise he made me when I was thirteen to buy me a pony."

He leaned on the rail. The music had faded as they'd wandered away, the scent of pine replacing the aroma of burgers on the grill. "I remember that promise," he said.

She sighed. "They seemed to think a horse

would somehow make up for lying to me for thirteen years about the fact my mother was really my aunt, and my real mother was doing twenty-to-life for murder."

He winced at that, and she looked over at him. "Oh no, Ben. I don't think Audrey is going to be upset—"

"I'm afraid that when we tell her, she'll want nothing to do with me, she'll be so angry with me for missing so much of her life."

"Ben!"

But he walked away from her. "What if . . . maybe we should just leave things well enough? She likes me, Kacey. And maybe that's enough."

He'd reached the barn, and Snowy met them at the rail, having responded to Kacey's whistle. She nudged her muzzle into his hand, and Ben ran his other down her forelock.

Kacey had followed him, silent. "I understand— really, I do. Every time I come home from a deployment or am on leave, I wonder if this will be the time Audrey won't forgive me. She'll suddenly discover that I wasn't enough mother for her and decide I don't have a place in her life." She reached up, petted Snowy. "Sometimes I go back to that decision to join the military and wonder what would have happened if I'd stayed. Maybe gotten a job in town, taken classes at the community college . . ."

"Or if I hadn't left." He turned, leaned against

the railing. "If I hadn't been a coward and believed you'd be better off without me."

"Not followed your dream? No, Ben—"

"That wasn't my dream, Kace." He took her hand, tugged her to him. Then he reached up, touched her cheek. "You were. You, and Audrey."

Her beautiful eyes widened, so much raw, eager vulnerability in them, and for the second time that night, she simply swept his breath from his chest.

Somewhere inside that tough soldier exterior was the girl who believed in him, who saw him as her hero. Who had loved just him, without the number one singles, the awards.

"Can I ask you something?" His thumbs ran over her cheekbones.

"Mmmhmm."

"How did I get so lucky that you're not married to some other guy?"

She looked down, away from him. Shrugged. "Because there's never been anyone else but you, Ben."

Oh. Her words could simply unravel him. "Wow, I love you."

It just leaked out, and he didn't care. Just dove in, his heart suddenly thundering to break free. "I never stopped, never could escape the idea that someday, somehow I might be able to earn your forgiveness." His voice thickened. "Please forgive me for leaving."

She looked up at him, her green eyes thick with emotion. "Forgiven." She touched her forehead to his. "If I am."

She leaned back, and he curled his hand behind her neck. Searched her face, then settled on her lips. His throat thickened. "Absolutely."

He pulled her to himself and kissed her. Nothing tentative this time. He knew what he wanted, and fueled by his memories, his touch contained the longing of missing her, and his hopes of healing the raw, open, fourteen-year wound between them.

He kissed her like she belonged to him, and him to her, smelling the afternoon sun on her skin, pulling her closer, tangling his fingers into her soft, cascading hair.

And she pressed into him, moving her arms up over his shoulders, kissing him back as if he might be her entire world.

The way it was supposed to be.

"Oh Kacey," he whispered as he came up for air. It scared him a little how easily he opened his heart for her to walk back into. How much he could taste this life that should have been his.

That *would* be his. "Let's tell her tonight, after the party."

She met his gaze, her breath a little broken, and nodded.

"You've *got* to be kidding me."

Ben stilled.

Kacey's eyes widened.

Not again . . .

He grimaced as she untangled herself from his embrace. "Daddy—"

"I thought you were smarter than this, Kacey." Robert stood just outside the shadow of the barn. He'd removed the apron, his shoulders rising and falling as if holding in something akin to what churned through Ben's brain.

But he wasn't a scared seventeen-year-old kid anymore. *Let's have a go, sir.*

He found Kacey's hand and clasped it.

"Judge—"

Her father held up his hand, his face grim. "Listen, I know you two think you're rekindling the past, but in truth, you're just headed for heartache."

"How's that?"

"When Audrey finds out what's happening here—"

"That her parents have finally found their way back to each other?" Ben said. "That she has a *father?*" He kept his voice down and bit back the diatribe that threatened to emerge.

"No. That her father is a big country star on a pit stop through town, and as soon as he's got a better gig, he'll be on his way. And she'll be heartbroken again. As will my daughter."

"That's not—"

And that's when he spotted her. She was dressed

in short cutoffs, a lacy cream top, a cowboy hat, designer boots, and a thick turquoise necklace dangling from her neck. Hollie Montgomery. And, of course, she was attracting an entourage.

He had no words as his country costar marched right up to him, past Robert, ignoring Kacey, put her arms around his neck, and kissed him on the mouth.

And that's when Kacey let go of his hand.

For all her military training, and in ten years of working in a combat zone, Kacey never had the dark urge to pull out her hand-to-hand combat skills until this very moment.

Except she didn't exactly know where to focus her attack. On the slinky blonde who held Ben's face in her grip, grinning up at him as if she might give him another smack on the lips.

Or Ben, who had Hollie by the arms, as if to steady her, maybe even pull her back in.

His words broke through her haze of shock, however, and forestalled her response.

"Hollie, what are you doing here?"

Here. Not what are you *doing?*

Yep, she should hit Ben. But hadn't she known, deep down inside, that he had something going with Hollie? Anyone who read the tabloids could figure that out—they didn't all lie.

So she was the foolish one for believing he hadn't had feelings for Hollie. If she thought about it, he hadn't really said they'd dated. But hadn't clarified that they hadn't either. Just called her cotton candy.

A lot of people liked cotton candy.

She deserved this horrible, humiliating moment. Still, she managed to fold her arms akimbo, listening for Hollie's answer.

"Benji—I told you." Hollie dropped her hands from his face and grabbed his wrists. "I was wrong. I need you." She even affected a little pout, and if he fell for this, then—

"It's not a big deal—"

"Oh, I knew you'd forgive me!" She flung her arms around his neck, knocking him backward.

Not a big deal?

That's not how he'd made it sound.

Kacey took another step back, felt her father's presence next to her. His hand went around her arm.

Ben set Hollie down, held her at arm's length. "No, Hollie, listen. That's not what I meant—"

"What, you don't forgive me?" She stepped back, and that's when a flash went off.

Ben flung up his hand, and Kacey glanced in the direction of the light.

A cell phone, one of the kids. In fact, it seemed the entire party had followed them out here to watch the reunion of country duo Montgomery-King.

"Not here," he growled and reached for Hollie's arm, but she wrenched it away.

"No. Are you still mad at me?"

And despite her own fury, Kacey saw him glance at the kids, over to Audrey, and she recognized a man trapped.

He metamorphosed before her eyes in a blink, into Mr. CMA, affecting a drawl Kacey had heard on too many country music interviews. "Of course not, honey."

Superstar Benjamin King had returned. As if to seal the deal, he tugged on Hollie's hat, gave her a wink. "I could never stay mad at you, darlin'."

She gave him another hug, more cell phones flashed, and Kacey turned toward the house.

She just might be ill with her own stupidity.

But she hadn't pushed far through the crowd when she heard Ben's voice. "Kacey!"

She didn't want to turn, but she didn't want to make a spectacle either, and end up going viral on social media. So she stopped. Waited.

Ben came striding after her, and she manufactured the same smile he boasted—fake, wide. Nothing to see here, folks.

"You need to meet Hollie Montgomery," he said, but his eyes were searching hers, pressing in.

I'm sorry.

She shook her head, ignored his plea. Instead she stuck out her hand to his petite costar. Cotton candy, indeed. "Lieutenant Kacey Fairing. I'm an old pal of Benjamin's."

Hollie pumped her hand. "When Ben's manager

emailed me and told me he was here, I thought—
what fun to visit him in Montana! I stopped by
his house, only to find out he was here. I love
birthday parties! So I called your house and
your dad said I should come over. Where's the
birthday girl?"

Kacey had frozen, unable to move. But she heard
Audrey's voice rush up behind her. "I'm here."

And Kacey just couldn't ruin this moment
for her starstruck daughter.

"Glad to meet you, Audrey," Hollie said. "I got
you something." She held out a tiny gift bag,
and Audrey reached inside, pulled out a silver
chain with an MK engraved in it.

"For Montgomery-King," Hollie said, stating
the obvious. Then she posed with Audrey for
more selfies.

Ben had grabbed Kacey's elbow, attempting to
pull her aside.

She yanked it away, but it lacked gusto.

She didn't know where she might spend the
night tonight, but she had a great urge to simply
get in her Escape and head for the border.

He stepped close, spoke in her ear, below the
murmur of the guests. "Kacey, I don't know why
she's here, but I promise, I meant what I said—"

"Stay away from me. And Audrey."

He drew in a breath as if she'd slapped him,
and she regretted her words.

Still. She cut her voice low. "Ben, I don't know

what to think—but I do know that I don't understand what just happened—"

"She has stage fright."

Hollie was taking more snaps and laughing with fans.

Kacey looked at him. "What?"

He kept his voice low, managed to keep his smile and wave as Hollie called his name. "She can't sing in public without, well, me."

Kacey looked back at Hollie, now climbing up on the fence with her fans for an epic shot. "You've got to be kidding me."

"I'm serious. She's got a great voice and is a fantastic performer, but only if she has someone—me—to sing with her. I guess she forgot that part when she launched her solo career."

"With your songs."

"Half-written songs."

Hollie slid off the fence, came over to Ben and Kacey. "I brought you a gift too."

Kacey tried not to look horrified. "Me? Why?"

Hollie glanced at Ben, and Kacey's heart fell.

What exactly had her father said to Hollie? That she was Ben's ex—someone Hollie had to woo like an ex-wife?

She suddenly saw a very messy tabloid article, with her and Audrey in color, above the fold.

Hollie had pulled out an envelope. "I have an extra ticket to tomorrow night's concert in Kalispell."

Ben stared at her as if she'd spoken German. "What?" He took the envelope from her.

"I got us a gig—at the Great Northern Auditorium. It's a smaller venue, but—"

"You got *yourself* a gig. This ticket says the Hollie Montgomery Band."

She shrugged, made a face. "I'm sorry, my manager put it together before I told him I'd never leave you."

Kacey looked at Ben, a little unnerved at his expression, like he was trying not to use military moves on Hollie too.

"Please, Benji?" Then Hollie looked so stricken, even Kacey couldn't imagine Ben saying no.

"Fine," Ben said. "But just this once."

"You know you can't quit me." She winked and looked at Kacey. "See you tomorrow night. We're having an after party too—stop by."

Then she blew a kiss at Ben and left. Kacey followed her exit, saw an SUV sitting in the drive, a bald, tattooed man standing by the door wearing jeans and a white print tank waiting for her.

He lifted a hand to Ben.

"Who's that?" she asked.

"That's Harley, my drummer," he said quietly.

Oh.

He sighed, looked at Kacey. The kids and her parents had migrated back to the party. She stood there, her arms wrapped around herself. "I can't believe my dad did this."

Ben looked beyond her, into the horizon. "I can. He's still trying to protect you from me."

Probably.

"Are you okay?" She didn't know why she cared—she wasn't the one who'd kissed her like he'd forgotten his former life only to dive into another smooch minutes later.

Only, seeing as Hollie had attacked *him,* Kacey could maybe forgive him for that.

"You two never dated?"

He met her eyes then. Sighed. "Not really. We had a moment, but . . . Kacey, she's nothing to me. It's an act, I promise."

A moment?

"Why, Ben? I didn't peg her as your type."

He looked away. Sighed again. "I told you how I came home the summer Ian's niece went missing."

She nodded.

He looked at her then, his blue eyes steady in hers, his voice soft. "I came home for you. I wanted to show you I'd made it, and that maybe I was worth . . . Maybe you'd finally forgive me."

His words left her stripped.

He shook his head, casting his glance away.

"I was so ashamed of myself, that I'd not only broken all my vows to God and gotten you pregnant, but that I'd left you. I wanted to make something of myself—and I finally had. So I came home."

"And I was gone."

He nodded. "I didn't know you'd moved away, and then Sam mentioned that you'd joined the military, and since I didn't know about Audrey, I thought you wanted nothing to do with me. My mom told me it was time to put the past behind me. So she told me to go back to Nashville, to do something with my life. I went back, and Goldie, my manager, decided I needed something fresh, so she paired me with Hollie in the studio for a couple songs. We sounded so good together, it just happened."

"You were never in love with her?"

"Are you kidding me? She drives me crazy."

She laughed, and it felt good to finally let go of the fist in her chest.

Then her smile dimmed. "I should get back to the party."

He stiffened then. "I don't think tonight's quite the night to tell Audrey about . . ." He swallowed. "I think there's been enough excitement for one night."

She hated the look on his face. But she nodded anyway.

"What about the concert? Will you come?"

"Aw, Ben, I don't know—"

"Please. You've never really heard me sing . . ."

"Are you kidding me? I grew up hearing you sing. I still hear you sing, all the time."

She wasn't sure why she let those words escape,

but she felt his smile, the way he searched her face.

"I really want to kiss you right now," he said, a tone in his voice that slid under her skin, turned it to fire.

However, she put her hand on his chest. "Not in view of the children. Or their cell phones."

He made a face but closed his hand around hers. "Fine. But I get a dance tomorrow night, at the after party."

"Does that mean I'm your date?"

Oh, crazy words issuing from her mouth tonight. But she couldn't seem to stop them.

"Wear a dress." Then he let go of her hand. "Thank you for tonight. And for . . . understanding. You sure you don't want me to stick around, have a chat with your dad?"

The question caught her off guard, and the protectiveness in it stirred warmth through her. "No. I'll talk to him."

"Tell Audrey good-bye for me."

Behind them, she heard the intro music for *Star Wars*.

"Go, must I," he said.

"May the force be with you."

She laughed as he walked out to his truck.

Her father was gone when she returned to the backyard.

She debated tracking him down, but she wouldn't let her anger destroy Audrey's night.

Kacey found her and flopped down next to her on the sofa, curling her arm around her. To her shock, Audrey leaned into her embrace.

Princess Leia was running from Stormtroopers on the screen, and the speakers were pumping out the sound of lasers.

"Do you like him, Mom?"

Kacey glanced down at her. "Who?"

"Benjamin King. Because I think he likes you."

Kacey let her breath trickle out slowly. "I don't know."

Audrey looked up at her. "I know I've never said, but sometimes I think it would be cool to have a dad, you know?"

Kacey bit her lip. Nodded. "I know."

"Do you think he thinks about me, sometimes? My real dad?"

Oh. She kept her voice soft, easy. "I'm positive he does, honey. How could he not?"

Audrey sighed. "Well, he missed an awesome party tonight."

Kacey gave her a squeeze.

R2-D2 landed on Tatooine.

"Mom." Audrey leaned up. "I hope you know I didn't mean it. About you going back to Florida. I'm really glad you're here." She put her arms around Kacey, gave her a kiss on the cheek. "Best birthday ever."

— 12 —

"I feel silly." Kacey stood in front of the standing mirror in Sierra's bedroom, smoothing the mini dress that showed way too much of her legs, if anyone cared about her opinion. Which, apparently, they didn't.

"If that's what the military can do to my body, sign me up!" Willow sat cross-legged on the bed behind Audrey, braiding her hair into French braids.

"You do have amazing legs, Mom," Audrey said. "You should show them off."

Kacey glanced at her in the mirror. "Enough from you."

She turned to check out where the shimmery purple and orange sleeveless dress landed on her thighs, noticing of course the scar high across her shoulder. But her hair mostly covered that up.

"I'll need a jacket," she said. "In case it gets cold."

"Right. In an auditorium full of screaming fans. You'll probably spend the entire night on your feet, jumping up and down. I promise, you won't get cold." Audrey grinned at her, eyes shining. "I just can't believe you're actually going on a date with Benjamin King!"

Sierra looked up at Kacey from across the room, where she was rifling through her jewelry box. Raised an eyebrow.

Kacey gave a quick shake of her head.

"It's not a date," Kacey said, turning back around. "Actually, Hollie gave me the ticket. And Ben and I are just friends."

"I wish she'd invited me too."

Willow finished the second braid, secured it. "You have band practice. But frankly, I'm with your mother. I heard Hollie's new release, and I think maybe she's courting an older audience."

Audrey shook her head, climbed off the bed. "I'm *fourteen*."

"And I'd like to keep it that way," Kacey said.

"We need to get going. Nate and the others are probably already at the church." Willow reached out for her hand, but Audrey clasped her mother around the waist.

"Have fun tonight, Mom."

Kacey kissed the top of her head, seeing Sierra's smile.

She came over, holding a gold necklace. Downstairs, the door shut.

Kacey took the necklace, tested it. Gave it back. "I don't need any bling. Or these crazy high heels." Three-inch platforms, and they only posed a health hazard. "I'll wear my boots."

"For the record, I agree with Audrey. You have great legs."

"The last thing I need is Ben noticing my great legs. That's probably how we got into this mess." She leaned forward, checked out her makeup. Too much, probably, but—

"Hardly. Ben and you were—are—soul mates. Yes, you made mistakes in high school, but Ben never had anything but long-term intentions with you."

Kacey stared out the window, watching as Audrey climbed into Willow's Jeep parked on the road. The driveway still glistened with mud, and Sierra's poor deck lay in pieces across the side and backyard.

"I know. I've always known that. It's just that he said something last night about being ashamed he'd gotten me pregnant."

"Of course he was. He was a preacher's kid, and here he was not only sleeping with his girlfriend, but he got her pregnant, proof of his sins in front of the entire town."

No wonder he'd proposed. Kacey had never felt like she'd trapped him, not really, but somewhere in the back of her mind, the thought lingered.

"He wasn't the only one. After everything my parents did for me—taking me in when my mother went to jail, raising me. They gave me everything, taught me right from wrong. Yet when I found out about my mother, I felt so betrayed. Ben was the only one I would listen to. He was my best friend before he became my boyfriend.

I can still remember how devastated I felt, giving birth to Audrey without him there."

"I'm sure he felt the same way."

She hadn't thought about that before, but knowing him now—yes, he had to have been bereft at his decisions, that he'd let his anger, his pride keep him from the most important moment of his life.

"You know he got in a fight with Cash that night —that's why he didn't show up. He was in jail."

"That fight was a long time coming, Kacey," Sierra said. "I'm not sure he was in the wrong— seems to me he was defending your honor."

"And his."

Sierra conceded with a nod.

"And, in his defense, I did consider giving Audrey up for adoption. My dad wasn't lying about that."

"You did?" Sierra approached with a container of perfume, misted it in the air.

Kacey walked into the mist. "I just kept thinking —what if I turned out like my mother? In a crazy fit of anger, I'd destroy someone's life, and then Audrey would grow up with the same horrible fear, that deep down she comes from bad stock."

More silence, and finally Kacey turned.

Sierra wore concern on her face. "You don't think that, do you? That you're somehow innately flawed?"

"I know I am. Ben might have felt shame over

breaking his Christian vows, but I didn't. I just wanted him to love me. For me to belong to someone. He was ready to bring me home that night. I'm the one who . . . I said yes before he even asked. I got us here, just as much as he did. I probably deserved that word written on my car. And Ben paid the price.

"The fact is, I *am* flawed—I'm selfish and afraid, and right now, not a little messed up. I still can't sleep through the night without sleeping pills. And while Audrey and I are better, I'm not a good mom. I'm a part-time, Fun Mom. And maybe that's all I'll ever be."

Kacey turned, surveyed herself in the mirror. "I'm not this girl. I'm really good at one thing— flying choppers. And maybe I need to accept that."

Sierra had sunk down onto the bed. "And Ben?"

Kacey wrapped her hands around her waist. "I want it so much it scares me. When he kisses me, I'm suddenly not the daughter of a murderer, or a mom who leaves the hard jobs to others, but someone whole and clean. I'm again that girl who sat in the audience, believing he was singing only to me."

"Maybe he was. Maybe he is."

"No. He's singing to his fans—his songs aren't his own anymore. Frankly, he's as lost as I am. Maybe our mistakes are unfixable. It's not like we can pick up the pieces, make everything brand new."

Sierra slid off the bed, came over, and put her chin on Kacey's shoulder. "Listen. You're just scared. You've gotten a taste of what you want, and you're tempted to run. Instead of telling yourself you can't have the happy ending, why don't you let go of all your dreams—and your fears—and let God show you how it ends. He's the master of happy endings—let him figure it out."

She leaned back, turned Kacey around. "When you found out about your bio mom, it blew your world apart. I was there, I remember. And Ben was there too . . . and he helped put you back together. And then he left and you had Audrey and you were still sort of in pieces. And I know the military gave you glue for your life. You're an amazing chopper pilot. But then that world blew apart. And now here you are, still holding the pieces, right back asking the question, who am I and where am I going? And I have one answer for you, the one that's been there the entire time. The only one who can give you the answer to all your questions is God. He is the object of your searching. We find ourselves and our happy ending by finding him and realizing the grace, the love he has for us."

Sierra caught her hands. "You thought you were coming back to save your daughter from making your mistakes. But what if God brought you back here to save *you,* to redeem *your* mistakes? To put that heart of yours back together, delight you and reunite you with the one man you've always loved, only this time in wholeness?"

Sierra pulled her close, hugging her. "Don't be afraid of letting go and walking into all God has for you."

Kacey longed to believe Sierra's words, to lean into them.

To believe that God might forgive her for her mistakes, her gut-wrenching decisions, and somehow make something beautiful out of the pieces.

Sierra let her go, and Kacey found her cowboy boots. These, she could dance in.

"Thanks for taking Audrey for the night. I'll probably come back here after the show and crash too."

"Okay. I'm going over to Ian's to see if we can track down any more information on Esme."

"You're going to Ian's?"

"Please don't look at me like that. I'm not working for him—I'm just helping him contact guests who might have stayed at Saint Mary Lodge when Esme arrived, maybe given her a ride somewhere."

"So you're giving him your time for free."

"We're friends—and again, stop looking at me like that. Can't friends help friends?"

Kacey finger quoted. "Friends?"

"Yes." But a blush pressed Sierra's face. "He's alone right now, and he needs someone who cares about him. He can't move on until he finds out what happened to her."

"That, or he can't let you go."

"Trust me, he can let me go. After all he's been through, I should have never thought there was anything between us. Ian has no room for anything in his life but finding Esme."

Kacey raised an eyebrow. "Please don't let him hurt you."

Sierra shook her head. "He won't. But I do need to pick up a pizza on my way." She picked up her cell. "Have fun at the concert."

The parking lot at the Great Northern Auditorium was already full when Kacey arrived, a warm-up band stirring the crowd with their country ballads, a little rock and roll thrown in. She found her seat on the front row, a little dazed by the giant Hollie Montgomery banners hanging from the ceiling of the venue. She hoped Ben hadn't seen them—until she saw his own banner, a giant square right over the stage, a magnificent picture of him sitting on a stool, playing his black Gibson, wearing his brown Stetson, his dusty curls dragging out behind the brim. He wore a white T-shirt, something that outlined his superstar physique, a tantalizing smatter of beard, a hint of a smile as he leaned into the mic.

Oh boy.

"Don't be afraid of letting go and walking into all God has for you."

She raised her hands, clapping along with the band, swaying into the song.

You've got a wild side
Something like mine
But when we're alone
Gonna take my time . . .

When she heard the lyrics, she knew she'd made the right decision keeping Audrey at home. The band stayed for an encore, then relinquished the stage to Montgomery-King.

Apparently Ben's people had a chat with Hollie's new manager, because the MK graphics flashed on the Jumbotron.

And then the fireworks began.

Hollie and Ben came out from the wings, singing their signature song, the one she'd deleted off Audrey's playlist.

Ben looked like his album cover photo, except in a black T-shirt outlining his poster-boy physique.

Hollie picked up the second verse, looking at Ben like he might be her true love.

Kacey tried to let the words of the song bounce off her, but she hated the way he gazed into Hollie's eyes as they dove into the chorus.

Let's start a fire
Let it burn brighter
I'll show you how to light up the night

So maybe this wasn't the right concert for her. She clapped her way through the song and found herself cheering when Ben turned to the audience and treated them to a guitar solo.

But Hollie's gaze on him had Kacey's chest burning.

Worse, to her eyes, Ben seemed to be enjoying himself. And why not—cheering fans, a cute girl singing to him like he alone could, well, light up the night.

Kacey held on to the rail. Audrey was right. She'd probably stand the entire concert.

Unless she left.

She was looking for the exit when she heard Ben step up to the mic.

"It's awfully nice of Hollie to let me crash her party tonight. I know you all signed up for a Hollie Montgomery show. I hope you all don't mind me taggin' along." He said it in his fake yet convincing and sexy drawl, and the crowd roared their approval. She wondered what it cost him to say it, however.

"But Hollie said I could sing one of my favorites, especially since I'm back to my old stompin' grounds. This is a little song I put together back when I was dreaming of following my dreams to Nashville."

Hollie had scooted him up a stool, and now he sat on it, propped his leg up.

Kacey couldn't move when he started picking out the tune.

No . . . oh *no.*

He leaned into the mic, and suddenly she was back in the Gray Pony, watching him fight the crowd for attention.

Early riser, gonna catch the sun
Gotta start 'er early, gonna get her done . . .

She pictured herself sitting on a high-top, tracing the afterglow of the sun on his face, seeing him in his worn cowboy boots, faded jeans, a clean T-shirt.

She didn't care what he said about her being his dream—he'd wanted to sing his songs for as long as she'd known him.

After the big game, the bonfire's on
I got my pretty gal, not doin' nothing wrong
Wishing on stars, hoping in the night
Someday everything's gonna work out right

Someday. She nodded. And it had, really, for him. He'd crafted an amazing career, charmed millions with his songs, including his own daughter.

The crowd cheered as he added a riff to the end of the verse, diving again into the chorus.

Believin' that the dreamin's gonna get me far

It had. And it still could, if he wanted it. His voice could still make her shiver; the smoky heat

tunneled under her skin, awakened emotion—
hope, joy, even longing—inside her. Probably he
did that for all his fans.

In his last stanza, the fiddler and the drummer
dropped out, leaving just Ben and his voice, his
guitar, lonely and poignant on the darkened stage.
His song lifted, sweet and sad, falling upon her.

Somewhere back there, the mountain waits
Sorry, darlin', but I'll be home late
I've got a song to sing, the dream demands
C'mon, boys, let's warm up the band

He let the last notes drift out, falling on silence
before the crowd erupted. She stood there, her
cheeks wet, her eyes blurry.

The dream demands.

He stood up, looked out in the crowd, and she
couldn't tell if he was searching for her or not.

But how could he see her, really, against the
bright footlights of the stage? And he wouldn't
notice, either, if she slipped out.

In fact, amidst all the applause and the triumph
of the evening, he probably wouldn't even miss
her.

She waited until he and Hollie started their
next song, jamming hard into something about
blue jeans, cowboy boots, and blondes, and
headed for the door.

He was wrong. Ben might be able to come back
to Mercy Falls, but Benjamin King could not.

For the first time since Ian fired her, Sierra could admit that perhaps this was better.

Sitting down to pizza with him as her equal, if she could ever call Ian that, helping him with his search, filled a place inside her she hadn't quite realized was empty.

More than him being her entire world—they'd finally become real friends.

They sat on the leather sofa, the pizza box open on the coffee table, a list of the guests of Saint Mary Lodge in front of them, procured by her after pleading Ian's desperate case and, of course, adding Ian's generous donation for an updated dining room. It helped, too, that Sam had called, verified their official search needs.

Sam had been checking in with her too. Even stopped by last night after she got home, a late-night pizza in hand. Poor guy put in too many hours as the town's deputy.

She had called nearly all 116 guests of the lodge, cabins, and motel rooms. "I left a message with the Lefevres and the Williamses—and I'll keep calling the Jansens, but we're getting to the end of the list, Ian."

He had kicked back on the sofa, his bare feet on the table.

She noticed the wounds on his knuckles had healed, finally.

She desperately hoped Ian had heard her words

about God not punishing him. About wanting to set him free.

"I know," he said, reaching for another piece of pizza, sliding it on a paper plate, licking his fingers clean of the sauce. "But we'll figure out something."

We.

See, a team. Friends. Equals.

She dished up her own piece of pizza. "I'm sorry we haven't been able to spend more time on this."

"Your new job seems to be working out." He said it without rancor, his tone genuine. She had to admit feeling a hint of disappointment that he hadn't asked her to work for him again.

Then again, she spent practically every off-hour helping him keep the search alive.

And this was better, anyway.

"I like working for the team. Now that we've joined with the local EMS, I'm helping dispatch with 911 calls, I've put together a training schedule with the volunteer fire department, and Deputy Brooks has been bringing me up to speed on SAR terms, policies, and protocols."

He got up, walked over to the kitchen. "Do you want another drink?"

Her cell phone rang. "I think this is one of our callbacks," she said as she picked it up. "Hello?"

"My name is Megan Lefevre, and I have a message from someone named Sierra?"

"That's me." She motioned to Ian as she filled Megan in on their search. "So, we were wondering if you might have seen a girl matching that description—blonde hair, possibly wearing a Mercy Falls Mavericks sweatshirt, maybe looking for a ride?"

"Maybe. I remember the blonde hair, but not what she was wearing. We gave her a ride to East Glacier."

Sierra was on her feet, snapping her fingers at Ian. "I'm going to put you on speaker."

She pushed the button, lay the cell on the table.

Ian came over, wearing an enigmatic expression. Hope? Disbelief?

"Go on," Sierra said.

"She was desperate to leave—we actually picked her up on the highway. She was hitching, of all things, and I told my husband that she looked like she might be in trouble, as if she'd been in a fight. She had a bruise on her jaw, a swollen lip. She looked like she'd been crying. It made me worry about her—that's why we picked her up."

Sierra had grabbed Ian's arm. "Do you remember where you took her?"

"Yeah. We bought her something to eat at this little café and tried to find out who she was. She said she'd come to the park with her boyfriend, and they got into a fight. My husband wanted to call her parents, but she said she was eighteen and on her own. We finally got her to agree to take the train home. In the end, we gave her some money and dropped her off at the Amtrak."

Ian had taken Sierra's hand and was now tightening his grip.

"Is there anything else you can remember? Did she say anything about the fight, or maybe do you remember if she mentioned any names?"

"No. She was quiet, maybe even a little skittish, and—oh yeah, I remember. Some cops came into the café, and she suddenly put up her hood, as if she didn't want them to see her. So yeah, she must have been wearing a sweatshirt. I thought about it later—it made me wonder if she was a runaway. I should have never let her get on that train. I admit, it haunts me."

"You helped her—thank you for that," Sierra said, glancing at Ian. "And you did all you could for her. Some people just . . . well, you can't force them to accept your help."

"I'll ask my husband if he remembers anything, and if he does, I'll call you back."

"Thank you again." Sierra hung up and turned to Ian.

He stared at her, and a slow smile crawled up his face.

She matched it.

Then suddenly, his arms were around her, picking her up, whirling her around. "We found her!"

She had no words—too caught up in the sense of being in his arms, crushed to his chest, the air out from under her feet.

He smelled good, and she'd forgotten how strong he was, that aura of power that had always intrigued, delighted her.

"You did this." He set her down, caught her face in his hands. "You did this, Sierra. We're going to find her!"

And then, suddenly, he leaned down and kissed her.

Not a quick kiss, either, but something thorough, as if it might be long-awaited.

Shock turned her still; her body froze under his touch.

He tasted sweet, like the soda he'd been drinking, smelled of the soap from his shower, his touch solid as he cradled her face in his hands.

And then she was kissing him back. Her hands fisted in his shirt, pulling him closer. Practically inhaling him, throwing away every bit of hesitation, that old caution that held them apart torn asunder.

More than friends—*finally*.

He angled his head to deepen his kiss, moved his hands behind her back to pull her closer, a little sound of desire issuing from the back of his throat.

Ian. Her brain could hardly catch up with the

feel of his honed body against hers, the sense of this amazing, powerful man letting himself go in her arms.

When he moved away, he seemed to be breathing hard as he searched her face. A smile tipped his lips. "Okay, so I admit I've been wanting to do that for a while."

She touched his wrists and he caught her hands, entwined his fingers into hers.

"How long?"

"Five years?" He lifted a shoulder, as if suddenly sheepish. "I didn't want to be that boss that stalked his beautiful employee."

Beautiful? And suddenly the fact that he hadn't rehired her made her want to sing. She could barely speak with the emotions clogging her throat. "I've wanted to kiss you for a long time too."

He moved his hands behind her back, still holding hers. "Really?" He stepped closer, touched his forehead to hers. "Because I always thought I'd offended you that night . . . when—"

"Hardly."

"I wasn't myself." He leaned down, kissed her neck, and a shiver went down her entire body.

And this *was* himself? Oh boy. She swallowed as he found her eyes again.

"Maybe you're right. Maybe God is done punishing me."

He kissed her again, sweetly, and she decided

not to correct his theology. As his kiss deepened, she sensed the well of emotion that he'd kept banked for so long.

It occurred to her that was why she never saw a woman on his arm or even overnight, at the house. Because Ian never did anything halfway, and he simply wouldn't dive in without giving his whole heart.

And he wasn't the kind of man to give that over easily.

She kissed him back, her own emotions sweeping over her.

It wasn't until he broke away that she noticed he'd moved them over to the end of the sofa. He sat on the arm, putting his arms around her. She propped her hands on his shoulders, touched his curly dark hair. The lamplight illuminated the strands of amber, a few russet hairs at his temples.

Although he'd shaved, late-afternoon copper whiskers graced his chin. She ran her fingers over them and he grinned, touched her cheek, ran his thumb down it, eliciting a trail of sparks.

"Thank you for not giving up on me—or Esme. Even if I'd hired a PI, he or she would have given up by now. But not you, Sierra. You cared enough to keep looking. Now we just have to get ahold of the Amtrak office, see if we can figure out where she went."

She frowned, put her hands on his muscled shoulders.

"Ian, I thought you just wanted to make sure she was okay. Alive. We did, and now maybe you need to let this go."

"I just need to find out where she is, and then I can walk away."

"But . . ." She ran her hands down his arms, caught his hands. "What if she doesn't want to be found?"

He frowned. "What are you talking about?"

"I just think that maybe she wants to stay lost."

He stood up, and she backed up to give him room. He let go of her hands. "Why would she want to stay lost?"

"Think about it. Why did she go to the east side of the park, instead of back to Mercy Falls? It looks like she's running."

"From what?"

His tone brought her up, and she stiffened.

"I don't know. Maybe she saw something or was a part of something—you heard what Megan Lefevre said about her weird reaction when the cops came into the café. Like she didn't want to be noticed."

"Are you saying she did something bad?"

He let go of her hands, walked away from her.

"I didn't mean she had something to do with Dante's death, but whatever it was, she didn't think she could come home. And it sure seems like she doesn't want to be found."

He held up a hand, walked away from her.

"What if she needs my help? Megan also said it looked like she'd been beat up. I can't just . . ." He blew out a breath. "I can't just leave Esme out there alone."

Sierra schooled her tone, tried to keep it gentle. "Not everyone needs your help, Ian. Or wants it."

That brought him up short. A muscle tensed in his jaw.

"I know you've helped thousands, but—"

"You don't understand, Sierra." He rounded on her. "That's why I'm here, that's what I do. If I don't help them, who will?"

She paused then. "God?"

"Oh, please. Really? Listen, I got to where I am today because I didn't let my mother's choices keep me from going to school, didn't let my poverty keep me out of college, didn't let Katrina destroy me. I helped myself to where I am today. And I can help Esme."

"Even if she doesn't want your help?" She didn't mean for her words to emerge as a challenge. Her heart filled her throat as she stared at him, gauging her words. But she saw his future tunneling out into a fruitless search, the what-if holding him hostage. "You need to let this go."

Quiet. The room cooled. He walked over to the list on the coffee table, picked it up. Closed the lid on the pizza box. "I'll find her on my own, Sierra. Thanks for picking this up. You want the leftovers?"

And just like that, she was dismissed. She stared at him, stripped.

He met her gaze, and the emptiness in it brushed down her spine.

She shook her head at the pizza, her eyes burning. "Okay, Ian. You win." She walked toward the door, grabbed her boots, slid them on. "But despite what you believe, you can't save everyone. You can't protect everyone. And you can't make the world obey you."

He stood in the glow of the lamplight, the darkness of the window pressing in around him, his eyes dark, his chest rising and falling against her words.

"And you're a fool to think that you got here on your own. God has had your back every step of the way, and someday you might actually get your ego out of the way enough to see that."

She put her purse over her shoulder and pulled the door shut behind her.

She made it to her car before she bent into the steering wheel and sobbed.

"What do you mean, you can't find her?" Ben stared out at the remnants of the crowd from the wings of the stage. He'd expected Kacey to be lingering after the show, had sent Hollie's new manager to find her. "Did you check with security—maybe she tried to get backstage?"

She wasn't waiting in the crowd, nor by the

door to the stage in back. He'd left two messages on her phone, texted her.

Nothing.

He packed his guitar into its case, disappointment like a fist in his gut.

"Benji, you were ah-*mazin'*," Hollie said, putting an arm around his shoulders. She pressed a kiss to his cheek.

Yeah, he just might have given the best concert of his life—mostly because he'd dreamed of exactly this night. Him at the mic, staring down into the crowd, the woman he loved singing along.

He knew Kacey had been there—the minute he took the stage, he looked for her seat, found her standing at the rail, smiling, clapping.

And then the music swept him away. That, and Hollie's crazy performance. He had never seen her quite so flirtatious on stage, her dance moves just a little too forward, her voice sultry. He'd never really considered the lyrics of his songs—but suddenly they all sounded way too suggestive, especially when he thought about Audrey singing them.

For the first time ever, he felt a little soiled after a gig.

He shut the guitar case, picked it up. "Gotta run."

"What? No, you have to stick around. I wanted to work on that song I heard you singing during warm-up. What was it?"

Kacey's song. The one that wouldn't leave his brain. He'd written nearly the entire thing, just needed an ending, had been reaching for the lyrics in his dressing room with the band, anticipating singing it to Kacey after the concert.

Turn around, listen to your heart
I need you so much, don't tear me apart
I was wrong, you were right
Nothing between us but this darn fight

And yes, Hollie had come in, humming along as she read fan tweets on her phone, but he didn't think she'd actually heard him.

"It's nothing," he said and shrugged out of Hollie's embrace. Last thing he needed was her finishing the song and claiming it.

She grabbed his arm. "But what about Billings? The tour? Me?"

"I'm not on tour with you, Hollie. You started this project alone, remember? You'll have to figure this out on your own."

The flirty, dangerous look had vanished. Instead, she glared at him. "You can't leave me."

"Oh, I think I can."

"No, you can't. Because without me, you're nothing, Ben. You were heading down has-been lane when I came along. And you'll be right back there when I leave you here in this back-water town."

"Have a good tour," he said quietly.

She made a sound of disbelief. "You think you can come back home, fall in love with your high school sweetheart—yeah, I'm not blind. I know exactly who you're hanging out with. But she'll never love you the way you need to be loved. The way the music, the fans love you." She advanced toward him. "Face it, Benji, you gave your heart to the stage long ago, and you're fooling yourself if you think you can leave it behind."

He shut the door behind him, his entire body burning with Hollie's words.

"You gave your heart to the stage long ago, and you're fooling yourself if you think you can leave it behind."

He clutched his guitar and strode out of the building to the back parking lot, the cool wind swilling down from the hazy black outline of the mountains. Overhead the stars winked down at him, and he inhaled the sweet scent of pine.

He put his guitar in the truck, then pulled out his cell phone, hoping for a text.

Nothing. He put his truck into drive.

She hadn't texted by the time he pulled up to her parents' home. He got out of his truck, wishing he knew which window was hers.

But he wasn't a high school boy sneaking around anymore.

He walked up to the porch, his heart banging.

Why did you leave?

The words practically breached his mouth even before the door opened, riding on a wave of adrenaline.

His words stopped short at the sight of Judge Fairing in the frame, dressed in his jeans and a flannel shirt, as if he might have been waiting up.

He opened the door. Stepped outside, onto the porch, his jaw tight.

Ben drew in a breath, stepped back.

"What are you doing here, Ben?" the Judge said in his quiet, reasonable voice. The one that had convinced Ben that leaving town was the best possible course.

Last time.

"Is Kacey here?"

The Judge shook his head. He didn't elaborate, just met Ben's eyes with his own, bearing a dark challenge.

Fine. "I love her. I never stopped loving her."

"That was never in doubt. But the question was—and still is—is that enough? You have a big life, Ben. A superstar life. One that doesn't have room for Audrey and Kacey. Or are you going to give that up?"

And now it all made sense. "That's why you invited Hollie to the party, isn't it? Because you thought by bringing her here, I'd get sucked back into that life."

The Judge just stared at him.

"Maybe I don't have to give it up," he said, surprised at his own words. Because, really, being a performer didn't mean he couldn't have a family.

"And that's the problem, isn't it? You don't see the big picture. Never have." The Judge shook his head. "You only see what you want. Not what is best for Kacey, or Audrey."

"I'm what's best for Kacey and Audrey."

The Judge tightened his mouth into a grim line, and the disapproval could choke Ben if he let it. Finally, "Go home, Ben. If Kacey has left you, it's probably because she's finally come to her senses. If she wanted to see you, she would have told you where she was."

He closed the door behind him as he went inside, leaving Ben standing on the porch. The lights went off inside the house.

He pressed a hand to his knotted chest as he got back into the truck. He pulled out his cell phone, hoping for a text. Nothing. But he sent another.

I missed U tonight. Sry if I did something wrong. Call me.

She hadn't texted by the time he pulled up to the ranch house.

"She's finally come to her senses."

The swing on the deck called to him with the urge to just sit, watch the starlight glisten on the wet rocks, feel the night air cool on his sweaty skin.

He didn't hear the door open until he heard the thump of his father's walker, the click of Jubal's nails on the porch. He turned, alarmed.

"You're not supposed to be up walking without supervision."

Chet ignored him, easing down on the swing next to him. Jubal lumbered down at their feet, put his head on his paws.

His father stared out at the water, the shape of the faraway mountains. He rubbed his chest. "Got a little indigestion, can't sleep. How was the concert?"

Ben shrugged. "I invited Kacey, but she didn't stick around." He tried to keep the hurt out of his voice, but it hitched, betraying him.

Chet nodded.

"I went to her house. Her dad said that . . . he said that I only wanted what was good for me—not her. I do want what's best for her. But what if it's not me?"

Chet just sat staring at the sky. "Your mother and I used to come out here at night, especially near the end, and she'd look up to the heavens and reach for my hand. Squeeze it. I used to think she was afraid, but as we got closer to the end, she told me that she wasn't afraid of dying. Just of leaving me. Anticipation—that's what that squeeze was. Because once she knew the doctors had done all they could, she set her focus on following her heart home."

He pointed upward. "She'd long ago given her heart to God for safekeeping. Her hopes, her trust, her dreams—all in his embrace. People think that faith, especially as we face our fears, or hold on to our dreams, is for the weak, the pitiful. People who are afraid or indecisive. But in fact, having faith is the bravest thing we can do. It's the unwavering confidence that God loves us. That although we can't see the road ahead, we can see God. A God we know, a God that loves us—so much that he won't give up on us. Won't let us get lost, even when we think we are. Real faith takes everything you have—throwing your life, your heart, everything you are with complete abandon into the embrace of God."

Ben sat in silence next to him, the night shifting around them in the tang of the grasses, the rush of the river. He thought about his mother. The fact that he wished he had her kind of faith.

Maybe he simply wasn't brave enough to trust God with his and Kacey's future.

Finally, "You're supposed to let me help you with your rehab. It's dangerous for you to be shuffling around on your own—you could fall."

"I know. I just can't abide sitting in that chair. And you're busy."

"That's why I'm here. To help. I don't understand why it's so hard for you to let me step in—"

"Because I'm not weak, and I don't need help."

"But you do! Sheesh, Dad, you were in a

helicopter crash. You nearly died. And it's okay to need help—"

"From God, sure. But not from you."

"Why not?"

Chet looked away, and suddenly the drape of the moonlight etched out his wrinkles and grooves, frailties.

He sighed then. "Because I can't bear for you to see me as less than I was. I used to be your hero, a soldier, the man who taught you how to rope and herd cattle, to throw a football. When you rescued that hiker, I thought—he learned that from me."

"I did. You taught me how to survive in the wilderness."

"But now when I look in your eyes, I see a doddering old man."

Ben pressed his mouth tight. He wanted to correct him, but the reality of his behavior over the past few weeks reached up for a choke hold.

Yeah, he might have made his dad feel that way.

Chet finally reached out for the walker, eased himself forward, up.

Ben rose, ready to catch him.

Chet found his feet without help, though. Glanced over at him.

"Don't stay out too long," his dad said. "It's getting cold outside."

He'd been out for so long, he was used to it.

"I'll be in soon," he said quietly.

— 13 —

Kacey just knew that letting Ben King into her life—her daughter's life—would only break her heart.

Ben simply didn't have room for a family—and maybe the best thing for all of them would be for him to walk away. Kacey stood at the door to the deck of the PEAK ranch, drawn by the lure of the ribs in the hickory smoker, the sounds of laughter in the yard, where her daughter stood with Ty, who had decided to forgive Kacey for taking his job and to teach Audrey how to rope the imaginary steer attached to a hay bale.

Miles played with his three-year-old, chasing him, scooping the little bull rider up, tossing him over his shoulder, grabbing his arms to fly him around the yard. Miles's cute pregnant wife, Kelli, sat in an Adirondack chair, a hand on her rounded belly, and talked with Chet, who sat rubbing his arm as if he might have a stiff muscle.

Pete tossed out a Frisbee for Jubal to catch in a flying lunge. Gage and Jess filled the cooler with ice and tossed in cans of soda.

The perfect Sunday afternoon arched high and bright, the sky so blue she could dive in, the mountains in backdrop standing sentry and majestic over their day.

She could hardly believe that two weeks ago, they were wading through floodwaters and rescuing kids off mountaintops, with her trying to find her footing after discovering thirteen years of betrayal.

But maybe this team could provide a new kind of camaraderie—the kind she'd found in the military, only closer to home, with Audrey in her life every day. The place to build something safe. With these people, she didn't need Ben to move forward.

"Ben just pulled up," Sierra said from behind her. She held a bowl of potato salad and was heading outside, but nodded toward the front drive. "Just giving you a heads-up."

"I figured he'd show up sometime."

"It'll be okay. Just tell him that you had a headache—"

"I'm not going to lie to him, Sierra. He deserves to know, to move on. We just don't fit into each other's lives anymore."

Sierra shook her head, but Kacey cut her off. "We make much less sense than you and Ian do."

"Not true. Ian sees me as his employee—he always will. More, what is a hippie's daughter doing with a billionaire? Like that would ever work. He saved us both—"

"He kissed you!"

Sierra glanced outside, back to Kacey. "Ix-nay on the issing-kay. I don't want the team to know.

Besides, trust me when I say it was just a moment. He didn't mean it."

"But you did."

Sierra lifted a shoulder, a contrast to her slightly reddened, still swollen eyes. "Again, imagine if he hadn't cut this off before he became my entire world." She made a face, something of horror in it, and Kacey laughed.

"Okay. Whatever. But Ben has never been my entire world—I made sure of that."

"And now who's lying? He's been your everything since you were thirteen. You've just been living in denial for so long you think you can live without him. Or maybe you think you don't deserve him."

Kacey ignored that. "I *can* live without him. I have you, and"—she gestured to the team out-side—"these guys."

Ben came up on the porch holding a couple bags of chips, and the sound of his boots made Audrey turn.

"Yes, you do," Sierra said. "But what about—"

"Mr. King!" Audrey exclaimed. "I didn't know you would be here."

"Audrey," Sierra finished quietly.

"I don't know yet," Kacey said. "I agree she should know, but I don't want to disrupt her life. You know she's going to want him to stick around . . ."

And she couldn't help but wince as Audrey

came up on the deck and actually put her arms around Ben's waist. He responded with a quick hug, and Kacey's heart just about tore in half.

Sierra, too, said nothing. Sighed.

Audrey leaned back, looked up at Ben. "Can you teach me that guitar lick? I brought my guitar."

A quick *no* died in Kacey's throat when he nodded, and Audrey headed inside to retrieve her guitar.

Sierra stepped back to let her inside, and Audrey shot her mother a wide smile, her eyes shining. "Benjamin King is here!"

"Yes, he is."

"Do you think he's here to see you?" She grabbed her guitar case from where she'd parked it near the sofa. "Did you have fun last night?"

Audrey had been asleep on the foldout in the family room when Kacey sneaked back to Sierra's house last night, her heart in her hands. And this morning she'd successfully dodged any questions as she helped Sierra prepare for today's barbecue.

Now, she found a smile. "Great concert."

"But the after party—did he try and hold your hand?" Audrey held her guitar like she might a teddy bear, one arm around the neck, the other hand on the body.

"No, honey. I told you, we're just friends." The words came out almost without a hitch.

Audrey frowned, a shadow of disappointment across her face. Then, "It's okay if he teaches me, right?"

Sierra's eyes on her made Kacey nod.

And when Audrey opened the door, Ben turned, his blue eyes fixed on Kacey. No welcoming grin, no warmth in his eyes. Just a tiny twitch of his mouth, as if he wanted to say something.

Anything.

She gave him a tight nod, aching. But this was for the best.

Sierra went outside, and Kacey walked over to check the cookies Sierra had baking. The house smelled like something out of a storybook—homey, comfortable.

Ian was an idiot to push a woman like Sierra out of his life.

Kacey donned her hot pads and pulled the cookies from the oven. She felt ultra-domestic as she scooped them off the tray.

Jess came in as Kacey was finishing with the cookies. "Have you tried roping yet? Ty's giving lessons. Ben already showed off. I didn't realize he could rope."

"He used to work as a hand on his grandfather's ranch," she said, not wanting to think about the cowboy in Ben, the way he seemed just as natural on a horse as he did onstage.

What didn't he do well?

As if in answer, she heard the sound of a guitar,

and she spotted Ben outside sitting on the deck, leaning over the instrument, his fingers flying over the fretboard.

She watched as he handed the guitar to Audrey. He leaned over her, positioning her fingers, one at a time, picking out the pattern for her on the strings.

"She bites her lip the same way he does," Jess said quietly, also watching the pair. "How are they getting along?"

Kacey hearkened back to her conversation with Jess in the dim light of their bunk room. "I haven't told her yet."

Jess glanced at her. "I know it's none of my business, but why not?"

"Well, look at him. He's a big star. Has fans everywhere, and a life in Nashville. Imagine if you suddenly found out your father was someone famous. You'd feel like you'd have to compete with his fans, wonder if you were enough, if he'd choose you. And then there's the fact that he would be in and out of your life, bringing chaos and media attention when that's the last thing you'd need to live a normal life. Not to mention the fact that if he did pick you, you'd always know that you'd held him back."

"Hmm," Jess said. "I guess I'd think, 'Wow! I have a dad.' But you're probably right." She picked up the plate of cookies. "I think the ribs are ready."

Perfect. Kacey turned off the oven and followed Jess outside, pasting on her game face. She didn't have to make a big deal about last night—maybe Ben had already figured out that their worlds didn't mesh.

From the sound of it, Audrey was catching on to the lick. Ben's hands were now off the strings. He didn't look at Kacey as she came out.

Fine.

Jess set the cookies on the picnic table covered by a red-checked tablecloth. Chet rolled up the ramp, with a friendly push from Pete. Gage carried the tray of ribs.

Miles propped his three-year-old on his neck, holding his legs. Ty came over, coiling up his rope.

Sierra took the ribs from Gage, added them to the table already filled with potato salad, watermelon, cookies, chips, and a cake with "Welcome Kacey!" in the center.

A truck pulled up behind them, and Kacey spotted Sam Brooks getting out. He waved a hand as he walked toward the house.

"I invited Sam because he's just as much a part of us, now that we're working with the Mercy Falls EMS," Sierra said.

Kacey didn't miss the flare of disapproval from Pete. He stuck his hands in his back pockets, looked away toward the mountains as Sam greeted everyone. Huh. She would have thought they would have gotten closer after the death of their father.

Chet cleared his throat. "It's a new season, with Kacey joining us at our weekly barbecue. But it'll be a good season, and until I'm back on my feet and Ty is back at the helm, she'll be running operations alongside Miles."

She smiled and maintained her military bearing when Ben glanced at her, his face blank.

"We don't pray for dinner—we praise." Chet gripped the arms of his chair, his voice rising. "The Lord is my shepherd; I shall not want. He maketh me to lie down in green pastures: he leadeth me beside the still waters . . ."

In unison the team recited the familiar psalm, and the words awakened inside her, just like they had when Howard had spoken them. Now, as then, she found her mouth moving with the rest of the team.

"He restoreth my soul: he leadeth me in the paths of righteousness for his name's sake."

She glanced at her daughter standing next to Ben, the words innocent on her tongue.

"Yea, though I walk through the valley of the shadow of death, I will fear no evil: for thou art with me; thy rod and thy staff they comfort me."

She closed her eyes against the picture of God, the Good Shepherd, using his weapons to protect her.

It might not have felt like God was with her on

that mountain in Afghanistan, but she *had* discovered a measure of comfort—he'd brought her home, deepened her relationship with Audrey.

And she had survived the mountain, hadn't she? That thought settled deep.

"Thou preparest a table before me in the presence of mine enemies: thou anointest my head with oil; my cup runneth over."

Yes, maybe she'd request a release from active duty, move home during her reserve term, and get on with building a life here in Mercy Falls.

Because this was more than enough, really, if she were to look around at the team, the friends she'd already made.

"Surely goodness and mercy shall follow me all the days of my life: and I will dwell in the house of the Lord forever."

And it would be enough for Audrey too.

They chorused an amen, and while the guys grabbed plates, Audrey went to put away her guitar.

"Honey, you should put that in the house when you get done eating." Kacey reached for a paper plate but suddenly heard Ben's voice in her ear, low and strident.

"We need to talk."

She glanced at Audrey, then back at Ben. "Now?"

"Everyone's busy eating," he said. "They won't notice we're gone."

So maybe she owed him an explanation. Kacey

backed away from the table, headed toward the house, Ben on her tail.

Inside, away from prying ears.

She walked past the kitchen, toward Chet's office. Ben came in behind her, and when she turned, he'd already worked up a lather.

"I don't understand. Why didn't you stick around?" He shook his head. "I've been going through this all night. Was it Hollie? Or the music? I get it—I do. I know it's not . . . it's what sells, Kacey. And it might not be where I started, but it's where I am now and—"

"Stop, Ben. You don't have to justify anything to me."

That brought him up short.

"You and Hollie were amazing out there. She's a great performer—not a hint of stage fright."

"Oh, trust me, she was practically shaking before we got on stage. But—"

"But you're right. She needs you. And you put on an amazing show. I was so proud of you up there."

Again, he just blinked at her. And it occurred to her that he'd never seen himself like she saw him last night. Small-town boy making good on stage. Living out all his dreams.

A thread of warmth slipped into her words. "You were brilliant. And not just your voice and your guitar slinging, but you. You glitter up there. You were made for the stage, Ben. I always knew it, and last night—I was just so proud of you."

"I . . . I thought you left because, well, because I'd offended you."

Oh. She let out a sound, something like a laugh. "No. I mean, I didn't expect the songs to be quite so . . . I think I'll need to take another look at what Audrey listens to."

He made a face, then ran a hand behind his neck.

Her voice turned soft. "I loved 'Mountain Song.' " She hoped he could see it in her eyes, how it touched her to hear the song he'd written for them. For Audrey. "I was caught in time. It was beautiful."

"Then why did you leave?" Some of the anger had fallen from his expression, leaving only hurt.

It made her want to reach up, touch his face, run a thumb along a smattering of golden brown whiskers.

"Because I already realized that I can't let you give this up. You've worked too hard to make a career."

He looked stricken, and her heart went out to him, just a little. "I don't understand. I said I'd stay."

She stepped closer, reached out to take his hand, softened her words. "Ben, please. You have too much music in you to stay. We both know this."

His mouth opened. The hurt was gone, replaced with an expression that hit her straight on.

She was right.

He blinked, looked away.

So she pressed in the truth.

"Think about it, Ben. You live in Nashville, and no matter how much you say we can work it out—and probably yes, you could fly back and forth. But in the end, your daughter is only going to feel like she's making you choose. And she feels either guilty or resentful."

"And is it too much to ask her—you—to move to Nashville?"

She drew in a breath. "Seriously? Her life is here. You want to take her away from her grandparents, her school?"

His gaze was sharp. "What are you saying . . . you've changed your mind about Audrey?"

She let his hand go. But he had to see the obvious.

"I don't see how it doesn't turn out badly. We just don't fit in your life, Ben. I know you want us to, but you can't see the sacrifices you'll have to make. And maybe that's what my dad saw— you're bigger than this town, than us. And I need to . . . let you go."

"No—"

"We have a family here, Ben. Your dad is here, and the team is great. We're going to be okay—"

"*I'm* not going to be okay! I need you, Kacey. I love you—and Audrey. We're a family—or we could be."

And now he was simply being stubborn. Her voice slid to something low, blunt.

"And what's that going to look like? You going to take us on the road with you—"

"Maybe. Or maybe I do quit country music. I can. I only did it for you, anyway. To show you that I could take care of you, become the person you always saw." And now his beautiful eyes were filled with a sort of angry desperation.

She put a hand on his chest. "I know—and you have. Wow, you have. You're this amazing, breathtaking man. Kind and protective—and yeah, of course I'll always love you. But I can't let you quit."

He just stared at her, as if trying to sort out her words. So she found the ones he needed to hear.

"Ben, I don't need you anymore. You're free to go. We'll be fine."

His mouth closed, jaw tight.

Then he nodded. "Of course you will be." He turned away as if to go, and she finally let out a breath.

There. Over. Good.

"But I won't be." He whirled back around, and she hadn't taken a breath before he had his hand around her neck, pulling her mouth against his.

And then, all thought left her as he kissed her, such desperation in his touch that it shattered the tight control she had on her emotions, barreling right through her reasons, straight on to grab up her heart.

Oh, how she loved this man. She tasted her own tears as she kissed him back, her arms around his neck, losing herself in her hope of what-if, the fairy tale that she longed to be theirs.

He had backed her up to the wall and now braced his arms on each side of her head as he leaned back from her, meeting her eyes. His glistened, and she grasped his shirt in her fists, not sure if she should hold on or push him away.

Her heart thundered, her lips bruised, aching to kiss him again.

"Babe, I know you don't need me. You've made this amazing life. You're a hero, a pilot, an awesome mom, and frankly, I'm so blown away by you I can hardly find the words. But that's the thing—with you I *do* find the words. You and Audrey are what's been missing, all this time. We belong together, you and me and Audrey. She's my daughter, and I love her. And I want to be in your lives."

"What did you say?"

Kacey stilled, and by the way Ben's eyes opened wide, he'd heard her too.

Audrey, standing in the doorway, holding her guitar.

Probably bringing it in the house, just like her mother told her to. With a groan, Ben leaned away from the wall.

Kacey broke away from him, headed toward Audrey. "Honey—"

"What did he say?" Her eyes were wide, her voice shrilling. She looked at Kacey, accusation on her face, then to Ben.

"We were going to tell you—" Kacey started, but Audrey wasn't listening.

She had rounded on Ben. "You're my dad?"

Ben stood there, let out a breath.

Then he nodded.

Silence thundered as Kacey watched Audrey's reaction. Then her eyes filled, her jaw tightened. "You lied to me. You both *lied* to me." She turned to her mother. "How long have you known?"

Kacey didn't quite know how to answer that. "All your life?"

"Yeah, right—all my life. You knew that Benjamin King was my father. And yet you acted like he'd abandoned us—me. Like he didn't want me."

"No . . ." Kacey started toward her but Audrey held up her guitar as if it were a weapon.

"Of course I wanted you," Ben said. "I just didn't know—listen, it's complicated. And we'll tell you everything, I promise, but—"

"I don't want to hear it. I don't want to know. You lied to me for two weeks, acted like you were my friend, when all this time . . . What, were you trying to figure out if I was good enough to be your daughter?" She looked at the guitar then, and Kacey could almost see it in her eyes.

She flung the instrument at Ben. He barely caught it as it hit the floor, banging, issuing a sound of discord.

"I don't want your stupid guitar. And I don't want you." Then she turned to Kacey. "How could you do this to me? I wish you'd never come back!"

Then she stormed back outside, slamming the door. It banged on the sill.

"Audrey!" Kacey started after her, but Ben grabbed her arm.

"I'll go."

But she shrugged him away, shaking. "Listen, I know you didn't mean for her to find out this way—but this is *exactly* what I meant. Stay away, Ben. Before you make it worse. I'm her mother. I'll fix this."

Her words turned to poison in her mouth, but she followed her daughter outside.

Audrey wasn't there.

In the driveway, her Escape fired up. She ran to the edge of the deck in time for her to watch Audrey peel out, dirt scattering as she hit the road.

"Yep, she's definitely your and Ben's daughter," Sam said, coming to stand beside her. "Does she have a permit?"

She held out her hand, and he handed her his keys.

"Stay away, Ben. Before you make it worse."

Ben came out on the deck on Kacey's heels, the words like fire in his brain.

"I'm her mother. I'll fix this."

Yeah, well, he was her *father*. And he wasn't going to let his daughter drive away upset.

"Kacey." He didn't know how many of the team had heard Audrey, but he didn't care.

Enough secrets.

But Kacey had jumped off the porch and was headed for Sam's truck without a backward glance.

He rounded on Sam. "Really?"

"I'll call the station, get someone to intercept her. But I know Kacey as well as you do—she would have wrestled keys from someone. That or taken the chopper."

Ben jumped off the deck, running after her. "Kacey!"

But she was ignoring him as she gunned the truck.

Down the road, Audrey had already kicked up enough dust to obscure her exit.

Nice.

He dug into his pocket, found his keys, headed to his truck.

"Ben!"

Pete's voice caught him, turned him around. He had come off the deck, running at a fast clip toward him. "Don't go."

"Listen, this is my mess—"

"I think your dad is having a heart attack."

Pete's words landed a half second before he turned, raced back to the house.

Chet was hunched over in his chair, one hand across his chest. "I'm fine." But his voice emerged strained, and he groaned at the end.

For a second, the physical therapist's words flashed in Ben's head. *"He also has a higher risk of heart failure, as well as blood clots . . ."*

"Get him in the house." This from Jess, who turned to Gage. "Get me the portable oxygen unit from the rig."

Gage took off across the yard toward the barn while Pete and Sam maneuvered Chet toward the house.

"I'm fine." But his voice rasped with pain.

"You're not fine, Dad," Ben said, holding the door open.

"I'll call for an ambulance," Sam said as he pulled out his cell phone.

Ben grabbed his father around the shoulders, easing him up, and to his shock, Chet held on to him, let him lower him onto the sofa.

Jess knelt beside him, leaned him back onto a pillow. Gage came in, holding the portable tank. He pulled the plastic off the mask, handed it to Jess, who affixed it over his face.

"Just breathe, Chet."

His father's face tightened.

Sierra appeared with the first responder kit, and Jess opened it, dug out the stethoscope.

Ben stepped back, arms crossed, thunder in his ears as Jess listened to the heart.

She shook her head. "There's no arrhythmia. Let me get his blood pressure."

She wrapped the cuff around his arm, pumped it up.

Sam came through the door. "Ambulance is on its way."

"I told you I'm—"

"Stop talking, Dad," Ben said.

Chet looked at him.

Ben met his gaze. "Let us help you."

Chet drew in a breath, closed his eyes.

Behind him, Gage was raising Chet's feet onto a pillow and covering him with a blanket.

Ben went to stand on the porch and wait for the ambulance. Sam came out beside him. "He's going to be okay. It could be angina, but we have to treat it like an AMI."

"I know." He pulled out his phone, debating a call to Kacey. Put it back. "I should have never come home. He doesn't need me—he has you all. And I just made everything a mess with Kacey. And Audrey."

"What are you talking about? Of course you're needed here. Your dad needs you, even if he can't say it. We can't get him to shut up about you. And Kacey—well, she needs you, too, even if she says otherwise."

Ben shook his head. "No, she doesn't. I've never met a more capable person in my entire life. Everybody tells the story of how we rescued that hiker on the McDonald Loop—but it was Kacey. She kept him calm, stayed awake the entire night watching him. It didn't surprise me at all that she'd earned a bronze star—she always knows what to do. But me, I just keep screwing things up. Kacey, my career, my dad—I don't know why, but I just kept thinking that if I made something out of myself, I could prove to them all that I wasn't—"

"The preacher's kid who got his girlfriend pregnant?"

Ben looked at Sam, who raised an eyebrow. "Well, yeah, not to put too fine a point on it."

In the distance, he could hear the ambulance whining.

"You know why I wasn't there the night Audrey was born?"

"Yeah. You got in a fight with Cash Murdock. Who, by the way, is doing a nickel in Crossroads for possession."

"Mmmhmm. But the *reason* I got in a fight with him."

"Didn't he spray-paint a word on Kacey's car that, well, pretty much labeled her as some-one who played fast and easy with her virtue?

By my vote, he deserved that broken nose."

"He did, but I was the one who . . . Judge Fairing was right to tell me I had no business proposing. I had nothing to give her, I was just this kid who thought too much of himself."

"Aren't we all at that age?"

"Yeah. But the problem was, I didn't go after Cash for Kacey. I said I did, but it was because of the boots."

"The boots?"

"When I was ten, Murdock's had a pair of boots in the window for Christmas, and I wanted them. They were buckaroos—remember them? Taller shafts? And these were black and about a hundred dollars, so I knew it was a long shot, but I begged my parents for those boots. My dad wasn't a Christmas gift guy, see. He'd rather go out on Christmas Day and treat all the veterans to a turkey dinner, or maybe make food baskets for the hippies out at the artists community. There were years when I got nothing but a pair of socks, fresh underwear, and maybe a chocolate Santa under our little fake tree."

He glanced at Sam. "But that's the thing. Christmas Day came, and I couldn't believe it when I found boots under the tree. They weren't quite the same, but they were shiny, if not a little worn. They had the same black leather—buckaroos. I was in love. Until, that is, I went to school."

He could see the shiny lights of the ambulance

glinting against the sunshine as the rig barreled down the highway to the turnoff.

"Cash wore the same pair of boots to school—except his were definitely new. And worse, he took one look at mine and told me that they'd been his, and his parents had donated them to the Goodwill. He even proved it—he'd carved his initials into the boot heel. I was mortified—and angry. At my parents for embarrassing me, and at myself. I should have never wished for something so expensive. I was so ashamed."

"And knowing Cash, he made fun of you wearing secondhand castoffs. Which is why, when he spray-painted words on Kacey's car . . ."

"I thought I was protecting her honor. But her father pointed out, rightly, that I was just protecting my pride."

"If you feel any better, I was on board with the whole thing that night."

"I know. But you weren't the one who ended up in jail, staring at your sins. Ashamed again."

"I was faster." Sam grinned. "But I also had a good reason not to get caught. My mom couldn't take any more stress in her life."

"Yeah, well, no matter what I do, I can't seem to get it right. I thought maybe I could be someone my dad could be proud of. Someone Kacey might be impressed by."

Sam shoved his hands into his pockets. "What you have, and who you impress, does not make you who you are. And the crazy part is you taught me that. You gave up a football scholarship to play music. Nuts, right?"

Ben didn't correct him, but he'd given up his scholarship because of Kacey.

Because he'd wanted, more than anything, to be the guy who did something right.

The ambulance turned into the drive, and Sam stepped off the porch to meet them.

Ben headed back into the house. His dad lay on the sofa, eyes closed, Jess holding his hand, the team huddled around him. Miles and Kelli were packing up the ribs, Sierra supervising.

"We're going to the hospital with him," Sierra said as she came up to Ben and put her arm around him. "He's going to be okay."

The EMTs—a man and a woman he didn't recognize—came in carrying a stretcher. They took Chet's vitals, asked the pertinent questions, then put him on a stretcher and called it in.

They started to wheel him out, but Chet reached out, as if for Ben's hand.

He caught it, walked beside him, his throat tight. *Please, God.* He wasn't ready to say good-bye.

"I'll be right behind you, Dad."

Sam came up beside him, held out his hand. "I'm driving."

Ben pulled out his keys and got in the truck. "Keep up, Sam."

– 14 –

Kacey simply had to think like an angry teenager.

How had Audrey gotten so far ahead of her? By the time she hit the main road, her daughter had vanished. She only hoped she'd been heading to Mercy Falls. Kacey sat at the stoplight on Main Street, trying to decide if she should turn right, toward the road that led to the old river bridge.

Maybe her daughter had remembered an old story she'd told about her father, decided to visit the past in the hope of finding answers. Granted, she hadn't exactly been forthcoming with names and details, but had told her enough to spark her imagination.

Or she might have gone to Sierra's, although Kacey had driven past the old house, found the driveway empty.

She'd also searched the Last Chance coffee shop, the library, the bakery, and called home.

Her mother, of course, asked too many questions, and Kacey had to hang up without an explanation.

The last thing she needed was judgment from her parents about how she'd handled this way-too-delicate news.

"How could you do this to me? I wish you'd never come back!"

Kacey ran a hand under her chin, swiping at the moisture there, and took a right. The road took her past Mercy Falls Community Church, and the sight of the church stirred up memories of their youth.

S'mores and hiking with the youth group. Listening to Ben play his guitar on her front porch. Cheering for him as he threw touchdowns.

Agreeing to marry him, to love him forever.

"We belong together, you and me . . . and Audrey."

She *could* live without him. Kacey touched her lips, hating that she'd let him pull her close, that she'd kissed him back with so much—too much—desperation.

She stopped at the four-way stop. *Ben, I don't need you anymore. You're free to go. We'll be fine.*

Another swipe across her chin. Yeah, *sure* they'd be fine.

She went through the stop, traveled down another block, and spotted her old house, a colonial revival home, in faded red brick, with the rounded covered entry porch. It sat back from the sidewalk in a grand landscaped yard, slightly raised from the level of the street.

She stared at her room, the end window, and for a moment saw Ben standing below, calling up to her.

"He's been your everything since you were thirteen. You've just been living in denial for so long you think you can live without him."

She shook her head as she drove past the house.

When she'd been thirteen, distraught and angry, the first person she'd run to had been Ben.

She pulled over, found her phone.

She noticed the four texts Ben had sent, the three missed calls. She ignored them and dialed Willow's number.

"Hey—"

"Willow. Where does Nate live?"

Ten minutes later she rolled up to Nate's parents' ranch house, located a few streets over and across from the football field of Mercy Falls High.

She couldn't escape memories of Ben, no matter which road she took in this town.

Her Escape sat at the curb. She spotted Audrey in the driver's seat, her hands over her face.

Nate sat in the passenger seat, worry in his expression.

The scene felt so familiar, Kacey just sat there.

I can't believe they lied to me all these years.

Her words, to Ben. And, she had no doubt, her daughter's words to Nate.

She got out, walked across the street.

By this time, Nate had alerted Audrey to her mother's presence. Kacey tapped on the window.

Audrey didn't move, but Nate leaned over her, rolled the window down. "Hello, ma'am," he said. "Uh, Audrey is pretty upset."

"Thank you, Nate. I think we need to talk, don't you, Audrey?"

Audrey lifted a shoulder.

Kacey looked at Nate, who gave her a grim nod and reached for the door handle.

Audrey put a hand on his arm to stop him. "Don't go."

But he put his hand on hers. "I'll be in the house if you need me. But it's your mom, Audrey."

Okay, now Kacey liked him, just a little. Nate got out, gave her a look she couldn't read, then headed for the house.

Kacey put her hand on the driver's window. "Why don't you let me drive? I want to show you something."

Audrey sighed but got out, left the keys in the ignition, then walked around the car.

Sat down, turned herself away from Kacey.

Kacey drove without words, retracing her route back to Main Street, then over the bridge and out of town toward the old river bridge.

Maybe her daughter needed a glimpse of the past.

"I'm not going to say anything about driving without a permit, especially in front of Sam Brooks."

Audrey lifted a shoulder. "Let him arrest me."

Oh, this would be fun.

"You know, just for the record, Ben wanted to tell you right away. It was me who held him back. So your theory that he wanted to see if you were worth him claiming you as his daughter is wrong. He was thrilled to find out he was your dad."

Audrey shot Kacey a look. "Find out?"

Kacey nodded, turning off onto the dirt road. "He thought I'd given you up for adoption."

"I wish you had," she said. "Then at least I'd have a father and a mother, a normal home."

And *that* didn't hurt. "You do have a father and a mother," Kacey said. "And grandparents who love you."

Audrey lifted a shoulder again.

"And a great life, by the way. Safe, provided for."

Audrey looked out the window. "Don't forget abandoned and lied to."

Kacey tapped her brakes as she pulled up to the bridge. She shoved the gear into park. "That's enough, Audrey. I know you're angry, but you don't know what you're talking about."

"Then why don't you fill me in!" Tears filmed her reddened eyes.

"Fine. Get out."

Audrey's eyes widened.

Kacey's voice gentled. "I want to show you something."

An old one-lane car bridge spanned a narrow

in the river. The forty-foot drop was just high enough to take Kacey's breath away when she'd jumped, back in her youth.

And, of course, under the starlight, it had become a different kind of bridge, between innocence and adulthood.

"What is this place?"

"It's the bridge your father used to take me to when we'd go stargazing." She stopped in the middle, stared down at the river, blue, cool, refreshing. "It's where we fell in love, where he asked me to marry him."

"Why *didn't* you marry him?"

Audrey had settled beside her, not too close.

"I said yes. And I wanted to. Then the night you were born, he got into a fight and was sitting in jail, and I was so angry that he didn't show up for your birth that I refused his phone calls. So he left town. I didn't know that . . ." She cleared her throat. She didn't want to destroy her daughter's relationship with her grandfather. "That Ben thought I'd given you up for adoption. I thought he'd abandoned me."

"He did," Audrey said, her voice sharp, on the edge of tears.

"No, baby, he didn't. He tried to call me, but I wouldn't talk to him. When he left town, he thought you were gone. And when he found out I'd kept you, he was distraught that he'd lost all those years with you."

Audrey rounded on her. "Then why didn't you let him tell me?"

Kacey swallowed. "Because I was afraid what it would do to you to find out."

Audrey frowned.

"He's a big country music star now, and he has a life in Nashville, honey. One we're not a part of. And I knew he'd go back to that, and I feared it would break your heart."

Audrey's mouth quivered. "I'm not a baby."

Okay, she could do this. "I know. But I remember what it felt like to be rejected, to be lied to . . ."

Audrey stared at her, shook her head.

Kacey turned back to the river, translucent to the stony depths below. Took a long breath. "Grandma and Grandpa are not my real parents. They're my adoptive parents." She glanced at Audrey. "My mom, Laura, is actually my aunt. My real mom died when I was thirteen . . . in prison."

Some of the hardness in Audrey's face softened.

"I'm not sure they would have ever told me, really. But I got a letter when I was thirteen from the Montana Women's Prison in Billings, where my birth mother was serving time for killing my father. I don't know how or why—I never wanted to know—but she was dying of cancer and wanted to see me. I was three when she committed the crime, so I didn't remember her at all—but my mother decided that I should see her. Probably compassion on her part for her sister, but it destroyed me. Suddenly I wasn't the daughter of Judge Fairing and his pretty wife but the offspring of this thin, bitter prisoner who had no hair."

She had lost herself in the telling, remembering standing there at the bed in the hospital ward of the prison, the odor of sickness and regret swilling the air, the sickly yellow skin and sallow face of a woman who'd made one too many mistakes. "The worst part was that they let us into the hospital ward. She took my hand and told me I had her eyes. And maybe I did, but in that moment, I only heard a prophecy that I was going to end up just like her."

She blew out a breath. "Audrey, I made big mistakes, I know that. I should have told you about your dad the minute he came back. I'm so sorry for hurting you." She wanted to reach out to her, take her daughter's hand.

Audrey did it for her. "Mom, I didn't mean it when I said I wanted you to go back to Florida. I just . . . sometimes I want it so bad, it hurts. And then suddenly, I saw it, right there, and it scared me."

"Want *what* so bad?"

"A family. You, here. And a dad. And our own house, like what Nate has. Maybe even a brother or sister." She gave a shaky smile. "I even thought, well . . . I thought maybe Benjamin King would fall in love with you."

Kacey gave her a small smile. "Why did it scare you?"

"I don't know. I guess I just thought that it would never happen. And it was wrong to want it so much, because you're right. I *do* have a good life. And it felt wrong to wish for more."

Kacey touched her cheek. "You deserve it all, honey. All the good that life has to give you."

"So do you, Mom." A smile tweaked up her face, mischief in her eyes. "Were you really kissing him? 'Cause it looked like it when I walked in."

Kacey's face heated. "Yeah."

"You still love him, don't you?"

She looked at her daughter's hands holding hers. Sighed. "I do. But . . . that's the thing, honey. Ben's life is different now. He is—"

"I know. A big country star. But he's also my dad. And I don't care if I can't see him very much. I can see him now. And maybe . . . maybe he'll come back sometimes?"

So much vulnerability on her face. Kacey reached out, pulled her close. Audrey's arms went around her, and she tucked her head against Kacey's chest. "I think he would like to, if you say it's okay."

Audrey nodded. "It's okay." Then she leaned back. "Do you think he'd stay if we asked him to?"

Her heart fell for her beautiful daughter, so

much hope in her voice. "We can't ask him to do that, Audrey. It's not fair. He's worked so hard for his career—and it's at a pivotal place right now. He needs to be in Nashville, and on tour with—"

"I don't like Hollie Montgomery. She's not very nice. You should see her tweets. She sometimes calls Benjamin 'the geezer.'"

"The . . . *geezer?*"

"Yeah, like he's old or something." She reached into her pocket, pulled out her phone, thumbed open her Twitter account. "See?"

Geezer and I are writing a new song—here's a clip! #holliemontgomery

The post linked to a video, and Audrey opened it.

A home video, grainy, hard to see, but Kacey immediately recognized the voice, the tune, if not the words.

Turn around, listen to your heart
I need you so much, don't tear me apart

No. He did *not.* She schooled her voice, her throat tight. "That's enough, honey."

Audrey turned it off. "She's not a nice person, even if she did give me a present."

"I know."

Ben certainly hadn't given Hollie his—their— song, right? *"It's what sells, Kacey."*

"Do you think he's still at the ranch?"

She nodded. "Could be." She pulled out her phone, thumbed open the texts. They all said the same thing.

Are you okay? I'm so sorry. Call me if you need me.

Maybe.

We belong together, you and me and Audrey. She is my daughter, and I love her. And I want to be in your lives.

She pressed dial and put the phone to her ear, running a hand down her daughter's hair. The phone rang, then again.

Then someone picked up. She heard the fumbling. "Ben? It's Kacey."

"Oh, hi, Kacey."

Not Ben. A female voice, and Kacey froze. "Who is this?"

"It's Hollie. Are you looking for Ben?"

A retort found her lips, and she bit it back. "Is he there?"

"Sorry, he's not available right now. Want me to have him call you back?"

Kacey was shaking her head even before she answered, managed to find her voice, something cool, stable.

Thank you, US Army. "No. Tell him that . . . nothing. It's okay."

She started to hang up, but Hollie stopped her. "Kacey, you should know something. I know you're in love with Ben, but he'll never love you as much as he loves his music. Trust me on this. I know."

Kacey said nothing.

"Are you there?"

She hung up, forced a smile for her daughter. "What?"

"I think Ben's a little busy right now. But we'll catch up with him later." She winked, despite the urge to cry, and remembered her words. *Stay away, Ben. Before you make it worse.*

Please, don't let him be obeying her. Not this time.

"Let's go back to Sierra's house. I think she has some more of that potato salad tucked away in her fridge."

Audrey turned on the radio when they got into the car, pulled out her phone, and connected it to the radio. And of course, pulled up a Benjamin King album.

Perfect.

Audrey's voice lifted in the cab.

I've spent so many nights wondering where you are
What you're doing, how I let you get so far

Are you dreaming of me, out on your own
Are you thinking of us, and our own song

Are you wondering if I miss you too
Are you hoping that I'm just as blue

Please, oh please, come home

She turned to Kacey. "Do you think he was thinking of you when he wrote that song?"

Kacey drummed her fingers on her steering wheel, tightened her jaw against a wave of pain. She would have liked to think that. "No, honey. It's just a song."

She parked her car in Sierra's empty gravel driveway. She got out and walked toward the house, the ground spongy under her feet.

"Hello?" She pushed open the door. The benefits of living in a small town—Sierra never locked her house.

In the kitchen, the refrigerator hummed against the silence.

Audrey pushed past her, to the kitchen. Opened the fridge door and pulled out the bowl of extra potato salad. Set it on the counter.

Kacey grabbed a couple spoons.

Outside, she heard the rumble of a backhoe, clearly repairing damage at one of the neighboring houses. A whine, breaking timber.

Suddenly the floor began to shake, the house rumbling. Kacey grabbed the counter, holding on, her hand reaching for Audrey.

"What—"

And then, the house gave a moan as the timbers overhead shifted and the walls began to tilt. "It's collapsing!"

Kacey grabbed her daughter, pulling her to herself as she lunged for the front door. The floor gave way beneath her, the joists ripping as the weight of the house bent under the torque.

Then she was falling back toward the kitchen, sliding under the table, Audrey in her arms. She grabbed for purchase—anything—but the floor opened up and they fell toward the dank, black depths of the basement.

She landed, hard, the breath whooshing out of her, pain splintering through her shoulder, her arm.

Audrey.

But her daughter had fallen out of her grip. She reached out, groping for her as the entire structure buckled, then crashed down over them.

"You can't make the world obey you."

Ian slammed his right fist into the heavy bag. The bag rebounded back at him, and he brought his fist back up, exhaling hard.

Sierra's words from yesterday still ricocheted through him.

He didn't expect the world to obey him. But maybe some acknowledgment that he was only trying to help.

He kept his feet moving, shuffling in, out around the back, his hands up. He threw another strike.

The bag jerked back, then swung toward him. He pivoted out of the way, shuffled around it, saw himself ordering Sierra from the house, and landed another punch.

The bag shuddered, came at him, and he jabbed three quick rights and a left, a power shot.

That was for the idiot he'd been when he'd told Esme that if she didn't want to make a mess out of her life, she'd dump Dante, take his offer for schooling, and stop being a fool.

Yeah, he'd been a real hero. No wonder she'd confided in Sierra and planned on running away without a word to him.

He followed the bag around, pummeled it on the backside, ending in a power shot that burned through his knuckles. He probably should have taped up, but frankly, too much tape meant he got sloppy, less technique, more adrenaline.

And he'd already lost his head enough over the past two weeks. In fact, ever since Sierra had told him that Esme had come to her with secrets, he'd felt his life unraveling.

Except for the days she'd come over, helped him sort through the names and numbers.

Helped him pick up the search, again. Not that he couldn't make a phone call—he'd somehow managed to get his calendar under control, talk with all his branches, even postpone the quarterly Shaw Holdings board meeting.

But having Sierra back in his living room,

looking at him with those eyes that told him everything would be okay . . .

He hit the bag again, then let it fall back and caught it, breathing hard.

He shouldn't have kissed her. That might be the worst part—remembering how she'd kissed him back, her arms around his neck, her perfect body against his, kissing him like he'd only dreamed of for the past five years.

Finally.

Until . . . *"You need to let this go."*

He'd spent the better part of today arguing with the Amtrak office, threatening, cajoling, and attempting to purchase the security footage that might give him a clue as to what train Esme might have taken.

And dissecting just why Sierra's words tore at him.

Maybe he didn't want to let it go—because he didn't want to let *her* go.

Ian walked away from the bag, sweat streaming down his chest, and picked up a water bottle.

"You can't make the world obey you." Maybe that was it—if she didn't have to search for Esme, there was nothing pulling her to him but . . . him. And he knew how that worked out.

Ian sprayed water into his mouth, then grabbed a towel and wrapped it around his neck, scrubbing it up into his hair, rubbing away the heat.

He glanced at the bag, debating another go.

At least it felt better than leaving another voicemail with Sheriff Blackburn asking about the coroner's report.

He was reaching for his free weights when the doorbell rang, a resonant boom through the house. He came down the hall in his bare feet and athletic shorts, the towel around his neck.

Sam Brooks stood on his doorstep.

"Please tell me you're here with a coroner's report."

Sam shook his head. "I just got back from the Kalispell hospital. Chet was having chest pains."

Ian pulled the towel off, wiped his face. "Oh no. Is it a heart attack?"

"They're still working that out, but I thought you should know."

Ian held the door open. "Come in."

Sam stepped inside, and Ian closed the door behind him and headed to the kitchen. "Want a drink?"

"Sure." He slid onto a high-top chair. "I thought Sheriff Blackburn called you about the coroner's report on Dante."

Ian grabbed two bottles of water and closed the fridge. "No."

"Hmm. Well, the results were inconclusive. Probably Dante drowned—but the coroner said he also suffered a skull fracture as well as a broken shoulder. Although that might have happened in the fall."

"And what about the other body—any identification?"

Sam shook his head. "But Blackburn is on duty today. Give him a call."

"I've called five times. He's probably avoiding me." He handed Sam a bottle, opened his. "I wish Sierra were here. She always had a way of making people talk."

Sam let one side of his mouth slide up. "She sounds like the KGB."

Given the secrets Ian had told her, she could be. "No, I just mean she could get things done."

Sam took a drink, then considered his bottle for a moment. "So, you two are . . . I mean, she's not working for you anymore, right?"

Ian had thrown his shirt over a chair when he'd gone to work out, and now retrieved it. "No."

"And so you're not . . . I mean, there wasn't anything between you two, right?"

Ian turned, looked at him. "Why? Did she say something?" He felt a fresh heat curl through him, the memory of her in his arms suddenly bold in his mind.

"No. But sometimes, well, I thought maybe you sort of liked her."

Ian pulled on the shirt. "No. We're just . . . no."

Sam stared at him, his expression enigmatic. "Okay. So you don't mind if I ask her out, right?"

Ian tried not to stiffen, to keep his voice casual. "Sure. Why not?"

More silence then. "Okay. Good. I just wanted to make sure I wasn't overstepping."

"Nothing to overstep." Ian took a long drink of his water, tried not to let it choke him. Cleared his throat. "She's a great gal." Normal voice, and he managed a smile.

"I agree. I've known her almost my entire life, but something about her—ever since she started working at PEAK. She's just always so cheerful, and she has the most amazing hazel-green eyes."

"Blue. Her eyes are more hazel-blue than green."

"It depends on the light, maybe."

Ian finished off his drink, crushed the bottle in his fist. Refused the urge to argue.

"She's had a rough go of it, with her mother," Sam said. "She practically raised Willow on her own. And then she dated Rhett Thomas for a long time."

"The hockey player? For the Minnesota Blue Ox?" How did Ian not know that?

"Yeah. They dated four years—and then he left for Minnesota and got engaged three months later to one of the cheerleaders on the ice crew. Sierra took it pretty hard. The worst part is that they were engaged for three of those four years. I think he was just trying to hang on to her. But he took four years from her that she can't get back."

Ian stared at him, hoping he hadn't flinched at Sam's words.

"She's always been an amazing godmother to Audrey, Kacey's kid. She'd make a great mom."

"Sam, you haven't even asked her out yet, and you have a ring on her finger?" Ian didn't mean for his voice to emerge quite so brusque.

"No, dude. I'm just saying that she'd be a great catch. And maybe I'm the one to catch her."

He didn't mean it in such a way that Ian should want to hit him.

Except, he did.

Sam finished off his water, handed the bottle to Ian. "Thanks." He slid off his chair.

And something like panic flamed in Ian's chest —a sense of losing something he might never get back.

Yeah, I mind. The words formed in his head. *I want to date Sierra.*

He opened the recycle bin, dropped the bottle in.

Sam headed toward the door.

"Sam."

He turned. "Yeah?"

Ian came around the counter, trying to find the words. "About Sierra."

On his belt, Sam's cell phone buzzed. He answered it. Listened. "Oh no. Was there anyone inside?"

Sam shot a glance at Ian, and he didn't know why, but his gut tightened at Sam's expression.

"Okay, I'm on my way." He hung up, his jaw tight as he looked at Ian.

"What?"

"That was dispatch. Another house collapsed in Mercy Falls." He swallowed. "It was Sierra's."

"And was there someone inside?"

Sam hadn't finished nodding before Ian swept up his shoes and headed out the door.

"So he's not having a heart attack." Ben stood at the desk, down the hall from his father's ER cubicle, trying to tamp down his own heart attack after two hours of pacing, panic, and not a little frustration at his own helplessness.

It hadn't helped that Kacey hadn't answered one of his texts or returned his calls.

He'd left the team in the waiting room when the ER doctor pulled him aside. He should probably update them.

Although, frankly, the doctor should have probably talked to Pete or Jess. After all, it seemed they knew his father better than he did.

"No. Your father's EKG came back normal. But you need to follow up with his primary care doctor to see if he'd like to run a stress test."

"So I can take him home."

"We just need his discharge paperwork."

He was nodding when he spotted her. Oh, for crying out loud. "Hollie, what are you doing here?"

She wore a pair of cowboy boots, a ripped sweatshirt falling down one shoulder, a glittery baseball cap, and leggings that outlined her petite frame. "You left this in the waiting room."

She held up his phone, and he took it, pocketed it. "You didn't answer my question."

"I stopped by the ranch. I wanted to talk to you. A nice woman named Kelli sent me here. Is your dad okay?"

"He's fine."

"Oh, that's good. I was so worried."

He frowned but let the words bounce off him. "Thanks. I gotta—"

Her hand on his arm stopped him. "I came to see if you were okay after last night. You seemed so upset."

Really? "I'm fine."

"Because I love that song you were working on before the concert. I took some video of you playing it and posted it on Twitter. It's already trending."

He stared at her. "What?"

"It's a good song, Benji." She broke into a hum. "Hollie—"

"Just come back home, Ben. We'll go back in the studio, make that music magic we do."

"I gotta check my dad out of the hospital." He pushed past her, toward his father's cubicle.

But Hollie's voice trailed after him, lifted to carry down the hall. "She doesn't want you, Ben."

He stilled.

Turned.

Hollie shrugged. "I'm sorry. She called while

you were in there. And she said that she didn't want you to call her."

He stared at her, searching for venom in her tone, her expression. She just gave him a sad smile. "Sorry. I really am."

"I have to get my dad home."

"Our flight doesn't leave until later tonight. I have a ticket for you." She shrugged, a sudden vulnerability in her expression he hadn't expected.

It reminded him of their early days, when she hung on his every word, when he'd thought they might be a real duo, partners.

"Just in case you want to make great music," she finished.

He headed to his father's cubicle.

Chet sat on the table, already wearing his clothing. "I told you it was just the barbecue."

"Dad, don't. You really scared us."

Chet nodded. "Sorry. I guess I scared myself a little." He winked. "Thanks for sticking around."

"Are you kidding? Dad, c'mon. I'm not leaving you. But you need to take better care of yourself. This might have been a shot across the bow."

"I know."

He did? Ben expected a fight, but the old man gave him a crooked smile.

"Edamame and quinoa for me."

It took a second, but Ben let out a laugh. "Okay, Dad. Let's find you a wheelchair. The team is waiting to take you home."

"Good. Then let them. You go find Kacey."

"No. Kacey was right. I just made it worse. And now she doesn't want me around."

"So? You're Audrey's father."

"I haven't been her father for thirteen years. So why do I think I have the right to be now?"

"And that's your problem, son. You've let shame tell you how to run your life. You have since the day Cash Murdock made fun of your boots."

"You knew about that?"

"Of course I did. I'm your dad. And I was proud of you that I didn't have to pick you up from the principal's office. You turned the other cheek."

"Until I didn't."

Chet frowned. "You were young, Ben. And angry. And, frankly, afraid."

Ben flinched at that.

"Stop blaming yourself. You were barely eighteen. And Judge Fairing made it very easy for you to walk away. And you let shame tell you that you should. Shame is a powerful voice." His voice softened, and he looked away. "I know. Because I'm ashamed that I failed you."

What? "Dad, how did you possibly fail me?"

Chet looked away, and the fluorescent lights turned him thin, old. "Because you've lost so much of yourself, and I did nothing to stop it."

Oh. "Dad, if you're talking about my career choices, they aren't your fault."

"Yes, they are." He looked at Ben, his jaw tight. "Maybe not all of them, but I've had thirteen years to figure this out. You needed me, and I wasn't there for you."

"What are you talking about?"

His father's barrel chest rose and fell. "You called Judge Fairing that night you landed in jail instead of me. And I knew it was because you thought I'd be disappointed in you."

"I . . . you always said it wasn't worth fighting over. And in retrospect, it probably wasn't."

His father shook his head. "I should have been the one you called. Instead of thinking you disappointed me, you should have trusted in my love for you. That I would be on your side."

"I didn't blame you, Dad. I did something wrong —I didn't expect you to come to my rescue."

"But you *should* have expected that. I'm your father—and regardless of whether I agreed with you or not, my love for you doesn't change. But you thought it did, and for that I am ashamed. I should have stood beside you. I knew Kacey better, and I should have said that I didn't think she'd give up her baby for adoption. But I was also embarrassed in front of our town, and let that shame rule my decisions. I admit I wanted you to leave, and for that . . . I'm so sorry, Ben."

A fist had tightened in Ben's chest.

Chet managed a tight, small smile. "You're

not the only one longing to fix your mistakes."

Ben looked away, eyes burning.

"When you came home that summer, I thought you'd stay. I admit it—you started working on the SAR team, and suddenly I had this chance to fix everything. I thought maybe we could just forget what happened, start over. But then I realized you'd come home for Kacey, and it would only tear you apart to stay. Your mom thought maybe it would be better for you in Nashville."

"She's the one who told me to go back. I really wanted to make her proud."

"She had all your albums, Ben. She loved them."

Ben blinked, nonplussed.

"Even . . . the last one?"

"She knew your heart, your mom did." His voice fell. "There's no pressure to stay, Ben. But don't leave because you think you're not wanted here. And don't let shame drive you away. Or tell you that you can't be a dad to this little girl who needs you."

"She doesn't need me, Dad."

"All children need their dads, Ben. It doesn't matter how old they are."

Ah, shoot, he was right. Because Ben just stood there, longing like a stupid kid to fall into his father's embrace.

As if his father knew, Chet shot him a sideways look. Ben met it, nodded.

Then Ben said softly, "I have no idea how to

be a dad to Audrey. I see her with Kacey, and she just . . . she just knows what to do."

"I saw you today, teaching her how to play the guitar."

"That was ten minutes. That's not the rest of her life."

"You don't have to figure it out today. You just have to start. Like physical therapy, right? Progress, one day at time, leaning on God for the steps, the strength, the healing."

And, of course, it came right back to God. "Dad, why would God help me? I got myself into this mess. He's not going to get me out of it."

"Ben. That's *exactly* what God is going to do. That's what he means when he calls himself the Good Shepherd. He restores your soul, gives you new strength, and then he leads you in the right direction. And it has nothing to do with whether you've made a mess out of your life. He is the Good Shepherd for all the sheep who call his name—whether you're a white sheep or a black one."

Ben closed his eyes.

"So, son, you have a choice. You can keep trying to fix this on your own, or you can give your trust —your heart—to God. Every day, one day at a time. And don't let your mistakes tell you that God isn't for you, that he won't help you fix them."

He slid off the table, used it to balance himself, and put one hand on Ben's shoulder. "How about this—let's not let our past determine whether God loves us or not. He does. And we'll never get it right without him."

Ben swallowed, wanting to believe him.

His father suddenly pulled him to himself, holding him. "I love you, son. And I'm so proud of you."

Ben closed his eyes, letting the words find root. "I'm so sorry, Dad. For everything. I embarrassed you and I cost Mom her grand-child, and I just want to do this right."

Chet didn't let him go. "You will, Ben. Because it's time to come home. Because you finished your song, right?"

Ben leaned back, met his dad's eyes. "You heard me on the deck last night."

Chet nodded. "I forgot how much I love listening to you sing."

Before he did something embarrassing like burst into tears, Ben ducked his head out of the cubicle, spied the orderly with the wheelchair. "Over here."

He saw Pete, Jess, and Gage sneaking in behind the orderly.

"He's good to go."

Thankfully, no sign of Hollie.

His dad shrugged off his help getting into the chair. But he grinned up at Ben, winked.

He held up his hands in surrender as the orderly wheeled him out.

Pete had run ahead and now pulled up his F-150.

He came around to help, but Chet was climbing into the cab on his own. Pete had brought his crutches from the house and now threw them into the back.

"I'll catch a ride with Gage," Sierra said. Gage was twirling the keys to his Mustang around his index finger.

"Ty also drove," Jess said, nodding toward Ty's Silverado. "I'm sure he has room."

"Wait, guys—"

This from Pete, who held his phone up to his ear. "Hey, Sam . . . Yeah, I got your text, what's up?"

He looked at Sierra, then Ben. "She's here . . . No, I don't think Ben tracked them down yet, why?"

Ben looked at him, and Pete's face seemed to lose a shade. He swallowed. "I don't know." He looked at Ben. "What kind of car does Kacey drive?"

"A silver Ford Escape."

"Yeah, that's hers," Pete said solemnly. "Yeah, we'll be right there. You want us to stop by HQ—right. Okay." He paused again. "I'll tell him."

He hung up, and a hush hung over the group. Pete looked at Sierra, his face tight. "Your house collapsed."

Sierra stared at him. "What?"

"And . . ." He swallowed. "They think Kacey and Audrey are inside."

Ben couldn't breathe.

No . . .

A hand tightened around his arm.

"Get in, son," Chet said, scooting over. He glanced at Pete already moving to the driver's side. "We're on our way."

— 15 —

"C'mon, Kacey, pick up." Ben listened to her voicemail message, wincing, then hung up, fighting the urge to throw the phone.

Beside him, his father braced his hand on the dashboard as Pete cut down Main Street, then turned left onto Sierra's road.

The flashing lights of a police cruiser splashed red over the debris pile that once formed Sierra's house. Ben spotted a couple figures in the yard—recognized Sam, out of uniform, and Ian Shaw, and even Sheriff Blackburn and Miles, just getting out of his truck.

From this vantage point, it seemed the house had collapsed in on itself, simply folding in, one wall falling, then the other, the roof settling on top. Electrical wires dangled from the overhead poles, snapping.

And sure enough, Kacey's Escape sat in the dirt driveway.

His father was speaking. "Ben, trust my team.

They know what they're doing. Wait for us to assess—"

But Ben had the door open before Pete pulled up to the curb. Gage's Mustang slid in behind his.

Ben ran across the lawn toward the house. "Kacey!"

Sam intercepted him, hands to his shoulders. "Stay back, buddy. We got a call in to the electric company—they're turning off the electricity." He pointed to a couple live wires dangling dangerously near the soggy ground.

Ben shucked him off. "She's in there, Sam, I just know it."

"My house!"

Sierra had arrived on the scene, now stood with her hands over her mouth. Jess came up, put her arm around her. "It'll be okay."

"Are they in there?"

"We don't know," Sam said. "But we think so."

"We thought it was you," a voice said. Sierra looked past him, and Ben followed her gaze to Ian Shaw, who was staring at her with a raw, almost palpable, relief on his face.

"It's not me, okay? It's my best friend and her daughter! And we have to do something!"

Ben's exact thoughts. "Somebody turn off that electricity!"

As if on command, a voice came through Sam's handheld, confirming his request. He swiped it off his belt, asked the ETA of the volunteer fire department, his hand going back to brace against Ben's chest. "What do you mean, they're on a call? Then call Kalispell! Or Whitefish."

Ben pushed Sam's grip away, advanced on the house.

He didn't know where to start. The cement steps suggested where the front door had once stood, but from there, the house flattened. The dormer windows were still intact and sitting atop the rubble of the roof. Underneath, the walls stacked like pancakes, the windows shattered, two-by-fours and plywood protruding like matchsticks.

Shadows pressed into the crannies, recesses where she might be trapped, deepening under the twilight descending into the valley.

He crouched in front of a space between foundation and collapsed roof. "Kacey! Can you hear me?"

He closed his eyes, listening. Heard only the terrible thunder of his heartbeat.

"We need a layout of the original structure," Miles said as he stood beside Sam. "So we can figure out how this fell, where there might be natural voids where she might be trapped."

"Audrey's in there too," Ben said in a choked whisper.

Please, God.

He got up, turned to Sam. "We've got to get in there!"

His father had gotten out of the cab, and now Chet stood, balanced on crutches with Sam and Miles, watching Sierra draw a map of her house on the back of a napkin someone had fished out of their car.

He joined them.

"It's a small house—the kitchen is here, and across from that, the family room. A bathroom in the back. Two bedrooms upstairs. And a basement."

"What kind of basement?" This from Pete, who stood next to Sam, hands on his hips.

"It's a dirt basement. And it's been wet since the flood."

Ian hovered over the group. "Your deck washed away?"

She nodded. "The mess is in the backyard. I haven't had a chance to clean it up. It's a swamp back there."

Ian pointed to the drawing. "If the water collected here, around the foundation, the house could have collapsed at this point, near the kitchen." He held up his hands, demonstrating. "The foundation wall drops, and the floorboards buckle. The opposite wall caves in as the floor opens up, and then the roof collapses in on top."

"These old houses are balloon-framed," Pete said. "Which means if the wall torques, it'll rip off the ledger board, which is just nailed on, and the entire floor will collapse, in pieces."

"Which makes the debris pile highly unstable," Ian finished. "We go in there blind, start moving things, the house could collapse further into any void they might be in."

Ben thought he might be ill. He turned back to the house, breathing hard. "We don't have time for this! We can't just disassemble the house like Legos—we have to get in there."

A hand pressed on his shoulder. "Ben, take a breath. If we want to do this right, without costing lives, we have to do it smart. My team knows what they're doing. Now you have to start trusting God."

Ben walked away from his father's grip, his jaw tight.

"I'm not sure, but there might be a natural void here, along the wall where it first collapsed," Pete was saying, forming a visual with his hands. "As the floor fell, it's possible the wall came in on top, creating a pocket."

Ian was staring at the house. "Sierra, was your second floor an attic with knee walls or a full second floor?"

"The attic. We finished it ourselves." She had a hitch to her voice, her arms around her waist.

"Okay, then from my rough measurement, there is definitely a lean-to void in the basement area. Otherwise, the roofline would be further down," Ian said.

"What if we got a line around the top edge of

the roof, peeled it back," Pete said. "Then, at least, we'd have less pressure. And we could get a better look, maybe send someone in."

"Me. I'm going in," Ben said.

No one argued with him.

"Here comes Ty," Miles said, and Ben turned to see the Silverado pull up. Jess jumped out, then pulled gear from the bed. "I sent them by HQ to pick up equipment."

Jess came over, dropped a duffel at Miles's feet, breathing hard. "I didn't know what to grab, so we got everything—flashlights, ropes, helmets, uniforms, gloves, radios, the litter from the chopper —anything I could think of."

"Did you get a cable?" Miles asked.

"I have a lot of climbing rope."

"I'll get my truck," Pete said.

Sam was back on the radio, getting an update on the fire department.

Ian had walked over to stand by Sierra. Ben noticed how he put a hand on her shoulder.

She shrugged it away and walked over to Ben. "We'll get them out, Ben. Kacey's smart and tough. And she isn't going to let anything happen to Audrey."

In the distance, the finest whine of a siren haunted the dusk.

Ty and Gage began to loop rope around the far edge of the roof, back underneath, climbing onto the edge of the house. Miles shouted directions as Pete backed his truck into the yard.

Jess handed Ben a pair of overalls, a hard hat, gloves, and a harness. "We'll belay you in. In case something goes south, we can find you."

He couldn't think that far, to the what-if of something going "south."

It seemed south enough from his vantage point.

Gage and Ty looped the rope twice, secured it with a knot, and Pete attached it with tow strapping to his truck's hitch.

"Oh please, let's not make it worse," Jess said, also wearing her uniform and a helmet, the first responder bag at her feet.

Pete got in the truck. "I'm just going to ease it off at an angle," he said, putting the truck into drive. Miles gave him the go-ahead, watching the lines.

The truck chewed at the lawn, the tires scrabbling for purchase in the soft grass. The top layer of the roof began to move, sliding over the pile, toward the front lawn. Ty and Gage walked with it, easing it off, testing the rope. Wood splintered, groaned, and Ben felt the moan of it to his bones.

The bundle finally hit the grass, with the boards cracking and splintering. Pete nudged it further from the house, but it didn't want to give.

"Hold up!" Miles said, and Pete stopped.

The siren peaked and a fire engine came down the road.

Ben took a look at them, then turned and headed for the house.

"Ben, we need to get you geared up." Jess scrabbled behind him.

He ignored her, climbing over the debris to the front steps. Without the roof, the damage could be more easily assessed—good call, Ian and Pete. The walls had indeed pancaked in, but Sheetrock and flooring jutted up, as if propped by the interior walls below.

He dropped to his knees. "Kacey!"

He couldn't hear anything over the sirens and the sound of the truck pulling up.

He turned to Jess. "Hook me up. If I don't go in now, they won't let me go." He glanced behind him. "And I'm going to find her."

Jess clipped a carabiner onto his harness. "Just don't die in there."

He pulled down his eye protection, strapped his helmet under his chin, and flicked on the lights on his hard hat, the beam shining into the crannies of the house. The siren had died, and he heard shouting behind him telling him to wait.

He pointed to the cranny between the foundation and the collapsed outer wall. "I'm going in here." He moved a two-by-four, and the house creaked. But he leaned over the edge, found an opening between two ancient two-by-sixes. "Kacey!"

Nothing, and the rank smells of the ancient basement wafted up at him. He wedged himself into the pocket between wall and floor and climbed down, moving aside beams that crisscrossed his path. The light illuminated dangling electrical wires and crushed Sheetrock. He found a pocket under the kitchen table wedged against the kitchen counter, the electric stove on one side, propped against the wall, bracing the table. The table held up the fridge, which loomed above him like an anvil.

"Kacey!"

He listened, holding his breath. Then he heard what he thought might be a moan. "Kace—I'm here!"

He worked his way through the space under the table, found it blocked by the laminate flooring. The moaning seemed to emanate from the other side.

"Hold on, baby." He could turn around, and now looked up at Jess, some seven feet above. "I need a pry bar. I think she's under the floorboards here."

He lay at a slant, and he propped himself against the oven as he tried to find an opening in the floorboards.

"I'm right above you, Kacey. I'm coming down."

No more sounds, and he hoped he hadn't imagined it.

"Ben King, is that you?"

He looked up, didn't see the owner of the voice, but recognized it as Sheriff Blackburn.

"You need to come out of there and let the rescuers down there."

"I'm a rescuer. And I'm here to get my daughter —and my . . . the woman I love. So hand me down a pry bar or get out of here."

More voices, arguing, and Jess reappeared. "Pry bar coming down," she said as she leaned over and lowered it down on a rope.

He caught it, untied it. Outside, the sun had set, and only the glow of his head lamp lit the boards as he pried up the laminate flooring. It came off in a sheet, and he shoved it into a recess, then wedged the bar in between the floor joists. Already weakened, they broke free, and he pried one up, fighting it free.

It created a gap about as wide as his shoulder. He tried to angle his light into the gap, but he couldn't see around it.

He stuck his arm down, shoulder deep, and felt around.

His fingers barely brushed the ground—or what he supposed might be the damp, pliable basement floor. "Kacey!" He moved his hand around, searching in an arc, but hit only air.

Then, just as he was about to pull back, something grabbed his hand. The slightest pressure, just at his fingertips.

Squeezed.

"I got something. Or someone!" He pressed his face to the boards, trying to position himself further without letting go.

The hand slipped away. He searched for it again,

praying he hadn't been dreaming, but nothing caught him. "They're down here!" Or at least one of them was.

He pulled himself back up. "I need a saw!"

"I'll get one from the rig." Jess disappeared, and he heard Pete's voice.

"We're going to move the other wall, Ben. You need to get out of there."

"Forget it. I'm not leaving her. She's right below me."

"The entire place is unstable. There's a three-hundred-pound refrigerator just waiting to collapse on you."

"Five minutes. Just give me five minutes—"

"I've got the saw," Jess said and handed him down a rescue saw. He adjusted the guard, turning it only deep enough for the joists, yanked on the pull-start.

The saw buzzed, bit into the wood, and sawdust bulleted up at him, pinging off his glasses. He opened up a space big enough for him to crawl through and handed up the saw to Jess.

"If she's not there, you're coming out," Pete said. "That's direct from Miles."

Ben tightened his jaw, then leaned down and slid into the opening.

The space was tight, reeked of mold and rot. He braced himself on his arms, lowered himself down, and maneuvered to his hands and knees.

No one. "Kacey?" He met a wall of Sheetrock

and wood, more debris behind him, a wall of rubble to his left.

Nothing.

"Dad?"

He stilled. "Audrey? Where are you?"

He felt a tug on his boot. He turned and wanted to weep when he spied Audrey's hand snaking out from a pile of litter and dirt. He grabbed it.

"I'm here, Audrey. Hang on." He tunneled away the dirt when he saw her lying under the cradle of the laundry sink. Dirty, her eyes huge, her face smeared with tears, but she gave him a quick smile. "I thought that was you."

He grabbed her hand, hunkered down next to her. "How badly are you hurt?"

"I think I'm okay. I'm just wedged here." She pointed to a beam lying across her legs.

Oh no. He managed his voice. "Can you move your legs?"

"No. I can move my feet, but they're caught—"

"You're not in pain?"

She shook her head, but her face started to crumple. "But I'm scared."

He wanted to cry too at her desperate expression.

"I can't find Mom. She was right beside me."

He didn't want to tell her about the destruction, the rubble in every direction.

He was having a hard time breathing with the immensity of it all.

Oh God—please.

"Dad, are you okay?"

He bent down, found her gaze. "Yeah. I'm fine." He managed to keep his voice quick, solid. "We're going to get out of here." *All of us.*

"Having faith is the bravest thing we can do. It's the unwavering confidence that God loves us. That although we can't see the road ahead, we can see God."

He had started to shake.

Yes. Please, God. Give me the faith to trust you.

Creaking and then Pete yelling, boards breaking, and Ben barely had time to brace his body over Audrey's before the refrigerator crashed down, crushing the table, and splintering through the floorboards.

It brought the rest of the kitchen floor down around them in a cloud of dust and debris.

They were shooting at her again. Or maybe grenades, but explosions jerked Kacey awake. How could she have fallen asleep when her men needed her?

Pitch dark. She could smell the dust, and more—something foul. But she couldn't move.

Had she been hit? Kacey searched for light, anything, found herself pinned, something heavy on her legs, unable to move her arm. Oh—her breathing tumbled out, and bile filled her throat. Don't let them find her—don't—

Light. It flashed above her, quick and fast, just a sliver before it flickered away.

She didn't want to move. What if the others were dead? If she just lay here, they'd never know.

She closed her eyes, willed herself not to move, not to cry out. She didn't feel hurt, but maybe that was simply shock.

The voices died out, leaving only her heartbeat thundering inside her.

Alone.

So alone. Blackness. Trapped. Tears filmed her eyes. *God, it can't end this way—please.*

She didn't know where the thought came from, but she leaned into it, reaching for something. *The Lord is my shepherd; I shall not want.*

Yes, that. She fought for the words.

He maketh me to lie down in green pastures: he leadeth me beside the still waters.

She heard shuffling around her, stiffened.

They were out there. Somewhere, waiting for her.

He restoreth my soul: he leadeth me in the paths of righteousness for his name's sake.

Strength, yes, she needed strength. She stilled, centered her breathing.

Yea, though I walk through the valley of the shadow of death, I will fear no evil: for thou art with me; thy rod and thy staff they comfort me.

Protection. Trust.

In the blackness, she heard something heavy fall—a body? One of her teammates?

Please, God, for Audrey, bring me home!

"Kacey?"

Her name. She opened her eyes, listened.

"Kacey, can you hear me?"

That voice . . . And then, with a jolt, it all rushed back. *Ben.*

She *was* home. And the last thing she remembered was sliding through Sierra's house as it imploded on her.

Oh no—Audrey.

She opened her mouth, but her voice barely emerged a whisper. "Here. I'm here."

"Kacey, if you can hear me, make a noise, anything." Again, Ben's voice. What was he doing here? And he sounded so desperate it made her ache.

Her arm stretched out on the floor in front of her—she couldn't move it, her legs too—and it stung her that maybe she didn't feel anything because . . . oh no, she *couldn't* be.

How badly was she hurt? Please, she couldn't be paralyzed.

Her breaths came in fast, hurdling over her. "I'm—here." Her voice barely dented the pitch, fell back to her without breaching the walls around her. She closed her eyes.

Don't panic.

Oh, she was way past panicking. She heard it in her breaths, the rush of her pulse, her thundering heart.

It wasn't fair. Yes, she'd made a few mistakes, but she'd been trying to fix those. To make up for them, to yes, deserve something good, like Audrey said.

Clearly, God disagreed.

"But what if God brought you back here to save you."

Sierra's voice, in her head, and she wanted to laugh, but the irony just burned.

What if God brought her back to remind her that she could never have the life she longed for?

That sounded about right. And really, that's what she deserved, for keeping Ben from his daughter, abandoning that daughter, even letting the world think she was some kind of hero, when really, she was a coward who'd simply let fear take over.

"Mom? Are you there?"

She nodded, tears dripping off her chin.

Above them, she heard more voices, but they were muffled and she felt herself start to shake.

Then, softly, she heard a voice. Not Ben's deep rumble, but something sweet and soft, familiar.

Beautiful.

Singing.

When you need a friend
A shoulder you can cry on
Someone who understands what you're going
    through
Just look over here, see me standing closer

Audrey? Except it didn't sound like her daughter's voice. It came from inside, a heartbeat.

The song she'd sung in Afghanistan. It had come to her in the middle of the night from the hidden places of her heart, with Duffy moaning six feet from her, O'Reilly on the other side, shivering, swearing.

Perhaps God hadn't left her in the dark then. Or now. More, he'd redeemed the past, used it to carry her through the darkness.

"He is the object of your searching."

She heard Sierra's voice as clearly as if she'd spoken to her through the darkness.

"Don't be afraid of letting go and walking into all God has for you."

Kacey closed her eyes, feeling the sob rise inside.

Words floated to the top, and she latched onto them.

Please, God, I need you.

I need you, I need you . . .

And that's when she felt it. A warmth passing through her, sinking into her, settling her heartbeat.

A presence. A voice.

"Nobody will love you the way I do."

And just like that, the fear whooshed out of her.

"Kacey!"

Her eyes jerked open, and fractured light broke through. A hand grabbed hers.

She blinked as the light revealed the man peering at her through the boards.

"Wow, you're beautiful," Ben said. His face was nearly black with grime, and his blue eyes glowed, so much relief in them that they started to glaze over.

"What happened? Where's Audrey?"

"I already found her. She's okay. We didn't know where you were, but then the fridge came down. And when it did, it broke open this wall." His voice shook, just a little. "Listen, I'm going to get you out of here."

He turned as if to go, but she gripped his hand. Pain sliced through her, and she cried out.

Clearly not paralyzed. She wanted to weep with relief.

He turned back to her. "It's fine. The fridge landed vertically. It's actually holding the floor up." He let out something of a sound of disbelief. "We're going to be okay."

"Yeah, we are—but only if you don't leave me." She realized how awful, how pitiful that sounded, but she didn't care. "Please, Ben, don't leave me."

She should have said it thirteen years ago instead of listening to her hurt, the lies that told her she didn't deserve the happy ending.

She was *not* her mother.

"Don't leave me, Ben. And not here, I mean. Don't. Leave. Me. We need you—Audrey and I.

And if that means we have to follow you around the country, then—"

"Shh." He reached his other hand through the grid of boards, touched her arm. "I'm not going anywhere. You and Audrey are my life—and we'll figure it out. I promise. But let's do it after we get you out from under this house, okay?"

She gave a feeble, pitiful laugh, and he smiled, white teeth against the grime. Except—

"Audrey—"

"Is fine, really."

"Is she . . . was she singing?"

Ben shook his head. Glanced back. "I think she might be praying, though."

Kacey gave another laugh. It ended in a groan. "I guess we did something right."

"That we did, baby."

What if it were Sierra the rescuers were fighting to extract from the rubble of her house? That thought kept shuddering through Ian as he watched the Whitefish then the Mercy Falls FD work with the team to extricate Audrey and Kacey from the tangle of wood, plaster, appliances, fixtures, and furniture.

Spotlights turned the now-rutted front yard to midday, and with all hands on deck, he'd donned a rescue jacket and helped with the assembly line that tore apart the house, creating a hole big enough for Jess and Pete to climb in and help Ben move Audrey to a stretcher, despite her assurance she felt fine.

She looked like a Chilean miner, her body covered in grime. But she possessed her mother's fighting spirit because she refused to leave the site until her mother emerged.

Sierra, too, had joined in the efforts, despite a heated argument with Sam, one Ian recognized as all too familiar.

No one got between Sierra and her desire to help.

Which, really, made them too much alike, probably. Because he recognized his own frustration in her tone, the same frustration he'd leveled at her.

"We're ready to move her!" Jess's voice came through the walkie-talkie in Miles's hand, and he nodded to the team to move into place. They positioned themselves strategically along the recovery path to move her stretcher hand-by-hand instead of trying to climb out with it in tow. Safer for everyone. Ian lined up across from Gage, next to Ty, who positioned himself nearer the hole to grab Kacey's litter, across from Ben.

Ian felt for the guy, understood his grim, almost desperate expression as he resigned Kacey's care to Jess and Pete.

The team had affixed ropes and a pulley system to stabilize the litters as they came out. Miles and one of the firefighters from Mercy Falls worked the system as Pete and Jess wrestled Kacey up to the rescuers. They'd stabilized her with a collar, secured her tight into the litter, cocooned in a blanket, her shoulder, which they thought she'd broken, secured to her body.

"I got you, Kace," Ben said as he put a hand on the portable stretcher. Ty took the other side, and Ian moved in to assist.

Kacey managed a smile at Ben as they passed her along, out of danger.

Ian and Gage carried her out to the ambulance, Ben scrambling out of the rubble after them.

Audrey came up to her, a blanket around her shoulders. "Mom!"

"I'm okay, honey," Kacey managed, and then Ian handed her off to the waiting stretcher and the EMTs from Kalispell.

He stood there watching as they packed her up, as Ben demanded a ride, finally conceding to ride in the other rig, with Audrey.

What if it had been Sierra?

Ian blew out a long, tired breath. Turned and spied Sierra now staring at her house.

She needed a home. A friend. Help.

He came up next to her, not sure how to offer anything off that list. "I'm sorry about your house."

She glanced up at him, her face dirty, her eyes reddened. He barely stifled the urge to reach out, pull her into his embrace.

"It's just a house."

"You worked on that house for five years. It's not just a house."

"It was old, and the foundation was crumbling, and I should have had it inspected after the flood." She rubbed her hands on her arms. "I'm so grateful that Kacey and Audrey are okay."

"Me too," he said. "But where are you going to sleep tonight?"

She gave him a smile. "Jess offered her place."

"What? I've seen that place. She's sleeping in her living room. It's barely habitable."

Sierra held up her hand. "It's fine. It's a roof over our heads."

"Stay with me, Sierra. I have lots of rooms—"

"I don't think that's a good idea, Ian." Her smile was tight. "But thanks."

"If you're worried about . . ." He swallowed. "What happened, it won't . . ." Shoot. "It won't happen again."

But the sense of her in his arms, those lips kissing him . . . He had to blow out a breath, add a smile. "Really."

She considered him a long moment. Then, finally, "Thank you for your offer, Ian, but I don't want your help."

She, too, manufactured a smile. "I need to move on, stop thinking you need me. You don't, and I know that now. But if I stay with you—and believe me, I appreciate the offer—I'll just jump back into your world. I can't help it, really. So I need to say good-bye and let you do what you need to do."

He stared at her and couldn't flush the frustration from his voice. "Why are you so stubborn?"

She recoiled, stepped back. "I'm not stubborn. But you can't be my entire world anymore, Ian. I should have seen that earlier, but believe me, I'm seeing clearly now. And the one thing my mother taught me is how to say good-bye, to walk away and stand on my own. So I'm not being stubborn. I'm moving on. And so should you."

But he didn't want her to move on. She was his entire world too.

"I'm not ready to say good-bye," he said quietly.

"I know." She touched his arm, squeezed, compassion in her eyes.

No, she didn't. "Sierra—"

"No, Ian. I wish you the best on your search. I really hope you find out what happened to Esme. But I can't be a part of it anymore." She gave him a sad smile. Then she walked away toward Jess, who had just climbed out of the house debris and was debriefing Miles.

Leaving him there with her words. *Move on.*

But how exactly could he? Not without her. But maybe she was right—not until he was able to say good-bye to Esme.

Behind him, he heard the ambulances pull away.

"I'm glad I caught you, Ian." Sheriff Blackburn

stepped up beside him. "I wanted to give you an update on that body we found. The coroner is still searching for a positive ID. She suggested that she could compare DNA to Esme's if you still had a sample."

"I'll find something."

"Good. Because she found something on the body we wanted you to take a look at." He pulled out his cell phone, scrolled to a picture. Handed it to Ian.

Ian stared at it. The sight of the necklace on a tray hollowed him out. A diamond pendant inside a heart hung on a tangled tarnished silver chain.

"I gave Esme that necklace on her eighteenth birthday," he said quietly.

Blackburn took the phone back. "I'm so sorry, Ian."

"Then who was the girl that Lulu gave a ride to Saint Mary?"

"I don't know what you're talking about."

Clearly, Sam hadn't updated the sheriff on the search. Ian filled him in. "We even talked to someone who picked her up in East Glacier—it sounded just like Esme."

"I'm sorry, Ian. I don't know what to tell you. The necklace isn't a positive ID, of course, but I think you should prepare yourself for the likeli-hood this is your niece. I'm so sorry."

He pocketed his phone, walked away.

Ian looked back at Sierra.

Of course, his first urge was to update her, to tell her that . . . Well, maybe it was over.

He didn't know how he felt. A jolt, yes, the sense of grief for his revived hope.

But for some reason he also felt as if a grip had loosened around his chest.

This could be over. All of it—and then he could let go.

Figure out how to move on.

He started toward Sierra, a crazy, wild stirring inside him.

Sam joined their group, sidling up to Sierra.

He put his arm around her shoulder, something loose, like a friend would, and that wouldn't have stopped Ian except for the way she looked up at Sam.

She laughed, something sweet that lit up her entire face. Then she gave Sam a funny punch, and he, too, laughed.

The shine in her eyes made Ian stop.

Move on.

He turned, shoved his hands in his pockets, and headed for his truck.

Apparently, she already had.

— 16 —

Daddy.

Audrey had called him that twice in the last hour.

Ben's heart still rushed to the name, something sweet and bright inside him. And it only grew as she cuddled up on the hospital sofa next to him, settling her head on his shoulder as she fell asleep.

He could hardly believe she'd escaped with only a few bruises. Or that Kacey had only suffered a broken collarbone, a dislocated shoulder, and a few broken ribs.

He glanced at the clock. Nearly an hour she'd been in surgery as the orthopedic surgeon reset the bone in place and attached a plate.

He closed his eyes, which were still burning from the dust of the house. He longed for a shower but had no intention of moving from Kacey's or Audrey's sides. Ever.

Audrey shifted beside him, sighing.

He pressed a kiss to her hair, still feeling her hand clutch his as they'd ridden together in the ambulance. *"I knew you'd come for me, Daddy."*

He ran a finger under his eye.

"Is she out of surgery yet?"

The voice alerted him, and he steeled himself

as he spotted Judge Fairing at the nurse's desk in the hall.

Thankfully, he hadn't had to make the call—he'd left that to Sierra, who had clearly taken her time.

Maybe knowing the inevitable collision of wills.

Well, he hadn't just found them only to lose them again. Ben eased Audrey down onto the sofa and got up, then walked across the room, into the hallway, stretching his neck, his aching back.

Laura stood nearby, listening as the Judge interrogated the staff.

"She's probably in recovery by now," Ben said to him.

Robert Fairing turned to him. Unshaven, wearing a sweatshirt and a pair of jeans, he'd never looked so ruffled. But it only took him a second to regroup. "What are you doing here? I thought you would have left with your band."

"Not my band. Hollie's band. And good try, but I'm not leaving."

The Judge's mouth tightened around the edges. He turned to the nurse on duty. "I'll be in the waiting room. Let me know when she's out."

He glanced at his wife, who followed her husband into the room. Audrey was awake, sitting on the sofa, her knees drawn up. She sprang up when she saw them, went to the Judge, and wrapped her arms around his waist. "Oh, Grandpa, it was just terrible."

Ben watched as Robert pressed a kiss to the top of her head, a softness on his face that belied his tone in the hallway.

Laura, too, gave her a hug. "I'm so glad you're okay."

However they felt about Ben, they clearly loved their granddaughter.

Laura looked over at Ben, then back to Audrey. "Do you need something to eat? There's a vending machine down the hallway."

"Really?"

"Just this once." Laura winked, and Audrey left the room with her.

Judge Fairing turned to Ben. "You know that technically you're not family. We can forbid you from seeing her."

Just try it. But Ben managed a tight smile. "I know. For now. But you won't, because you know that Audrey wouldn't allow it. Or Kacey."

"Just because you've stuck around to save them doesn't mean that you're here for the hard stuff—"

Ben held up his hand. "We're not doing this again. You cost me thirteen years—"

"I saved you both. Gave you a chance to grow up, find your way. Look at you—you're a big star. You should be thanking me."

Funny, he actually sounded serious.

Except . . . Ben blew out a hot breath, schooled his voice. "I will thank you. For taking care of

436

Audrey. For loving her and giving her a good home. And I admit I was an idealistic kid back then, scared, and yeah, I did believe that maybe Kacey was better off without me. Not anymore."

The Judge shook his head. "You think you know what's best for her, but—"

"No, I don't know what's best for her. And probably Kacey doesn't either—so we're going to trust God to figure it out. To put our lives back together. One day at a time. I don't know what that looks like, but I do know that I'm not going to let my fears—and my mistakes—keep me from being the dad I want to be. The husband I want to be."

Judge Fairing looked away, walked over to the picture window, where a light shone down over the parking lot.

Ben knew the view—he'd stared at it for a long time after their arrival, praying.

A lot of praying.

God, protect my heart, because I'm giving it to you.

"You can't blame me for wanting the best for her," Robert said quietly. "I was just trying to protect her."

Ben said nothing. Sighed. "Me too."

Robert turned then, met his eyes. "Kacey—and Audrey—are my entire life."

"Again. Me too." He refused to look away and met the Judge's gaze without flinching.

"What about your music career? Your tours. Nashville."

He took a breath. "I've been kidding myself for a decade. There is no music career without Kacey. Not one worth having. I love her and Audrey, and if that means giving it all up—I will. My dad is here. Audrey is here. And I'm hoping I can convince Kacey to stay too."

"She will, Dad."

Audrey stood in the doorway, holding a Snickers. "She loves you. She just doesn't want to destroy what you worked so hard for."

"That's the thing, Audrey." He came over to her. "It all doesn't matter if you don't have someone to work hard for." He took her by the shoulders. "Someone who you love to sing to."

He kissed her forehead, and she grinned.

"But . . . this old geezer, as Hollie likes to call me, still has a few tricks up his sleeve."

"Really?"

"You can tweet that, if you'd like. Hashtag *new release* from Benjamin King."

She pulled out her phone, and he laughed.

A nurse opened the door. "Judge Fairing, your daughter is in recovery and coming around."

Audrey turned to go, but Ben shot a look at Robert. The Judge hesitated a moment, then finally nodded.

Ben followed them into the room, watched as Laura kissed Kacey's forehead. Kacey was just rousing from the anesthetic. Her face was battered, her shoulder wrapped, an IV plugged into her hand.

She appeared so fragile and sunken into the bed that his heart just about broke in half. He put a hand to the railing to brace himself.

"Audrey?"

"Right here, Mom." Audrey grabbed her hand. "And Dad's here too."

The word, so natural coming out of Audrey's mouth.

He stepped up to the other side of the bed. "Hey, beautiful."

She opened her eyes, found his, and managed a febrile smile. "You're here."

"Of course I am. And I'll be here when you wake up, for the rest of your life, if you'll have me."

She blinked, licked her lips. "Is that a proposal?"

He had her hand, now rubbed his thumb against hers. "Well, I already proposed once, so maybe it's just a reminder."

"I'll have you," she said softly, her lips tilting.

He pressed her hand to his mouth, then leaned over and gave her a soft, quick kiss.

When he moved away, she looked past him, to her father. "Daddy."

"Hey, honey." He touched her leg, squeezed. "We'll take Audrey home. You need to get some rest."

She nodded, and Audrey leaned over, kissed her good-bye. "I'll be back in the morning."

Kacey formed a smile until they left the room. Then she looked at Ben, and her expression seemed, for a moment, stripped.

"I was lying there, in all that blackness, and . . . I thought I heard you singing. But it wasn't you, and it wasn't Audrey . . . But I felt as if—as if someone were with me. That I wasn't alone."

"You weren't alone." He kissed her hand again.

"But I mean—"

"I know what you mean, Kacey. I knew it as soon as the dust cleared and I saw you lying there—God crashed down the house to show me where you were. And maybe that's his MO—using the debris of our mistakes to show us how he can save us, rescue us from our dark places. We just have to have that crazy faith that he'll do it, despite our mistakes, our fears, even our pride."

She bore so much hope in her eyes, he couldn't help but lean down, kiss her again softly. "I love you so much, I feel like I need to shout."

"I love you too." She sighed. "I'm so tired, but I don't want to sleep."

"Shh, babe. It'll be okay. I'll be right here when you wake up." Ben hooked a chair with his foot, drew it over. "Let me sing you a little song I just finished. I think you'll like it."

He started to hum.

"I think I know this one," she said quietly. "It's one of my favorites."

He sat, so much emotion in his chest he couldn't breathe. "Yeah, you do. You've always known it. But it took me a while to finally find the ending. I borrowed a little from Audrey's song. See if you like it."

Years gone by, my eyes are dry
But the echo of my heart won't tell a lie
I'm coming home to the one I love
Second chances, given from above

When you need a friend
A shoulder you can cry on
Someone who understands what you're going
  through
Just look over here, see me standing closer

I never knew a love like this . . . 'til there was
  you.

"Just this once, Audrey. Don't get used to this— it's a school night." Kacey lifted a hand to Gina behind the bar of the Gray Pony. "Can we get a refill on the root beer?" She passed the mug over to Gina, who filled it from the tap.

Audrey sat on the bar stool next to her. Gina handed her the mug.

"Your guys ordered some calamari. I'm slammed. Can you bring it back to them?"

Kacey glanced to the stage, where a hopeful crooner played a ballad about country roads and going home. Clearly influenced heavily by his mentor.

"Yep, I have time."

"Great. It'll be right out," she said.

The smells of grilling burgers, tangy barbecue, and crunchy fries swelled out from the kitchen as Gina opened the swinging door.

"I think you should homeschool me so I can go on tour with Dad next year," Audrey said.

"We'll see. We have the entire summer ahead of us to negotiate."

But she and Ben had already had that conversation about next summer, and it included a large custom bus with a bedroom for Audrey.

Their daughter was already pushing for a winter wedding.

She noticed Audrey glance back, over her shoulder, and followed the glance to spot Nate sitting nearby with his parents.

Interesting.

Gina returned with the calamari.

"Stay here, I'll be right back," Kacey said. "Save my seat." Because, well, that was exactly where Ben would look the minute he took the stage.

The crowd parted for her—thanks to her sling. The private-ticket-only event had the entire town of Mercy Falls buzzing.

It wasn't every day that Nashville picked up and moved to the shadow of Glacier National Park, decided to set up a studio. Ben had already cut his first track, a love song she'd helped title.

In fact, one could say she'd provided inspiration for the entire thing.

She set the calamari on a table in an alcove by the door, in a rounded booth reserved for her cohorts. Ty, in his cowboy hat and designer boots, pulled the calamari toward him. "I love these rubbery things."

"Squid, Ty."

He waved the curly deep-fried appetizer at her, wearing a rare smile.

Recovery had given her time to review the details of Chet and Ty's chopper accident—no wonder Ty struggled to climb back in the cockpit.

But her accident had given him the nudge he'd needed to use the simulator. PEAK Rescue just might have a pilot back in the cockpit sooner rather than later.

Once her request for separation from the military came through and her reserve status was confirmed, she could put together a training schedule for both of them.

"Bull's-eye!" Pete's voice rang out over the crowd from where he and Gage waged a war with the darts.

Next to Ty, Jess was thumbing through pictures on her cell, showing them to Sierra.

"What are you looking at?" Kacey asked.

"Sierra's got some ideas on how to remodel the kitchen."

"I think you need to finish one of the bedrooms first." This from Sam, who had returned from the bar with his order of nachos. He set the food on the table, slid in next to Sierra.

Sierra glanced up at him, something warm in her expression.

Interesting.

Especially since Kacey had seen Ian at the bar, talking with a pretty, crunchy-granola park worker.

Miles came in, holding Kelli's hand, making a way for her and her pregnant belly through the crowd. He helped her off with her jacket, and Sam moved in to make a space for her. Miles turned the chair at the table around backward, straddled it. "Did we miss anything?"

She glanced toward the stage, over the heads, and saw the warm-up singer just finishing.

"No, but I need to get back to my seat."

"What are you, Benjamin King's good luck charm?" Jess said.

"Something like that." She added a wink. Then worked her way back to the front. Slid into the high-top seat at the bar.

Audrey's was empty.

"She said to tell you that she'd be right back," Gina said. "She has a surprise."

But that's when the lights dimmed from somewhere onstage, and a low, deep voice spoke softly into the mic. "Are you ready to get this party started?"

It was Ben's voice, low and rumbly, and a shiver thrilled under her skin. Her man knew how to put on a show.

From the lonely stage, out of the darkness, a quick guitar lick twined through the air. A fast country flavor, the Benjamin King signature.

The crowd cheered and the lights flicked up.

Kacey's mouth dropped open when she saw Audrey standing onstage, her beautiful ne guitar over her shoulder. She was dressed in a new pair of boots, a fringed black dress, and her own cowboy hat, her beautiful chestnut hair long and in waves.

Clearly, Audrey had been the musician, her hands still poised on her guitar, her smile wide as she looked over at her mother.

"Sorry. That was planned," Gina said.

Kacey could only shake her head, grinning.

Then Ben stepped up to the mic, wearing his signature Stetson, hair curling out the back, jeans, a black Mercy Falls Mavericks T-shirt, and her dog tags hanging from around his neck.

"Hey, Mercy Falls! Thanks for having us tonight. I'd like to introduce you to my newest act—the beautiful and talented Audrey Fairing!"

To the applause, Audrey played another lick,

this one longer, raising the applause of the audience.

So this was what she and Ben had been up to all those days, killing time at his house while she'd been recuperating or reading up on past SAR missions.

And here, Kacey had thought she'd been only getting to know her grandfather, helping him with his PT, and playing with Jubal, the dog she'd immediately adopted as her own.

Audrey found Kacey's gaze again, her eyes sparkling. Then, she stepped up to the mic. "Actually, the name is Audrey King." She turned to her father, her eyes bright.

He wore so much joy in his face, Kacey had to blink away the moisture in her eyes. Her own heart was so full, so whole, she could hardly breathe.

Then Ben joined his daughter in a final, quick solo, a grand flourish at the end.

The crowd came to their feet as Audrey parked her guitar and hopped offstage.

"What did you think, Mom?"

"Like father, like daughter," Kacey said, taking Audrey's face in her hands. "I'm so proud to be your mother."

Then she kissed her forehead.

Audrey climbed onto the stool as Ben took the mic again.

"Tonight's a very special night. Most of you

know, my dad was in an accident a few months ago. He's back on his feet, but it helped me realize it was time to come home."

A hand on her shoulder made her turn. Chet stood behind her, leaning heavily on his crutches.

She slid off the stool. "What are you doing here?"

He raised an eyebrow. "Came to see my son sing, of course." A man at a nearby table vacated his chair, and Chet eased himself into it. "Thought it was time."

She glanced to the stage, and Ben was watching them, wearing an expression she couldn't place. For a second, a muscle pulled on his face, emotion rising in his eyes.

He cleared his throat. "So tonight I'm here to give you back what you gave me. A home. A family. A song to sing. And by the way, I'll be stickin' around—because I'm starting my new label right here in Mercy Falls. It's called Mountain Song Records."

Cheers, and he lifted his hand to quiet the crowd. "But the real reason I'm back is to marry the girl I've always loved. Kacey Fairing. This song is for her." He lowered his voice, something husky in his tone. "It's called 'Kiss Me.' "

A few hoots from the crowd, and her face heated.

Ben strummed the first few bars of his song, then looked up, his beautiful blue eyes finding her in the audience.

And then it was just him and her, the world slowing as his song reached out to twine around her, capture her, reel her in.

Bring her home.

— Author's Note —

Amazing grace, how sweet the sound, that saved a wretch like me. I once was lost, but now I'm found, was blind but now I see.

"Amazing Grace." As I was creating the theme of this series about a search and rescue team, this hymn kept returning to me. Searching and finding. God opening our eyes to his care for us. Sometimes I feel like we have a hard time taking those words into our hearts. Making them personal.

How do they apply to mistakes—even sins— we've committed? Actions that have far-reaching consequences, that affect lives and futures? Does God really offer us second chances? And what happens when we feel that we've either out-sinned God or maybe simply turned our back on him so long that he couldn't possibly want us around?

That is where Kacey and Ben find themselves as this story opens. And, while I understood the mind of Kacey—being a mother who longs to protect her child—I struggled with Ben. I wasn't sure what Ben's state of mind was—a famous country music star with shame in his past.

As I was writing, I was listening to a lot of country music. One singer in particular kept appearing on my Pandora lineup—Chase Rice.

Most of his songs are pretty wild—not unlike Ben's!—but then I heard one that changed my entire story. Called "Jack Daniels and Jesus," it's about a man who knows he's not living right, but even in his darkest places, he hears Jesus calling to him through the twenty-third Psalm.

See, we often believe that since we've sinned or made mistakes that God can't possibly want us, be on our side, run after us. Love us. But we are his sheep—and if you follow the metaphor, he knows we need him. That we'll be lost without him, even if we don't realize it.

Which means that God is not satisfied to sit on the sidelines of our lives—he wants to guide us and protect us, to give us a fresh hope every morning. Too often we spend our lives searching for redemption—like Ben, and even Kacey—when it is freely offered, right there in front of us.

In fact, as I was writing this book, God confirmed this in words I'd already written, in Ben's song.

When you need a friend
A shoulder you can cry on
Someone who understands what you're going
    through
Just look over here, see me standing closer
Nobody will love you the way I do

Nobody.

Surely goodness and mercy shall follow me all the days of my life; and I will dwell in the house of the LORD for ever.

If you're caught in darkness today, believing God doesn't want to rescue you, I challenge you to reach out and see that the Good Shepherd is already pursuing you. Already protecting you. Already willing to give you a fresh start and bring you home.

Thank you for reading *Wild Montana Skies*! The epic adventure continues in the next book, *Rescue Me*!

Grace to you!

Susie May

— Acknowledgments —

Thanksgiving of 2014. I flew out to Montana to visit my parents with my oldest son, David, and we were sitting around the breakfast table talking to my father, who was reading the paper. He showed me an article about the rescue via SAR chopper of a hunter who'd been shot.

"You know," Dad said, "that might make an interesting book series—an SAR team out of Glacier National Park."

It just so happened I was already noodling on that idea. Having loved my Team Hope series (a SAR series), and my Noble Legacy books (set in Montana), I wanted to combine my love for the "family" series (The Christiansen Family) and small-town life (Deep Haven) with something more along the lines of romantic adventure.

I went upstairs to his bonus room armed with big sheets of Post-it paper, markers, and my son, David, who is an amazing storycrafter. Three days later, we'd fleshed out the entire series, with characters, theme, and book blurbs. Montana Rescue, and the PEAK team, was born.

And it continues to grow—because it takes a team to raise a book, and I'm so grateful to those who helped bring *Wild Montana Skies* from baby idea to full-fledged novel. My deepest gratitude goes to:

MaryAnn Lund, my beloved mother, who loved the PEAK Rescue idea, handed me magazines and ideas, and cheered us on as we plotted. Wow, do I miss you—and I know you're still cheering me on in heaven.

Curt Lund, for your support and enthusiasm for this project! I love the way you think! Thank you for your continued ideas.

Ken Justus, ALERT chopper pilot. Thank you for the answers to endless questions and for what you do every day to save people. Any mistakes are all mine.

Tobi Leidy, reader friend who suggested the name Jubal Sackett for Chet's dog! Thank you for your excellent suggestion—Jubal it is!

David Warren, brilliant storycrafter, encourager, and plotter. Thank you for sticking in the brainstorming fight with me, seeing my vision, and helping me flesh out characters and scenes. I know I've said this before, but really, you're brilliant.

Rachel Hauck, writing partner and best friend. Thank you for being on the other end of the phone with the answer to the question: what next? You, too, are brilliant.

Andrew Warren, who knows the right answer to the question: what's for supper? (You decide! And, um, can you fix it too?) I am so grateful for your support and encouragement. With you, I'm home.

Noah Warren, Peter Warren, and Sarah and Neil Erredge, for giving me a reason to finish my deadlines so we can all have fun!

Steve Laube, for loving the Montana Rescue series, and being in my corner.

Andrea Doering, for seeing my vision and for having the enthusiasm to bring it to life. I am so grateful for you!

The *amazing* Revell team, who believed in this series and put their best into making it come to life—from editing to cover design to marketing. I'm so delighted to partner with you!

To my Lord Jesus Christ, who, in every scene of this story, showed up, my Good Shepherd, to lead and guide me. To fill my cup to overflowing and to remind me that he is always there to rescue me.

— About the Author —

Susan May Warren is the ECPA and CBA bestselling author of over fifty novels with more than one million books sold. Winner of a RITA Award and multiple Christy and Carol Awards, as well as the HOLT and numerous Reader's Choice Awards, Susan has written contemporary and historical romances, romantic suspense, thrillers, romantic comedies, and novellas. She can be found online at www.susanmaywarren.com, on Facebook at SusanMayWarrenFiction, and on Twitter @susanmaywarren.

Center Point Large Print
600 Brooks Road / PO Box 1
Thorndike, ME 04986-0001 USA

(207) 568-3717

US & Canada:
1 800 929-9108
www.centerpointlargeprint.com